Firebird

Harriet Castor sold her first book, *Fat Puss and Friends*, to Puffin at the age of twelve, her second when fifteen and her third when she was twenty. She joined a professional dance school and performed for the Scottish Ballet and on TV until aged fifteen she decided to quit and enrol in a normal school. Since graduating from Cambridge University she has worked in publishing. Now aged twenty-six, she has written her first novel.

Firebird

Harriet Castor

PAN BOOKS

First published 1998 by Pan Books

an imprint of Macmillan Publishers Ltd
25 Eccleston Place, London SW1W 9NF
and Basingstoke

Associated companies throughout the world

ISBN 0 330 34815 9

9 8 7 6 5 4 3 2 1

A CIP catalogue record for this book is available from
the British Library.

Typeset by SetSystems Ltd, Saffron Walden, Essex
Printed and bound in Great Britain by
Mackays of Chatham plc, Chatham, Kent

For Helen

Firebird

Harriet Castor

Chapter One **London, 1989**

It was a filthy plastic bag, shredded in places as if a porcupine had tried to wear it. Now it was trying to wear Laura's ankle.

'Blast!' She kicked her foot out to the side and the wind, after a thoughtful tug, picked up the bag again and tossed it down the pavement. It was May, for goodness' sake. What had happened to warmth and sunshine and a bit of cheering blue sky? Laura grimaced, picked a stray strand of hair out of her mouth, and plunged into the Institute.

Four floors up, where the ceilings got lower and the windows smaller, she found her secretary hovering outside her office.

'Yes, Maria?'

'It's Mr McIntyre.' Maria nodded towards the door and lowered her voice. 'I'm, sorry, Madame. I tried to persuade him to wait outside—'

'All right.'

Laura's heart sank. This was the member of her staff she least wanted to see, but also, as the most famous, the one with whom she must exercise the most care. And this morning, the nasty little man had undoubtedly come to crow. Laura set her face in a tight-lipped smile and opened the door.

'Alexander!'

'My dear *Madame*. Good morning.'

A pair of pale eyes, enlarged by spectacle lenses, faced her from across the room. Alexander McIntyre was standing just beyond the window; as she came in he stepped forward into the light, straight and trim as a military man, his white hair and clipped white beard immaculate.

Laura pushed the door shut behind her and drew in a breath. Her smile was holding. 'Well,' she said, setting down her briefcase and turning to hang up her coat, 'my congratulations on last night's documentary, Alexander. Were you pleased?' She tugged at the sleeves and turned again. 'Hm? What did you think of it?'

The old man tilted his head the merest fraction and smiled a delicate smile. 'Let me see.' He considered. 'The tributes . . . were of no consequence, of course. I shan't pretend I don't deserve them – if there's one thing I can't stand it's false modesty – but I can safely say that those five minutes of stinking slander were worth the whole of the rest and more.' As he met Laura's gaze, his eyebrows arched in amusement. 'You expected me to be angry, hm?

Oh, no – no, no, no. It was the *coup de grâce* . . . You did *watch* the programme, I take it?'

'Fifty minutes of prime time honouring "the most gifted choreographer of his generation" – who just happens also to be one of my staff? Oh, Alexander . . .' Laura surveyed him calmly. She could hardly admit to having spent much of the previous evening barely able to see the television set, let alone make out anything on it, prostrate with a cataclysmic headache. But – stinking slander? Though she was well practised enough not to show it, Laura hadn't a clue what he meant.

'It quite tickled me,' Alexander was saying now, 'the way they blacked out the slanderer's face as if she were some terrorist or child molester. "A current student of Mr McIntyre's who wishes to remain anonymous" – anonymous, dear, dear! Did the girl imagine I had no brightness button on my handset? One touch – pzz!' He jabbed an imaginary remote control in Laura's direction, then described an arc above his head, his hands opening like a flower. 'There she is – revealed! Did you not think to do that, Madame?' He chuckled and wagged a finger at Laura. 'Well, I can solve the mystery for you. The culprit was indeed a student here. Can you guess? It was our little crock of – shall I say? – *questionable* talent, who just loves-loves-*loves* to make trouble . . .'

Laura, finding herself in front of her own desk, reached for the small hard chair she reserved for unwanted callers and gripped its back. She was thinking fast. The television crew had interviewed one of the Institute's students (*how? she had forbidden it*). And they had just happened to choose the one whose views were not only guaranteed to be slanderous, but who would relish broadcasting them to the nation. It was not hard to work out. 'Natasha Taylor,' she said.

'Who else? So.' Alexander folded his hands before him with an expectant air.

'So?'

'Naturally I rushed here, as the injured party, to hear the miscreant's fate. You must know, Madame, how long I have dreamt of seeing that little runt righteously struck down.'

'I know how unhappy you are,' said Laura evenly, 'with the parts she has been given in the graduation gala—'

Alex flapped a hand. 'Simply the latest in a long line of travesties of justice. I have marvelled at how there has seemed to be nothing – nothing! – that the Institute in its flabby wisdom cannot accommodate. How often has her arrogance, her insulting behaviour brought her to the edge of the abyss? Hm? And each time her talent is truffled up as the paltry excuse. Of course, the fault lies with your predecessor, Madame. You have, after all, been *notre maîtresse* only – what? Eight months? One cannot expect you to have come to grips with every area of your role.'

Bristling at the insult, Laura held his gaze. She said

icily, 'Yours is not the common view, Alexander. The rest of the staff—'

'Ach! That bunch of clowns—' He stopped, and touched his fingers to his lips. 'They wanted Miss Taylor to star in the gala. What could I do? Long live democracy . . . That is why, you will understand, it is so sweet to me now. She has been given a little rope and – chhk – has done the job my greedy fingers have been itching to perform for so long.'

'And what exactly,' asked Laura, 'are you hoping for?'

Alexander affected a look of innocent surprise and then, with a flourish, deep thought. Behind the posturing, Laura knew, he was watching her narrowly. He said, 'Well, now. I really do not think she can remain a student here, do you?'

Famous and influential he might be; Director of the Institute he was not. He had presumed too far. Laura said, 'Natasha Taylor is two months away from graduating. Do you seriously consider your reputation to be in danger? From one dissenting voice among so many?'

There was a pause. Alexander stepped forward and leant a hand on the desk's edge. 'This is a point of principle. I am not a vain man. But my work cannot be impugned. I will not have it.'

'I see.'

'Oh, I hope so, Madame.' He straightened, and inspected his fingernails. 'It would be unfortunate to discover such an important difference of opinion between us. Just as . . . for *example* . . . it would be a shame to hear, at this eleventh hour, that my friend – your benefactor – had withdrawn his funding for our first graduation gala, would it not?'

Behind the glinting spectacles, the gaze had lifted again. And brought with it a threat. For a moment Laura faced him in silence, as still as Lot's wife. Then she walked around the desk and let herself smoothly into the high-backed chair behind it. Silently, she was calculating the implications.

'You want this new gala to stamp your mark upon the Institute?' Alexander went on. 'I do not condemn it, Madame. But I understand it, however much you might like to tell yourself it is for the glory of the school. Remember, I knew you before – in your other life. I know the strength of your ambitions. You tasted great success once, and you want to again. So you and your Institute shall rise together, hm? Well, indeed. So it should be. But do not forget it is my friend you depend on for money. And without money, your little publicity machine will grind to a halt.'

Laura's voice in reply was perfectly steady. She said, 'My gratitude will hardly allow me to forget, Alexander. Your friend's generosity has saved the gala.'

His smile broadened. 'I am only trying to help you, Madame. After all, you will have to give reasons to the rest of the staff for Natasha Taylor's departure – and, bless them, they are but simple-minded folk. So here is the neat choice you present: they may have their gala *or* they may have their sluttish little star. But – *quel dommage!* – with no gala the star cannot be the star *of* anything, can she?'

At this he gave a snort of mirth and advanced, jaunty as a man half his age, around the desk towards her.

'We have built a tower of bricks and somehow I seem . . . to have my hand on the bottom one. Madame—' Quick as a tongue, that same hand darted out to grasp Laura's. She felt a brush of lips and clipped beard, then he released her fingers and smiled. 'I know you will do the right thing.'

LAURA SAT STARING fixedly at the closed door. On the other side of the wood, carried on his rasping little pumps, Alexander was skimming away from her down the corridor to the stairs. But the unease cast up by his presence hung about the office still, like dust from a powder puff. Laura drew a deep breath and dug her fingers, hard, into her eyes. The skin felt papery; it felt old.

'Maria—' she said, emerging from her office a moment later. 'You saw it, did you? Last night—'

Maria was sucking a lollipop. 'The documentary?' she said, removing it. 'You bet!'

'Then tell me,' said Laura, 'what *precisely* is Mr McIntyre so bothered about?'

Beneath the lurid red fringe Maria's eyes widened. 'You mean you don't . . . You didn't—'

'Not all of it, no. Something came up.'

'Well.' Maria pulled open a drawer. 'Why not see for yourself?' In her hand, held out, was a video-tape. Laura took it and shot her a quizzical look. 'I set the study room machine on the timer. For the archive.'

'Full marks, Maria. Study room free now?'

Maria spun on her chair to look at the wall-chart behind her. 'Uh – yep. Till eleven. But don't forget you've got the second-year girls in studio two at half past. And – ' The phone rang. As she picked it up, she slapped her hand on a pile of papers. ' – there's a mountain of post you should definitely see. London Ballet Institute, good morning?'

Laura headed for the door.

'Madame?' Maria had jabbed her lolly on the mute button.

'Take a message.'

'But it's the *Daily T*. About that documentary.'

Silently cursing, Laura started back for her office. As she passed the desk she thrust out her hand for the pile of post. And turned back in the doorway. 'Ring Dr Debenham and make a date for dinner tonight. Or, better still, lunch. Don't let on it's urgent. Say I've been meaning to call for a while – '

' – but you've been *so* busy and now you've just had a cancellation.' Maria grinned stickily. 'Raphael's at one?'

'Perfect. But whatever you do don't let her put it off.

And, Maria, find Natasha Taylor. I want her up here by the time I'm off the phone.'

'THE PROGRAMME INCLUDED some pretty serious allegations, Miss Douglas,' the reporter was saying. 'And the name Natasha Taylor has been mentioned to me. Can you confirm?'

'It was an anonymous student.'

'Ah. I see. You'll be protecting her, then?'

Risking a cricked neck and shoulder by clamping the phone between them, Laura dropped the pile of papers onto the desk and let the tape slither from under her arm. 'I'll be protecting no one,' she said. 'An internal inquiry is in hand.'

'So you're going to punish this mystery student simply for speaking her mind?'

Laura mustered a patronizing sigh. 'Mr Shaw. If criticism is levelled at a member of staff by a student in so public a manner—'

'You mean . . .' He was clearly searching through some notes. 'You mean like, "The man hasn't choreographed since 'seventy-eight. If he ever had any talent in him, he ran out of juice long ago"?'

So *that* was the direction of assault. Laura raised her eyebrows at the cyclamen on the window-ledge. It ignored her.

'Is there any truth in the allegations?'

'None whatsoever.'

There was a pause. 'This Natasha Taylor, then. Is it true she's your best student?'

'Every student of ours is unusually gifted, otherwise they would not have a place at the school. We do not deal in superlatives.' It was almost a chant; policy line. Laura picked up a letter from Maria's pile and began to read.

But this journalist was persistent. 'Still, she's important to the, er, graduation gala you're staging?' he said. 'You must feel a lot hangs on it for you. New, higher profile Institute – you've a fat pay cheque to justify, after all. And they poached you from the Haycroft specifically to shake things up. Don't *you* lose out through this gaffe?'

At this point, Laura's patience left her. When Maria knocked on the door a few moments later, the call was over – one journalist chewed up, spat out and cut off – and Laura was deep in reading her mail.

'Madame? Drawn a blank on Natasha. Not signed in and even that Renée Aitchison swears blind she doesn't know where she is. Said she was going to see her father for the weekend or something. He lives in Oxfordshire, apparently.'

Laura nodded briskly, without looking up. 'As soon as she's in, let me know.'

When she heard the door click behind Maria she stopped reading and sat back. For some time she stayed like that, staring at nothing, lost in thought. She picked up the video-tape, put it down again. Then she slapped her way through the rest of the letters. Invitations to this and that, complaints from parents of failed candidates for next year's intake, inquiries from hopefuls for the year after. Laura read, struggling to concentrate, and one by one put the letters aside.

Thinking she had come to the last, she was about to reach for the tape when she spotted a final piece of paper she had overlooked. It was a letter, headed with a Parisian address. Laura scanned down the two brief paragraphs – and froze.

For how many minutes she sat there, she was hardly aware. Her face, slack-jawed in shock, wore an expression that neither Maria nor Alexander nor any other person at the Institute had ever seen.

A little later the sun came out at last, thin and cold and bitter, staining the building's grey stone walls and leaking through the pocked uneven window-panes. Unnoticing, Laura rose, placed the paper, apart, in a drawer and shut it softly. Then she reached for the video-tape and made for the door.

SHE WOULDN'T TOUCH IT. There was no one there to disgust or impress and so no point, either, in pretending to childish bravery. Squatting on her heels, breathing through her mouth against the smell, she stared at it. It would once have been beautiful: alive, the dark pattern would have been a brilliant rich blue suspended in a kind of milky sputum, now it looked saggy, rancid and dull-coloured.

Natasha turned and searched about for something to prod it with. To either side of her lay thick salt-stinking strips of seaweed, tangled up with old cans and plastic lids and bits, and broken shells encrusted with dried white scum. An arm's stretch away there was a half-rotted stick: pulling the end of her sleeve over her hand, she picked it up and turned back to the jellyfish.

It lay there like a big splattered eyeball. When prodded, it didn't burst like an egg yolk, or even ooze. Disappointed, Natasha paddled the stick on its surface for a while, then cast the stick aside, stood up and looked about her.

Away across the sand – cold and hard and ridged like a washboard – the sea slopped quietly to itself. Thin greasy layers ran in and retreated, and the heavy water behind merged, gun-metal grey, with the sky. A need for the sea was what had brought Natasha out of London on the coast-line train. She was finding it difficult, now, to remember quite why. Except that at the last moment she couldn't face Oxfordshire, or her father, accepting and unquestioning though he had learnt to be now, in his own bemused way.

Still, the guest-house had been all she'd hoped: balding raspberry-pink candlewick and lacy-edged fried eggs and marmalade in dwarfish jam jars. Saturday night she'd gone to bed early and alone – but for the bottle of Talisker on which she'd blown most of her money. She'd sipped it slowly from the tooth mug; salty like the sea, and stinging.

By last night – Sunday – the cash in her pocket had all but gone. She had money, plenty of it, but no plastic to get at it with, and she hadn't been able to face the train back to London – not yet. So she'd taken the rest of the whisky to the beach and several hours later had come to wish she hadn't. Even the sunrise, in that gnawing, joint-aching cold, had managed to look ugly.

Natasha turned her face into the wind. Cars on the headland road were moving, small and silent, in ones and twos, and someone in trainers was slogging down the promenade. It must be about seven o'clock. She wasn't even supposed to be anywhere yet; no one would be missing her. She gripped the battered suede coat tighter around her and made her way back up the beach.

A curling, grinning neon fish jutted out above the street. Natasha felt for the change in her pocket as she walked, drew out a fistful of coins and stopped to count them. Just enough.

Inside the café it was steamy and the air was thick with frying. The woman behind the counter wore a mohair sweater under her apron. 'Yes, love?'

Natasha ordered. Her stomach ached for the full breakfast, but her money stretched only to a lesser combination: sausage, egg and fried bread, plus a cup of coffee. As she slid into a plastic seat by the window, she had a vague awareness of curious looks being cast in her direction, but felt no need either to meet or to avoid them.

Was she scared of going back, she wondered suddenly – and was relieved, searching her feelings, to find that the answer was no. Bored, rather. Everyone was about to behave very predictably and she was going to have to be there to see it.

'WHOA! Not so fast!'

The waiter who had just served Dr Debenham the *moules marinières* banked round and approached the table again.

'I'll need more bread than this,' the doctor informed him, leaning back and plucking at his sleeve. 'Bring me thick-cut wholemeal. And butter. If it's in those bitty little dishes like usual you'll have to bring two.'

'Certainly, madam.' The waiter's nod was barely more than a blink. He turned and cast himself off into the sea of tables once more, dodging them with practised swerves.

Laura refilled the glasses. Margaret Debenham (Ph.D. Cantab.), sitting across from her at the polished block-wood table, was an art historian with a sizeable family fortune originating from plastic cake decorations. She was also the current chairwoman of the London Ballet Institute's board of trustees.

The bread arrived: several wholemeal doorsteps and enough butter to grease a Channel swimmer. Dr Debenham had just sucked a mussel into her mouth; she struggled with it and a stray length of something rubbery flicked its secretions onto her chin. Her face, which was pudgy with occasional ruching, looked much like a mussel itself.

'Now, tell me about the gala,' she said, dabbing with her napkin. 'The pre-publicity seems to have been set up extremely well, from what I can see. I trust the seats are beginning to shift?'

Laura knew she wanted figures: Dr Debenham's mind chomped on figures the way her jaws would chomp on the bones of the small, plump quails that were at this very moment being prepared for her in the kitchens. Laura prodded her *frittata*, feeling a little green, and set down her fork.

'With the time that's still in hand, I'm confident ticket sales will run pretty near to capacity both nights. We need eighty per cent minimum, even now we've sorted out the funding. The theatre's agreed to waive the fee for using the crush bar for the first-night reception, but only if we arrange the catering through them. I'm prepared to go with that, but I've told them they'll have to improve on the menu they submitted first time around.'

'What was it? Coronation chicken and pizza squares?'

'Not far off. It would have let us down badly. I'm calculating for a hundred and fifty people, and that's keeping it exclusive.'

'Just company directors and anyone with lots of cash. Good – so the directors have been nibbling, then?'

'We seem to have hit lucky. All the major people

from this country have said yes – and then there's a whole list of directors from Europe and the States who are either going to be there in person or sending a deputy.'

'Super. Well, hats off, Laura. You know what I thought when you first broached the subject of a gala – what the whole board thought. But you were absolutely in the right. Good for you!' Dr Debenham chuckled complacently. 'Oh – what's the word on the designs?'

'Looking impressive, but complicated. We haven't seen much more than the set model and swatches. Half the costumes'll still be clamped under the sewing machines an hour before curtain-up, I'd wager.'

'Front of house?'

'The set woman won't be interested in that – it's not her line. We'll have to get someone else in to advise.'

'Oh, just make it a decent florist. I can recommend if you like.' Dr Debenham sat back and wafted her napkin like an opera singer's handkerchief. 'I see flowers – everywhere. Where it matters, I mean, which is anywhere the people in the decent seats will go. It's madness, but you simply have to spend in order to make the stylish people think you're stylish enough to deserve support. Alexander, of course, will argue against me. He's such a purist. But then he can afford to be. What he doesn't quite see is what philistines half these people are. They like the notion of ballet, fair enough, but sit them down in front of it and they're bored as hell. Haven't a clue what they're looking at, most of them. That's why the buffet's got to be amazing. They'll go home with a much clearer idea of the quality of the vol-au-vents than the quality of the dancing.'

As may you, Laura thought uncharitably, watching her lunch guest wield knife and fork with the eager precision of a surgeon. 'Tell me, Margaret,' she said, ' what do you know about Aubrey Chancellor?'

'Aubrey? Our financial saviour? Not an awful lot. I've been stuck next to him at dinners a couple of times. We sat on a committee together once, too. Why? Is something wrong?'

'On the contrary. I have to pinch myself to believe quite what he's doing, stepping in to save the gala at the last minute like this. I just wonder about his motives.'

'You don't believe in the spirit of pure generosity?'

'What a quaint idea.' Laura smiled thinly. 'Do you think he might have backed us even without Alexander's persuasion?'

'Doubt it very much. Frankly, from what I know of Aubrey, charity's like garlic and the cross to him. I'm surprised he's being so generous even though he *is* a friend of Alex's,' said Dr Debenham, reaching for her glass. She swallowed, and shook her head. 'I can only think he owes Alex a favour. We're really very lucky.'

So, thought Laura, Alexander wasn't bluffing. Damn. But were there other options? She said, 'Just as I suspected. It means, of course, that we won't be able to rely on the same source next year – that's why I'm thinking ahead.'

She turned her glass-stem slowly. 'Did you know of any other contenders we might have chased up if Alexander hadn't produced Aubrey?'

Dr Debenham frowned. 'I think you're worrying unduly. Who's to say we'll have to grub around for backers? I don't see why, with a year in hand, we won't find a corporate sponsor. As long as the gala is good, of course. The problem this year has been that nobody knew what they'd be getting for their money. It's like trying to finance a new company no one's ever heard of, full of dancers no one's ever heard of. Worse, in fact, because a graduation gala, you know, translates to those business types as just some end-of-term gang show.'

'I'm aware of all that. But in my experience it's never too early to worry about money. So – other backers?'

Dr Debenham sat back and ran her tongue round her teeth. 'None would have bitten this year. If Aubrey hadn't stepped in we would have been looking at cancellation, for certain.' She dislodged something from a tooth and swallowed. Then she said, 'It just goes to show that Alexander's name on the staff list is the most valuable asset we have. And it never ceases to amaze me how many of the top-brass types he knows. I can't imagine how he does it, though I suppose all that time he spends at Sotheby's and Christie's in aid of his collection helps. Still, he gives me the shivers sometimes – have you seen him at work? He's a shape-changer. There really seems to be something diabolical about it. But I suppose there's something weird about everyone who's got that much talent, don't you agree? No wonder I'm so normal!' She hooted at this, and a small wet spray coated her Peter Pan collar and parts of the tablecloth. 'No, if Alex wasn't on the fund-raising remit we'd be jiggling around one very empty hat. The only thing that would be a real disaster for us is if he decided to call it a day.'

Laura felt her spirits slide. Dr Debenham was, after all, a fairly reliable barometer of board opinion. And whether or not this view of Alex's importance was correct, Laura would find it very difficult to get rid of him if he had solid board support.

'Oh, lord! That reminds me,' said Dr Debenham suddenly. 'The documentary! Do you know who it was? That student?'

'I'm afraid so,' said Laura. 'Though I haven't admitted it to the press.'

Dr Debenham took the hint and lowered her voice. 'They've been on to you already?' She grimaced. 'Bad luck. So?'

'Natasha Taylor.'

There was a pause. Then, 'Isn't she that dark-haired thing with the weasely face?'

'Probably.'

'Can't say I'm surprised, in that case. I saw her when I sat in on a class eighteen months or so ago. She was terribly good – a proper little whirlwind. But the most obnoxious brat I've ever met. What is she now – third year?'

Laura nodded.

'Has she much to do in the gala?'

'Some choice variations. Kitri in *Don Q, Pas Classique*.'

'Lord! How unfortunate. I always said that Alan, sainted man, was just too soft on student discipline. The whole board was petrified the Institute's standing might start to slip.'

Alan Hoyle had been Laura's predecessor as Institute Director. 'He did have his eye on Natasha Taylor,' she said. 'He warned me about her when I first took the job. It seems she's been a royal pain in the arse ever since she joined the Institute. Poor attendance record, lack of discipline, overall a highly questionable attitude to her work.'

'That does make it easier, then.' The quails had arrived. A gobbet of cooked flesh quivered on Dr Debenham's lower lip: it dropped as her mouth stretched into a smile. 'We made such a good choice in you, Laura. Strong hand on the tiller and all that – hm? Just what we needed.' She beamed and helped herself to the last of the Merlot, her sleeve, unnoticed, dragging a stray dob of butter in its wake.

NATASHA HAD BEEN ASLEEP; the slam of the front door below made her start.

A moment later Renée, her flatmate, flicked on the

light switch, in what she supposed was an empty room, and met the beady glare of something dishevelled, squinting crossly at her from the sofa. She yelped. 'My God! Natasha. If you have to lurk, try not to look so fiendish about it. Where have you *been* all day? Ouch! What was that for?'

Natasha, who had thrown the cushion accurately and quite hard, smiled savagely. 'Grassing on me, you little trollop.'

'I never—'

'You robbed me of the pleasure of going and owning up, heroically saving the whole school a week-long detention.'

'I never said anything.' Renée dumped her bag, stripped off her coat and went back into the hall to hang it up.

'Well, who did, then?' Natasha shouted after her. 'I only told you about that interview. Who did *you* tell?' There was a packet of fags on the floor. She stretched one leg off the sofa and kicked it within reach.

'No one,' said Renée, coming in again. 'I didn't need to. It was perfectly bloody obvious to everyone watching who the mystery – haha – person was.' She opened the fridge and bent to inspect its contents, then pulled out a Diet Coke bottle and took a long swig. 'You've been into school, then? No one said they'd seen you.'

'Lunchtime. Came straight back again. Maria collared me before I even got to the canteen.'

'Did she haul you in front of Madame?'

Natasha shook her head. 'Her Graciousness was off whining and dining. But she'd left instructions for when I showed my face. Whole bloody questionnaire. Did I get paid for it? Did I approach them or did they approach me? Blah blah blah. Spanish Inquisition stuff. Maria said there's a staff meeting tomorrow and I'm going to be summoned to it when they've decided what to do with me. Lamb to the slaughter.' Feeling in a pocket for her pen-knife, Natasha bent up her knees and started on her feet. The nails on her big toes were thick and ridged and the colour of candle wax; the skin around them red and peeling with hardened patches she'd been cultivating lovingly for some time. She hacked at one of the nails with determination.

Renée slumped on the sofa beside her, swilling the last of the Coke round the bottom of the bottle. 'What will they do?'

'Don't know. They'll want me to lick Alex's boots and declare that it was a mental aberration, that I was having a seizure involving temporary loss of marbles.'

'They'll chuck you out.'

'They won't. *Ouch.*' Natasha had cut off the nail too close to the quick. The skin beneath stung badly, so she bent her head and stuck the toe in her mouth. It tasted of sea-salt. 'Okay,' she said round it. 'They might.'

'You're bothered.'

'I'm not.'

It wasn't convincing. Renée was regarding her with a look of irritating perspicacity. But Natasha was feeling too fragile to confide. She parried with a change of subject. 'Seen Raoul today?'

It worked. Renée groaned. 'Spoke to him in the canteen. It was *awful*. I went totally tongue-tied and stupid again. I should stop kidding myself – there's just no way he's interested.'

'Oh, well. His loss,' said Natasha breezily. 'If he hasn't the good sense to tell steak from hamburger, as Paul Newman might say, you should drop him. He's not worth wasting your time on.'

A cushion clamped over Renée's face. There was a muffled whimper from beneath it. 'But he's *sooo*—'

'*Cuute!*' Natasha finished for her, getting up and padding towards the bit of the room they called the kitchen. 'He's bloody not, Renée. He's got a face like a sun-dried tomato and the bedroom skills of a hormonally imbalanced orang-utan. As I, unfortunately, know.'

'Don't rub it in.'

'I'm not. I'm making a concerted effort to put you off. You've brainwashed yourself. You only want him because he's ignoring you. Try lusting after the yucca instead – you'll get much the same response.'

Natasha rummaged in a cupboard, found a pillow-sized bag of tortillas and settled herself on the floor with it.

'Thank you for your wise words, Natasha "No Hang-ups" Taylor.' Renée got to her feet. 'And if you're seriously considering sitting there and chomping your way through that *entire* bag of saturated fat, I shall refuse to watch. I'm going to have a bath.'

The taps gushed for a considerable time, and the pipes joined in with a strange contrapuntal knocking. By the time Renée could be heard shifting about in the water, which from downstairs sounded like heavy, juddering scrapes against the bath-bottom, Natasha had got half-way through the tortillas and stopped. Overtaken by a sudden and profound weariness, she thought she probably needed a drink. Quite possibly several.

She hid the tortilla-bag under the nasty sixties coffee table with the detachable legs. She was, she calculated, just near enough to the fridge to reach it if she stretched out full-length. Lying back, she got her fingers to the door's edge and clawed it free. Inside, beneath an elderly egg and half a shrunken lemon, stood several brown bottles, quietly sweating beads of condensation. Natasha had learnt, long ago, to remove bottle caps with her teeth; it was surprising how often it came in handy.

Later – much later, when Renée had reappeared, pink and steamed and wrapped in towelling, and had gone up again to bed, and when three brown bottles had fallen jumbled in the wastebin and three more from the crate stood chilling in their place – Natasha found herself by the window, clutching the neck of a fourth and a cigarette, and staring out into the dark.

It wasn't regret, this feeling. Alex had made her life hell from day one at the Institute; he deserved all she could throw at him. But, still, she was troubled by the sneaking and uncomfortable suspicion that, this time, she might simply have gone too far.

A light went off in the flat below; the railings' shadow on the pavement disappeared. Natasha pulled on her cigarette; the curl of smoke, reflected in the window, caught her eye. Behind her the room showed up bright and sharp: a mess of magazines and books and *pointe* shoes, half-spilled ashtrays, limp flowers in yellow water. But in the middle of this, too close to the glass to catch the light, she was a blank – blacked out as she'd been on screen – a human-shaped hole in the fabric of the room. It was as if someone had taken scissors to a photograph and – carefully, neatly – snipped her out.

THE STAFF MEETING had been scheduled for two thirty; the time likely to cause the least disruption to classes.

Strictly speaking, Laura reflected as she made her way to the staff room, she did not have to do this. Officially, she had sole charge of disciplinary decisions and was answerable for them only to the board, to whom appeals could naturally be made by staff or students if they wished. But Alan Hoyle had knitted up his own kind of woolly democracy, and its forms were still expected even if its substance had gone.

The Institute sprawled over two buildings: a tall

merchant's house on the end of a terraced row, the top floor of which housed Laura's office, and next door, neat and grey in its own walled plot, an architecturally disembowelled nineteenth-century church. The staff room, which she entered now, was the bell tower's old ringing chamber: it was cold and dark even in summer, with two measly arched windows, their glass interrupted by a lattice of lead-work. Only one of the bells remained, forty feet above and out of sight, and though its rope and all the others had disappeared, eight empty eyelets still punctured the ringing chamber's ceiling like air holes in a travelling box for mice.

Below, at the level of scuffling activity, the staff room was a grubby, genial mess, littered with full ashtrays and stained polystyrene cups, and seventies square-cushioned chairs, like outsize chewy sweets in unwholesome citrus flavours. Even today, when two tables (of different heights) had been pushed together in the centre space, it was hardly a room that encouraged anyone to feel business-like or efficient, but it was the only place in the school where a full staff meeting could comfortably be held.

Not that the staff were so numerous: eight in total – part-timers and Director included. All of them, save Alexander McIntyre, had contested Laura's appointment: she had earned herself a reputation at the Haycroft for ruthless efficiency. Well, thought Laura now, shutting the door behind her and surveying the room, much good had it done them: she was here, and she was not, she knew, about to to win any hearts with this little performance.

Still, she would lead them into it gently.

'Since we're meeting today,' she began, when everyone was at last seated, 'I would like to treat this as a replacement for Thursday's regular session, and deal with a few items before we come on to the main business in hand. I see no point in meeting twice in one week.'

Six pairs of eyes blinked at her, impassive. The seventh, belonging to an irritating thirtysomething named Frank Schwartz, was trained incuriously on the ceiling.

Laura made her way briskly through the items listed before her: the upcoming weekend's final auditions and interviews for September's intake; the rota of staff who would be sitting in with her for them; the schedules for the dress and technical rehearsals for the gala, and precisely whose attendance she would expect there.

'And news on the first-night reception is excellent,' she added. 'We're pulling in the big names like flies to a fly-strip. I'll be hosting the reception in the crush bar afterwards, as discussed. If anyone can't make it, let me know this week. Excuses, I hardly need say, had better be gut-punchingly good.

'Oh, and still on that subject, I've had a letter.' Something made Laura check in her file, though she knew she hadn't brought it with her; it was still in that drawer of her desk. She swallowed quickly. 'A letter.' Looking up again she smiled, a smooth smile, professional and unamused. 'From Milan Novák, whose name, I am sure, is familiar to us all. It seems he's having a second go at setting up a company in Paris. He's coming to trawl the London schools and wants a special look-in here. Needless to say I'll refuse. I can't stop him coming to the gala, but I won't invite him to the reception, or let him sit in on classes. This is simply for your information, should he speak to you at the theatre. Any questions?'

'Absolutely.' Opposite Frank, Ellen Ellmore leant forward. She was ex-New York City Ballet, and tended to speak her mind. 'If he's got jobs to offer, why not see him in the same way as anyone else?'

'Who knows if he has or not? You'll remember, I'm sure, what happened at his last attempt. All the sponsorship money mysteriously disappeared and there was strong reason for believing it went straight up his nose. Anyone thinking of backing him again might as well tip their money down the drain. And their dancers. I certainly wouldn't recommend any of our students to take up a post with him.'

'He should at least be acknowledged.'

'Should he? By all means strike up a conversation at the gala, then. I believe you're most likely to find him in the nearest bar.'

Ellen did not reply. She looked at Laura with a thoughtful expression, then sat back.

Laura said, 'Now we come to the principal matter in hand. Natasha Taylor and her interview in Sunday night's documentary. But first, a warning: anything you wish to say on the subject must be said here, now, to me. Once the meeting is over and we leave this room, the matter is closed. There is to be no discussion with anyone else. If internal school business is leaked to the press, I shall be severely displeased.'

It was not so much the press, in truth: what Mel Shaw couldn't get hold of he would happily manufacture. Rather, the seven must have their say now so that dissent would not grow like canker in the Institute's corridors and darker corners. Or so that if it did, Laura would know in advance its nature and, with some certainty, its source.

She looked round at her staff. Given the impossibility of finding alternative funding for the gala, there was, she had concluded, no way out. But she knew they would fight her. She said, 'As you very well realize, the girl, in casting a slur upon a senior member of staff, has attacked the entire Institute. The conclusion seems to me quite plain. She cannot remain a student here.'

The silence thickened. Laura sat minutely still.

It was sudden, when it came, a burst of energy from a surprising source. 'No. Absolutely not. Categorically. It's mean and vindictive and, if that's what you see as justice, it stinks.'

'I would advise you to sit down, Mr Schwartz, or I shall have to ask you to leave and take no further part in this discussion.'

Frank, apparently surprised to find himself on his feet,

sat again abruptly. Beside Laura, Bara Floris, a mild woman and one of her most valued Classical specialists, gestured across the table. 'Perhaps the person who has been wronged should give his view?'

Laura turned to Alexander now with interest. But he held up a hand in pious self-denial. 'No, no. By no means. I am the victim – a witness, perhaps? – but neither judge nor jury.' His eyes, which had been modestly downcast, now trained themselves on Laura. 'I shall humbly submit, Madame, to whatever is decided.'

Bastard, thought Laura. Manipulating bastard.

Bara spoke again. 'But, Madame, so close to the gala? Natasha is just the smallest step away from the end of the course.'

'And look, we've given her the top roles in this thing,' said Frank, sprawling his arms across the table. 'She's six weeks away from the best showcase a kid her age could have. Anywhere. You *cannot* take this chance from her at the last minute.'

'*Cannot*, Mr Schwartz?'

'What about her talent, then?' put in Ellen. 'How can we discuss Natasha Taylor without mentioning it? Has any of us ever taught someone so sublimely gifted? Be honest, now. Put considerations of her personality to one side.'

There was a grim laugh; it came from Alexander. Ellen looked at him quickly. 'We're all used to good students here,' she said. 'Very good students. But Natasha Taylor – is something rare. I'm not usually one for words like this, but I'd even say there's something of genius in her.'

Alexander said nothing, but Laura was painfully aware of him beside her. She could sense the impassive gaze; something behind those pebble-thick lenses seemed crouched and grinning like the stone grotesques on the guttering outside.

'There must be alternatives,' said Bara steadily. 'How about withholding Natasha's graduation diploma?'

At this Alexander could not suppress a snort. 'A paltry piece of paper?'

'Then why the hell do we bother giving them out?' said Frank.

'Or tell her that a report of her conduct will be included in all her references,' suggested Bara.

'Yeah, why not?' Frank shrugged. 'The kid has the good sense not to care a fig for references. She knows full well that the minute she has a chance to show what she can do, no one would notice if a reference made her out to be sodding Hannibal Lecter.'

'So you're saying, Frank, that anyone who sees Natasha Taylor dance will give her a job?' said Laura. 'Surely that means we're not, as you suggested, ruining her career by excluding her from the gala? We're simply inconveniencing her, and also, perhaps, making a public gesture of discipline – to fit her public gesture of defiance.'

'Okay. Forget the effect on her. Granted, I think she'll get a job with no problem. Maybe we're even helping her by chucking her out – giving her publicity.' Frank frowned at his own reasoning and shook his head. 'Whatever. But if you won't think of her, maybe you'll think selfishly. A hell of a lot hangs on this gala for us, right? If we want to prove we're as good as the Haycroft it needs to be fantastic, right? But, just like a company show, a school show needs stars. Who the hell, someone tell me, will take on Natasha's roles?'

Bara nodded agreement. 'Year three this time just haven't turned out as strong as we'd hoped. Lucian James has come on well, and Evan and Michael have promise. But the girls, on the whole, are disappointing. I think any one of us would admit it. Year two are better, but they're looking green, and as things stand they've not much to do on the night.'

There was a knock at the door. Maria appeared. 'Excuse me – Madame? Don't faint but she's actually turned up on time. Do you want her to—'

'Tell her to wait, Maria. I'll call her in a moment. Just make sure she doesn't disappear.'

'If what we're talking is principles here,' said Ellen, when the door had closed, 'why not go down the route of scrupulous fair play? Give the girl a chance to apologize.'

'Apologize?' spluttered Frank. 'She wouldn't. Not if I know the kid.'

Ellen ignored him. 'After all, when was that programme filmed? Months ago. Maybe she's regretted it.'

'In which case she could have withdrawn her contribution,' said Laura.

'Could she? How do you know she didn't try?'

'She was asked yesterday. She didn't.'

'Well, okay,' Ellen conceded. 'She's proud as hell. We all know that. But even Alex . . .' She paused and, wearily, corrected herself. 'I'm sure Alex wouldn't be ungracious enough to refuse an apology—'

'We could formulate a letter from her to the papers too,' put in Bara, brightening.

All eyes were on Alexander. His expression was sickly sweet, almost sorrowful. He said, 'On a personal level, an apology naturally . . . is one thing. But Madame is concerned for the Institute.' He looked at Laura, and allowed the sparkling gaze to betray his confidence. The others had turned towards her too. Looking round, Laura saw unwilling hope, mistrust, and judgement – and realized, with some surprise, how much she had to lose.

A moral question – and not, perhaps, such a gamble. 'If I know the kid,' as Frank had said. And did he? Did *she*? This might be a way to placate the staff – and to find out. Laura placed her hands, calmly, one over the other. The flat stone of her largest ring felt cool against her palm. She said, 'Very well. Let us call her in and witness this great apology. Full and unconditional. Here. Now.'

One face, rigid in shock, and a low voice: 'Madame—'

She turned her head coolly. 'Yes, Alexander?' When

he didn't speak, she looked away. 'Bara, could you tell Maria . . .?' Bara nodded and scraped back her chair.

'What if she won't?' said Frank.

'Then she will be barred from the Institute.'

Alexander's gaze had not wavered. 'And . . . if she *does* apologize?'

'Then – we consider the casting.'

'Casting for *what*?' he asked softly. No one else heard.

NATASHA, SLOUCHING THROUGH the door, observed the Council of Eight from behind her chair. She'd decided to bring with her the irritating, inarticulate persona she had used to good effect over three years of Alexander's classes. 'The old bugger believes,' she'd explained to Renée early in its career, 'that all dancers are thick as pig-shit. And I do *so* like to confirm a screaming prejudice where I can.'

From the faces before her, she understood with some satisfaction that there had been an argument. Bara seemed anxious, Ellen watchful, and Frank, waiting till he thought she was looking, rolled his eyes in jaded amusement. At the far corner, Alexander seemed to have a bad taste in his mouth. His neck, where chicken-skin met a crisp white collar, strained forward; his head was inclined, tense and listening.

Only one person was completely impassive. As she listed the particulars of the crime, the woman at the head of the table sat straightbacked and still. Dressed utterly plainly, except for several rings on her delicate fingers, 'Madame' was a strange figure: small, slender and commanding.

Natasha caught a rising tone, and realized she'd been asked a question. It was repeated, testily. 'Why were you not in class this morning?'

'No point going to *his*. 'Specially now. He can't take it if you don't toady to him. That's his trouble.'

'And your trouble would seem to be cowardice. Among other things.'

'Bullshit. *I* was honest. Loads of people think the same as me.'

'You've done a survey?'

From behind the hair, Natasha's gaze was withering. 'Yeah, right.'

Madame looked back at her, unblinking. 'Your conduct has been unforgivable. To have made such slanderous comments in so public a manner demands that your place at this school be immediately forfeited. Only a full and sincere statement here and now that you regret your actions might persuade the Institute to consider a reprieve.'

'You what?'

'An apology, full and unconditional, to Mr McIntyre and to the Institute.'

'And if I don't?'

'You will no longer be a student here.'

'I get it. Kicked out.'

'Expelled. You are aware of the full implications, I suppose?'

Natasha nodded grudgingly.

'So? Your answer?'

Outside, the rain had stopped and started again; Laura realized, with surprise, how dark it was. Silent and still in the half-light, the room waited and watched, all eyes on the girl.

'You want me . . . to say sorry, right?' A hand emerged from a cuff's-end and hooked back half the curtain of hair. One rodent-sharp eye was revealed, staring straight at Laura. For an instant she thought she saw laughter in it. But the mouth was resolutely straight.

'It is entirely your choice.'

Beside Laura, Alexander stirred. His white hair gleamed dully; his fingers, laced together on the table, gripping tight.

The girl glanced at him. 'Yes. Well. You've got a long wait, then.'

'Am I to take that as a refusal?'

'I've wrung you lot dry already anyhow.'

'Meaning?'

'You work it out.'

Laura surveyed her. She said, 'Natasha Taylor, as of this moment you are no longer a student at the London Ballet Institute. You will attend no more classes here. You will not, needless to say, perform in the gala.'

The girl shrugged. And in a moment she had gone; had turned and headed, with no sign of either haste or unwillingness, for the door. It did not slam; there was no show of adolescent temper; it hung on its hinges, ajar, until Ellen slipped smoothly from her place and pushed it shut.

'Well?' said Laura. 'Do we not have classes to go to?'

The other figures around the table began to move stiffly as after a long vigil. Hands on her chair, Laura rose.

Back in her office five minutes later, she slipped out of her shoes and padded across the thin nylon carpet to the window. Far below, she heard the front door thump and watched as a figure emerged unhurriedly and sloped across the road. A coat had been pulled on over the mound of clothes; above it the drooping black hair flapped as the girl moved, like curtains at an open window. Laura tried to read something in the walk – was there an emotion detectable there? Something different from the way that same figure might have trudged to school that morning – or lunch-time, or whenever it was she'd deigned to turn up? But none was discernible. None whatsoever.

Laura tapped her fingers impatiently on the window-sill, cracking a small bubble of paint that fluttered down onto the carpet. There was something her staff did not know. Something that for much of the last year she'd been trying damn hard to forget herself. And it was this:

Natasha Taylor, the 'odious little person', the 'nasty brat' beloved of nobody, who might, just *might*, have a place in the category of greatness labelled genius, was the one student in the school who did not just call Laura 'Madame'. She also called her Mother.

Chapter Two **Oxfordshire, 1963**

'. . . spend so much of the time feeling downright ugly. Really, it is the most confounded chore.'

'What is?'

'Having children, darling. Babies, I mean. But then they grow up into these lovely things and you feel so *proud* of them, don't you? Even when they cause such frightful trouble. Who's winning?'

A shout drifted across to them from the tennis court. Laura hoped for an instant that Lydia and her mother might go over and see how the players were getting on, which would mean she could climb down before they all came back for tea. She shifted her bottom on the branch to brace herself in readiness.

But her mother simply stood, cradling the butter dish in one hand. She said, 'Harry hasn't made a fuss?'

Lydia Trafford-Taylor, mistress of the estate and one of her mother's oldest friends, was unwrapping a large fruitcake. She looked at Laura's mother sharply, then shook her head. 'They were holed up in the study a good long while the first day he was back. But I think Oliver had had his fill from the school already.' The hamper that had been brought from the house was empty now; she flipped down the lid and pushed it to one side. 'We're just trying to keep the details away from the village – you know how medieval their morals are. So we've let slip that forthright journalism in the school rag was Oliver's undoing. The story seems to have shot round already – Dr Palgrave told me yesterday one of his patients in Wittcombe repeated it to him as Stop Press news . . . Is that everything? Do you have enough knives on that side?'

The trestle table, shrouded in a white cloth and positively groaning under the housekeeper's heavyweight baking, stood some way from Laura, in the shade of an enormous and venerable cedar. Her mother sat down on one of the wooden chairs beside it. 'But what about the girl's parents?' she asked. 'It must have been public knowledge in the town . . . They're not pressing for marriage?'

Lydia looked at her in wonder. 'Johanna! Did I not tell you?'

'Tell me?'

'Dear heart, this isn't some young slip we're talking about. Lord! He might have been disciplined for that, but I doubt they would have given him the boot.' She sighed fondly. 'No – Oliver was caught *in flagrante delicto* with the wife of his house master. And the worst of it was, by all accounts, she was absolutely smitten. Oh, look, here they are . . .'

Laura turned her head. Four men in whites were heading up from the eastern side of the house, where the tennis court lay tucked behind the stable block. Lydia's husband Harry led the way, with the elder of his two sons beside him. Richard Trafford-Taylor – responsible, dependable and, at nineteen, the heir by two years – was six foot three and built like a rugby player. By contrast, at the rear of the little party, Laura's father Tom was portly and fifty-one, with round shoulders and a spreading bald patch. His face wore a fixed smile. He has lost, thought Laura, and he's furious. The thought gave her a small shiver, but hardly detained her for long: her attention had strayed to the middle of the group, to the fourth figure, and would brook no distraction. She gripped the branch in front of her and leant forward to get a better view.

You could hardly look at him *and* breathe. Taller than anyone, save his brother, he was lightly built, with shoulders straight as a yard-arm and hair improbably pale and thick and curling. Laura hadn't quite understood all that her mother and Lydia had said, and the mention of marriage had given her a nasty shock, but looking at him now a dawning, flooding certainty washed over her: Oliver, the Trafford-Taylors' younger and more beautiful son, had been dragged into something not at all of his making. House masters sounded pretty important, so their wives would probably order people about a lot. This one was clearly a wicked, scheming woman: she had probably threatened to have Oliver expelled or something if he didn't kiss her. And now the worst of it was he'd been expelled because he *had*!

'How did it go?' called Lydia as they approached, installing herself elegantly in a chair and lighting up.

'Dad and I won, but it was a close-run thing,' said Richard.

'Not at all,' said Tom. Attempting nonchalance, he added, 'You packed me the wrong racquet again, Johanna.' He swiped the air with it in a dummy forehand pass.

'Did I? Sorry, darling.'

Laura considered her father. He looked curiously trussed up in shorts. His belt, unsure whether to ride above or below his fleshy belly, had chosen above and this pulled on the legs, so that they stood out at the front like cropped clown's trousers. Thinking he was unseen, he shot a fierce look at Johanna and murmured something as she brushed past him. Johanna shook her head.

'Don't worry, darling, I'm sure she'll turn up soon,' said Lydia, who had observed the exchange and guessed its subject.

The business of tea was started on seriously after that. It was hot. The dainty breeze that had been twirling beneath the trees and flapping at the edges of the tablecloth gave up under the weight of the thick June air. On the table, the butter sweated and began to slide decorously to the bottom of its dish, and crumbs of sticky fruit cake glistened on plates and napkins, attracting the notice of flies. Laura was suddenly painfully aware that she hadn't moved for an age, and her knicker elastic was digging into her tummy.

Her plan, it had to be said, had not worked out well. She liked climbing trees, she liked being up above everything – but today she'd only done it to get out of tennis, because she was humiliatingly hopeless at it even when her father wasn't there, and a hundred times worse when he was. He would point out all her mistakes and that would make her nervous and clumsy, and then he'd call her a mutt, and then maybe she'd cry – and that wouldn't make him nicer and sorry for her, it would make him worse. So she'd planned instead on disappearing for a bit, and turning up nonchalantly on the terrace once it was too late to be roped in; it was simply bad luck that her mother and Lydia had chosen to set up the tea things in the very place she'd disappeared to. At first she hadn't come down because she knew she'd be told off for climbing – and then they'd started talking and would have told her off for eavesdropping too. And she certainly couldn't come down *now*, or she'd be made a worse fool of than she would have been at tennis, and she simply couldn't bear that – not today, not in front of Oliver. So she was stuck.

She shifted gingerly along the branch, peeling the bottoms of her legs off the bark, taking care not to rustle the foliage with her feet. Her dress was olive green and brown – a good camouflage. But perhaps, in the tranquil air, the soft sound of her movement carried. At any rate, when she peered down once more at the table, one person, his mouth crammed with the last of the last fruit scone, looked up and saw her.

Still as a cat, she stared back at him, hardly breathing.

There was a pause. Interminable. Then Richard's eyes crinkled at the corners to communicate an invisible conspiratorial smile, and his jaws resumed chomping. He turned again to the conversation; no one had spotted him look away. Relieved and grateful, Laura – though he couldn't see her – smiled in reply.

'HERE – I SAVED YOU a bit of cake.' He unwrapped a napkin as they walked and held it out to her. 'I imagined you were a bit stuck.'

'Thanks.' Laura took the napkin carefully: nestling in the middle was a small piece of Dundee cake, rather crestfallen and mostly crumbs.

'You were up there when they brought the table out, were you?' said Richard, pulling at a bush as he passed it. 'Must have been torture watching us demolish all that food.'

Laura shrugged and lied that it hadn't been so bad.

'What were you hiding from?'

'Tennis.'

'Hate it that much?'

She nodded and picked at the cake. Then she said, 'Didn't you want to go with the others?'

'To the stables? Not really. I've already had a good look at this new horse and I know exactly the rigmarole Dad's going to give them about it.' He smiled. 'Heard it all before. Where are we heading?'

Laura looked up. They were climbing a gentle incline, taking them further into the woods, away from the Hall and the lawns and the formal gardens. 'Up to the Bath House?'

'All right.'

They trudged on, Richard measuring his strides carefully so that Laura could keep up. It was an unlikely friendship, really, when you thought about it, but ever since Laura could remember she and Richard had got on well. She'd never quite worked out, though, why he bothered to be nice to her. Each time he'd gone off to school – and to college, now that he was doing this Land Economy thing – she'd expected him to change. To realize that she wasn't worth bothering with. It would happen one day, of course. But she was glad it hadn't quite yet – he could be an important source of information. He was, after all, Oliver's brother.

'Are they really not letting him go back to school?' she said now, a little out of breath.

'Bro? Seems not.'

'What will he do? He must be terribly upset.'

Richard laughed. 'Not really. You know Oliver.

They'll send him to some crammer in Oxford, I expect, and get him into university that way. He hasn't burnt his boats.'

They had almost reached the Bath House now: a single-storey folly built in a Victorian's idea of the Romanesque style, all colonnades, portico and friezes, with a row of deities in moss-covered marble staring blank-eyed from the parapet. The designer had even gone so far as to create an artificial knoll, so that it sat like a cherry on a turf-covered fairy cake.

Richard took the grass bank in a couple of paces, and Laura scrambled after. There was a fine view from here on a clear day, with the first houses of the village, Denham Ford, just visible through the trees to the east. Among them, a chimney stack and the corner of a grey slate roof announced the presence of the Old Rectory, Laura's home. She didn't bother to look for it now.

The Bath House doors were shut fast, but Laura knew where to find the key: two statues stood in niches on either side of the entrance, each carrying a water vessel – she ran to the left-hand one and plunged her arm into the pot. She passed the key to Richard and, with some expert jiggling of the lock, he coaxed the doors open.

'Want to swim?' Inside his voice echoed off stone and still water. 'I think there's a couple of costumes hanging about somewhere.'

Laura followed him across the threshold. It was cool and shaded. The panelled glass roof lent a greenish shadow to the light, making the whole room seem under water, and eerily cut off from the sunny day outside.

'It looks *slimy*.'

'Don't worry, it's fine. Bro said he had a dip yesterday, and he doesn't seem to have caught anything.'

Oliver. Laura imagined him down there in the water before her. He had a scar on his back from an accident at school, a pale, curving line, just below his ribs—

It wasn't, of course, that she was truly expecting a seventeen-year-old to fall for someone who was still only twelve. But one had to start somewhere. He would become very fond of her and then later on, when she was older and the gap didn't matter so much, he would find himself desperately in love and would laugh and say to her, 'Do you remember how often we used to see each other back then, and hardly even notice? Who would have thought that one day . . .?' And then she would smile, and stroke his glorious hair, and admit that she had always known . . .

'How about this one?' Richard, standing by the cupboard at the far end, was holding up a lilac all-in-one. It was ancient and knitted and, dangling from his meaty fingers, looked extremely small.

'I – I don't think it'll fit.'

Richard considered. 'Probably be too big for you, but you may as well try it.' He crunched it into a ball and threw it over. 'Not very nice, I know, but I'm afraid it's all there is.'

Laura slipped into one of the rudimentary cubicles and dragged the curtain across. The costume, it turned out, was roughly the right size, but it looked as shapeless on as it had off, and she felt silly in it. Richard was already in the pool when she emerged, his head – a much dustier and duller blond than his brother's – ploughing competently through the water. Laura sat down hastily on the edge and sloshed her feet, then stuck them out in front of her and studied her legs with severity and a sinking heart.

Would Oliver *really* fall desperately in love with her? That was the question. Even when she *was* older, and could do what she liked with her hair? Laura wished someone could give her a definite answer now: it would save years of worrying. The thing was, if progress so far was anything to go by, the chances of her turning into something elegant and glamorous seemed pretty low. Currently, Laura knew she was plain, skinny and dull. Who was to say it would ever change? With sudden irritation she pushed herself into the pool.

'WELL, WELL, WELL! Guess who's turned up.'

On the terrace, the french windows had been thrown wide, and metal chairs and small wicker tables set out. Oliver was first to spot the returning pair. He'd stretched his magnificent limbs to fine effect on the sun lounger, and now the edges of his mouth curled softly as he announced their arrival. Laura, skin still damp under her dress, shivered.

'Where *have* you been?' asked Lydia, not at all annoyed. 'Oh, silly question – look at you! Richard, that shirt is positively indecent – run and get changed at once.'

'Sneaking off together – '

'Lemonade, darling?'

' – were you waiting for him at some trysting place?'

Johanna stretched out an arm, but couldn't reach Oliver from where she sat; her fingers patted the air. 'You're a terrible tease! She's only twelve.'

Oliver lowered his lashes slyly, and Johanna laughed. Laura felt in sudden danger of crying. She turned away hurriedly and, seeing an empty chair, went and sat in it.

They were all drinking some reddish-brown stuff Laura recognized as Pimm's; there was a great jug of it on the table next to Lydia. Laura had been allowed to try some last summer, and it had tasted strange – not in the least how its colour had made her expect – and the mint leaf floating in it had felt all wrong somehow, as if a bit of the garden had fallen into your drink when you weren't looking.

'Your hair's sopping!' Laura looked up to find her mother's attention on her again. 'You'll catch your death.'

'Not in this weather, darling,' said Lydia. 'She'll be fine.'

'We should be going, in any case.'

'Should we? Oh, Tom . . .'

There then followed a disagreement that stretched on for some time, with Lydia urging that everyone should stay for supper and Johanna taking up the idea with hopeful enthusiasm. But Laura watched her father prevail, and deny, politely but firmly, that they should be waved off from the front drive.

Johanna, disappointed, moved to get up and then sat down abruptly. She blushed and giggled and caught her balance the second time.

'GET IN.'

Their car, a black Rover, was parked in the gravelled area in front of the stable block. It had been in some shade but wasn't now, and the back seat felt as if you could fry an egg on it. Laura crawled in and wound down the window.

'. . . falling all over the place,' said her father, yanking his door shut far harder than was necessary.

'Oh, Tom, I wasn't, surely? I only had—'

'Whatever you had it was too much. You embarrassed me.'

There was a pause, during which the engine started up. 'I'm sorry, Tom.'

He jabbed the gear stick, missed reverse, found it, and stalled. '*Sod* it!' he muttered. Laura stared out at the gravel: it was the expensive sort, of a uniform sandy colour and spitefully sharp. She wondered why her father hated coming to the Hall so much.

He checked the mirror. 'And it was downright rude

of you, Laura, not to join in with the tennis. God knows, you need the practice.'

'It might be for the best, Tom. She doesn't want to sprain something so close to the audition.'

'The audition?' Tom changed gear, and pulled away too fast. The tyres screeched complainingly. 'Are you *still* blathering on about that bloody dancing school?'

'I thought we'd agreed she should try.'

'We agreed nothing of the sort. I told you not to let her waste everyone's time.'

A month before, Laura's ballet teacher, Miss Chubb, had swooped on Johanna after class and delivered a long tirade about how Laura *must* be allowed to try for the West London Ballet Academy, which was a boarding school in Chiswick, apparently, and top notch as far as training went. It was run by a friend of Miss Chubb's – one Hermione Lawrence (the sort of name, Laura felt, that only a terrifying person could have) – and she would be visiting shortly to view a hand-picked selection of pupils.

Considering how completely she *didn't* look the glamorous ballerina type, Laura was astonished that Miss Chubb seemed to think her worth considering. Though ballet was the only thing she was the slightest bit good at – she was terrible at sport and couldn't sing *or* do French – still, she was positive she wasn't half good enough to pass anything so grand as an audition.

'But what harm would it do?' Johanna was saying now, more insistent than usual. 'She should be given a chance.'

'To humiliate herself?' said Tom. 'Well, if that's what it takes for you to recognize that our daughter is *clumsy* and *talentless*, Johanna, she had better go through with it.'

They were gathering speed now; gravel had given way to tarmac. Laura shut her eyes against the warm rushing air.

'. . . in their right mind could possibly think the child is going to be a dancer?' she heard her father say, and had the pleasant sensation that she was somewhere else entirely, and just happened to be listening in. 'She's about as graceful as a stick insect.'

There was a short silence. 'Miss Chubb thinks she has promise,' said Johanna softly. 'It'll transform her, Tom, you'll see.'

'That woman's grip on reality, Johanna, is no better than yours.'

THE AUDITION, as it happened, was scheduled for the day before the only other significant event the summer seemed likely to offer: the Denham Hall annual fête. On the Thursday of the following week – one day before the audition and two before the fête – Laura came out of the school gates to find her mother's green Morris Minor drawn tightly up to the kerb. As she crossed the pavement, the door swung open.

'We're due at the Hall this afternoon, remember?' said Johanna, leaning across. 'Lydia's rung – there've been rows, apparently, about what's going where, so everything's miles behind.'

Laura registered something different about her mother's face, but couldn't quite put her finger on what it was. 'Lovely,' she mumbled vaguely, getting into the car.

The Denham road took them swiftly out of town and onto the country roads. The sun shone with the confidence of summer; the clouds were plump and scudding as they should have been, the trees full-leafed, the crops tight-packed and pointing proudly skywards. Days like this were too perfect: they made Laura convinced, unfathomably, that disaster loomed. She frowned, cross with herself for foolish thoughts, and snatched a sideways glance at her mother. This time she spotted what was different. Eyeshadow. Not much of it, but definitely there. Pale blue: the colour of airmail paper. Her father, she recalled absently, hated make-up.

The road narrowed and curled to the left as it passed through the edge of Denham Ford. The body of the village lay down a right-hand turn, but they missed it and motored on, past the post office and the policeman's house, and over the hump-backed bridge. The right side of the road became wall after that, and in the wall were several gates, serving varying purposes: the one they took led onto a driveway that meandered up through the parkland, giving glimpses of Denham Hall's façade – row upon row of oblong, blankly staring eyes. Coming to the stable block at last Johanna swung the car round and parked.

'Darlings!'

It was Lydia, at the wheel of a large old Zephyr. She crunched to a halt alongside them as they got out and stuck her head through the window. '*Complete* mayhem. The tent needs patching, the red canopy's got mildew and Mrs Palgrave is ready to do murder over the Lost Offspring rota. *I* am going to town in search of a very large pot. But go and join in, do! I've even persuaded Daphne to help for the first time in her life. I swear to God it gets worse every year – *such* fun!' She grimaced and smiled and rippled her fingers, and was gone before anyone else had spoken a word.

'Come on, sweetheart.'

Laura followed her mother under a small arch to the rose garden and then, turning left, along a border ablaze with oriental poppies. This brought them to the back of the house. Johanna spotted Lydia's twin sister straight away and headed up the terrace steps: Daphne Devereux lay prostrate at the top on the sun lounger, struggling with what looked like a misshapen paper rugby ball.

'Only looked at the blessed thing and it fell apart. I was absolutely convinced I'd got it right! You do it, Johanna – the hook has to fit onto this wire bit.'

Laura hung back.

Her mother, completely unperturbed by the uncon-

ventional greeting, accepted the handful of coloured paper
and bent to press a cheek against Daphne's, each side in
turn, making tiny smacking noises with her lips. 'I didn't
think you'd be here until Saturday,' said Johanna. 'Lydia
told me you had guests in London. What *is* this, by the
way?'

'A blasted lantern – one of hundreds, Lord help us, for
the trees. Someone must be hoping for a forest fire. And,
believe me, darling, I wish I *hadn't* come till Saturday. I
can't imagine what possessed me. Laura!' Daphne pointed
with her cigarette holder – the thing that Tom called a
Pathetic Affectation. 'You look quite different from when
we last met. What has happened to your nose?'

Approaching the vision in black, which had a fearsome
beak itself, Laura stated with certainty that there had not
been any face-altering incidents, and Daphne said no
matter, she liked the new version and it must be so
exciting, mustn't it, Johanna, to have a face that was still
growing?

Johanna, who'd been fiddling ineffectually with the
lantern, gave up, murmured a distracted agreement and
turned to look out over the grounds.

Daphne followed her gaze. 'It's been hell, darling,' she
said equably. 'A garden full of beastly people running
around sabotaging each other's hopeless little projects and
calling it helping. The malice behind the neighbourly
smiles is terrifying – it's as bad as Christmas.'

On closer inspection, the scene on the lawn did seem

a little strained. The space was large, running from the border below the terrace right out to the brow of the wooded rise, cutting a wide channel between the formal gardens, nearest to the house, and, further away, the shrubberies and trees – the lawn had been planned originally so that occupants of the Hall's main bedrooms could enjoy an unimpeded view across the small valley to the Ridgeway hills beyond. Unadorned for the rest of the year, the grass was now studded with wooden pegs, heaps of rope and metal scaffolding poles. Plots for booths, not yet erected, were marked out with umbrellas, lengths of garden twine and fearsome military precision – each plot's occupants squinting jealously at their neighbour's, imagining hitherto unsuspected advantages in position or aspect that had undoubtedly been secured by foul means. In the centre of it all a large marquee, spread out but not yet pitched, lay on the grass like a vast disappointed soufflé.

Laura leant over the stone balustrade. Below, a little apart from the rest, stood a trestle table. Great sheets of paper were spread on it, bucked and furrowed where they had been folded, and two figures bent across them, their backs to the garden. Two blond heads: one dusty pale, the other bright as buttercups.

'Why don't you help Daphne with the lanterns, sweetheart?' said Johanna, handing Laura the mess of paper and heading for the steps.

'Help me? She can take them over – my creativity is entirely spent,' Daphne declared, fixing a fresh cigarette into her holder. It was fuchsia pink and the filter, which she had snapped off, was gold.

'I'll just go and find out where I might be most useful.'

'Beware, darling! They'll have you digging trenches as soon as look at you!'

But Johanna had gone. Daphne's cigarette caught and glowed and she lifted her chin to exhale; the smoke carried sideways, in a column, and dispersed. Laura sat, and set about the misshapen paper lantern.

Voices carried up to them intermittently, distant and half caught. Daphne filled her glass from a jug on the table beside her: ice cubes teetered on the lip of the spout and then splashed in, all together. Laura sighed.

She was perfectly content to be left with Daphne. Daphne didn't believe in conversation for conversation's sake and would not, for want of anything else to say, ask how one was *getting on*, or what one had been *up to* recently; the sort of questions that required dishonestly neat, polite answers.

'Daphne,' Laura began, 'do you believe in . . .' She hesitated, thinking about the word. '. . . in *destiny*?'

Daphne cast her a sidelong glance and pursed her lips. 'That's a notion that comes in many flavours, darling,' she said. 'Do you mean the idea that some Higher Being is forever jiggling our puppet strings? Or character as destiny – in the Shakespearian sense? Or the Wheel of Fortune, perhaps? Fortuna? Tyche? The three daughters of Night?'

'Ye-es,' said Laura uncertainly.

'Well?'

'Any.' She shifted in her seat. 'No, actually . . . destiny as in . . . people being meant for each other.'

'Love-wise?'

Laura nodded, blushing and beginning to regret ever having mentioned it.

'That is called hindsight,' said Daphne, ignoring her embarrassment. 'A person finds himself "in love" with someone and it appears to work terrifically well, and the fact that they're together seems such a chance thing that he can't accept that that's *exactly* what it could be.' Daphne drew on her cigarette contemplatively. 'Lots of people, darling, like to think they're so *particular* that there are only a few souls existing in the world they could fall for. They're too vain to realize that in fact, as humans go, they're terribly run-of-the-mill and could have ended up with any number of equally run-of-the-mill people. Then they call it Destiny.' She smiled thinly. 'Except, of course, when they wake up five years later and suddenly call it frightful bad luck.'

'No,' said Laura. 'I didn't mean that. I meant . . .' She frowned. 'Sort of . . . knowing in *advance*.'

'Ah,' said Daphne, eyeing her now with an expression Laura didn't like to interpret. 'That is something else. That, my dear, is called wishful thinking.'

The housekeeper, Mrs Brett, appeared at the french windows. Clearly disappointed to find Daphne the sole lady to hand (she included her in that category only with the utmost reluctance), Mrs Brett explained she had reached a critical point in her preparation of the weekend's comestibles, but had omitted to check with Mrs Trafford-Taylor whether the lamb or the beef would be preferred. Daphne swung her legs down with the air of someone about to put on a big show of practicality while in fact making the wrong decision – *on purpose* – and followed the housekeeper indoors.

Laura abandoned the lanterns. She'd sort of got it right; the wire rings joined up properly now, and the concertina bit was almost straight, although it had got a little ripped in Daphne's struggles so she wasn't sure that it would really do. She balanced it carefully next to Daphne's drink and went back to lean over the balustrade.

The marquee was going up. Half a dozen men from the estate were pulling on ropes and dragging out canvas, and the whole thing was heaving and lurching like a drugged elephant. Oliver directed the operation in the manner of a maestro, waving his arms about and shouting at people and not doing a great deal. Someone called to him; Laura didn't hear the voice but she saw him turn and cross to where several large stalls were taking shape. Her mother was there, struggling with a roll of fabric, and Oliver, laughing, took it from her and helped measure out a length for an awning. Johanna put her hand on his shoulder and touched her forehead to it briefly. She hasn't the faintest idea, thought Laura, her stomach tightening a little. And oh, that smile – why can't he turn that smile on me?

AT THE BREAKFAST TABLE the next morning, the newspaper snapped and rustled and reinvented itself as a small thick oblong. Tom propped it against the milk jug.

'You eat that properly, Laura, or you do not take it onto your plate in the first place.'

Laura jumped. Convinced her father wasn't looking she had been surreptitiously attempting to remove the lines from her marmalade; now she put them back. This faced her with a fresh dilemma: whether to pile them all onto one corner of the toast, so as to get the horrible part over with in one awful disgusting bite, or whether to scatter them as they would have been *au naturel* – which was less gullet-challenging, but on the other hand spoiled the whole slice and lengthened the ordeal. Laura opted for the single nasty dose, but then found that however much she chewed, the peel would not go down. She sat, her mouth full, and wondered what to do.

Tom shovelled dripping spoons of cereal into his mouth. His coffee arrived; he reached around the paper for it.

'Christ!'

All at once he was up, cup in hand, and disappearing through the door; Laura heard her mother's voice from the kitchen: 'Sorry, Tom . . . so sor – I *know* . . . not thinking—'

And her father's: '. . . perfectly simple task . . . *warmed* cup or there's no bloody point . . . *everything* myself . . . dreaming about?'

With the opportunity now, alone in the dining room, to dispose of the marmalade peel (back in the jar? hidden in her handkerchief?) Laura found that it had gone.

Tom reappeared, self-righteously aggrieved. A fresh cup of coffee – in a warmed cup – followed him.

Johanna sat at the place she'd laid for herself. Secretly, around her toast, Laura watched her. Everything bubbled to the surface of her mother's face unchecked these days, like small bits of vegetable in a fast-boiling soup: worry, self-doubt, apology, a kind of passive resentment. The skin held the shapes of past expressions, all ready to be used again: the two little uprights between her eyebrows, the uneven music stave on her forehead, a line from each nostril curving round to the tips of her mouth and meeting there diagonal darts, stronger than the rest, pulling everything downward.

At last, cereal finished, Tom got up to go. Laura watched Johanna get up too and follow him to the hall, where she would, Laura knew, reach for his jacket and his briefcase and be told not to fuss, would hold the edge of the open door as he went through, not kissing her, would watch him go down the steps and cross to the car.

On the table Johanna's own breakfast – a solitary slice of toast – sat untouched, stiff and cold as cardboard. Laura stared at it blandly.

'All packed for school?' said Johanna, appearing in the doorway.

Laura nodded. ''Cept my ballet stuff.'

Suddenly Johanna looked stricken. She sat and offered her hand across the table. 'Oh, sweetheart, I'm sorry. He meant to wish you luck, I'm sure. It must have slipped his mind.'

Laura was quite certain that it hadn't. But she did not care. She knew she would be better off without her father's kind of luck, since it could only be the ill kind. He was the driest type of academic: he made up his mind about things for a living, and he liked nothing better than to be proved right. His hypothesis in this case was that his daughter had no more chance of getting into a London ballet school than she had of swimming the Atlantic, or marrying royalty, or one day turning into somebody worthwhile.

Laura sometimes caught herself hoping her father would choke on his morning Grape Nuts. She was afraid this meant she was very wicked.

'REMEMBER: BACKS STRAIGHT, point those toes every time you jump, and *smile*,' Miss Chubb pulled an exaggerated leer to demonstrate. 'And whatever you do, don't fidget between exercises. I shall be sitting with Miss

Lawrence, and I shall ring a bell when she wishes the next group to come in.'

Miss Chubb shut the studio door behind her. Inside were four girls from the Thursday class; the four from the Tuesday class were left in the corridor, shivering, hopping from one foot to the other, and pulling on their socks so regularly the elastic was losing its spring.

'I couldn't eat anything at lunch time.'

'I bet you'll faint, then. Right in front of Miss Lawrence. In the middle of *pliés* – crash!'

'*Hilary.*'

'My class made me a good-luck card,' said a girl called Penny, who went to the convent school. 'I'm missing a spelling test this afternoon.'

'I'm missing history,' said another – Clara, 'which is a real swizz because it's my favourite. Are you nervous?' she asked, turning suddenly to Laura.

'No,' Laura lied. She felt sick.

'Nerves are good,' said Penny. 'They make you do it better. Come on – we haven't done our numbers.'

Someone last year – it had been forgotten exactly who, though several people claimed the credit – had started a tradition of bestowing luck by crossing the first two fingers of your right hand and tapping the other person on the breastbone to the total of their lucky number. The recipient then had to do it back or it didn't count.

Penny's lucky number was three, Clara's was seven

and Hilary's, defiantly, was thirteen. Laura, who had been asked her lucky number before she'd found out the reason, had on the spur of the moment chosen a hundred. Not many people were therefore willing to wish her luck, and kept a step away in case she sprang at them with her fingers crossed and they had to return the favour. But today Clara, who was nearest, took pity on her. 'Do me first,' she instructed wearily. Laura obliged. Clara crossed her fingers. Her taps were very fast and rather heavy, and Laura wondered whether the skin above the neckline of her tunic would be prodded raw by the time she had finished.

'That was curtsies! Already!' whispered Hilary, who had bent down to listen at the crack under the door.

'Fifty,' said Clara, concentrating. 'Don't worry. They won't call us in straight away.'

But she'd only got to seventy-two when the bell rang.

THE NEXT AFTERNOON, baking beneath the tiles in the attic of the Old Rectory, Laura dressed with care. The audition, in the end, had passed without disaster. Miss Hermione Lawrence had turned out to be a tall woman with large flat hands like ping-pong bats and feet so immensely long you half expected her to pick them up high when she walked, like a clown or someone in diving flippers. She'd said nothing to the candidates, of course, except 'very *nice*', and 'thank you *so* much for coming,

girls'. Laura had spent the hours since in a state of certainty
– certain both of failure and of success, in alternating
moments. It was thoroughly exhausting.

Now she checked herself in her small dressing-table
mirror. She had picked out her sleeveless blue cotton dress
with the ribbon sash (darker blue); it lent her eyes – an
indifferent slaty grey most of the time – a reflected colour,
and when she wore the matching ribbon in her hair the
overall effect was not too bad. She had a white cardigan
for when it got cooler – not practical, but her mother
would insist she took one and it was the only one that
went with the dress. But now, turning back to the bed,
she found her cat Mr Noah curled plumb in the middle of
it, feigning deep sleep and no doubt moulting as prodi-
giously as ever. She lifted him, still curled up, and moved
him further down the bed.

Her father had already left for the dinner at his college.
Now Johanna called up the stairs, 'Ready, sweetheart?'
just as Laura started down them. 'You do look nice,' she
said, as Laura reached the second flight and came into
view.

Johanna turned to fluff her hair in the hall mirror. She
was wearing a dress Laura hadn't seen before. It was pale
green, with a stiff, flared skirt that just reached her knees.
She'd curled her hair carefully, and her shoes were the
low stiletto slingbacks she kept for best. 'And will I do?'
Johanna asked, facing Laura again and seeming genuinely

anxious to know. Laura hugged her cardigan to her midriff
with sudden vague unease. But she nodded.

A BLISTERING AFTERNOON had mellowed into an early
evening unusually warm and sweet, even for the beginning
of July. In the grounds of Denham Hall, the scent of
honeysuckle and roses hung heavy in invisible clouds, and
with the pungencies of the garden were mingled other
scents – of charcoal smoke from the barbecue, of baked
potatoes and pasties and pies, heating in a makeshift oven
beside it. On the fringes of the lawn, the trees were strung
with paper lanterns – well-made, clearly not by Daphne –
in reds and blues and greens, and the bright colours were
picked up, too, in the striped awnings of stalls and the
little flags of bunting that scooped along the edges of the
tables. There was a coconut shy and a lucky dip, a 'guess
the weight of the cake' booth and a stall selling feathered
and sequinned masks; and here and there trestle tables
displayed a world of sweet delights, sugared almonds and
biscuits and raisin buns, jelly shapes and home-made stick-
jaw toffee.

Laura and Johanna wandered at a stately pace; Laura
slipped her hand into her mother's and let herself be led,
stopping when Johanna stopped to look at a display or to
chat. She saw Miss Chubb in the distance, with her spaniel
tugging on its string. She caught a glimpse of Daphne too,
in emerald silk trousers wide enough to catch the wind
and a turban topped with Carmen Miranda fruit; beneath

it, the bony face seemed paler and stranger than ever. Then Laura spotted a peacock's head complete with tiny crown-like crest approaching from the direction of the house. It was attached to a short cocktail dress and the unmistakably shapely legs of Lydia Trafford-Taylor.

Johanna had seen the peacock too. She squeezed Laura's shoulder, and said, a little too eagerly, 'I expect you'd like to explore, sweetheart, yes? Find some of your friends?'

Laura drifted away as was required. She could see Penny, Clara and Hilary huddled together by the barbecue, whispering and sucking their drink straws. Laura had no wish to join them and knew, in any case, that they would quickly contrive to lose her if she did. She turned and headed in the opposite direction. Smaller children were chasing in rampageous circles around trees and stalls and clumps of talking adults, giggling, staggering, panting and occasionally crashing face-first onto the grass, only to be rescued and carried away, tears and mucus sliding down crumpled chins. The big ones, the teenagers, were slouched behind the marquee complaining about the middle-aged music being played inside.

Giving them a wide berth as she rounded the marquee, Laura found on the other side the stall where masks of all shapes and sizes were strung up on hooks like the spoils of an exotic shoot. She felt for her purse in her cardigan pocket: Johanna had given her a little money.

'Yes, dear?' said the stallholder, whose chins wobbled

beneath the upper face of Marie Antoinette, complete with beauty spot and cardboard powered hair.

Laura considered. Marie Antoinette's smile became fixed and then testy.

'How much is that one?' said Laura at last, pointing to a bird face, with red and yellow feathers sprouting like flames from its brow and a sharp hooked nose that reminded her of Daphne. Its tag had twisted round.

'Half a crown. Have enough, do you? It's all to St Peter's roof appeal, so I'm not giving reductions.'

Laura counted out the money carefully. Marie Antoinette counted it again. Then she reached up, grudgingly, to unhook the mask. It was one of the nicest and she seemed unwilling to part with it.

Laura stretched the elastic over her head and pulled her ponytail through. Her breath was loud and hot behind the cardboard and her lashes caught against the eye-holes as she blinked.

Setting off again, she came next to a game stall, where a central island stocked with knitted toys, bottled fruit and baskets of lavender bags turned gently round, and players attempted to hook things from it with fishing rods. Supervising the frustration and the prize-giving was Richard. Beside him stood someone in an owl mask, leaning against the canopy pole and talking to two of the older girls from the estate cottages. It was an owl with yellow hair.

To her own surprise, Laura was gripped with a sudden panic. Her instinct was to plunge straight back into the crowd. But Richard had already recognized her. She was glad of her mask.

'Hello there, Laura. Want to fish?' he called. 'Three goes for sixpence.'

Laura hesitated, then started forward. Though he was facing away from her, Oliver was so near as she took her three goes that her nostrils tingled: sweat and warmth and a hint of cologne. She wasn't doing well.

'Last time round, this . . . Ah – never mind! Good try, anyhow. Who's next? Philip? Come on, then – here you are, have Laura's rod.'

She stepped back, and a group of boys pushed in front of her to the counter, laughing and shoving and arguing. In a moment Oliver was laughing with them, his teeth flashing white below the owl feathers. It was her he should be speaking to, she thought. If only she could make him laugh like that. But he hadn't even noticed she'd been there. Laura turned away.

As THE LIGHT BEGAN to fade and the windows of Denham Hall flamed red with the reflected sunset, all about the gardens voices became louder, gestures more expansive. The grass underfoot was strewn with paper cups and raffle tickets and streamers. Laura felt peculiar. The evening hadn't turned out as she'd hoped – though she didn't know quite what she *had* hoped. All she knew was that she felt flat and disappointed, dull amid the tinsel-bright reflections and the tipsy laughter.

In the marquee, the band was sawing doggedly at a quickstep. Laura stood just inside the canvas wall and caught the first glimpse of her mother she had had for some time: among the twirling figures, rising and sinking somewhat erratically in step with the postman, Mr Flegger. Johanna's face was ruddy and shiny and her expressions exaggerated: she flopped about in Mr Flegger's grip like a rag doll, leaning over one arm and then the other to talk to dancers skimming past. Mr Flegger looked nervous, as if he'd been left with the care of a too-boisterous dog.

Usually, by now, Laura could expect her mother to be fretting about her bedtime. But Johanna looked as though thoughts of her daughter, of going home, of sleep, could not be further from her mind. Laura left the tent, pushing against a crowd of villagers who were on their way in.

Outside the air had chilled. She struggled clumsily with her cardigan as she pulled it on, straining to see the buttons past the beak of her mask. She was jostled and bumped and, as soon as the crowd thinned, began to run. She had nowhere to aim for, only a sudden need to get away from the noise, to seek space and solitude.

She found them at the beginning of the wooded slope. The trees were unadorned here; no lanterns or streamers, no bunting. She came to a twisted yew, and swung herself up into its branches. The bark was dusty-dry.

Climbing as high as she dared, Laura turned back to look out over the gardens. Distant shouts and shrieks drifted on the air, claps and cheering and snatches of music. It was half in her mind that she would be missed, sooner or later. That her mother would have to come looking for her. That she should, if she were sensible, climb down and go back. But instead she sat dangling her legs and watched as the sky darkened.

Some time later she heard voices. She stiffened, suddenly alert, and strained her eyes to make out who it was, and where. Two figures were stumbling up the grass incline, falling in towards each other and staggering away again, giggling and whispering. Laura glimpsed them, lost them, saw them again through the lattice of branches. They came among the trees not directly beneath her, but lower on the slope.

'Johanna—'

A man's voice — it must have been Mr Flegger's — carried indistinctly.

So she *was* looking for her. Laura was about to call out, but heard a sound and wondered if her mother was crying. No, it was laughter — strange: soft, continuous. It lent Johanna's voice a tremor as she spoke.

'W-what? Where've you gone?'

'Come here.'

'No-o-o.'

There was fumbling, and more laughter — low laughter, so it must have been his — and Laura couldn't tell if she was dragging or he was pushing, but then they were on the ground, with Mr Flegger half kneeling, half lying on top of her mother. Johanna's hands were tugging at his clothes. Her legs were ugly, apart and bent up like that, and one of her suspenders had come undone.

They shifted, out from the deepest shadow beneath the branches. There was a mask pushed up over Mr Flegger's forehead, sliding back – it would fall off soon as he moved – and she saw the hair beneath that glimmered in the half-light; in the greys of the half-light she caught its colour.

Yellow. Glorious, golden yellow.

She swallowed. A strange feeling rose in the pit of her stomach. She smelt a smell again: salt sweat, warmth, a breath of cologne.

All at once, the yew tree seemed to lurch. The branch below swung up sickeningly towards her, and Laura felt herself falling.

Chapter Three **London, 1989**

The sheets were twisted. Natasha pulled at them irritably and rolled onto her back. What time was it, anyhow? These curtains were so thick it was like a blackout. Was it morning or still night? She'd heard the door slam – when? An hour ago? Two? Had that been Renée, heading off for the Institute? Hardly the first morning that Natasha had been still in bed when her flatmate left but these days lying in didn't feel so good. There was nowhere she was supposed to be.

She put out her arm and located the cigarettes among the mess of magazines and books and bog roll. She'd drunk too much again last night. And smoked too much, most likely, though she hadn't kept a count. She felt for the right end of the cigarette and lit up.

Jumbled, fractured thoughts were turning fast in her head. It seemed the restless monologue had carried on all night: she was exhausted. Where was her mother? Right now, this minute. Was she thinking of her? Please, don't

make me *laugh*! Christ – Natasha had even made it easy
for the woman: everything she'd said about Alex on that
blasted programme had been *true*, any imbecile could have
seen it. But what had she expected? Selfless support?
Natasha smiled grimly into the darkness. Her mother was
incapable of any kind of selflessness. Oh, yes, she'd have
the world believe the opposite: she'd have it believe she'd
made the ultimate dancer's sacrifice and given up her stage
career for the sake of husband and child. But that was a
lie, Natasha knew.

Laura had not retired until Natasha was six. By then
Natasha had already wished her real mother was the
nanny, not this woman who flitted home for brief visits
between tours. And Laura had only retired, even then,
after yet another ankle operation had failed and it had
become obvious that in any case the end of her career was
imminent. So much for selflessness. Natasha wished now
that Laura had never come back to live at home at all.

As she lay still in the dark, her thoughts slid again to
the Institute. She found herself floating above the buildings
and, looking down, saw the studios, the changing rooms,
canteen and corridors crawling with students. Those
huddled groups, whispered conversations – were any of
them about her? Some of the girls in her year must be
crowing – plum roles in the gala up for grabs. All that
work she'd put in, for nothing. And why had no one
rung, damn it? Why had no one rung and said this was

mad, all a mistake, they couldn't let *her* go, of all people? Why was everyone else carrying on pretending nothing had happened? To spite her, was it? To—

Natasha shook her head and half sat up. She took a breath, a slow one. It was okay. It wasn't anything she couldn't handle.

She had another fag before she got up. It made her feel sick. She groped her way to the bathroom and splashed some water on her face, then shuffled back and pulled on an old paint-stained T-shirt and jogging bottoms. Holding her thoughts off the Institute with an iron grip, she tried very hard not to turn them to the other subject that was biting at the edge of her consciousness: exactly how, from here on in, she was going to spend her time.

Breakfast. Breakfast was the thing. She didn't normally eat it, of course, never up early enough. What the hell? She did now. She headed for the kitchen. God, she was stiff – she had to get to a class. But not today, she couldn't do anything today.

She made the instant coffee too strong. It was foul, but she drank it anyway. Fried an egg; looked at it; chucked it in the bin. Then she flicked on the TV and lay on the sofa.

Some day-time garbage; she let the gabble wash over her. Summer fashions for the larger lady – smiles bright and hollow as the studio sets. The colours blurred, the figures swam and merged, and Natasha was surprised to feel hot salt tears stinging the corners of her eyes. Angrily, she scraped a hand across them. But there was no one there to see her – for once, no need to pretend.

AT LEAST THE AUDITIONS had gone relatively well. Laura hung on to this fact like a floating spar as she made it back up the stairs to her office. One hundred and nine candidates competing for twenty-six places in next year's intake. The stars of the gala in three years' time, though it might as well have been twenty: Laura could no more imagine getting through the next three days or months than the next three years.

In the outer office Maria sat at her desk, headphones on, typing at virtuoso speed. She plucked out an earpiece as Laura approached. 'That stuff for Health and Safety's nearly done, Madame. Want to check it through?' But she got no response.

Laura walked into her office and closed the door. The next stage, she told herself methodically, was to draw up a short-list of the candidates they'd want to see again for a final audition. She could sift through the applications tonight. But, then, she still had the gala recasting to work out. It was madness to put it off any longer – there was little enough time as it was. Laura opened her door again. To speak with her usual firm clarity now seemed to require a supreme effort. 'Maria,' she said, 'get me some videos of year three classes, the most recent you can find. At least two general classes plus *pas de deux* and *pointe* work.' Year three classes were the last thing she wanted to watch just now but there was no time for squeamishness.

'Yes, Madame.' Maria sprang up quickly and left the room.

The gala recasting. And that letter from Paris, too. From Milan Novák. She had to reply. Laura went to the desk and opened the drawer, took out the letter, read it again briskly. It was addressed to Alan Hoyle – Milan didn't even know she had taken over the Institute . . . or was that deliberate? She shook off the thought with impatience. He only asked to come to the gala, after all. Was that so terrible? Her gut instinct screamed yes. She *couldn't* see him. She couldn't bear—

'Madame!'

A voice behind her. Laura dropped the letter into the drawer, snapped it shut and turned. The sight of the old man on the threshold – spry as a gentleman cricketer in knife-crease trousers and blazer – gave her a sudden shiver. Conjured out of thin air again. She wished his shoes squeaked.

'At last,' Alexander said, inclining his head with graceful politeness. 'If I didn't know you better, Madame, I should have said you'd been hiding from me since that little drama of ours on Tuesday.'

Laura struggled to muster the last resources of self-control. He was counting it a victory: the spring in his step as he came forward said everything.

'But I'm so glad I've caught you. I've been to Sotheby's and made a most glorious addition to my collection. You will simply love this.' He had a fat, glossy catalogue in his hand. Flicking rapidly through, he found a page and held it up. '*Regarde!* Nijinsky's costume from *Schéhérazade*. Isn't it to die for? Some cretin on the telephone from Japan was bidding against me but I buried him in the end.'

The costume consisted of a pair of flowing Arabian trousers and a close-fitting, beaded top. Neither looked in very good condition but, to a serious collector like Alexander, the illustrious name would be more than enough. He had been hunting down and buying ballet memorabilia ever since Laura had known him; she had begun to wonder where he put it all. Now, looking from the photograph to the eager, wrinkled face before her, she said, 'Will it fit you?'

'Very droll, Madame. I have a tailor's dummy on which to display it. Not quite the divine figure of my dreams, but, then, faceless, which is an advantage – if one can't have the head of the Golden Slave himself, that is. Stuffed, and on a pole. Figgis!'

Figgis had followed Alexander into the room. An over-pink, damp-looking young man, he was writing a thesis for his master's degree on the Life and Work of Alexander McIntyre: Choreographer and Teacher, and was trailing his subject round the school like a rejected lover. For the last few moments he had been lumbering to and fro by the weeping figs, taking photographs of his hero in conversation. Now Alexander, who seemed to consider Figgis a personal servant, handed him the catalogue. Where on earth, Laura wondered, watching the boy juggle it uncomfortably with his camera, had Alex found such a toadying spineless specimen?

'And a morsel of news, Madame.' Alexander leant towards Laura confidingly. 'I have been invited to choreograph in Berlin.'

'Willkommen, bienvenu, *welc*ome.' Laura smiled with unfeigned pleasure. 'How wonderful! You would like to arrange a sabbatical, perhaps? When do you go?'

Behind the spectacles the white brows lowered. 'Such equanimity!' he muttered sharply, then bared his teeth in a smile. 'But I don't believe I shall go. Life is so very *interesting* here. I should hate to miss anything.'

'*He hasn't choreographed since 'seventy-eight. If he ever had any talent in him, he ran out of juice a long time ago . . .*'

A harsh note sounded in Laura's memory. What was Alexander's motive? Surely he would not put petty Institute concerns before his own greater glory. What – and the idea was hardly comfortable – if Natasha had been right?

With a formal bow, he retired. On his way to the stairs he met Maria returning. With exaggerated deference she moved aside to let him pass.

Laura stood for a moment, breathing carefully. Then reaching for her chair, she let herself slowly into it.

Maria came into the office, and set down two videos on the desk. 'That one's February, that's April.'

Laura nodded and dismissed her. She did not like to think of Alex for long; right now, it was almost more than she could bear. His had been a temporary victory, but one for which he would pay. Eventually. And, in the short term, she had come to a decision: she would find a way to help Natasha. It was possible, though she couldn't move directly. She needed some sort of go-between. Her own part in the business had to be hidden, or Natasha wouldn't want to know. And Laura could hardly blame her for that. So, whom could she use? Leaning back in her chair, Laura assessed the options. They were neither many nor varied.

'Maria?' she called.

The vermilion bob reappeared round the door.

'Book Ellen to see me, will you?' said Laura. 'Private chat. Monday morning.'

WHEN RENÉE GOT HOME from the Institute, she clocked the living room litter and reckoned Natasha had been lying on that sofa all day. Still, she asked, without hope, 'You find out about classes?'

Natasha groaned and aimed the TV handset. 'Off my back, Aitchison.'

'*Nat*. Remember the old saw: miss one day's class and you notice, two days and your teacher notices—'

'Three days and your frigging arse falls off. What's the big fuss? It's hardly as if I'll have a problem getting a job.'

'Hello. This is me you're talking to, not Alex or Madame. You can cut the swagger.'

Renée began picking up the foil trays, crisp packets and empty cans, then shook her head and dumped them in Natasha's lap. 'You can't be that confident, seriously?' she said, ignoring the growls of protest.

'Why not?' said Natasha, and then frowned, puzzled. 'You aren't?'

'There are never enough jobs.'

'For the mediocre. Real talent always gets snapped up.'

'For a cynic like you that shows remarkable faith in the system.' Renée brought the bin bag from the kitchen and held it out. 'Look,' she said, tying up the ends, 'even if you're right you've still got to get yourself seen. No one's going to serve up your glittering future on a plate. Find a regular class, pronto. And try any audition that's going.'

Natasha flopped back against the cushions and shook her head. 'I'm not going to take just *anything*. I want to be sure I'll make the biggest bloody splash I can. It'll be my way of settling a few scores.'

It had sounded good in her head. But Renée didn't seem, somehow, so impressed. Natasha thought she almost looked sorry for her.

MONDAY MORNING. Ten o'clock, or thereabouts, saw Ellen Ellmore rap on Laura Douglas's office door and,

answering the summons, proceed inside. At fifteen minutes past the hour, Ellen was still sitting on the small,
uncomfortable wooden chair opposite the large,
unfriendly wooden desk. And she was looking surprised.
Natasha Taylor was not a subject she had expected her
employer to introduce, still less the business of putting
some undercover favours the girl's way. Ellen had had to
reshuffle her views on recent events, on Madame, too,
quicker than a card-sharp. Her face, intent, assessing, had
shown it all. Laura smiled. Straight-talker, quick-thinker:
she liked Ellen.

'And one more thing.' Laura opened the drawer beside
her and drew out a sheet of paper. 'Since – from what
you said at the meeting last week – you seem to feel so
strongly about it.' She turned the paper round and pushed
it across the desk.

'Milan Novák?' said Ellen, picking it up, surprised
again.

'I took your point about an outright snub, and I
thought you might like to deputize for me if he comes to
the gala. I'll have enough on my plate buttering up the
directors who *do* have decent jobs to offer.' *If* he comes to
the gala. Laura listened to herself. And if he *does*, what the
hell will stop me running, screaming, out of that theatre?
Her hands were clasped, lightly. She realized that one nail
was digging into her palm. She shifted her grip.

Ellen read through the letter. 'You still won't let him
come to the Institute, though?'

'Certainly not. And he won't be invited to the reception. I wouldn't trust him not to . . . disrupt things. And I wouldn't particularly like the impression of us that his presence would give.' Absently, Laura picked up a pen and turned it in her fingers, apparently unconcerned. 'But you could write and let him know you're the person he should speak to. If he wants to speak to anyone, that is.'

'You can't stop him inviting students to audition for him, anyway.'

'I'm aware of that,' said Laura. 'But what I'm not going to do is give him official encouragement or his putative company any sanction. Feel free to tell him why, if you like.'

Laura wondered whether Ellen thought this strange. It was likely she remembered that Laura and Novák had worked together once. But, along with most people, Ellen had probably forgotten what had happened afterwards. Laura's career and Novák's had both been colourful enough since then, thankfully, to erase that episode from the public memory.

'Any student tempted to work for him deserves to be warned,' Laura said now, leaning forward and tapping the pen to make her point. 'If his company folds like it did last time, they could find themselves with nothing, having turned down other offers. It should be a last resort.'

Ellen shrugged. 'If there's a chance Novák may have solid jobs to offer, it's still worth their while.'

Holding herself still and impassive, Laura watched

Ellen get up and cross to the door. She was a strange-looking thing: the canvas slacks, the man's shirt rolled up to the elbows, the windblown hair, which, from the look of it, she went at herself with a pair of kitchen scissors. And the orange toe-nail polish.

Laura said, 'You worked with him at some stage, didn't you?'

Ellen turned. 'Only briefly. New York in the late seventies.' She shook her head, remembering something. 'Weird guy.' Then she cracked a generous smile. 'But watch him dance and you'd forgive him anything, wouldn't you?'

Laura opened her mouth to ask another question. But then she thought better of it and shut it again.

RENÉE'S WORDS HAD HIT home. Both of them knew that behind the bluffing Natasha listened to her advice and, in her own time, tended to act on it. And so, that same Monday, as Laura faced Ellen in her small sunlit office, Natasha was occupied in finding herself a class. After only a little hesitation, she took the easy option and signed on at the Sweat Shop, a serve-all supermarket of a dance school just off Garrick Street. Name registered, money paid, she shouldered her battered holdall and descended into the sweaty underworld of the changing room. This one was large, low-ceilinged and crowded, with a stench of Deep Heat, talc and hair-spray so thick her nostrils constricted in protest. Nevertheless, Natasha barged her way in, shoved up the bags on the nearest bench and dumped down her belongings, ignoring complaints. The room was a jostling mass of elbows, knees and bony bums, protruding hip-bones, vertebrae countable as building blocks, scabbed and blistered feet, all moving to the sounds of popping, grinding cartilage, as bodies slipped out of baggy clothes and into clinging ones. Natasha dragged on ancient frayed leggings, leotard and sweatshirt, twisted her hair and jabbed it in place with a pin, cursed herself for not having had another fag to damp down the hunger pangs that were clutching at her gut and bolted for the studio.

By the time the class started, she was already wishing she hadn't bothered turning up. It was an all-women session, ostensibly for professionals, but that seemed to be a euphemism here for the out-of-workers, the never-been-*in*-workers, the not-a-hope-in-hellers. It was worse than an open audition for a West End musical. The young ones didn't disturb her so much: the girls with soft teenage faces and bright shimmering leotards who looked in the mirror only to admire themselves; the girls with soft feet, whose legs trembled in a long piece of *adage*, who stopped when they got tired and rushed to their water bottles and to blot their make-up with their neatly folded towels.

Pausing now between exercises, Natasha peeled off her scruffy cotton top and wiped her face on it. Sweat had stained a dark channel down the groove of her back and in the hollow above her bum and across her leggings at the front, either side of her crotch.

No, it wasn't the young ones: it was the older dancers who made her freak. From the far side of the pit they might have passed muster but up close they were all joints and stringy gristle: the necks looked like skinned-over electric cabling; the rib-cages were toast-racks; the eyes swivelled in hollows deep and empty as buckets. They worked like buggery and their gaze clung to the mirror in hope and not a little desperation.

'Look at them,' said a voice at Natasha's shoulder as they paused between exercises. 'Look at me. This is the scrapyard. This horse-meat'll end up in cans.'

She turned. A woman stood beside her, breathing hard and plucking at her plastic sweatpants with yellow-stained fingers.

Natasha shrugged. 'Guess it's hard to give up. When you used to be professional.'

The woman looked at her strangely. 'Used to be? I wouldn't know.' She turned back to the class, then added as an afterthought, 'I'm thirty-one.'

Natasha stared at her. Then she stabbed a *pointe* into the floor and pressed over on the arch, studying her foot. She felt sick. It was appalling. The lines were etched too deep, the skin was too rough, she looked too . . . *tired*.

They were called back, then, to the centre of the studio. Natasha saw the woman smile at her in the mirror, amused. She stared back, watching; she was strong – the plastic-wrapped legs held without tremor their respectable angles, 90 degrees, 100 . . . 135 on a *développé* in second. Whatever, Natasha thought, rattled. Get to that age and you were past it, that was all. You just had to know when your time was up. Go get yourself a life. *Another* life.

It was less disturbing to put on the blinkers and focus. After the latent anxiety of the past week, Natasha found she relished the chance to push herself. The pain was immaterial – a lot of your average class did hurt, and by no means moderately. But the eccentric restrictions of this most eccentric dance-form gave Natasha, conversely, an intoxicating sense of freedom, an emotional release like a drug-rush, and there was more of her soul in the simple controlled extending of a leg than there had ever been in any verbal exchange she had had in her life. Renée was right: Natasha had to get to regular class. But not for Renée's reasons – fitness, auditions, getting a job, all that was peripheral. If she didn't dance, Natasha felt she was suffocating. It was a physical need. If the thought hadn't appalled her, she might have said it was in her blood.

Still, Natasha reflected, this place was no good. The teaching was crap, her classmates were worse. As she towelled off on her way to the showers, she decided to pay a visit to a few company headquarters on the way home, and check out the plan B Renée had suggested: company classes.

*

'BASTARDS!'

'Well, hello to you too,' said Renée, upside down. She was lying on her bedroom floor with her bum against the skirting board and her legs splayed sideways in either direction; in this posture she was also managing to darn the end of a *pointe* shoe. 'Which particular bastards,' she said, 'among many, admittedly, would these ones be?'

'They wouldn't see me.' Natasha sat down heavily on Renée's bed, looking accusatory.

'Who wouldn't?'

'You said to check out company classes, right? See if they'd let me join in, kill two birds with one stone. I get class, no skin off their nose, and they get to see if I'm any good. Which, of course, I am and so I get hired, right? No need for all that audition shit.'

'Right.'

'*Right.* So, after the Sweat Shop I go to the Metropolitan, don't I? Only they won't have me. Stupid cow on reception says they're not taking anyone into classes for the foreseeable future.'

Renée, upside down, raised her eyebrows. It looked peculiar.

'So I try the EBT,' Natasha ploughed on, 'and, just for the hell of it, the Southern. Same story. I never got past the hallway.' She thwacked Renée's duvet in disgust. 'Cretins! Hasn't it occurred to them they might be missing something? But if they won't bloody see me I can't show them. Can I?'

'Stick with the Sweat Shop, then.'

'I am *not* going to that dump again. It was like freak night at the Bell and Butcher. Gave me the willies.'

'So what are you going to do?'

Loath as she was to admit it, Natasha was genuinely worried. 'Don't know,' she said quietly.

Renée extricated herself from her uncomfortable position, reached into a bag and slung a newspaper across the floor to Natasha. 'Here, I picked this up on the way home.'

It was the *Stage*.

'Any auditions?'

'Well, nothing you'd want.'

Twenty-four hours had changed a great deal. Natasha took the paper eagerly and began to flick through.

THAT SAME EVENING, a little after eight, Laura climbed the front steps to her house, paused at the top and put her key in the first of the door's big locks. Wandsworth had turned grey and greasy in the evening light. It was raining, in a vague, pettish sort of way; wet leaves in small front gardens bore the same sheen as plastic signs at the filling station across the road. A dog, well fed but matted, pattered up and stopped to sniff the bottom step where stone gave way to railing. Approvingly, it cocked its leg and a twist of warm, acrid scent drifted up to Laura as she pushed against the door and went inside.

The lock clunked behind her. Without bending, she

levered off her shoes. She listened for a moment, heard nothing, and put down her bag softly. The house smelt empty, waiting, cool as glass. Only the cats moved silently through the rooms, past the windows, hardly rippling the air, like phantoms going about the business of another world.

She was tired – no, tired didn't even begin to describe it. Her eyes seemed to turn in sockets lined with sandpaper. She was drained, utterly, and with a sour taste at the core of her: sick at heart, sick of herself.

Slowly, she sat on the hall chair. The mirror opposite showed her half a picture – a landscape, Oxfordshire – the edge of the sitting-room door, nothing, thankfully, of herself. She was afraid to see her face. How on earth did she do it? How did she function all day, walking and talking, never breathing a word of what she felt? She was afraid even to think of it: it gave her a sensation like nausea, as if her feelings, once unleashed, would spew out uncontainably, stinking with fear and distress, disgusting, horrifying.

Laura shook herself a little, stood up. There were things to do. Those year-three videos were in her bag, still unwatched, and the decision about the gala casting had to be made. Tonight.

Glass of wine; pad of paper; pen. She set them on the low sitting-room table, picked up the first video, put it down. She took the other, weighed it for a moment, slid it into the machine. Then she sat, straight and unrelaxed on the settee, and began to watch.

The light wasn't so great. It was studio one. There were the free-standing barres, pushed to one side, the piano in the corner, the rosin box beneath. There was that ginger-haired girl, on the front row as usual – she paid too much attention to the mirror. What was she called? Sarah – Sarah Cunningham. That was it. She wasn't bad. Nice line but she turned poorly. Laura glanced down at the paper and scrubbed out the name.

The girls were *piqué*ing from the corner, picking their way across the room on *pointe* like so many dressage horses. Two passed across the screen and disappeared, then a third, a fourth – all decent dancers, technically accomplished, though none with a great deal of flair. There was, Laura noticed, a figure at the back who had not taken her turn. She was in shadow, a murky shape, so slender she looked heart-breakingly fragile. She was bending down, rubbing her shin and adjusting a shoe. The teacher – it was Bara, Laura could hear her voice off-camera – summoned them into the centre and, unseen, marked out an exercise.

Now Laura wasn't writing any more. The pen, disregarded, hung loosely in her fingers, its tip just catching the cuff of her other sleeve. Slowly, stealthily, the blue ink was seeping into the linen. But still Laura didn't look down. On-screen, the figure at the back had moved out of shadow, been called to a place near the camera and, along with half a dozen other members of the class, was dancing.

The body was astonishing; a little taller than average and perfectly proportioned. The joints seemed endlessly pliable: the limbs twisted, swung, knew instinctively where lay the most beautiful lines, the curves and angles that most pleased the eye and hit them every time. Above them the face was not quite pretty: the features were too sharp, too straight-set for that. But, still, when the girl danced, her dark gaze shone with a kind of savage enjoyment, an unapologetic pride that was mesmerizing. When she was on the screen Laura could look at no one else. No one but this girl – this young woman. Her own daughter.

And that daughter would have been surprised to see her mother's face at this moment: to have seen there open wonder, mixed with pain and something softer – regret? All were emotions to which Laura could not admit, for fear of what might follow. Self-control seemed, these days, to be her chief and constant aim.

Still, as she watched the tape, alone, Laura allowed her thoughts to roam a little. How, she wondered, could it have been different? She and Natasha had stood no chance right from the beginning, she saw that now. The circumstances of Natasha's birth had been too terrible, the depression afterwards all-consuming. Laura remembered how desperately she had wanted to escape, back to the stage and her old life. How could she have bonded with the demanding bundle of flesh that prevented it? And yet, the question had tormented her, what sort of mother was she, what sort of woman, if she could not? She had tried, one grim day, to end her own life. No one knew of that. But it was what had pushed her, at last, to find work again.

Abruptly, Laura took the handset and shot the picture from the screen. She watched the grey electric fuzz for an instant, then took her glass and headed back to the kitchen. She poured another measure, drank half of it in a single gulp and filled the glass again.

A cat, sensitive to kitchen sounds even from the garden, nosed daintily through the cat flap and sat by its bowl, expectant. Laura spoke to it, conversationally, and sat down to rub her ankle. Something caught her eye. At this level she could see beneath a Sunday colour supplement to where the answering machine was flashing in silent alarm. She reached out and flicked it onto Playback.

An eternity of beeps. A pause. A sigh. Then a voice she hadn't heard for quite some time: 'Darling, it's me . . . God, I hate these things. Why can't you just be *in* at a reasonable hour of the day?' Another pause, the sound of cigarette smoke being exhaled. 'Look. Give me a call, can you?'

And then a clanking thud. Daphne's telephone, Laura knew, was ancient, and hanging up sounded like she'd flung it across the room.

Laura held out her leg and turned her foot gingerly,

drawing circles in the air. The ankle was loosening up but her head was beginning to pulse. Unwisely ignoring it, Laura picked up the phone and dialled Daphne's number.

RENÉE'S NEEDLE HALTED; the thread dangled. 'Was that our door?' she said.

Deep in the *Stage,* Natasha grunted. 'Dunno. Christ, there really is *nothing* in here.' She turned the page.

There was a pause. 'I suppose *I*'d better see, anyway.' Renée got up.

'Nat!' she called a minute later. 'It's . . . someone to see you.'

Natasha frowned, shoved the paper aside and stumped down the stairs. Before she reached the bottom a thought had occurred to her and, for one awful instant, as she walked into the living room she half expected to find her mother waiting there. It was with a strange relief that she saw the figure of Ellen Ellmore.

Renée, looking embarrassed, was making hostessly offers; Ellen declined them all and remained standing in the centre of the room. There was a short, awkward silence.

'Renée mentioned . . .' Ellen began, then hesitated, clicking her keys in her coat pocket.

'What?'

'That you'd not got any specific plans.'

Natasha nodded genially. 'Renée knows shit,' she said.

'Oh. You have a job?'

A pause. 'No.'

Another pause. 'But I've got a bunch of leads I haven't had a chance to follow up yet,' said Natasha. 'This time next week I'll be sorted.'

'If you think so.'

'I know so.'

The three women eyed each other. Ellen ran a hand through her hair. 'Look,' she said to Natasha, 'you're going to public classes, I presume?'

Natasha could feel the look Renée was shooting her; she pointedly didn't meet it. 'What is this, the third degree?'

'I'll take that as a yes.' Ellen sighed. 'But if you really want to do yourself justice at these auditions you have lined up, I reckon you might be able to use some extra coaching. I'm offering.'

Natasha raised her eyebrows, archly amused. 'Got some quarrel with Madame, have you?'

Ellen looked back at her, blank-faced, and then said heatedly, 'I was thinking of you. Look, you brought this expulsion on yourself. But I still think it was a tough decision. Some of us have put three years' work into you, remember.'

'Right.' Natasha smiled falsely. 'Well, I can manage fine, thanks. I don't need charity.'

'Natasha!'

'It's all right, Renée.' Ellen waved a pacifying hand. 'I can't say I'm surprised.' She looked towards Natasha again.

'But don't imagine you can put me off with your little attempts at offending me, either,' she said evenly. 'My prediction is that you'll want the coaching. But you'll come to that in your own time.' She paused. 'I might, you see,' she said, 'be able to set up some auditions for you. Some *more*, I should say.'

Something in the set of the shoulders told Ellen she'd got Natasha's attention, though the girl was looking at the floor, her face hidden behind her hair.

'Who with?' came a wary voice.

'I'd have to see. Can't promise.'

'Madame's the one who talks to company directors.'

'Not always.' Ellen hesitated, then took a decision. 'I'm heading up the Institute's dealings with Milan Novák, for example.'

Now, for certain, Natasha was alert. There was a rapid glance of honest interest. 'Milan Novák? He's working again?'

'Setting up a new company. Yes.'

Natasha shifted uncomfortably. Novák's name had touched off spreading ripples of association in her mind. The famous Czech defector: sublimely gifted, recalcitrant, wholly unreliable. A chance to audition for *him* . . .

'So here's my number,' Ellen was saying, scribbling on a small notebook she'd produced. She tore off the page and stuck it under a lighter on the mantelpiece. Then she smiled at Renée, with something like reassurance. 'I'll see you tomorrow.'

'You will.'

Natasha was still trying to think of what to say when they both left the room.

With Ellen shown out, Renée returned, fairly fuming. 'You might at least have sounded grateful. She's trying to help.' She sat down, and then stood up again. 'Natasha! For God's sake, they might even sack her if they found her bailing you out.'

'Who told you to go running to her anyway?' Natasha said, but it was delivered half-heartedly and Renée didn't even bother to reply.

Why, Natasha reflected, could she not bring herself to say 'yes' and 'thanks'? Why was it so hard to take a hand held out to her? She felt unsettled by Ellen's visit, and frustrated and cross. And perhaps, somewhere, pleased too. But all she said was, 'That woman thinks I can't sort myself out. Like everyone else at the Institute, I'm sure. The last thing I need is Ellen bloody Ellmore sticking her nose in.'

Renée, already half-way up the stairs, came down again to the door and fixed her friend with a steely glare. 'Don't give me that crap, Natasha Taylor. She's going to make it easy for you. And that's just what you wanted. Well, isn't it?'

'No, DARLING. I'm just a little concerned, that's all.'

The voice at the end of the line echoed. Laura could picture Daphne, a tall, straight figure standing in the cavernous Blue Drawing Room at Denham Hall, robed in something long and shapeless, cigarette in its wand-like holder permanently to hand. It was three years now since she had moved into the Hall. The original plan had been to set up home with her sister in the East Wing. But Lydia had died six months too soon, so Daphne lived there alone – independent, by her own wish, of the rest of the household.

Laura, in the somewhat different surroundings of her Wandsworth kitchen, realized that the communication she craved tonight was beyond her reach. She said, 'It's not like you to interfere.'

'New hobbies do so invigorate one in one's declining years,' said Daphne, unperturbed. 'You'll discover this later on. Now, we both know what a banshee you have for a daughter, so I don't for a moment expect she's told me the truth of the situation. "Expelled" was the word she used.'

There was a pregnant silence. Laura knew this was Daphne's preferred method of digging and did not want to respond.

'Ah,' said Daphne.

What could Laura do? Tell Daphne that she'd asked Ellen to help? What if Daphne told Natasha, for her own wrong-headed reasons?

'You want me to explain,' said Laura, goodwill ebbing. 'Frankly I don't see why I should but I may as well tell you that it was all scrupulously fair. I treated Natasha as I would have done any other student.' This was sophistry. There *were* no other students as offensive, bloody-minded or downright talented as Natasha so how could any of them receive the same treatment?

'Exactly the problem,' said Daphne. 'If the press knew she was your daughter . . . Or even if your staff knew, come to that—'

'Is that a threat?'

'Mmm.' Daphne gave a low laugh. 'I wish I were as Machiavellian as you seem to think. No, darling. I'm simply saying that, in large measure, Natasha's own wilful obstinacy in keeping the connection a secret has made life easier for you.'

'Her choice.'

'Made when she was thirteen.'

Gripping the phone against her shoulder, Laura pulled at a bunch of newspapers and started piling them neatly. It just wasn't that simple any more. It had been too long, gone too far. And Daphne knew it.

'I doubt many people even remember your married name,' added Daphne, after a brief silence. 'But still she dropped half of it in case anyone made the connection. Going to such lengths – didn't it worry you?'

'Why? She could have changed her mind at any time. I have respected her wishes.'

'In part. You still took the Institute job, remember, when you knew she'd gone there instead of that Haycroft school precisely to keep away from you.'

'Would you prefer me not to step outside the house in case I bump into her?'

'Now there's a thought. Darling. I'm simply concerned for your – dare I say it? – spiritual well-being. And Natasha's.'

'A little too late, perhaps.'

'Damned and content to be so, I see.' There was a pause. 'I may be being insufferably dull, but my little brain *does* cling to the notion that life could be simpler than this. Crass of me to say it I know, but why *not* sort things out between you? Forget the Institute just for five minutes.'

'If you ask me to forget the Institute, you can ask Natasha to forget her career, too, and thus her expulsion.' There was no way Laura could tell her: this was Daphne at her most dangerous, convinced she knew best for everyone. 'She's better off without me, Daphne. I worked that out a long time ago.'

'Isn't she the best judge of that?'

'Frankly, no. But even if she were . . . Don't you think she agrees with me?'

'She may think she does but, then, she thinks plenty of silly things. You only have to reach out to her, you know. The girl is desperate for maternal approval.'

'Ah, yes,' said Laura heavily. 'Let me see . . . the refusal of all contact since nineteen eighty-four has been a sure sign of *that*.' How it smarted still. And how well she knew, in moments of scalding clarity, that the rejection was deserved.

'She may have refused to see you, darling, but she has also mysteriously decided to follow in your footsteps. Come on, it doesn't take much working out. You should be able to fathom what she's up to even if she can't. And it may be inconvenient if she bears a grudge, but it's hardly surprising, is it?' There was a short pause. Then, more quietly, Daphne said, 'You, after all, know what it feels like to have no mother.'

'She has a mother.'

Daphne sighed. 'One she hardly saw for the first six years of her life. One who then came home for a stretch of marital disharmony and depression and, ultimately, a divorce. The girl was bound to blame somebody some time, rightly or wrongly – and it's easier, wouldn't you agree, to choose the parent you see twice a term rather than the one you see every day? Darling, aren't you big enough, now, to sacrifice a little to make amends? What's any work consideration worth, after all, if it's at the expense of—'

'Forgive me for interrupting, Daphne, but how would you know? What work consideration has ever impinged on your life? What have *you* ever achieved? It may be amnesia but, frankly, I cannot recall a single thing.'

Silence. Laura heard her own breathing, quick and uneven. The cat, impatient now, chirruped faintly.

'Oh, my dear,' said Daphne at last. 'Achieved? I believe we differ in our definitions of the word. I have been happy. I'm not sure that is something one has ever been able to say about you.'

The phone in Laura's kitchen slammed down so hard it bounced.

THAT NIGHT, NATASHA THREW the scrap of paper with Ellen's telephone number on it out with the rubbish. It had only been half on purpose: Renée's mothering had started to get on her nerves. But she'd known it was stupid even as she did it. And the next day, as she hung head down in the dustbin, rummaging, she cursed herself and her silly childish temper.

She couldn't find it. *Shit.*

And thus Natasha found herself waiting, three days later, outside the newsagent's on the pavement opposite the Institute, hovering, immobilized, in the precincts of the hated place. Ringing the school would have been easier – but might they have recognized her voice? Besides, she remembered enough of Ellen's timetable to be able to estimate, not too roughly, what time she would emerge.

Sure enough, after fifteen minutes or so, Natasha spotted her quarry. Unwilling to approach too near the school buildings, she followed down a side street and intercepted Ellen as she reached her car.

The plain, scrubbed face, looking up, registered interest rather than surprise. 'The lure of old haunts, eh?'

A few retorts suggested themselves to Natasha, but instead she said simply, 'That coaching.' Ellen remained still, her fingers tucked under the handle of the car door. Natasha frowned. 'You said you were offering.'

Ellen seemed to consider. 'Ah. Is this a yes-please?'

'Suppose so.'

'Your enthusiasm and gratitude bowl me over.'

Natasha said nothing in reply, but shifted uncomfortably. When her hair slid forward from behind one ear she didn't retrieve it.

Ellen looked away, calculating, then squared up to Natasha again. 'Thursday. Half past eight. I teach till quarter past in studio two and there's no one else in the building afterwards so I lock up. Make sure no one sees you. Wait till a bit later if they're taking their time. I'll hang about for you.'

'And can you . . .' Natasha cleared her throat. 'I want an audition with Milan Novák.'

'Oh. Yes.' Ellen frowned. 'I'm not sure.'

'You said you could get me one.'

'Maybe – *maybe* – I could, but he was just a for-instance. You must know Novák's reputation, and what happened the last time he tried to set up a company. The question is always whether or not he's clean. This time, who knows?'

'Who cares?'

'Natasha. Believe me. You would.' Ellen's brown gaze

was direct and serious. 'Anyway, I'm not the only one who's concerned. Madame doesn't want any of the graduates going to work for him.'

Natasha's eyes sharpened. She had a vague hunch her mother and Novák had worked together once, though she couldn't remember it – maybe it'd been when she was a baby. Trust Laura, though, to disapprove of him: it was probably because he'd outshone her. She said, 'Really?'

'At first I thought she was being over-careful, but the more I consider it the more I guess she's right.' Ellen shrugged apologetically. 'It's not worth it, Natasha. You can do a hell of a lot better.'

'I want an audition.'

'There'll be others.'

'Whose career is this?'

'Okay, okay.' Something like a smile tugged at the corner of Ellen's mouth. 'If you're sure.'

'I'm sure.'

'I'll see what I can do. But I'm not promising.'

It only occurred to Natasha as she was walking down into the subway on her way to the Tube that she hadn't said a word of thanks. Firmly, she pushed away her misgivings. It could wait.

Chapter Four **London, 1965**

'Give me my bag.' One hand still gripping her half-unplaited pigtail, Laura thrust the other out in front of her, palm up, fingers splayed.

The girl opposite moved not a muscle, except for those needed to pull a sardonic sneer. 'Well, well, well,' she said. 'It seems that Little Miss Perfect was never taught to say please.' She clicked her tongue disapprovingly, and behind her someone sniggered. Though they were all fourteen, Frances Pidgeon seemed far and away the oldest. Everyone else in the year looked up to her: they didn't dare do anything else.

Frances now turned Laura's bag – slowly, oh, so slowly – upside down. Hairgrips, Elastoplasts, handkerchiefs and socks rained down onto the cold green matting, followed by a carefully folded school blouse, opening like a parachute. Laura watched them fall while her teeth grated small patches of skin from her lower lip.

'Maybe Little Miss Perfect should learn some manners.

It'd give her a break from polishing her halo every night. When she's finished darning her shoes, that is, with those incy-wincy fairy stitches of hers.' Laura's gaze shifted to Frances's stout feet. Flouting school rules, she hadn't darned the ends of her *pointe* shoes: she'd cut the satin away from the toes instead. It was quicker, but the edges frayed. Laura's head tilted to one side, considering. Frances, however, had not finished. 'But, then, no wonder Laura Douglas was brought up so badly,' she said. 'How many people here know that her mother was a *tart*?'

She slung the triumphant word out, her lips gripping the sound with relish. The rest of the girls in the changing room had been brushing their hair, jostling for space in front of the tiny wall-mirror, but she had their full attention now. Gasps were half swallowed before they sounded; eyes flicked from Frances to Laura, and back again.

'Had an affair, didn't she? But, get this. *He* was only seventeen. And Laura saw them at it!'

There were gasps and sniggers. An impressed '*Did* you?' Then a hard nudge and hissed reprimand: '*Shirley!*'

But Laura's gaze had turned elsewhere. In the far corner a girl named Monica shuffled with discomfort, her face and neck blotching deep crimson. 'Sh-she made me tell,' she stammered, eyes brimming. 'I never meant to say anything, honestly!'

'It's wicked to speak ill of the dead, Frances,' said another girl.

'Why? Mrs Douglas going to come and *haunt* me, is she?' And Frances Pidgeon ran at her critic with a whooping, wailing cry, both arms aloft like a cartoon phantom. As the whole room erupted into laughter, Laura shot forward blindly, head down, stumbling across her clothes on the floor, buffeted by colliding shoulders and elbows, one cheek whipped by her dangling plait. Making for the stairs, she smashed her foot on each step as she ran up them to block out the hateful noise.

The door to the basement changing room banged shut behind her. Laura's breathing was loud and ragged in her ears. She bolted through a door to her right. It led into one of the classrooms – the one where they'd just had their lesson; the mirrors were partly misted and the room smelt fuggy and stale with adolescent sweat. She thrust her knuckles into her eyes, then grabbed her plait and tugged on it hard – three times, four – jarring her head, making the scalp tingle and sting. One person, she'd trusted one person. After all this time in the school she'd thought she'd found a friend. How stupid! She yanked again, jerking her head sideways. And now they all knew . . . and that horrible Frances Pidgeon . . .

She let her hands drop to her sides. A dull ache had set up in her ankle from slamming up the stairs; it was her weak ankle, the one she'd broken falling out of the tree that terrible summer. Even her body seemed trying to torment her with the memory.

Looking up at her misted reflection, Laura took the

plait and folded it over the other on top of her head, removing a pin and jabbing it back in place, scraping the metal end across her scalp. Her *fouettés* had been hopeless in class today. She should be practising them.

She stepped into the preparatory position and snatched herself up onto *pointe*, the bad ankle beneath her, its ache converting to a sharp stabbing pain. As she spun, she overbalanced. No! Again. She prepared, turned. And *again*. She gritted her teeth. At last, a better one. Good. Now to try them in sequence – without straying from the spot . . .

Ten minutes later the studio door opened. It was the headmistress. Laura stopped in mid-spin, stumbled, and sat on her bottom, hard.

'Laura! What on earth do you think you're doing?' demanded Miss Lawrence, making no gesture to help as Laura scrambled to her feet. 'You know the rule, no unsupervised practice.'

Laura, upright now, kept her eyes firmly on the floor and stammered out a rapid apology.

'Laura?'

'Miss Lawrence?'

The tone had softened. 'Are you quite well, my dear?'

'Yes, thank you. Quite well.'

Behind Miss Lawrence the door was ajar. Laura watched as a stream of her classmates emerged from the changing room and filed past, nudging each other. As it was Saturday, classes were over for the day, though it was still only lunch-time. Civvies were on under the school macs – short A-line dresses, square-toed court shoes and nylon tights. The macs would be bundled into bags by the time they reached the bus stop.

'You have a pleasing dedication but . . .' Oblivious to the exodus behind her, Miss Lawrence sighed. 'Don't push yourself quite so hard, my dear. I think the half-term holiday has come at the right moment for you. Have a nice rest this week, hm? You *are* making good progress. Give yourself time, now, some breathing space. I'm tempted to recommend you stay at home an extra week.'

'Oh. No – please. I'll be fine. I couldn't possibly . . .' Laura's voice trailed off in confused anxiety. She fixed on Miss Lawrence a pleading look. The headmistress, against her better judgement it seemed, smiled and, placing two heavy hands on Laura's shoulders, propelled her from the studio.

Laura went back to the changing room. It was empty now, littered with a few stray hairgrips and scrunched paper tissues. She tried hard not to picture Frances Pidgeon over by the coat pegs, and tried not to hear an echo of her taunts. I will never, Laura decided, confide in anyone again. Ever. But what if Frances found someone else to tell, and they told other people and it spread? Was the grown-up world like a great big school where everyone got to know things, sooner or later? Because still, two years on, Laura was the only person in Denham Ford who knew what had really happened that awful August day.

It had been particularly hot, she remembered. Oliver said later – much later, as he had been in no fit state to speak for some time – that he had met Johanna by chance in Oxford and had offered her a lift home. The fact that the car was found on a road that would have been some way off their route appeared to have been passed over in the confusion of grief. There had been no other vehicle involved. He had taken the corner too fast, that was all, and Johanna, on the side that took the impact first, had been killed, they said, almost instantly. Oliver had spent three months in hospital.

At the time, it had seemed to Laura quite obvious that it was her fault. If she had told someone what she'd seen on the night of the fête – if she'd only told her mother that she knew – it would never have happened. But she hadn't. The morning after the fête, lying in bed with her ankle in plaster, Laura had noticed Johanna watching her warily, the anxious lines between her eyebrows deepened. And Laura had taken the decision there and then, her insides still churning with shock and abhorrence, to hide her feelings and pretend she remembered nothing. Johanna had been easily convinced: her joyous relief had cut Laura to the quick.

Thus, Laura had been forced to watch the events of that summer in silence. Alone, she had understood the real reason for Johanna's day-long shopping trips to Oxford, and sometimes to London, from which she would come back sparkling with happiness but with almost nothing bought. Alone Laura had understood why Johanna was suddenly able to meet Tom's complaints with laughter and a new confidence. And at Denham Hall gatherings why Johanna ignored Oliver as she had never done before, and yet was so animated in his company. Laura had seen everything, and had hated them both for it – her mother and this golden boy she had once believed she loved. She had prayed for it to stop. She hadn't specified how.

And then, one day that August, her wish, in the most horrific way, had been granted. How could she not blame herself? She was as guilty as Oliver – as guilty as Tom and Lydia and the rest of them. They'd all been hatefully stupid; they'd let it happen. The grown-up world, the grown-up love she had thought she wanted disgusted Laura now. She wanted to escape it, to run away. And she had the perfect chance: Miss Lawrence had offered her a place at the West London Academy. As soon as her ankle healed, she would go. Suddenly, ballet had seemed the only important thing in her life.

That at least hadn't changed, thought Laura, unplaiting and brushing out her hair. The last thing she wanted from Miss Lawrence was extra time off school. The dance studio was her haven: it was the only place where what had happened had no power to harm her. She need trust no one but herself there, and all she had to do was work –

push and push and push herself to perfection. Frances Pidgeon or no Frances Pidgeon, she would not stay away a minute longer than necessary.

Swiftly now, Laura stripped off her leotard and pulled on her vest and her school blouse and skirt. Then she sat on the bench and began to pick at the knots in her shoe-ribbons. Her right foot, propped across her knee, felt warm and slightly squelchy. Unravelling the ribbon from her ankle, Laura pulled off the shoe: where the fabric of her tights covered the knuckles of the third and fourth toes, it was soaked with blood. She examined the shoe, holding it up close to her face. There was a fair amount of blood inside and it had seeped right through the paste-hardened layers to the outer covering of satin. But Laura was less interested in the browning patch than in the darning at the shoe's blocked end. She'd sewn it differently this time and wanted to see whether it was wearing better.

Good progress, Miss Lawrence had said. Laura smiled softly as she put the shoe away.

DURING HER FIRST YEAR in London, Laura's home had been the school boarding house in Chiswick. She had not, however, thrived there, and when Daphne Devereux had made the offer of a room in her spacious Little Venice apartment, Laura had gladly moved in. This had depended, of course, on the sanction of her father, who did not like Daphne. But by then Tom had sold the Old Rectory in

Denham Ford and had moved permanently into his college rooms in Oxford; for that reason, among others, he did not want to risk an unhappy daughter appearing on his doorstep expecting to live with him once more. And, besides, Daphne's rates had turned out to be pleasingly cheap.

As for Daphne, her offer might have surprised some who knew her, but if they thought her motivated by any desire to cast herself in the maternal role, they were mistaken. Sympathy for this child, whose mother had been taken from her by a sudden violent accident and whose remaining parent was, in Daphne's opinion, unspeakable, was accompanied by a certainty that bringing Laura to live with her would not change her own lifestyle one jot. On this last point she was, not unexpectedly, able to prove herself right.

It was nearing two o'clock when Laura let herself quietly into the apartment and, padding down the hallway, peeped round the half-open door of Daphne's bedroom. The room showed signs of recent chaotic occupation – clothes, ashtrays and dreg-drained glasses strewn haphazardly across carpet and furniture – but otherwise stood empty. When she tried the bathroom, Laura did find a body, but not Daphne's. A young man lay prostrate in the waterless tub, resplendent in purple velvet trousers and apparently asleep. Closing the door softly, Laura went back down the hallway to the drawing room.

There, on the chaise longue, Daphne was draped, a

chiffon scarf spread over her eyes. She had heard Laura enter and, without stirring, she said in a low tone, 'Someone is dancing a flamenco on my forehead, darling. Did I stay out *very* late last night?'

'You were back by five. I saw your light on.'

'Oh, good. Now,' the chiffon shifted slightly as her brow, beneath it, furrowed, 'I'm *almost* sure there was someone here, but I can't think where I put him.'

'He's in the bath.'

The edges of the scarf wafted gently as Daphne gave a cautious nod. 'Unquestionably the best place.' She inhaled and, jutting out her lip, blew upwards, so that the scarf hovered for a moment, an inch above her eyes. 'He smells of *violets*,' she confided, meeting Laura's gaze with a look of some significance. 'Now, time for Daphne's magic medicine, I think.' She attempted to raise herself. 'Good lord.'

'Stay there,' said Laura. 'I'll make it.'

Daphne's voice followed her into the kitchen. 'You are an angel, darling, but where is Inge?'

'It's Saturday,' said Laura, assembling eggs, milk and brandy on the work surface. Saturday was the maid's day off.

The information occasioned, in the drawing room, a pause. Then the voice came again: 'Are you *sure*?'

Living with Daphne for the last twelve months had been an education of a sort very different from that offered by Miss Lawrence's Academy, yet just as instructive – and possibly more vital. From her Maida Vale windows, Daphne took a view of life unique in Laura's experience: she considered herself beholden to no one, and saw the single-minded pursuit of the satisfaction of her own desires to be a perfectly legitimate lifelong occupation. Not that she lacked conscience – not a bit of it. She had scruples, of her own particular variety, and, when questioned, an invariably cogent philosophy. But she did not waste thought on whether in the general run of things, she was *liked*, and that of itself set her apart from the vast mass of her fellow human beings, and saved her, it seemed, from many of their worst follies.

This unusual lady, moreover, drank gin as if Prohibition were imminent, rarely got up before lunch-time, and had a string of lovers, many of them less than half her age. Through it all, nevertheless, she managed to maintain a sublime air of dignity and unimpeachable good taste.

The magic medicine Laura was now preparing was an indispensable feature of the routine. It was truly, thickly revolting, and Daphne swore by it. Having pumped it to a glutinous yellow gloop in the Horlick's mixer, Laura took a tumblerful through to the drawing room and then slopped out another measure and headed for the bathroom. There the recumbent figure was exactly as she had left it; she couldn't see whether or not the man opened his eyes behind his large plastic sunglasses as she came in. But he didn't move, so she set down the glass carefully on a small rickety bookcase filled with damp-swelled paper-backs, and then retreated.

When Laura got back into the drawing room, Daphne was reciting poetry sonorously from underneath the chiffon.

> 'Pale beyond porch and portal,
> Crowned with calm leaves, she stands—'

Abruptly she broke off. 'How was school?'

'Fine,' said Laura automatically.

'Hm, better, but not entirely convincing,' said Daphne. 'You must work on your lying, darling. It's a great and useful talent.'

Laura looked at Daphne consideringly. She said, 'I'm supposed to be going to Denham tomorrow.'

'God, it's not another holiday, is it?' Daphne pulled the scarf from her face and then suddenly pressed it, crumpled, to her forehead. 'Oh, *blast*.'

'What's wrong?'

She heaved a monumental sigh. 'Vignettes of last night are dribbling back to me, darling. I have an awful feeling I may actually have sacked Inge. Blast, blast, blast.'

IT WAS THE SPRING HALF-TERM. Laura changed trains at Oxford and took the little stopper to Denham Ford. There, in front of the station, a Triumph Herald was parked, waiting for her. Leaning against the side door, hands in pockets, stood Richard Trafford-Taylor. He was twenty-one and, since he'd failed his degree and had a father who believed in heirs apparent knowing their plough-shares, he was working full time on the Denham estate. Enormous and sturdy as ever, he also looked impossibly fit.

'Hello,' he said now, surveying her with interest, 'you've grown again. Upwards, that is. Sideways you've shrunk. Aunt D not feeding you?'

'Daphne doesn't feed her*self*,' said Laura.

'I imagine not.'

The early March winds were cold, so the car roof was up. Laura slipped in underneath it, pushed her bag over onto the back seat and sat quite still while Richard started the engine. He's getting old, she thought, watching him surreptitiously as he drove. The skin of his face had lost some of its fresh bloom and his hands on the steering wheel were chapped and roughened.

The silence was an easy one. After a while Richard said, 'Mother, I warn you, is in something of a tizz.'

'Oh?'

'It's Bro.'

'He isn't back?' Laura imagined, with sudden dread, that Oliver might be at the Hall now, there when they arrived.

But Richard shook his head. 'Still in Manhattan. And still refusing to come and take up his Balliol place. The college, apparently, is threatening not to hold it open unless he signs in blood by the end of this month to say he still wants it.'

'Oh.' Laura's relief had passed quickly into self-protective indifference. She looked out of the window.

'Anyway, Mother's frothing about it,' Richard went on. 'With one academic failure in the family she's looking to Bro to make up the slack. I think she has some mad idea he should wind up as a college professor. Poor sod.'

'Like my father,' said Laura quietly.

'Sorry, meant nothing by that. It wouldn't suit him, that's all.'

'It's okay. I don't think it's done Dad much good either.'

Laura reflected, without pleasure, that she was supposed to be visiting her father this holiday. All in all, she rather wished school terms could be year-long, endless and break-free.

When they got to the Hall the wind had picked up. It blew low and fast, wrinkling the skin of the puddles blotched about the gravel drive. Richard took Laura's bag and followed her up the front steps of the house.

'I think Mother's in the library if you want to say hello.'

Laura didn't particularly, given what Richard had told her. She hardly allowed herself to think about Oliver – it always turned into some childish kind of waking nightmare – so she certainly didn't want to discuss him with Lydia. She hoped he never would come back from New York. She said, 'Am I in my usual room?'

Richard shrugged. 'I should think so.'

'I'd just better run and unpack, then,' said Laura, and held out her hand for her bag.

THE NEXT MORNING DAWN crept across a flat grey sky. Laura awoke early, roused by a wild and gusting wind. Mr Noah, her cat from the Old Rectory and now an elderly resident of the Hall, had spent the night in the crook of her knees. Reluctantly, she shifted from his patch of warmth and stole out from beneath the covers without disturbing him.

Swiftly, hopping from one foot to the other on the cold floor, she pulled on her practice clothes. Then, taking her *pointe* shoes, she made her way downstairs to the long gallery. The housekeeper Mrs Brett must be up already: the curtains had been drawn. Looking out, Laura could see right across the gardens to the rise where the trees parted and the grey, rain-drizzled haze outlined the shadowy slope of the Ridgeway in the distance. It was a familiar landscape but felt no more like home, now, than the streets of Chiswick or Little Venice. Turning away from the view, Laura put on her shoes, tested her grip against the polished parquet, and began work.

'DO YOU THINK YOU could kill someone?'

An hour must have passed, perhaps more, when a voice broke through Laura's determined, sweaty silence. At the bottom of an *arabesque penchée*, she promptly lost her balance and put her hands to the floor.

'Damn!' Upside down, she looked past her leg and saw Richard leaning against the gallery fireplace. 'I'm sorry,' she said quickly. 'You gave me a shock. What did you say?'

'The look on your face when you're doing that . . . *thing*,' he gestured vaguely, 'is terrifying. Murderous.'

'Well, it shouldn't be. But it hurts.'

'I dare say it does.'

Laura stood up and prepared to try the *adage* sequence again. 'Anyway,' Richard added, 'I thought this was a holiday.'

Laura shrugged. 'My choice.'

'Can't say I find that comforting.' He smiled, and was silent for a while longer, watching her work. At length he said, 'It's like being a nun or something, isn't it? Vocation and deprivation and scratchy underwear and cold stone floors.'

The light tone was riling. 'You haven't a clue.'

'No.' He dropped his arm from the mantelpiece. 'No, I expect you're right.'

She saw him turn to go and, feeling a flash of guilt for her bad temper, called after him hurriedly, 'Listen, I'm supposed to be meeting my father for lunch today. You couldn't—'

'Give you a lift into town?' said Richard, turning to walk backwards. 'Course I could. Just name the time and your chauffeur will be waiting.'

Laura smiled uncertainly at his retreating form: if she'd

offended him, he was quick to forgive. But frustration mixed with her relief. Richard, for all his kind intentions, thought her dancing a quaint little enthusiasm: he didn't even begin to understand.

THE DRIVE INTO OXFORD took three-quarters of an hour. Laura barely spoke through the whole journey. She sat, gripping her small leather bag tightly in one hand and smoothing her dress over her knees with the other. It was new, fine grey wool with white collar and cuffs and mother-of-pearl buttons, and she had picked it out specially as a style least likely, she calculated, to irritate her father.

She saw him so rarely now. The theory was that they should meet every holiday, but so often when she was back at Denham Tom was away, giving a paper at a conference or collecting material for his research in some distant record office or library. She had seen him last just before Christmas: the visit had been more enjoyable than usual, since he had taken her to the service of nine lessons and carols in the college chapel, which had obviated the need for – usually awkward – conversation. That had been their last contact until two weeks ago, when she had received a curt postcard arranging this visit.

Richard dropped her at the entrance to her father's college. A squally shower was just petering out as she made her way through the imposing gateway, turned left into Chapel Court and followed the rain-swilled path around to B staircase. The door there was reinforced modern glass fitted into an ancient, low and narrow archway; she pushed it and, mounting the stairs, was met by a waft of some smell akin to boiled cabbage.

Dr Tom Douglas's rooms were on the second floor. Laura stood on the landing. It was odd: each time, just before she saw him, she felt a surge of foolish, inexplicable hope.

'You're late. I've got a committee meeting at two.' The inner door had sprung open under her knock and she passed through into the dark apartment beyond.

Sitting room, bedroom, cupboard-sized kitchen (what don could be expected to cook for himself?) and bathroom opened off a tiny hallway over which watch was kept by a long-dead bewigged gentleman in a gilt frame. The canvas was so overlaid with grimy varnish that he seemed to peer in sinister fashion from the deepest shadows and Laura made a point, as she passed, of avoiding his gaze. His living co-habitee, her father, stepped before her into the sitting room, muttering, 'I suppose you'll want lunch somewhere. I'd really rather go into Hall.'

'Hall would be fine.' Laura clasped her bag against her legs and wondered where to sit. Books and papers covered every available surface in neat, important-looking stacks.

Tom grunted and looked at his watch. 'We'll go down at five to, then,' he said, and sat. Laura perched where she could and surveyed him. Never slight, Tom's thick waist had blossomed into a paunch, college port had begun to stipple his cheeks and nose, and his hair was thinning markedly on top, revealing shiny skin as smooth and pink as blancmange.

'Another new dress?' It was an accusation.

'In the sales,' said Laura. And not bought with your money, either, she added to herself. The allowance her father sent each month barely even covered the darning thread and ribbon for her *pointe* shoes.

Silence descended. Laura, because she could no longer look at her father, looked instead around the room. Little sign anywhere of anything but work. No flowers on the window-sill, no mirror above the dark iron grate; no ornaments save the photographs propped in little frames on the bookshelves. And all – she knew without needing to look – of her mother. Johanna smiling, Johanna laughing, Johanna serious; in sunshine and snow and cringing beneath a leaking umbrella. She was everywhere, including – Laura had peeped on one visit when Tom had briefly left the flat – beside his bed. 'My late wife,' she had heard him say countless times to colleagues in a fond tone he had never, as far as Laura knew, used to her mother in life. She could not bear it: she would have liked to turn every one of those photographs to the wall. What right did he have to Johanna's memory? What right did he have to ignore the living and lay claim to the dead? Laura sometimes wondered whether, if she died, her picture would appear on the bookshelves too.

The food at lunch was thick with suet and over-filling.

Tom had said, as they'd passed through the door into the dining hall, 'The Regius Professor may well be there today. Do try not to say anything stupid,' so Laura was opening her mouth only to admit the next forkful – and that as rarely as she could manage beneath her father's critical eye.

Diagonally opposite sat an old man with a baggy, rumpled face and enormous ears, behind which his two last remaining tufts of snow-white hair were lurking, as if he'd tucked them there for safe-keeping. Over the rhubarb crumble and custard he suddenly asked Laura, in a friendly tone, where she went to school. Laura described briefly the West London Academy, and when he asked whether she wanted to become a professional dancer, answered in the eager affirmative.

'You'll never be able to support yourself,' said her father, stirred into conversation. 'You're not naïve enough to think you'll make a *career* in it, are you?'

'I'd like to,' Laura murmured, abashed, prodding at her stewed fruit.

'Waste of time,' Tom said. 'After July, I'm not paying for another term at that school.'

This was not news. 'I told Miss Lawrence,' said Laura quietly.

'I should think so.'

'And she said that a bursary would be available if I needed it.'

Tom set down his spoon. 'It really is time you stopped all this nonsense. You need to get some qualifications. I doubt there's much you'd be capable of, but there must be some secretarial course you could manage. In London, of course. I'm quite certain your mother never envisaged you being at that place more than a year or two to shake you out of that terrible clumsiness.'

A blush of shame and anger had risen rapidly from beneath Laura's collar to the roots of her hair. 'You have no idea what Mummy would have wanted,' she said, making no effort to keep her voice down. 'You had no idea what she wanted when she was alive. You never asked her, and when she tried to tell you you never, ever listened!'

Faces along the table had turned in her direction. Tom looked at her, too, stony-faced and unflinching, his eyes, only, a little dilated. She longed, now she had begun, to tell him what she knew. She longed to scream at him that he had killed Johanna by pushing her away, pushing her towards Oliver – scream so loudly that the silver spoons down every long table in the room would be set rattling. She couldn't. 'Y-you always were beastly to her,' was all she stammered out instead. And, trembling, she stood up.

The scrape of the chair echoed to the rafters. As Laura walked down the Hall her footsteps rang out against the polished wood. She ached to look back, but she didn't. Only after the last table did she glance round. Far behind, a face was turned her way. It showed astonishment, and a melancholy confusion; at its side, behind the ears, two tufts of snow-white hair stood out. As for Laura's father, his back was towards her; his head bent to his food. He had not even troubled to watch her go.

Chapter Five **London, 1989**

'She's one vindictive twisted bitch. My God, and if there's anything she can't stand it's real talent.'

'Natasha—'

'She's as bad as Alex.'

'Natasha!'

Midway through a *soutenu* turn, Natasha came down off *pointe* and faced her teacher. 'What?'

'When you talk you lose all your *épaulement*,' said Ellen, leaning back against the mirror, half exasperated, half laughing. 'Can you shut up about Madame just for five minutes? You've left, remember. You don't have to see her again. Now get back to the corner and show me some decent *brisées*.'

Natasha coloured slightly beneath the film of sweat and did as she was told, for once, without a murmur. If she hadn't had to come back to this bloody building every week, sneaking in like a housebreaker, thoughts of her mother would never have entered her head. As it was, she felt Laura's eyes on her everywhere, as if she stared down from the wall of each studio like the Institute's own little Lenin. Every time Natasha turned a corridor corner her stomach tightened in readiness for a sudden meeting; she found herself whipping round in empty changing rooms, convinced of eyes on her back.

Anyone would think Natasha was hoping to see her mother. When, of course, coming across Laura was the last thing she wanted. No. When Natasha thought about it, it was always in terms of her mother wanting to see *her* – she imagined Laura anxious for contact, eager to explain. In her reveries, Natasha went into great detail, picturing exactly how she would brush Laura off, concocting ever better phrases of scorn and derision, painting to herself the crestfallen expression on her mother's face as she turned away from her, or, in another version, the desperate entreaties, scrupulously ignored.

But it'd been almost four weeks, now, and there'd been no chance meeting. Natasha was aware of a sense of frustration she could not wholly explain.

At last the *brisées* were completed to Ellen's satisfaction. Natasha's legs, strong as they were, felt beaten to a pulp; the sweat running down her back was cold. Breathing hard, she doubled up and leant her hands on her knees. 'So,' she looked up at Ellen, who was swapping her teaching shoes for sandals, and packing tapes and notes back into her bag, 'when are these auditions you're getting me?'

Ellen glanced up briefly at Natasha's reflection, then carried on with her packing. 'Jim Everett is thinking of holding an open audition, but he says he wants to go to the graduate shows first.'

'Shit.'

'The City look like they'll see you. Ditto the Western. I haven't managed to pin either down to a date yet, but I'm working on it.'

Natasha's mouth twisted ruefully. 'Well. My diary's fairly free.' She straightened up. 'And Milan Novák?'

Ellen turned. 'I tried to get in touch,' she said, with a tight little smile that indicated it had, perhaps, been a lengthy and not entirely enjoyable experience. 'He's only flying in on the afternoon of the gala. I'll have to speak to him there.'

Natasha glowered, chewing a fingernail. Ellen delved into her bag and, producing a small white envelope, held it out to her.

'What's this?'

Ellen didn't reply. Natasha opened it and drew out a small square of perforated paper, with a sketch of a familiar theatre façade in one corner. It was a ticket for the gala. 'Some sort of joke?' She passed it back and met a look of weary irritation. 'What?' she said in answer to it. 'You can forget it. I'm not going.'

'Well, you should. Watch some of the competition. I don't believe you ever really have in class.'

Natasha opened her mouth to remark that those losers

were hardly competition, but then realized, with an uncomfortable jolt, that Ellen had a point. 'All right. Hand it over, then.'

But Ellen hung on to the ticket and inspected her pupil soberly. 'Natasha. You have to promise. Stick to the back stairs, stay in your seat in the interval, and don't go anywhere near the crush bar either then or afterwards. I don't want you making trouble.'

Natasha smiled. 'For you.'

There was a short, uncomfortable silence. For an instant Natasha regretted the remark; this coaching was, after all, just what she needed. But when Ellen spoke, it was simply to say, 'For you, more particularly. I'm in no danger. You could, quite feasibly, have got hold of a ticket yourself. But the press'll be there and despite the half-hearted efforts that documentary team made at camouflage they just might know who you are.' This idea pleased Natasha: she pursed her lips to hide a smile.

'It wouldn't do you any favours,' said Ellen, understanding the look and frowning. 'And I shall be doing some quiet moving and shaking on your behalf so I don't want you showing your face at the wrong moment and causing a stink. Okay?'

The ticket was proffered again. Natasha took it, more respectfully this time. It was a shame: she fancied making something of a splash, and if she couldn't make one on stage, off would do. But she needed a job – and she needed Ellen's help. With reluctance, then, looking up almost sheepishly, she agreed.

THE GALA'S TECHNICAL REHEARSAL had overrun monstrously on the Friday night, so Saturday morning's dress rehearsal was rescheduled for noon. The costumes still weren't finished; neither were they, some of them, when Laura raced home at six to change, ready for the evening's performance.

She had felt fully in control all day. Everyone, in various stages of panic, had looked to her for reassurance and a steady hand; she was the barometer of how things were progressing – and it was essential she got the balance of invective and encouragement exactly right. She was steering the ship towards harbour.

She went up to the bedroom; the summer evening light showed softly through the windows, but she flicked on the harsh ceiling lamp and crossed straight to the wardrobe. She had already picked her clothes for tonight – and with care: she, of all people, knew the power of costume. Simple, flowing lines, subdued but flattering, the style understated, the quality ferociously high. Minimal jewellery, nothing flashy. To look as if you were trying to impress was a grave mistake, to be avoided at all costs. It was a game, of course, but it was surprising how few people knew the rules. Laura dressed swiftly and brushed out her hair. The brown was grey-threaded now, but she still kept it at a dancer's length, just skimming the shoulders. She no longer, though, ever wore it loose: expert fingers, working quickly, soon had it swept up and pinned into a smooth pleat. Just a touch of make-up to apply, and she would be ready. Disguise those smudged shadows beneath her eyes, brighten the pallid skin. She sat down at the dressing table and reached for her foundation.

The small tube was between her fingers. She looked at it for a second, suddenly still, then set it back on the glass tabletop. Her fingers felt icy: she saw, with some surprise, that they were quivering. A feeling of panic welled like bile in her gut. I cannot face this evening, she thought suddenly. I cannot pretend.

Taking a deep breath, Laura tried to search out, with hard-won rationality, the source of the panic. The gala? It would be fine. The girl who had taken over Natasha's roles was managing well. She hadn't the same talent, of course, but who would know what they were missing? She was good *enough* and the odds were that the show, barring technical disasters, would be exactly the profile-raising hit Laura had hoped for.

What, then?

Laura looked up into the glass. This was the face of the Institute Director, the face that went to meetings, discussed budgets and reprimanded students. Traced with fine lines, the eyes iron grey with exhaustion – no wonder. It was the only legitimate face of Laura Douglas now: she *was* her work. Wife no more, hardly a mother, and she could not count herself, truly, a friend of anyone — there was no space in her pared-down routine for that. And so she had no choice but to get through tonight. For if she could not be this Laura Douglas, who was she? And there were important people to see: directors, benefactors and parents. Proud parents — as she herself might have been, had circumstances been different. But she did not allow herself to think of that.

And, then, there was Milan Novák.

Laura applied the foundation quickly and fumbled for her eyeliner.

She did not know for definite that he would be there. But it was probable. And though she had arranged not to speak to him, he would, she knew, be watching her. She licked her finger and dragged at her eyelid irritably, then drew the line again.

But what if he didn't come, after all?

She reached for the powder brush. Hardly any need to answer that question. If he didn't come she would feel just one thing: relief.

Finished, Laura rose, turned, regarded herself in the full-length mirror. Then she crossed to the door and opened it swiftly.

THE SEAT WAS IN THE GODS, front row, near side of the right-hand aisle. Natasha fiddled with the slot on the opera glasses: you could save your twenty pence if you gripped the edge as you pushed it in. She barely had enough nail left, but managed it after a struggle. Thus equipped, she hung over the brass suicide barrier up to her armpits and studied the stalls in close-up. On detailed inspection the opulence of the theatre was decayed and fraying, tatty in the way that a stage costume, so glamorous from the auditorium, seems gaudy and disappointing close to. The people shifting along the stalls rows were, however, the real McCoy: the great and the good, in silks masquerading as sow's ears, most of them. God, what terrible taste half these people had! Natasha, too, had dressed up for the occasion: her jeans had no holes in them. And she'd even rubbed over her toecaps with a tea-towel on her way out.

By the time the orchestra had found its fully harmonious A, she'd spotted a significant empty seat in one of the boxes nearest the stage. A man she didn't recognize was sitting next to it and at the other side – she could just catch him in profile now and again as he leant forward – was Alexander McIntyre.

As the conductor entered and the house lights dimmed, Natasha kept the opera glasses trained on that box. She'd had to sit, now, so she couldn't see into it, the angle was too steep. But the light from the pit and the faint glow trained on the curtain was enough to show her, dimly, that a third figure had entered and taken its place. One pale hand was resting on the velvet-padded ledge of the box. No, not resting – Natasha looked again as the curtain rose and the stage-lights gave a stronger illumination – gripping. The fingers were bent, claw-like:

she could just make out the ridge of knuckles, the skin taut across them bone-white.

So Madame was nervous, was she? Anxious in case the gala did not reflect her well, did not further her career as she, doubtless, was hoping? That was her mother's problem, thought Natasha, she always put herself first. Always had and always would.

TRYING TO HOPE for disaster, Natasha found, as the dancers came on stage, that she could not. They were her friends up there, after all, some of them, and she only required that Fiona Tyrrell, the girl who had been given her roles, should not execute them as well as she would have done. On that point she was satisfied.

Immediately the curtain lowered for the interval, a buzz struck up about the auditorium. The verdict was positive: Natasha could tell from the pitch of the murmurs and chatter. People shifted and rose, bent to retrieve programmes and coats, straightened, picked their way past their neighbours *en route* for the bars.

Natasha slung her legs over the arm of her chair to make room for the people filing past. Ellen had told her not to budge from her seat, didn't want her to go 'making trouble'. Once her row was empty, she moved her feet to prop them up on the ledge in front of her. What sort of trouble did Ellen think she'd cause, anyhow? And did she honestly expect Natasha to sit up here like a lemon while the wheeling and dealing went on below? Jesus, there were directors down there! Talking about Fiona Tyrrell, no doubt, when they should have been talking about her. And she might run into Milan Novák, too. She could do herself some good. What if Ellen blew it, after all? The woman's intentions were sound, okay, but Natasha didn't much trust her technique.

Natasha got to her feet, and took the stairs up the gangway two at a time.

LAURA MADE IT INTO the corridor and turned in the direction of the crush bar. She'd excused herself to Alexander and Aubrey Chancellor as soon as the house lights had come up. Fortunately, there were enough legitimate claims on her attention to make this no dereliction of duty.

The gala, it was clear, was a great success. There was an evening's work ahead of Laura still, but she should have felt relaxed and confident. Instead, her smile was stretched taut as a drumskin over a mess of tense, confused thoughts. She had not even been able to watch the dancing properly. Training her eyes on the stage, she had made out no shapes, no formations and phrasings, not even whole dancers: just flailing limbs – ridiculous, funny, grotesque; parts of bodies, jumbled and disconnected, waggling feet, breasts like small jellyfish jiggling on xylophone rib-cages, hinging knees and elbows, rumps of rounded muscle. Laura had wondered whether she was going stark staring mad, right there in the darkness of the auditorium.

Now, as she headed for the crush bar, she saw a face emerge from the flow of people ahead and swim towards her. It was familiar, though when she had known it in, it now seemed, a former life it had not had quite those red-rimmed hammocks of skin beneath the eyes, nor that drooping salt-and-pepper moustache, that shock of grey hair above the dark brows. This was Dandy Franks, choreographer, company director, champion of the European dance avant-garde. Laura kissed him warmly and failed to listen as he gave her news of Munich. 'You know, we held open auditions three months ago and it was the most depressing experience of my life. Eighty girls, I saw, and not one of them had the strength to get through five minutes of *adage*.' He rolled his eyes splendidly and laid his hands on hers. 'So my main feeling tonight is relief. Thank God there are some, somewhere. Whatever you're doing, you should bottle it and flog it. You'd make a fortune.'

Laura smiled, said something appropriate, though she hardly knew what, and, with a parting squeeze, extricated herself from his grasp and moved on.

She knew she was sailing round the evening with apparent smooth aplomb. People were talking to her easily, respectfully, deferentially, and she heard her own voice answering in sane, normal tones. But inside her head there was a constant hideous jabbering, a monkey-devil crouched at her ear.

Where was he, for God's sake?

Was he here at all?

And if he was, did he want to see her?

COMING DOWN THE BACK stairs, out into the evening air and edging along a pavement crowded with audience overspill to the main foyer door, Natasha wondered whether she'd be able to recognize this Milan Novák. She'd seen pictures of him, of course – who hadn't? – but they all dated from at least five or ten years ago, before the drugs had truly taken hold. She hardly knew, now, what she was looking for.

There were plenty of other people she recognized. Critics, teachers, from the Institute and elsewhere, students from the lower years, a famous face or two, and Alexander, erect as a spring shoot, dressed head to toe in pea-green linen. Had she blenched, a little, at the sight of him? She had, at any rate, dodged behind a large woman sporting helpfully wide shoulder-pads and willed herself into invisibility as he passed. The scruffy street clothes were, perhaps, a little conspicuous – too many curious looks, and someone from the Institute was bound to recognize her. As yet, though, she had seen no one even vaguely resembling Milan Novák. Natasha lurked her way up the main staircase to dress-circle level, and took a breather behind a gilt-striped pillar. This was ridiculous. Perhaps Ellen had been right: she should have sat tight up in the plebs' gallery. She should go back – she would. Natasha heaved a deep sigh of irritation, tugged at the edge of her T-shirt and stepped out from behind the pillar.

She had turned in the direction of the stairs once more. It was a double flight divided by a small mezzanine landing where a high, opulent mirror rose against the wall, giving anyone at the top of the second flight looking down, or at the bottom of the first flight looking up, a good view of each other and of anyone else on the stairs. So it was that Natasha saw the two men before they had even reached the mezzanine; saw their faces in the glass as they climbed the first flight – and recognized one. The other was a boulder of a man. He had a nailbrush-bristle hair and wore a lounge suit voluminous enough to pitch as a big top. His great thighs kept his feet far apart as he planted them on each step: climbing did not seem the activity for which nature had intended him.

His companion – a man in the first half of his forties, she guessed – was of as impressive a build, but in an altogether different style. Lean where the other was corpulent, broad-shouldered and muscular where the other was simply fleshy, he nevertheless looked a wreck. The clothes, you'd say, had been filched from a flea-market then slept in for three days solid: rough V-neck sweater, no shirt; jeans, worn in places into patches of string; threadbare overcoat with hanging cuffs and enormous pockets. The hair was violently bleached, the face beneath as washed-out as the old denim: hollow, seamed with deep lines. Only the eyes seemed to gather the shimmering light and colour around them and give out a strange glimmer of their own; here was sharp observation, but no readable expression. Certainly, he did not look like the photographs. Even so, Natasha needed no one to tell her that she had found Milan Novák. And she was not alone in recognizing him. As he moved across the mezzanine, whispers and discreet but significant looks followed. His reputation, bright with brilliance, brighter still with notoriety, made him the focus of universal surreptitious scrutiny.

Natasha was still standing at the top of the stairs; Novák and his friend were climbing directly towards her. Taking a swift decision, she began to go down, her gaze on the floor as if oblivious to their presence. A step apart, she feigned a little surprise. The men had halted, and she lifted her face to find Novák looking full at her.

The next moment, Natasha's head dropped again; she muttered an apology and side-stepped, flattening herself against the wall as they passed. Then she raised her eyes quickly after them, in blank and complete astonishment. Chickening out wasn't in her repertoire. But she'd just had a perfect chance – and she'd blown it. What had happened?

AT THE END OF THE performance, to the thunderous sound of countless hands, held aloft, beating the air, Laura slipped out of the box, through a door marked Private and down the narrow corridor that joined the auditorium to the backstage area. Two more doors. Up the narrow steps. Into the wings. A crush of bodies; sweat, smiles and panting relief. Then out into the hot, dazzling glare for the next curtain call. The conductor had joined her; she raised a hand to him, and stepped aside, leading the dancers' applause. Then she turned to the students, her back to the audience, and flung up both hands, like Isadora Duncan at the Parthenon, in salute.

The air hummed and rolled with the noise. The students' faces, drenched beneath thick layers of powder, shone, and their arms stretched towards her, offering her, not themselves, up to the crowd. With majesty, Laura swept round to face her public. She held herself for a moment quite still, then dropped into a deep, graceful reverence. Her feet and knees and back might be killing her, these days, but she could still curtsy with the best of them.

In the black-out that followed, Laura sensed a presence at her side. Her hand was gripped, vice-like. 'My congratulations, Madame,' said Alexander McIntyre, as the stage lights came up once more and they acknowledged the ovation together. 'I believe we are a success.'

At Laura's other side, Dr Debenham appeared, her chins jostling to make way for a broad, gratified smile. 'Darling Laura!' she screeched, grasping and kissing her on both cheeks, to a crescendo of applause.

Laura beamed from one to the other. She felt like biting them both.

As the auditorium cleared, and the exclusive reception – the real work of the night – got under way in the crush bar, Laura found Dr Debenham still attached to her as if riding in a side-car. Holding forth on the quality of the buffet, and the importance of this to the evening's proceedings, she suddenly clutched Laura's elbow. 'It's Novák,' she hissed, spraying spittle. 'There – look!'

And there, indeed, he was. Invitation or no invitation, he had walked into the reception and was standing now to one side of the doorway, in the company of a fat, thuggish-looking man Laura did not know. Eyes on the people about him, without hint of either interest or enthusiasm, he was speaking, the fat man leaning in to catch the words. He had not seen her. And the feeling, as Laura looked at him, was bizarre. It was just a man, standing a room's width away. But it was a man Laura had thought never to set eyes on again in her life.

'I'm so glad you changed your mind about letting him come. You must introduce us!'

'You hardly need me, Margaret.'

'Don't be silly. You used to dance with him.'

'At least a century ago and I haven't seen him since.' Laura's heart was thudding. Not with Margaret. She couldn't face Milan, speak to him for the first time after all these years with this floundering, salivating woman at her elbow. She studied him: he was turned safely away from her. He looked . . . my God. He looked different.

'What a strange specimen he is. Can't he afford decent clothes? And the hair! He looks like he's been hung by his ankles and dipped in peroxide.' Dr Debenham, who had been using a stick of celery as a pointer, crunched on it ruminatively. 'Not what he used to be, eh? Saw him in seventy-two at the Met – don't think I've ever got over it. What a waste! He could be running a big company by now, and giving us a few von Rothbarts and Drosselmeyers into the bargain. Oh, do take me over, just for a minute.'

'Margaret, to be frank with you, I can't stand the man. If you want to talk to him, go right ahead.'

'But he might have some work for your students.'

'Which he can keep. Now, if you'll excuse me . . .' Laura moved away purposefully through the press of bodies, leaving Dr Debenham looking after her, an island of astonishment.

Laura headed away from Novák, and told herself, as she greeted and smiled and glanced undetectably over people's shoulders, that she was casting not one thought in his direction. Inexplicably, though, she found in time that her movements through the crowded room had described an arc around the spot where Novák stood. Now she was again barely twenty feet from him, and as people shifted and stilled, clustered into groups and broke away, she caught glimpses of him surveying the room, or commenting to his companion, or enduring, with chilling patience, the intrusion of an eager admirer. Looking again a moment later, she was horrified to see that he had turned towards her and begun to weave a path between the bodies that separated them.

She must have been seen. In an effort to cover her panic, Laura nodded and smiled at the elderly newspaper critic who was talking to her. She sought, desperately, an opportunity to step in and stem the flow, make her apologies and move, but the man seemed not to need to pause for breath. Damn, damn, damn. Hadn't Ellen told Milan that *she* was the one he should deal with? Or perhaps that was it: Milan had realized that Laura was avoiding him and was coming to confront her.

Her head was pounding. The room felt airless. The noise around her made no sense: it seemed too loud, fractured and raucous. She was looking about for her staff. Where *was* Ellen? He was almost with her now. Two people blocked her view of him on their way to the door, when they had passed he would be almost at her side.

Laura swallowed, watched the critic's dry lips open and close around his dentures, and heard not a word. A second or two, that was all. She counted them and, throwing a last dazzling smile to the old man, turned to face Milan.

But the space where he had stood was empty. He had gone.

★

'ALL RIGHT, I'VE GOT IT,' said Ellen two days later.

'Got what?'

'An appointment for you. With Novák.' She brought out her notepad, tore off the top sheet and handed it to Natasha.

There was a date, a time, and an address.

'The Sweat Shop? Eight *a.m.*?'

Ellen smiled narrowly. 'Only time I could get. It was damned difficult to persuade him, I'll have you know. And I had to book the studio myself.'

'I'll pay you back.'

'I'm not saying that. I'm saying you'd better turn up – *on time* – and do justice to the glowing PR.'

'Yes, yes. Of *course*,' Natasha said impatiently, folding the paper and tucking it into the knot she'd tied in her T-shirt.

'Would you like me to come with you?'

Natasha scowled. 'To hold my hand?'

There was a pause as Ellen considered her. At last she said, 'Your *petit batterie* looks like sludge today. Give me *entrechats* till I tell you to stop. *And*!'

IT WAS TOO EARLY in the morning: Natasha felt sick. She had walked the streets of WC2 on her way to the Sweat Shop in a weird state of outraged nervousness.

She did *not* get nervous – that contributed to the outrage.

She did *not* get up at seven in the morning – that contributed too.

And, finally, she did *not* want the Novák job that badly.

This last one was a lie. Maintaining belief in it was proving something of a strain.

Inside the Sweat Shop, the studio booked for Natasha was a small one on the top floor. She climbed the stairs, her bag slung across her back, and pushed her way through the swing doors, slamming down a bank of light switches with a passing hand. Somewhere else in the building office workers were trying to distract themselves from the day ahead by clattering their way through the Early Birds' Tap Class: strains of '42nd Street', thumped on a bullied piano, boomed up through the floorboards.

Natasha was already changed; she stripped off her outer layers and sat on the floor to jam sore feet into *pointe* shoes. A toe had got skinned two days ago and was still weeping; she wrapped a wad of lamb's wool round it, and across the sharply protruding big-toe joint too, red and shiny and agonizingly stiff. Then she warmed up. And she waited.

Ten past and no sign of Novák. The nerves were starting to dissolve in a kind of bubbling anger. *She* had bothered to be on time. Why couldn't he? Oh, yes, now she remembered: she was a nobody in need of a job and he was, potentially, the great provider. He could do what he liked and she should be grateful. The conclusion did nothing for her mood.

The clock was showing twenty past eight when the door opened and Novák walked in, freshly out of the shower, it seemed. The sprouting, dark-rooted hair was damp and standing in haphazard tufts where he'd pushed his fingers through it. Behind him came the big man Natasha had seen at the theatre. Neither looked at her; they crossed to the front of the studio, where Novak hooked a chair towards him with one foot and dropped into it. Standing before him, Natasha dipped her head instinctively in the movement that should have brought her hair falling across her face, except it was held back by an army of hairpins and most of a can of lacquer. She felt exposed.

'Warmed up?' Novák said to her, his English comfortable, the accent so light as to be well-nigh unplaceable. She was being stared at hard, like an animal on sale for its meat; she felt the expert gaze rake down the full length of her body and back again, without much interest. His eyes were strange: too pale. Reply, she told herself quickly, and managed to nod, not quite trusting her voice. Then Novák passed a hand over his face as if clearing his mind, and said, 'I'm not going to give you a class. Can't be arsed, frankly. Boring.'

Natasha didn't move.

'So, come on, then, Ms . . .?'

'Taylor,' put in the big man.

'Ms Taylor. Let's see what you can do.'

There is no worse basis on which to start an audition.

The thought that those few minutes, on that particular day, in that – God knew it – most uninspiring of settings, had somehow to be representative of what she could *do* was stultifying, paralysing.

Natasha's brow furrowed. 'I've got a Kitri solo from *Don Q*. And one from *Giselle*, Act I. Or . . . you can set something else.'

'Whatever.' Novák flapped a hand impatiently.

Natasha crossed to her bag and rummaged about in it. 'Where's the tape player?' she said as she surfaced, flushed.

The pale eyes pulled wide. 'Tape player?' said Novák. 'Do we have a tape player, Victor?'

'We don't,' said the bulk.

'We don't. Shall we hum?'

Christ, thought Natasha. She slung the tape back into her bag, took up her position, gritted her teeth, and began.

'I WANT TO SEE that again.'

Her rib-cage heaving painfully, Natasha fixed Milan Novák with a look of disbelief. 'Again? What, you mean now?'

'Do you have a problem?'

Do you? she wanted to ask, but somehow stopped herself.

This man is warped, she thought, as she pushed her lung-searing way through the variation for a second time. And if he's an ex-junkie, too, he certainly looks the part:

someone that age shouldn't be so lean and stringy – and those wrinkles are etched in acid.

The Kitri solo done – again – he asked to see the *Giselle*. Afterwards, Natasha felt she couldn't have so much as walked to the door if he'd requested it. She wasn't quite sure, as it was, how she was managing to stay upright. At least Novák's bored look had gone. His expression now seemed, at a guess, to indicate that he was pleased with her, but pleased because she amused him for some unspecified, humiliating reason. His look sent her fingers itching to her hair, her straps, the seam of leotard covering her bum, certain that something must be askew, poking out, sticking up, half undone.

Somewhere outside, Natasha could hear the crawling growl of the morning traffic; she longed to crawl away with it. Novák stretched, his arms in the air and his legs pushed out in front of him, and began speaking fast in very low tones to Victor. Natasha turned her head to the window, still breathing hard. She could see only sky.

'Okay, that's all,' said Novák, breaking off briefly from his conversation.

Natasha was half-way to her bag before she stopped and turned. 'Hang on,' she said. 'Aren't you going to tell me something about this company of yours?'

Novák sighed wearily, and pitched his head up and back in the vague direction of his companion. Victor leant forward, resting his baseball glove hands on his knees. 'Small company,' he said. 'And I mean small, six, eight dancers only. Varied repertoire base, new work whenever possible.'

'A dancers' company,' said Novák. 'None of this getting shat on by the management. No stars. No "in" people and "out" people.'

'No money.'

'Hahaha. Yes. No money and no place to rehearse and positively *no* help with expenses. Still interested?'

'You giving me a job?' said Natasha.

Victor shrugged. 'We'll let you know.'

Natasha kept her eyes on Novák. She wouldn't let him stare her down. She managed, if quietly, to form the word 'Well?'

'Like the man says.' Novák's arms folded across the flat, impeccably muscled stomach. 'I wouldn't rush me if I were you.'

'I guess I can wait.'

'No kidding.' It wasn't a question. 'You'll get a call.'

And that was it. Audition over. She had to go down to the piazza then and, squatting on a pavement's edge, smoke a shaky, fast-burned cigarette. Had she messed up? Had she done enough? What the hell was he looking for, anyway? Natasha found herself hoping – and doubting – so badly she frightened herself.

However great you were, you had to be employed. Employable. Shit.

★

'WHAT DO YOU KNOW about Milan Novák?' This asked of Renée, a week after the audition, as she and Natasha queued in Sainsbury's on the Liverpool Road.

'Novák? Okay.' Renée flopped over the front bar of the trolley and considered. 'Well, got to be one of the two, maybe three, best male dancers ever. Defected in his mid-twenties, danced with just about every major Western company you can name. Unstable character even, so they say, before he dropped out. Ten years-ish back, suddenly stopped performing, rumours of drug problems that he's never really shaken off. Tried to set up a small company about, what, five years ago? Fell through, mysteriously. Probably, I'd hazard, a sad and bitter has-been getting through his mid-life crisis with the aid of some well-chosen narcotics. Not *my* ideal boss.'

Natasha nodded and feigned a passing interest in the magazine rack. Renée was right – so why did she feel so bad? Her body, in which usually, despite its aches and pains, she found a certain satisfaction, now hung on her like an ugly suit of clothes; she felt for the first time its inadequacies more keenly than its strengths. She dragged herself through each day, working her muscles with a morbid, uninspired determination. Ellen had put her name down for every audition going. So what? She didn't want them. She wanted *him* to say yes, that was all. And maybe he *was* a sad and bitter has-been but she could find that out for herself. Because she had a hunch that this company of his would make your average classical outfit look as starched as a Victorian tea party. And that would suit her just fine. All she needed was a call from Paris.

Natasha stayed in a lot, and tried not to look at the phone.

IT HAD BEEN A LONG pause. Probably taking a drag on her cigarette, thought Natasha. At last Daphne's voice sounded down the line again. 'Pleased?' she asked, quite in her normal tone.

Natasha wound and unwound the flex. 'I guess.'

'And what does your mother say about this?'

'Haven't spoken to her.'

Daphne gave a short sigh. 'You're as bad as one another.'

'Excuse *me*!'

'Oh, but you are, my darling, you truly are. Two peas. You're playing the same game. Though, I will allow, your styles are slightly different.'

Natasha made a hideous face at the living-room carpet. But there was no point in arguing with Daphne. She said, 'Anyway, I start next week. Will you tell Dad?'

'You should tell him yourself. Come for the weekend. He'd like to see you.'

Natasha grunted.

'Repulsive child. Your father loves you to smithereens and you treat him like a mongrel with mange. You disgust me.'

'Don't worry, Aunt Daphne. It's mutual.'

When Natasha put the phone down, a few minutes

later, it was with a lifted heart. Daphne was a mad old bat, but they understood one another. It made a change.

'At first I thought she was going to turn down the coaching,' said Ellen. 'Talk about biting the hand. She's so bloody-minded.'

Laura made no response. She was sitting forward, her elbows on the desk, hands curled one around the other and her lips resting against them.

'And I got her seen by several people,' Ellen went on. 'Jim Everett, mind you, turned his nose up in the end – cancelled the open audition *and* said he hadn't the time to see students one by one. His loss, quite frankly.'

'So she did get some offers?'

Ellen smiled. 'Oh, yes. You could say that. She got offers all right.'

Laura said, 'Good,' briskly, and looked about her desk at the work spread there. Eyes upon it she said, 'Well, thank you very much for your help, Ellen. And your discretion. You'll find the overtime's been added to this month's pay cheque.' Choosing a sheaf of papers, she drew it towards her.

'You don't want to know which one she accepted?' said Ellen. Having declined to sit, she'd moved about the room as she talked and now had come to rest beside the window.

Laura looked across at her, then, for an answer, relinquished the papers and sat back.

Ellen said, 'I was pretty surprised, to be honest. Well no. Once I'd thought about it I realized it fitted Natasha exactly – you know, loves to shock, moves instinctively in the opposite direction to the one people would expect. But faced with the choice, I don't think many of our students would have been brave enough to jump the way she has. And I *did* warn her.' She looked as if she felt responsible. She sounded as if she was persuading herself as much as Laura. 'It may be the making of her,' she said. 'Natasha would hardly have been willing to start on the bottom rung of a classical company. She wasn't back-row-of-the-*corps* material, and I don't think anyone could have promoted her fast enough to keep up with her ambitions. So six months, eighteen months with this crowd might just wake her up.'

'Which crowd?'

'Oh, sorry. The Novák Company. She's signed up with Milan.'

A sudden, heavy silence. The two women held each other's gaze. Then all at once Laura threw back her head, her palms pressed flat together before her. It looked as if she were about to laugh: her mouth was open, stretched almost like a smile. But no sound came out – and whether it was the ceiling or something beyond it she was looking to, Ellen could not guess.

Chapter Six **London, 1970**

'The tour starts on May the eleventh. The list of venues is up on the board. Heather Spinks, our company manager, will fill you in on the travel arrangements. Back to London in mid-July, month off, then we start work on the new productions.'

The man behind the desk might have been an ill-preserved fifty with an unmistakable paunch, but to Laura he had suddenly taken on a heavenly aura. This is it, a voice in her head was telling her, you have a job. You – are – a – dancer.

'It's going to be a tough few weeks for you, learning all the *corps* work. But the move from school to a professional company is never easy.' The man held out a pen and prodded at the contract, showing her where to sign. 'Here – and here. And this copy's for you.'

The small dingy South Kensington office had suddenly transformed itself into a scene of triumph. Laura signed the papers eagerly and looked at the man with ill-contained enthusiasm. Max Norris, artistic director of the English Ballet Theatre, whom she had met at that first audition last week and thought just another balding ex-dancer with money worries and a company to run, was now to her a figure of significance, beneficence, and unlikely beauty. He had quite extraordinary eyes, she saw, flecked, grainy irises of a marbled blue that seemed made up of several separate layers of wafer-thin lapis, surrounded by the smoothest whites she had ever seen, like newly peeled hard-boiled eggs.

'Now, company class at ten on Monday. Heather will come and find you there. All right?'

Laura sensed the pause, started, and nodded, winding back in her mind to try to discover what he might just have said. His neckscarf, which on first sight had struck her as a definite mistake, turned out on considered examination to be rather stylish. Somewhere else in the building she could hear piano music, and the thumping of feet.

Max was looking at her, his top lip bulging as he ran his tongue over his teeth beneath it. Suddenly clammy under the arms, Laura muttered her thanks, blushing, and made to stand up.

'Hold on – you're not free for lunch, are you?'

'Er . . .' She was hunched half standing, gripping her bag in her lap.

'Yes? No? Come on.' He tapped the biro on the edge of the desk.

'Yes.'

'I'll meet you downstairs? One o'clock. Save any more questions for then.'

ONE O'CLOCK. COMPANY DIRECTOR. Her new boss. Laura panicked, raced into three different shops and came out of the last in possession of a large black hat, with a brim that undulated in front of her face. Thus armed, she met Max Norris for lunch. He took her to a basement café off the Cromwell Road with an enormous daisy painted on one wall and a fug of cigarette smoke that almost obscured it. Laura, letting Max order for both of them, felt quite certain she had died and gone to heaven. He must, she reflected, sipping the glass he had poured for her of a slightly sweaty-tasting white wine, be a very kind man to treat all his new dancers to a celebratory meal.

He drank rather quickly, and a patch of pink appeared high up on each cheek, like badly applied rouge. 'You know I'm married,' he said suddenly, staring bleakly into his plate and stabbing at a piece of chicken.

'Oh?' said Laura conversationally, who did. His wife was Nadine Kelly, the senior ballerina of the company. Too senior, some critics had ungenerously hinted. 'That's nice.'

He frowned at her for the first time. 'It's a sham. We barely see each other.'

'Ah,' said Laura, feeling foolish. 'I'm sorry.'

'Thought you should know since you're joining us.'

'Yes. Thank you.'

Laura wasn't used to wine. Her scalp felt as if it was shrinking slightly at the back, and she was conscious of some strange feeling in her stomach. It wasn't that she was attracted to Max exactly, she thought, looking at him again and complimenting herself on her analytical objectivity. The eyes protruded too far, as if he was having difficulty swallowing something large; the mouth was messy, slack and pulled off-centre . . .

But here was a man who ran a ballet company. The husband of Nadine Kelly. And he seemed, unless she was very much mistaken, to have spotted something in her. Her? The thought made Laura want to laugh. Mousy Laura Douglas? She chided herself for being so ridiculous. It was the wine.

The meal was over and they found themselves out on the pavement. Laura realized she had left her hat behind, went back for it and, panicking that Max would have disappeared by the time she returned, arrived on pavement-level again panting.

'There you are,' he said, putting one hand on her shoulder. 'Now I'm going to take you home.'

She felt something – was it expectation? – shatter and begin to slide, like an egg thrown at a window. 'Oh,' said Laura beneath her hat. 'Thank you. I mean – no need. I think I can get a bus from . . .' She searched about for the nearest stop and tried to consider on which side of the road she would need to wait. But Max was laughing. '*My* home, you idiot.'

The hand on her shoulder gave a squeeze. It was too hard, and hurt.

'Let's take a taxi. No pressing appointments, have you?'

She shook her head.

'Wait here.'

He strode off along the pavement, one arm held aloft at the passing traffic, scarf whipping out behind him.

Max found a taxi quickly, and Laura ran to meet it, one hand on her hat and the other clutching her bag. She felt madly happy, and rather gibberingly scared. Perhaps he just wanted to chat more about the company, after all. Surely he couldn't be thinking of . . .

As the taxi lurched off into the stream of the Cromwell Road again, Max lifted an arm around the back of Laura's shoulders, and pulled her in towards him. A film of sweat covered his upper lip and chin, and the damp stubble pressing against her face was scratchy.

THREE HOURS LATER LAURA was sitting on the edge of the chaise longue in Daphne's drawing room, lacing and unlacing her fingers. She bowed her head, and uttered a groaning whimper. 'I can't possibly go in on Monday. I'll have to go back to Miss Lawrence.' She half stood up; then sat down again as another thought struck. 'But I've signed the contract. Oh . . .'

Everything seemed to have gone heart-thumpingly wrong. She couldn't join the EBT. And mixed in somehow with this agonizing thought, the sensation kept coming back to her, as if she felt it still, of Max Norris lying on her afterwards, heavy, red, heaving and unpleasantly damp all over.

'But why can't you go in?' asked Daphne, with maddening simplicity.

Laura bit at her fingers.

'For goodness' sake, darling, whatever is the problem? How can you have been in this world for almost twenty years – five of them with *me* – and suddenly have turned into a little Victorian prude? This is nineteen *seventy*.'

'Daphne!' Laura's face twisted in frustration. 'Listen to me. I met the EBT's senior ballerina for the first time this afternoon as I walked naked down the corridor of her own apartment, having just made love with her husband.'

'Been screwed by, darling, been screwed by. From the sounds of things it was hardly anything more than that. What were you doing in the corridor, anyway? Admiring the décor?'

'I was looking for the bathroom.' Laura dug her knuckles into her eyes. She couldn't get Nadine's face out of her mind. That sardonic smile and that sweet voice, speaking barbed words: You've just joined the company? she had said. Welcome – and well done. Best to get the initiation rites over as soon as possible, dear.

Daphne, who had been walking about the room, now

faced Laura and sat. The embroidered silk of her kimono caught the light from the window behind her and glowed a glorious rich cyan. 'If he *does* sleep with everything that moves,' she said, laying her head back against the chair and fixing Laura with a narrowed gaze, 'his wife is hardly going to blame you any more than the rest of the – what do they call it? – *corps de ballet*, is she?' Laura groaned. Daphne went on, 'But perhaps he doesn't – did it occur to you that she could well be lying? The woman has a great line in put-downs – I should meet her some time.'

Laura could not believe the monumental proportions of her own stupidity. That she could have believed Max Norris would truly have seen anything attractive in her! He would probably say she had thrown herself at him. And by Monday it would be all round the company.

'Darling. Do you want that job?' Daphne cut through her thoughts.

'Yes.'

'Then for Pete's sake turn up on Monday and stop flagellating yourself about it.' She got up with decision, as if the subject were closed, and crossed to the sideboard. 'Now, darling,' she said in a fresh and brighter tone, 'gin?'

DAPHNE'S WORDS HAD STRUCK a chord. What if Nadine had been lying about Max? As the hours passed, the thought dissolved Laura's worst suspicions about Max's motives, and by Sunday afternoon she was half expecting that he might ring her. She had bolted so quickly out of his apartment, after all, hopping into her clothes as Max, still naked, argued with Nadine about exactly what times they had each agreed to use the flat. It was only when Laura was down in the street that she'd realized she'd left that blasted hat behind. Somehow it had been the last straw, and she'd cried softly all the way home on the bus.

But Max did not ring. On Monday morning, Laura gathered her somewhat confused courage and made the journey to South Kensington.

The company building seemed to have changed radically in appearance. She had left it in blazing spring sunshine, a worn but glorious centre of creativity and artistry. Now under a dull sky it appeared hunched and crouching, with a mocking expression about its windows and a lowering look to its guttering. Laura felt small, foolish and untalented. But she'd passed the audition; they'd taken her on. And nothing, in the end, would come in the way of that. Dancing, as she had discovered so often before, was all she could be sure of.

The dancers' common room was up on the first floor. Through the door, she was met by a wall of smoke. The room was full of bodies, lounging on chairs, sitting or lying on the floor in various contorted positions. There was a burst of laughter as Laura entered: she felt her cheeks instantly aflame, and, before she had time to think, had backed out again, with a grimace intended to indicate that she had made a mistake and come to the wrong room.

She checked her watch: fifteen minutes, still, before class. She couldn't go back in *there* – but where was the changing room? She should get to the studio and warm up. She looked each way along the corridor: there was no one to help. And that was how, without having consciously intended it, she found herself climbing the stairs to Max's office.

Now she was waiting outside the door. She had knocked and entered some time earlier. Max had been on the phone and had waved her out with a frown she hoped was meant for the person at the other end of the line.

The phone went down; Laura heard a shuffling of papers; then the scrape of a chair. A second later the door opened.

'Yes?'

'I—' Laura stopped. What on earth had she come to say? 'I just wanted to apologize for rushing off on Saturday like that,' she said, the words tumbling out while she listened to them, horrified. 'I mean, I—'

Max looked amused. His expression silenced her. He brushed his hand back across her forehead and brought it round to her cheek. She tipped her head to lean against it. Bringing his face close to hers, he said in a soft whisper, 'Thank you, Laura, but no. You're not worth it twice.' He paused, considering. 'I know you were doing your best, but did anyone ever tell you you're a cold little thing?'

The words took a moment to sink in. Laura jerked her head away. Her cheek was stinging as if he'd slapped her.

Max held his hand still in mid-air for an instant, then smiled briskly. 'I think you should be in class, don't you?' he said. He turned back into his office and shut the door.

LAURA STARED THROUGH the rain-streaked, ill-fitting window and wondered that she had not felt any different these past few days. For she was, in truth, a different person. Last week she had achieved an ambition for which she had ached and fought – against herself and others – and strained and cried and bled for years. She had taken the stage as a professional dancer; she had made, as those would have said who did not know the true lack of glamour of the situation, her début.

And now she was rattling towards Leeds on a draughty, cranky, dilapidated old train.

It had not been an auspicious début. She had had no spotlight or curtain calls or bouquets. Actually, that last was not quite true: Daphne had sent her freesias, with a note commiserating with her for having to venture as far as 'darkest Durham' (Daphne having no ambition ever to get further north than Oxford), and Richard a dozen white roses that had earned her looks of curiosity from the other girls in the morgue-cold and tiny *corps* dressing room. But no one in the audience, doubtless, could have picked her out from an identity parade of people they might or might not have seen in the English Ballet Theatre's touring production of *Swan Lake*. Laura had been a peasant girl, with a brown dress and a flower garland to carry, and then a swan, third from the back, upstage left, spending much of the evening standing stock still and willing herself not to get cramp. She'd had just two weeks to learn all her roles for the tour, and had only been glad afterwards that she hadn't bumped into any scenery, any*body* or fallen over.

The train was slowing: they were drawing into somewhere called Ulleskelf. Her carriage was empty and she wanted to keep it that way – she drew down the blinds on the corridor side and hoped not to be disturbed. She had work to do.

Laura settled back into the corner seat and studied her notebook. She had decided to try to teach herself as many of the other female roles as she possibly could, both in *Swan Lake* and in the other ballet they were alternating with it, Alexander McIntyre's *Romeo and Juliet*. She did not, however, particularly wish her fellow *corps* girls to know what she was up to. The prevailing fashionable attitude to work, at least in public, was decidedly blasé, and Laura had already caused irritation the night before by hanging around in the wings when she did not have a cue coming up. Nadine Kelly, who at thirty-eight was playing the supposedly young and nubile Swan Princess, had performed a *grand jeté* coming off the cramped and cruelly raked Durham stage and only narrowly avoided cannoning straight into Laura. For this Laura had been treated to a stream of ferocious and colourful obscenities, delivered in a whisper two inches from her nose by a face caked in about the same thickness of warpaint. She had retreated rapidly: she feared Nadine and tried, as much as possible, to keep out of her way. But the experience had not put Laura off her task. Back at her digs, she had sat in bed until the early hours, overcoat pulled around her in the unheated room, making detailed notes on the role of the Swan Princess. Now she was going over them, waggling her feet in front of her in echo of the steps.

Micklefield. Laura looked out at the station. The platform was practically deserted. It was May, and quite possibly the most miserable, rain-buffeted May she could remember.

The compartment door slid back and a face appeared. Marco Agnelli, one of the EBT soloists, glanced about the compartment, taking in Laura along with the empty seats and apparently making no differentiation between them. His head disappeared and she heard his voice in the corridor: 'This one's empty,' which brought a reply of 'Thank God!' and two other figures tumbling into the compartment. The three spread out, feet up on seats. The only woman, Eve Morrison, a delicate red-head and one of the company's youngest principals, said a quick, 'Don't mind, do you?' to Laura, at which she shook her head and quickly returned to her notebook.

A deck of cards was produced, and several packets of cigarettes.

'Nadine won't get first casts next season, I'm telling you.' This was the third member of the group, continuing a conversation that had started in the corridor. He was a tall, lugubrious-looking soloist named Dandy Franks.

'So who will?'

'Our very own Evie, of course!'

'Get away with you.'

'You shall, my sweet, or I will be lunching on my pyjamas.'

Dancer years, rather like cat years, put Nadine Kelly already on the edge of her dotage and the question of who would succeed her in the company hierarchy had been for some time, Laura knew, the subject of intense speculation. Among the principal dancers, hierarchy was dictated by cast orders. The system was simple: since to dance Odette-Odile or Prince Siegfried, Juliet or Romeo every night would have been impossibly exhausting, each major role was performed by three or sometimes more people on a rota basis. To be top of the rota – the 'first cast' – held by far the most prestige. The first cast performed at all the most important opening nights and galas and received, inevitably, the lion's share of press attention. Eve Morrison was currently second cast Odette-Odile, which meant Mondays and Wednesdays and ambitious impatience.

'But what about Francesca?' she asked now.

Laura listened intently, her nose in her notebook. This was Francesca O'Connor they were talking about, the second cast Juliet.

'Francesca's no competition for you. She has all the dramatic qualities of a steamed pudding.'

'Her extensions are good.'

'She's well practised at the movements, *chérie*.' Dandy opened and shut his legs; Evie hit him.

Some moments later Laura, glancing up, was taken aback to find Dandy looking her way. He was drawing on his cigarette, studying her thoughtfully, and seemed utterly unembarrassed to have been caught doing so. Laura dropped her eyes again quickly, feeling herself go pink.

'But when it comes to Nadine, darling,' she heard Dandy drawl, 'we must have a heart. She probably hasn't had a screw for *months*.'

Laura gave an involuntary wince, and wondered exactly where on the train Nadine was. Did she know how the other dancers talked about her? Probably. That she was a figure of resentment and jealousy, and therefore derision, was inevitable. As long as her claws were stuck into those first casts, she was keeping younger dancers out of the spotlight. But who, truly, could envy her? Perhaps she had one more season left – and then again perhaps she didn't. Even if she were lucky, what then? What would she have when the last curtain call was over? An empty marriage she'd stayed in for career reasons alone and a life equally empty because she'd given it to a profession that spewed out even its best by the age of forty.

Still, Nadine had, by any standards, been fortunate. There were dancers who had spent their whole career in the *corps*, who had started off full of the same hopes as Nadine but had had to settle, over time, for their thankless, punishing lot and were, for the main part, dying for a way out. And then, Nadine was lucky, too, to have lasted so long. The spectre of serious injury hung over them all, high and low-ranking alike, every day. As it was, at any one time half the company seemed to be struggling with incipient chronic conditions. Strap it up and ignore it, was the motto. It could cripple you in the end, of course. But the end wasn't right now. And meanwhile just one bad fall, one careless movement, one mistake from a tired or negligent partner, an insufficiently warmed-up muscle, a rake not at the angle you'd thought and you wouldn't just be gritting your teeth, you'd be in retirement.

So Nadine's fate – clinging to an old dream, fearful of the future – was the best any of them could hope for.

The prospect made Laura quail. But it would never make her change her mind.

THAT NIGHT'S PERFORMANCE was cursed with more than its fair share of mishaps. Nadine's swan costume caught on her prince's doublet as she was lowered from a lift, and they had to make a swift exit to unhitch themselves; a stage-hand broke his toe on a piece of scenery in a black-out; and Francesca O'Connor was taken ill just before the Act Three Spanish variation.

This last calamity was observed by Laura, pressed into the shadows of the prompt side wings. A little way along from her in the half-dark, a huddle had grown around Francesca, who was bent double with cramping stomach pains. Dandy Franks, her partner in the variation, had fetched Heather, Heather had fetched Max, and Laura watched now as Max's bulbous eyes swivelled anxiously to the stage and back as he tried to assess his options. He leant down to speak to Francesca. By way of answer, she vomited copiously into a fire bucket.

There was no way she could dance the variation. Calmly, Laura approached Max and touched his shoulder.

'What?' he hissed.

'I'll do it.'

He looked at her hotly. 'What are you saying? You know the part?'

'Yes.' Laura's heartbeat sounded in her ears like the timpani on overdrive; but she looked levelly at her employer.

Max raked a hand through his hair. 'Okay,' he said. 'Heather, get Francesca out of that costume. Now!'

Laura glanced about hurriedly for somewhere to change. She found Dandy suddenly at her elbow. The next instant he had Francesca's costume by the shoulders and was holding it open, ready for Laura to step in. 'Come on, then,' he insisted. 'Get yours off.' Seeing Laura hesitate, Dandy rolled his eyes. 'God, sweetheart, don't be a prude. I've seen it all before, I can assure you. And I'm going to need you on that damn stage in rather less than fifteen seconds.'

HULL. IT WAS DRIZZLING. Another dreary train ride to another dreary station. Exhaustion hung on Laura like a suit of iron, weighing down her cold muscles and aching joints. She could gladly have curled up on a bench in the waiting room and slept for a week.

No such luck. The first task, as ever, was to look for digs. Heather moved swiftly among the unsmiling dancers, handing out her list of recommended boarding houses.

'Ignore that,' said a voice behind Laura. She turned and was surprised to find Francesca O'Connor's cool blue gaze meeting hers.

'I'm glad you're better,' offered Laura, a little awkwardly. She had never, as far as she could remember, said more to Francesca than 'excuse me' in a crowded green room; and Francesca was not renowned within the company for her general friendliness. But the drama of the previous week had forged some link between them, Laura supposed.

At any rate, Francesca smiled. In combination with the forget-me-not eyes and the shining chestnut hair, it was an irresistible expression. 'Thanks,' she said, then waved the piece of paper that had been thrust into her hand. 'Heather doesn't know her arse from her elbow when it comes to finding digs. It's always either miles too expensive or a real hell-hole. Look,' she searched in her bag and produced a stub of a pencil, 'give me your list. I'll write down the best place for you. I stayed there last year – a real gem.'

'D'you want me to get them to keep a room for you too?'

Francesca wrinkled her nose. 'No, ta.' She nodded in the direction of her husband, another dancer. 'Colm's got some insufferable relatives here, worse luck. We've got to stay with them.'

'Oh – thanks, then. Thanks a lot.'

She's not nearly as bad as they say, Laura told herself, as she watched Francesca return to her friends. I really am too ready to believe the worst about people. It must be Daphne's influence.

'SLEEP WELL, DID YOU, DEAR?' Colm called out the next morning, as Laura walked into the ice-box of a church hall that was the company's rehearsal space for the week. 'How many bed-bug bites?'

Several among the group around him spoke at once. Laura made out the words: 'You didn't!'

'Course *I* didn't,' said Colm. 'Francesca.'

'No!' There were shrieks of laughter.

'God, the poor cow! I don't think anyone's been desperate enough to go to Mrs Fletcher's for years.'

'Francesca, you bitch! The kid's not that bad.'

Having spent a sleepless night on a damp bed in a room reeking of mildew, Laura barely had the mental energy to work out what was going on. She felt as if a steamroller had driven over her – twice.

That night's performance she only survived through sheer bloody-mindedness. Afterwards, there was to be a massed descent on the church hall for what had been advertised as a 'mid-tour desperation party'. The venue was inhospitable and Laura practically dead on her feet – but Mrs Fletcher's boarding house on Acacia Road was less hospitable still, so she went, and propped herself in the corner by the record player, trying to look plausible and hold a paper cup of punch without spilling it. For once, the fact that hardly anyone spoke to her all evening seemed a blessed relief.

Walking home listlessly just before three, she found herself behind a small clump of figures weaving an uncertain path along the pavement. They were instantly recognizable: one daddy-long-legs wrapped in a mac; one small red-head, dainty as a bird; and one dark, well-muscled Mediterranean. Dandy, Evie and Marco. They had spotted her too.

'Hey! It's my little partner!' There was a scuffle of whispering. 'What's her name again? Laura!'

Dandy turned, balanced himself carefully, and addressed her. 'You're not still at Old Bag Fletcher's, are you?'

Evie drew in a sharp breath. 'You mean the one with the bed-bugs?' She beckoned to Laura. 'That's more than body and soul can stand. Come back with us.'

'What?' hissed Dandy, flapping at her to keep her voice down. 'Evie . . .'

'She can share with me.'

'We'll never get her past Mrs Woolly,' said Marco.

'Woollam,' Evie corrected seriously. 'Course we will. Stop fussing. Come on, Fanny-Ann.' Marching over, Evie put her arm through Laura's and bodily dragged her along the street.

'WELL, THAT WAS WORTH IT just to see your solemn little face appearing over the window sill,' said Dandy later, pouring a large tot of brandy from a hip flask into a chipped mug. Laura looked at him quickly to see if she was being mocked, but the smile on his face seemed to radiate a genuine, if rather vague, friendliness.

'Can we keep it up for three days, though, do you think?' asked Evie.

'No need.' Dandy downed the brandy and poured another for Marco. 'Tomorrow Laura can present herself at the door in the normal manner. They won't turn down a few more days' rent, that's for sure.'

Laura, who was gripping her own share of brandy in a tooth-mug, looked from one to the other of them, feeling warmed by more than the alcohol. The climb up the drainpipe had shredded her nerves and a good deal of the skin on her knees but she hardly felt either discomfort now. This shabby, cramped room with its linoleum floor and candlewick-covered bed seemed a very fine place to be indeed.

'She's got guts,' declared Dandy, flopping back on Evie's bed, and flinging an arm in Laura's direction. ''S what I like. Guts. *Un*like Francesca O'Connor, who, you will remember, chucked hers up.' He thought for a moment, then heaved himself onto one elbow. 'You know,' he said, with the air of one who has come to a portentous conclusion, 'she wouldn't have bothered to be mean to you if she thought you were crap.' He nodded sagely. 'Mark my words. You'll get more soloist roles before this tour's through.'

LAURA DID MARK DANDY'S words and, though uttered in a state of considerable inebriation, they turned out to be impressively correct. A fortnight later Max tried Laura out in the Act Two *pas de quatre* and following that, she was given a week as a Verona prostitute in *Romeo and Juliet*, and then another as one of Juliet's maids of honour. And if the likes of Francesca O'Connor hated her the more for it, Laura now genuinely did not care: she had the armour with which to withstand such malice and wondered how she had got through life before the advent of Dandy, Evie and Marco.

In July, when the tour was over, the four decided to go on holiday. The vote had been in favour of Monte

Carlo. The reality turned out to be Brighton. But at least the weather was good. Laura learnt to smoke and drink bourbon, and watched her feet improve in the sun – dry out, harden and crust beautifully. One day Evie found her sitting on one of the sun loungers on the back terrace of the little hotel, staring at her toes balefully as she alternately flexed and pointed them.

'I've come to an important realization,' Laura said, when Evie asked her what was the matter.

Evie spread herself along the neighbouring lounger. The ice cubes clinked in her glass as she set it down and adjusted her extravagantly broad-brimmed hat. 'Spill,' she commanded.

Laura sighed, with a little catch in her throat of pure emotion, and turned to face her friend. 'I shall never,' she said, 'look good in slingbacks.'

Evie had a loud laugh for one so slight. She pointed her miniature pink umbrella cocktail-stick in the direction of Laura's toes. 'Absolutely true. But the battle scars do you credit. And I have a tip,' Evie added, after a contemplative pause. 'Wear the brightest bloody nail varnish you can find. It distracts attention from the bunions.'

For the duration of the vac, they all played at having far more money than they had. Dandy, though, spoiled the effect by being hopelessly mean. He'd found himself an ethnic pouch purse of quite microscopic proportions, and when it came to paying for anything or calculating spending power, he would lay the tiny bag on the table and count his pennies out of it with an expression of deadly serious concentration.

'I'll bet you anything you like he's got more money stashed somewhere else,' said Evie. 'Do you notice he always has about the same number of coins? He simply replenishes his stock.'

'How do you know?' Laura asked. 'He always gets out of paying for things so he doesn't need to.'

'Dear Dandy,' said Evie flatly. 'He's such a devious little trollop under that – that – devious little trollop exterior.'

Dandy's penny-pinching, however, never seemed to stop him coming up with fresh schemes for extravagance, which would inevitably end up as other people's. 'Listen!' he announced at breakfast, one morning, from behind a copy of *The Times*. Their table was the last left occupied in the dining room: Dandy believed in arriving at one minute to the nine o'clock deadline and spinning out his breakfast for as much of the rest of the morning as possible. In pursuit of this strange hobby he had developed a new and absorbing interest in prunes. 'The Czechoslovak National Ballet,' he said, when he had made sure of his companions' attention, 'is at Sadler's Wells next week. Who wants to come with me?'

'They'll be sold out,' said Evie flatly. 'They've got that wonderboy – what's his name? Milan somebody. Milan—'

'Novák,' said Marco.

'Novák, thank you. The press got in a right lather last time they were here. We wouldn't stand a chance.'

'So we'll get cancellations. Beg, bribe, shoot our way in. Oh, come on, anyone up for it?'

It was inevitable that they would be, and in the end they made a good show of it, with Dandy in his silk waistcoat and watchless watch-chain, Evie with a ferociously beaded full-length number and fur stole of dubious aroma, Marco sporting more frills down his chest than a turkey, and Laura. She had on a cocktail dress of her mother's, and was wearing it for the first time. They secured two returned tickets and the other two had to buy standing places. They swapped at the interval.

The 'wonderboy', as Dandy now insisted on calling him was no boy (twenty-five was the generally agreed estimate), but he did have his fair share of wonders to perform. The leaps suggested a personal denial of Newton; the *pirouettes* were to die for; the artistry of the performance was enough to engender in the breasts of these particular spectators an appreciative loathing. They ignored him in conversation and picked holes in the *corps* work instead.

'What's *she* doing here?' said Marco suddenly, as they stood in the bar afterwards. As a body, the three others faced the way he was looking and caught a quick glimpse of Nadine Kelly, before she disappeared down the stairs.

'Same as us?' suggested Evie.

'She has connections with everyone, darling,' said Dandy.

They drank up and wondered what to do next. 'Come on,' said Dandy, tugging at Laura's sleeve. 'I want to ask him what he's doing at the weekend.'

'Who?'

'The wonderboy, of course!'

'*Dandy!*' Three voices in unison.

'Oh, you spoilsports. Very well. I shall proffer my programme to be autographed and say please very nicely. Okay?'

On this assurance, Laura agreed to accompany him to the stage door. They'd waited there three-quarters of an hour before someone told them. The man they sought had already left.

THE NEWS OF WHERE Milan Novák had gone reached them with the morning papers. Laura had spent the night on the unforgivingly hard floor of Dandy's Finsbury Park bedroom rather than trekking back to Little Venice. The first she heard of the news was a screech outside the door. She pulled on Dandy's dressing gown and stumbled out into the hallway, expecting to encounter flood, plague, pestilence, or all three.

Dandy was squatting at the top of the stairs, ears between his spiky spider knees, the morning newspaper spread flat before him.

'What? What is it?' Laura asked, stumbling blearily

towards him and peering over his shoulder at the head-line.

'My darling,' said Dandy, turning a face up towards her on which surprise was mixed strangely with frustration, 'the wonderboy has defected.'

The report contained few details. A small reception had been held for Novák at a restaurant by, of all people, Nadine ('Connections everywhere, sweetest, I told you'). From this select social occasion Novák had managed to slip away, eluding his minders. He had been driven out of London by unnamed British friends, and was now holed up at a secret address, somewhere in the Home Counties, from which negotiations were being conducted with the Foreign Office to obtain political asylum.

'The Party of the Year,' said Dandy dourly, 'and I missed it.'

THE DRAMA OF MILAN NOVÁK'S defection set up a tremor felt throughout the dance fraternity. Its effect on Laura, though, was surprisingly practical. She moved out of Daphne's apartment.

The causal sequence was admittedly indirect. It ran thus: Dandy made a collage out of newspaper pictures of Novák and fixed it to his landlady's fridge with golden syrup (there being a lack of Sellotape). The landlady, a certain Mrs Semple, who did not appreciate the finer points of Dandy's artistic taste, tore it down. Dandy declared this act of sabotage to be the final straw, informed

Mrs Semple that he was terminating his tenancy agreement with immediate effect, and came to camp at Daphne's. Five days later he announced that La Devereux, much as he adored her, was out to ruin his lungs and his liver, and decreed that he, Laura and Evie should move in together. Marco, for his part, declined to be included in the plan though he did undertake, through family connections, to find them a flat.

It was situated above a chip shop in Muswell Hill. In the mornings, congealed fat dripped from the ceilings. The curiosity value of this phenomenon hardly made up for the lack of central heating, windows that shut properly or reliable plumbing.

'I just love it,' said Dandy, sounding the depth of a deep well of sarcasm. 'Whose idea was this, anyway?'

'Yours,' said Evie from the sofa, where she was curled around the warmth of a cigarette. 'Laura, you are so damn valiant, knowing you could trip back to darling Daphne at any moment.'

'Greater love hath no woman –'

' – than to endure a lard-drip for her friends. We're honoured.'

Laura reflected, bundling greasy bedding into a laundry bag, that it really was no hardship. But she knew better than to say so. Mawkishness was a cardinal sin in Dandy's book.

They christened the flat Bleak House and on a sudden optimistic whim decided to redecorate. Dandy wore his overcoat throughout the operation, refusing point blank to set foot on a ladder or to do any painting except the fiddly bits that required a small brush. He remounted his Novák collage on the fridge. Thoughts, as they worked, turned to the imminent end of the summer break and to hopes of promotion – for Evie to those longed-for first casts, for Dandy to the level of principal.

And then a trip made by Evie to the local hardware store brought some unexpected relevant news. 'Guess who I met in Carpenter's?' she said eagerly, setting down two paint pots big as milking pails.

'The Aga Khan,' suggested Dandy, standing back to frown at his handiwork and take a drag on his cigarette. 'Kennedy. Monroe. No, don't tell me – Adolf Hitler.'

'Heather,' said Evie, grimacing at him. 'And the news of the century is this. Milan Novák . . .' She paused, enjoying the feeling now of having Dandy's full attention. 'Milan Novák . . .'

'Yes? Yes?'

'Is joining the EBT!' finished Evie triumphantly, looking from Dandy to Laura and back again.

There was a short silence.

'Nadine's set it up, according to Heather,' she added.

'Ah,' said Dandy with slow-dawning realization. 'You know what this is, don't you? It's the Snow Queen's Revenge.'

'How so?'

'Well, Nadine's got Max over a barrel now, hasn't she?'

'Sounds painful.'

'Don't be vulgar. She's got to be screwing him.'

'Max?'

'Evie, Evie, get real. Novák, I mean. So, answers to all her troubles in the form of one man.' Dandy slung his paintbrush in its jam jar and sat on the sofa-arm. 'And I fear, Evie, that it's bad news for both of us.'

Laura frowned. 'Let me get this straight,' she said, sitting too. 'You're saying Nadine's done a deal. If she brings Novák into the company, she . . .' Laura shot a quick glance at Evie. It was clear she'd just worked it out as well: beneath the freckles she was porcelain pale. 'She has to keep her first casts?'

'*Naturellement*, my sweet,' said Dandy. 'And Novák is such good bait, what on earth can poor Max do but employ his wife and her lover? You have to take your hat off to Nadine. What an impeccable piece of engineering.'

'Oh, Evie.' Laura crossed to her and slipped an arm around the slender shoulders.

Evie said nothing, but readily accepted Laura's cigarette. Dandy got up and set about fixing them all dangerously strong vodka martinis.

'What I don't understand,' said Evie some time later, as they sat round what passed for the kitchen table, 'is why the hell Novák's muscling in on our grotty little outfit.'

'Evie. Some *amour propre* if you please,' said Dandy severely. 'He must be a stranger boy than we imagined. He must really be in the old girl's thrall.'

'Or on the run from the Czech version of the KGB. What are they called?'

'No idea.'

'Scuppers your chances, anyhow, Dandy.'

'I know, my sweet. Vacancy for a new principal dancer well and truly filled. But if I'm going to be trampled on in my inexorable progress to the top, I can at least be thankful that I'm only being trampled by the best.' He drained his glass and unscrewed the lid of the martini bottle once more. 'Besides, it may be a nudge from Dame Fortuna. I really want to choreograph, after all. So that's what I should be doing.'

An air of gloom had settled upon the room, and as the level in the bottle sank lower, Dandy and Evie both seemed to slump with it. Evie fished the olive out of her latest measure, sucked on it, and then spat it back into her hand. Dandy looked at her with deflated disgust. 'It was *off*,' she said, and lapsed once more into silence.

Laura wondered, blearily, why everything had suddenly gone so wrong. 'How can one person waltz in and wreck all our plans?' she asked, floating an exasperated stream of cigarette smoke on the air. 'I swear I hate the man already. And with such a will I'd be surprised if he didn't twist his ankle within five minutes of coming into the studio.'

Evie nodded at this and raised her glass in a toast. 'To bloody Milan Novák, then,' she said. 'And twisted ankles.'

Chapter Seven **Paris, 1989**

Natasha checked the scrap of paper. It seemed a pitifully small, uncertain thing on which to base her arrival. Today's date, that was right. The time: 6 p.m. – an odd hour of the day for company class by anybody's reckoning. And the address, which had brought her to this unpromising-looking street in the Pigalle district of the 9th *arrondissement*. She'd walked the length of it a couple of times before she'd spotted the right building. Now she gazed up at it; at the paint flaking off like dead skin, the bruisings of graffiti in black and blue spray, the blocked-off ground-floor windows, blind reflections of the shop fronts opposite. '*Permis de Démolir*' read a notice above the main doorway. Natasha's French was sadly limited, but she could work that one out. Christ, she thought. What kind of an outfit was this? But she pushed down the rising unease. After all, she'd hardly been to a dance place in her life that hadn't looked a complete dive from the outside.

A couple of plaques by the door announced a recording company on the *rez de chaussée*, and a clothes manufacturer further up – from the looks of it, they'd both deserted this sinking ship a while back. Nothing of Milan Novák, or any mention of a dance company. Natasha chose a bell at random and pressed. She tried another. Still nothing. She tried the handle. The door opened. Reluctantly, she went inside.

Half dark. Damp. A smell of cat's piss and mildew. Natasha stood in the murky gloom, tense for noises, voices, but there were none. She found a light switch, jabbed at it. To her surprise it worked. She made for the stairs.

Three floors up, and she'd passed no open doors, seen no sign whatsoever of life. A thick layer of dusty grit covered the floor; she could hear it sanding down the soles of her boots as she climbed. On the top landing, she stopped. The stairwell light, on a timer, clicked off. And from behind the door to her left she heard a vague shuffle of voices, echoing in a cavernous space.

'*Enfin, c'est lui!*' cried a voice from within, as she put her shoulder to the door and walked into a big bare room of almost warehouse proportions. Half a dozen faces turned towards her, expectant, laughing. A small group of people were lounging on the floor in the centre of the room. She saw a grey head among them, and stocky limbs as well as slender ones. Not dancers. And she was clearly not the person they had anticipated. The faces had frozen on the point of laughter and greeting, and they tightened now into battened-down expressions of mild curiosity.

Someone spoke again in French. It was a black woman, leaning on one arm with her legs sprawled out in front of her; thirtyish, bulky in sweatshirt and jogging pants. Natasha could tell from the tone it was a question, directed at her.

'I'm looking for Milan Novák's dance company,' she said, hoping one of them spoke English. 'Are they somewhere in this building?'

'They certainly are,' said a man at the front of the group in what sounded like a London accent. He was small, seriously small, with a wide, prominent forehead and a ring in each ear, standing out from the side of his face like cherubic golden curls. 'You've found them.'

Natasha stared. The little man grinned. 'Hard to believe?' he said, splaying his stubby fingers. 'What were you expecting?'

'A row of swans, Johnnie, a row of hellish little swans.'

The voice came from some distance to the right. Natasha recognized it and turned her head in surprise. In the far corner she saw a grand piano, in a state of quite extravagant disrepair. Beside it, leaning against the wall with his arms hugged close across his chest, was Milan Novák.

'And I hate to disappoint you, but you don't quite fit the bill,' he said, still speaking to Johnnie, and leaning down to a dog at his feet. 'If Fabrice doesn't turn up in the next two minutes we may as well start.' He released the dog, then, and it went scuttling across to greet the man called Johnnie, its tail whipping the air. Milan looked over to Natasha without apparent interest. 'What did you say your name was?'

Natasha, struggling to make sense of the scene, could only stare blankly. He couldn't have forgotten she was coming. So – what? Did he want to humiliate her? Why did she always feel with him there was a joke she couldn't fathom – and at her expense? She hoped this weird bunch of people were the joke – they *couldn't* be the company. She looked back to Milan and saw, with some irritation, that he was genuinely trying to place her.

Milan caught her look and his eyebrows raised. 'I forget things, a legacy of past follies. Not to be applauded, I know.'

'I'm Natasha Taylor,' she said tightly. 'You saw me dance in London.'

'I did? I did.'

'I got a call to say there was a job for me.'

'Ah, Victor and his wonderful optimism.'

'You mean there isn't?' Natasha stopped. She should have foreseen this. The anger rose in her throat. 'You've given it to someone else? Or maybe there never was a job? I get the picture. I'm wasting my time.' Snatching up her bag, she turned to the door. A murmur sounded from the group in the centre of the room.

'Hey . . . *hey*.' Milan's voice was quiet, but it stopped her. She looked back: he was watching her calmly. 'Now,' he said, nodding her forward. 'Refresh my poor addled memory.' Natasha turned, uncertain, clutching her bag in front of her like a shield. 'Your training?' said Milan. 'Just name the school, it tells me enough. Ah, yes. Injuries? Congratulations. Rare good fortune. General health? Okay, okay. And now remind me. Why did you want to join this – ' he looked, mildly, across the room ' – this limping band of sideshow freaks and self-abusers?'

Angry and uncertain, Natasha was in no mood to mention the glories of his reputation. Besides, if these people . . . if there was *any chance* these people really were his other dancers and she'd known it in advance, she would never have agreed to come. 'I wanted something different,' she said, with more than a hint of bitterness. 'I didn't care what people thought I *ought* to do.'

'Contradiction, Natasha Taylor,' Milan put in. 'You can't be a rebel unless you do care what people expect. And we're not what *you* expected, are we?' He smiled for the first time, but without amusement. Natasha felt a twist in her gut. 'Do I have it right?' he said. 'I see from your face that I do. Well, you can creep quietly home again if you like. We shan't tell a soul.'

Creep quietly home, having defied all advice to come here? How did Milan know? Or did he simply suspect, being aware of his own reputation? Damn his patronizing games! The weathervane of Natasha's pride had swung: he had prevented her from walking out as certainly as if he'd blocked the doorway. She stood her ground. 'I've turned down other things for this.'

'We're honoured.'

The tone chilled her: her anger and anxiety melted quickly into another type of fear. 'I only mean – look, tell me straight. Is there a job or isn't there? There's stuff I need to know. Rehearsal schedules, money – I've got a whole bunch of questions.'

'Ah, then, Victor is your man. Victor has *answers*.' Milan turned his head in the direction of a small doorway in the wall opposite. 'Victor!' he called, and another figure Natasha recognized – big as a buffalo – appeared. 'Reality is biting over here. Would you?'

At that moment someone else entered the room behind Natasha. There was a burst of derision and catcalling.

'Fabrice!'

'What was it this time?'

'We thought you'd died!'

The man thus hailed had sand-coloured dreadlocks and Bermuda shorts, and was evidently the pianist. Seeing him, Milan pushed himself off the wall, stripped off his sweatshirt, kicked it into the corner and made his way to the barre without giving Natasha another glance.

'Erik,' he said to one of the dancers, a tall man with close-cropped grey hair, 'are we in your hands this evening? Flay us to within an inch of our lives – I'm in a masochistic mood.' Milan rubbed his face, hard, with the flats of his palms. 'Yes indeed.'

NATASHA MISSED THE BEGINNING of the class. Victor, lumbering over, took her elbow gently and led her out onto the landing. As the piano started up to Erik's instruction she leant against the sharp edge of the window-frame, letting it dig into her shoulder.

'We play Paris for a month, mid-November to mid-December, *if* I can confirm the venue – God!' Victor, pasty-faced and sweating slightly, pulled at his hair. Some strands came away in his fingers, though he didn't seem to notice. 'Then,' he said, 'tour. The States and Europe, in that order. Perhaps. I'm doing my damnedest to persuade him to dance.' He nodded significantly towards the studio. 'Who's going to come and see us if he doesn't? The problem's so blasted obvious. No one'll give us venues and the backers'll be trampling on each other in the rush to pull out.'

Natasha narrowed her eyes. 'He doesn't want to *dance*?'

'Considers himself retired. Wants to direct and chor-eograph – nothing more. Only comes to class because he says it keeps him sane. Ha *ha*.' Victor pushed at his glasses, which were sliding down his nose, and blinked at Natasha. 'Anyhow. You wanted to know about pay? This is the not so good news, I'm afraid. Until September – that's, what?' He totted up on his fingers. 'Six more weeks? Seven? There is none.'

'*What?*'

'Hence evening class, rather than morning, so you can work during the day. Though I'd advise you to do it on the black. I know, I know, I should have said earlier.' He looked apologetic, but Natasha didn't suppose it had slipped his mind. 'There'll be some weekend rehearsals starting up soon for the stuff we're just restaging. Then, September, the real work kicks in. Full days here.'

'And what will the show be? What will I be doing?'

'What you'll do – not my province. The programme, at the moment, is this. Basically, two major new works. One by Milan, one by Quentin Faulkner – he's coming over from New York. Then, various things that've been done before, a couple of Milan's short works, a couple by other people, we want a programme we can shift about a bit. And then I want the solo Nick Casey choreographed for him too, but we'll see.'

'Will I have a contract?'

'Do you want one?'

There was a pause. Natasha felt royally confused. 'He wants me in, right?'

'We need another body. A couple more, ideally, but we can't stretch that far. Maybe he forgot you were supposed to be coming, but then,' Victor's shoulders shifted, 'maybe not. I wouldn't take him at his word. Milan has his own ways of . . . testing people. I think you just did another audition.' He smiled; it seemed genuinely friendly. 'Don't let it get to you.'

Natasha, riled by the unflattering pragmatism, nevertheless found herself smiling in return, suddenly grateful that someone, at least, was being straight with her. But what now? Rated as dancers, the people in that studio were freaks – Milan had said it himself. What was he doing? Maybe he was as unstable as everyone back home had said. And even if he wasn't, what kind of début could she expect in a company of no-hopers? Would she get a début at all if Milan wouldn't dance and the tour fell through? Natasha, muttering her thanks to Victor, felt as if every one of the whispering doubts spawned on her arrival in Paris was now screaming blue murder in her head.

She took a deep breath. Through the half-open door, Erik's voice could be heard giving instructions as he took the company through a warm-up at the barre. Natasha made a quick decision. She might not be a match for Milan in his conversational chess moves, but she could wipe the floor with any one of his dancers in class. She would make them take her seriously; she would make them gawp. And she would think later how to get out of this mess. Shrugging off her coat, Natasha crossed the landing and stepped back into the studio.

'OKAY, OKAY. That is all.' Erik nodded, satisfied, and ran a hand through his hair. It was sweat-soaked and stayed where his fingers pushed it, in spiky grey tufts.

Natasha walked slowly to the free-standing barre. She

bent over it, her arms dangling, her chest heaving uncomfortably against the wooden rail. 'Christ,' she said, when she managed to speak. She shook her head, marvelling, and drops fell from her nose and chin and forehead.

The class had astonished her. She felt dazed, humbled, mind-numbingly exhausted. Freaks they might be, this company, but they sure as hell could dance. Warming up quickly so that she could join the barre work, she'd noticed first how fit and lithe the seven bodies were. Though unaesthetic, all but Milan, by conventional dance standards, when they began to move she saw strange sculptures in flesh, scraped of fat like anatomist's models; she saw formidable strength and control and – yes – grace. Even Johnnie, who with his short limbs looked all corners, who had great solid sideboards of muscle for legs and a full kitchen cabinet of a chest, achieved a flow of line and an agility she'd rarely seen before.

Her sneering self-assurance had evaporated on the instant. She slipped into the class at the back, and bent her mind to her own performance. And found a second surprise. For Natasha, trained in a vocabulary which she had mastered quickly and young, and which had become second nature to her, this class was a foreign language, and it was tough. The style was eclectic: a magpie's nest of classical and contemporary techniques. The strength required, the stamina, the sheer bloody-minded hard work were terrifying. Thoughts of making the others take notice deserted her. Natasha felt herself floundering, and her confidence ebbed in the push and pull on her muscles of the unfamiliar movements.

'Christ,' she said again, raising her head.

'And he's put in a full day shifting concrete.' It was Johnnie, leaning on the barre beside her. Natasha frowned, puzzled. He nodded towards Erik. 'You wouldn't think our elegant Dane was a brickie by day, would you? He always has such clean fingernails.' He looked sidelong at her. 'Some of us'll be heading off for a beer, I imagine. You should come.'

An olive branch. Natasha nodded, half smiled. He grinned in return, baring a flash of gold tooth, then pushed himself off the barre and headed for the little doorway in the back wall. Natasha supposed that must be a changing room.

Her bag was near the other door. She crossed to it, and saw Milan slumped nearby, his back against the wall and a towel over his head. Had he observed her much in class? Against all her plans her performance gave her cause for concern: he had not, after all, explicitly confirmed that he wanted her to stay. Gently, trying not to advertise her presence, she pulled back her bag's zip. But Milan's dog hurried over, sniffed briefly at her ankles, then crossed to its master and nuzzled his fingers.

'And,' came Milan's voice from under the towel, as if he had only just paused for breath, 'you'll need to put on some muscle for double work. Lifting.' Two vein-ridged hands raised the towel delicately like a wedding veil. The face beneath was turned towards her.

'Muscle?' said Natasha, after looking about to check that there was no one else he might be addressing.

'Your arms, your arms,' said Milan impatiently. 'I don't think you could lift Johnnie without snapping them.' He smiled at her surprise. 'Oh, yes. It's equal opportunities in this company.' The towel fell back into place. From beneath it he added, 'Johnnie'll tell you which gym to go to.'

Johnnie, emerging from the changing room, had heard. 'The Chapelle. Tenth *arrondissement*. They know me there. And it's cheap.'

'You'll take your turn playing teacher? Bring us something of the schoolroom you've so recently left?' said Milan, rubbing his hair now and dropping the towel, neatly, over the dog. 'Not for a few days, perhaps. You'll need to find your feet.'

So I have a job, thought Natasha, pulling on a fresh T-shirt over her sweat-drenched practice clothes. It was something. Whether she wanted it or not was another matter.

Johnnie was ready. He hitched his bag onto his shoulder. 'You coming?'

Natasha nodded; she'd gathered there was no shower – but if she stank, at least everyone else would too. She grabbed her coat and followed Johnnie to the door, then glanced back over her shoulder. Milan was playing with the dog in earnest now; it yelped in delight, dragging the towel in dizzying circles. The rest of the world was forgotten; and the smile that lit Milan's face was new to her. She watched him for a moment, curious, then turned to go.

THE BAR JOHNNIE TOOK HER to was dark, bare and seedy, the floor sticky with spilled beer, the benches at the back cracked red plastic. All the company turned up except for Victor and Milan: Johnnie and Natasha; Erik, the tall Dane who'd taken class; Denise, the woman who'd first spoken to Natasha, and continued to watch her now with unhidden scepticism; Fabrice, the pianist; and Luc and Pascale, whom Johnnie described to Natasha as ex-circus artists, French and married. 'The beer here's watered-down rubbish,' commented Johnnie, 'but it's cheap as piss.'

Natasha concentrated on her fag, watching the others through eyes narrowed against the smoke. It was her tough-girl look, and she was in need of it: she was feeling shaky.

'So, how old're you, honey?' said Denise.

'Nineteen.'

Raised eyebrows. 'Brave, aren't you?'

'Meaning?'

'Not many people fresh from school'd sign up with a man like that.'

Natasha studied her. Then she said, 'Like what?'

Denise shrugged. 'He's not exactly your average boss.'

No one elaborated. Natasha lit a fresh cigarette. She turned to Johnnie. 'How long have you been in the company, then?'

'We're only just up and running,' he said, 'but I've known Milan for a while. I was in the company in eighty-four. The one that folded. You knew about that?'

'I heard.'

'And it doesn't bother you?'

Natasha watched him carefully. '*You've* signed up again.'

Johnnie grinned. 'Ah, yes. But it bothers me like hell.'

Natasha looked at him then, shocked, and he saw the look and laughed.

The talk turned to work – the lack of money, the likely rehearsal schedule, Victor's constant search for backers. Natasha let the curtain of hair swing down in front of her face. She wished heartily she were in London. You stupid, stupid bitch, she thought. You should have listened to Ellen, instead of your own contrary pride. Maybe if she went back she could contact Ellen without anyone knowing . . .

But why, exactly, would she be leaving? These people were good dancers – she couldn't deny that now. Would they think she couldn't hack the pace? And if Milan did dance after all and they got the tour, what, unemployed and in London, could she say to Ellen? Or her mother.

Who would hear of it eventually. And would be smugly unsurprised. Natasha, wincing, snapped her attention back to the conversation.

'Milan clearly thought we needed a nubile young body,' Johnnie was saying.

'Beauty and the Beast?' suggested Erik.

'I didn't screw him to get my place here, if that's what you think,' Natasha cut in quickly.

Gales of laughter erupted around the table. Natasha blushed in alarm: had she misunderstood?

'You have just, my child,' said Denise, reaching forward to pinch Natasha's cheek, 'revealed how little you know of our eccentric maestro.'

Natasha, feeling her dignity tottering, said coolly, 'Who does Milan sleep with, then?'

'Ah, now there's a question.' Denise drained the last of her beer, and added, 'Neither fish nor fowl, pumpkin-pie.'

'And does he never come out for a beer after class?'

'Never.'

'So what does he do away from the studio?'

'My God, what unhealthy curiosity! We've no idea. Don't you get any ideas about finding out, either.'

'Victor is the only one of us who sees more of him than you will,' put in Fabrice.

'Victor the minder – '

' – wet nurse – '

' – personal assistant – '

' – agony uncle – '

'Look,' Johnnie leant towards Natasha, 'Milan's in control when he's at work – he makes it his business to be. And as long as that's the case, nothing else is our problem, is it? He's a strange guy – so what? He's been looping the loop periodically all his career.'

'Oh?'

Johnnie nodded. 'First time was not long after he defected, apparently. Disappeared for months. Finally turned up on some Czech *émigré*'s estate in Canada. Then swanned off to New York and picked up the glittering career like nothing had happened. "Never explain, never apologize" – you know? That's why Victor's still hoping he'll dance, even though he hasn't been on stage for eight or nine years. There's no reason why he can't pull it off again.' Johnnie paused. 'If he wants to, that is.'

'If he doesn't,' said Natasha, 'I'm not going to stick around.'

Johnnie rubbed his chin, considering her. 'Well, well. You're a tough nut, aren't you? Nothing like the princess in a tutu we were all expecting.'

It took Natasha a moment to understand. 'So you *did* know I was coming?'

Johnnie's eyes disappeared in little crush-holes of amusement as he laughed, a full-throated, smoker's rip.

Natasha looked round the table. Every face was grinning, but with genuine amusement, unmocking. Then she was grinning too. 'You bastards,' she said, shaking her head. 'You bastards.'

IT WAS ONLY WHEN SHE WOKE up late the next morning and considered it, as she watched the yellow light shift across her tiny sloping bedroom ceiling, that Natasha realized the terrifying simplicity of her situation. She had invested all her eggs – labelled variously ambition, prospects, pride and self-respect – in one basket. And that basket – most probably a basket-case to boot – was Milan Novák.

The same Milan Novák who had a reputation for periodically looping the loop. The same Milan Novák who might or might not still have a drug habit capable of putting him in hospital and the rest of the company out of a job. Why would he not perform if that weren't the reason – that he couldn't trust himself?

She had seen him in class: no one could pretend that he was fit only for a graceful retirement. You glanced at him in the mirror at your peril: it was enough to ruin your own concentration, the instinct was so strong to stand, and watch, and marvel. Sure, he could no longer jump like he had at twenty-five – she had seen the films – but who was measuring? His technique was still razor-sharp, and the dancing, even at its gentlest moments, exuded a strange raw energy. It was hard to look away.

Natasha made herself reason it out. If Victor could

only persuade Milan to dance, and Milan kept himself healthy enough to make it through the next six months, she would have the best début she could hope for. After so long a break, Milan's appearance would whip press interest into frenzy, and with only seven dancers in the company she hardly risked obscurity on the back row of the *corps*. But Natasha wanted more than that: she wanted a major role, and her best chances were the two new ballets to be choreographed by Milan and this Quentin Faulkner. So, however much he wound her up or freaked her out, she was going to have to stay on the right side of Milan. And there were no promises that it'd be easy: Natasha was hardly accustomed to constraining her behaviour.

She hauled herself out of bed. If she wanted a shower she'd have to find a public swimming pool: this tiny attic corridor had no bathroom and the lavatory was just a hole in the ground shared between the grungy-looking inmates of half a dozen rooms. Sighing, Natasha reached for her jeans and her boots, and thought of the plus side. Stick with this dump, and she could get through to September, most likely, on her savings. The idea of getting another job did not entice her and, besides, she could not imagine a single thing she might competently do. She would settle for squalor and sloth. She simply had to ring her father to arrange for the rest of her savings to be transferred to her French account.

There was a telephone at the swimming baths. Richard surprised Natasha by being in. Sounding surprisingly close, he asked her how it was all going. Fine, came Natasha's reply. There was no point in trying to explain. Anyway, it *was* all fine, broadly speaking – for the time being at any rate.

And so, with evenings spent at class, Natasha's days were largely free. She soaked up the sun, sitting in the formal gardens of the 6th *arrondissement*, in the litter of low-slung chairs that circled every patch of smart grass, and puzzled over newspapers in an attempt to get to grips with the language. She bought postcards and frowned over them, too, trying to think what might best be said to Daphne, or Renée, or her father. And she left the postcards, unwritten, along with her debris of cigarette stubs and empty cups on café tables.

Some days she wondered, fitfully, what her erstwhile classmates were doing back in London, and whether they had found jobs. And sometimes, when she could not catch herself in time and bend her thoughts in another direction, she thought of her mother. It was a formless, inconclusive picturing, a touching of her mind upon a point of pain as a tongue might push at a loose tooth, and it made her cross. And then, since physical pain was a cure for the mental variety, she would go to the gym, obeying Milan's diktats only because her eyes were fixed firmly on the greater prize.

She felt, as she filled the days between class and class, as if she was marking time. It would have to pay off.

'THIS, CHILDREN,' SAID MILAN at class one evening, 'is Quentin Faulkner. You know what he's here to do. He'll be watching for a full week, so don't show off – you won't be able to keep it up.'

August, which had sent Parisians flocking out in their thousands to clog the *autoroutes* and call it a holiday, swept into the city a slight, balding and anxious New Yorker with irregular teeth. He had come, initially, to observe the company and get to know his raw material. Natasha was determined to dazzle. The weekend rehearsals had already begun for the pieces that were to be simply restaged. As she had foreseen, several of the dancers had taken part in these pieces before, and newcomers were being slotted around them. Her hopes rested with the new works.

Quentin sat on a chair throughout the class, balancing a notepad on his knees and occasionally scribbling.

'Doodling,' said Denise, out of the corner of her mouth as she passed Natasha on her way back from taking a slug from the water bottle.

'What?' hissed Natasha. Milan was taking class today; she kept a wary eye on him.

'Quentin. He's not actually writing anything,' said Denise. 'I looked.'

For the next exercise Natasha moved down to the front, just a few feet from his chair. Denise was right.

'So,' Natasha said to Quentin at the end of class, flourishing her towel in pretended nonchalance, 'what sort of work do you envisage? Will you, for instance, be using the whole company?'

Quentin bared his teeth in a crooked half-smile. 'No idea,' he said. 'I kind of like to . . . uh . . . dream it, and then let the subconscious flow in the studio. It's a kind of alchemy.'

Bullshit, thought Natasha, nodding sagely.

She was startled by a voice in her ear. 'Don't harass the choreographer, Natasha.' She turned. Milan stood a pace behind her, amused. Flushing quickly, Natasha swung the towel about her neck, and strode away.

One issue, at least, was not a mystery. From Victor's harried look, it was clear Milan was still refusing to include himself in the performance programme.

'Milan. We need to talk,' Natasha heard Victor plead the next evening in an urgent undertone as he and Milan came into the studio.

Warming up at the barre, Natasha was near enough to hear Milan's soft reply: 'I said no, Victor.'

'I'm not kidding. It may make the difference between the tour happening and not.'

'It would give you an easy job. Tough.'

'I'm serious.'

Milan raised a hand and patted Victor's shoulder. 'So am I.'

Natasha felt a shiver of mingled irritation and anxiety. It was clear from the work they'd started that the company was going to have a damn good programme with or without Milan and if they managed a month of Paris performances they should get decent press coverage. But what, then, if there was no tour? How could the company hold together? Natasha would be back on the plane to London, back to square one, and simply, for all she or anyone else knew, because Milan was too gutless to go out on a stage and perform.

Natasha hung in a forward bend, her arms wrapped around the backs of her legs, her face pushed against her knees. Doesn't he care about us? she thought. She didn't realize, until she heard a reply, that she had muttered the words aloud.

'Care?' snorted Denise, close beside her at the barre. 'That man cares for no one and no thing. 'Cept that damn dog.'

No one – was that true? Natasha wondered, looking across to Milan again. In the past she had never had much of a problem figuring out what made the men she knew tick. But this one was different: there were things about Milan that just didn't add up. And too much depended on him for it to stay that way. For the sake of her career, Natasha decided, she had better work him out – work out whether this investment was likely to pay off. And she'd better do it fast.

Natasha began to observe Milan closely, not simply the way he danced but the way he came into the room, the way he talked to that stupid dog, the way he watched the other dancers, when he did watch them; how he was on a good day, when he'd joke and horse around; and how he was on a bad day, when the dancers seemed to know without being told that he wasn't to be approached or bothered. And the way, on occasions, he slipped even his minder's leash. It happened the following week, after class. Victor had the keys to lock up, but had been waiting in the studio to talk to Milan. Milan, ignoring him, had been deep in conversation with Quentin. And now he had disappeared.

'Where the bloody hell has he gone?' said Victor, casting about in vain.

Natasha could see him. She was standing before one of the large grimy windows that looked from the studio onto the street. Now she twisted the catch, opened it and leant over the sill; below her, she had spotted Milan as he emerged from the building and started off along the pavement, his dog at his heels.

She felt someone at her shoulder. 'Johnnie, where does Milan live?' she asked.

Johnnie propped himself beside her on his elbows. 'No idea – Victor could tell you, except he wouldn't, of

course. But I don't think the big M's off there now.'
Milan was walking fast, in long strides, hands thrust deep
into the pockets of his battered old coat. 'He just walks,
far as I know, and it's not for the dog's benefit. He's a
night person. Doesn't like to sleep much.' Johnnie
shrugged. 'That may be old habits.'

Natasha thought of the solitary figure, pacing the
streets. 'Doesn't he get any trouble?'

Johnnie looked at her, amused and critical. 'You
haven't sussed him yet, have you?'

No, she hadn't. Suddenly Natasha ducked in from the
window.

Johnnie started. 'What's bitten you?'

'I'm going after him,' she said, and was half-way to
the door before Johnnie understood.

'Natasha—'

But she was already out on the stairs, racing down.
One flight, two flights, three. She smashed through the
front door onto the street, and set off, running, in the
direction Milan had taken.

She thought she had glimpsed him briefly some way
ahead, still on the same side of the road, but then people
had crossed her path, blocked the view, and when she'd
strained to see him again, she'd failed. As she ran and
swerved and dodged, she kept an eye towards the centre
of the road before her, to try to spot him if he crossed.
And each time she came upon a side road she stopped,

panting, at the intersection, to see if he had turned that way.

No sign. At a major crossroads she halted. Her shins ached with the jarring of her feet against the concrete and a flash of concern came to her that she might have done some damage, but she pushed it aside. The tall wiry figure she sought, with the little eager bundle of dog trotting behind it, could be seen nowhere. It was like a dream. She felt a pounding desperation that astonished her rational mind. What was she intending to say to him, after all, if she found him?

Natasha turned back, retracing her steps to the studio building. She stuck her head around the door of every bar she passed, earning looks of hostile curiosity for her pains. But Milan was nowhere to be found.

*

Dear Natasha

You have not, you pig, replied to any of my last three letters. How are you? I'm *sure* you're very well, in the midst of some wild affair, and wowing that Novák guy with your artistic genius (all your old comrades back here are just panting for your début). This, however, is no excuse for not writing to me. Your punishment is that you're going to be visited (just for two or three days – don't panic). I'm coming on October 1st, okay? I'm assuming the answer's yes – since I doubt you'll reply in time – and booking anyway. Hope you've got room for me. Oh and by the way, I'm going out with one of the soloists – can you believe it? He's called Jonathan and he's far too good to be true (damn talented, too, I don't mind saying).

Natasha sighed and pushed the card back into her bag. It was from Renée, who had a job now in the *corps de ballet* of a decent company based in Sheffield. The truth was, Natasha didn't want Renée to come to Paris, though she couldn't put her finger on why. The mention of a general air of expectancy about her own début should have been pleasing – they hadn't forgotten her, at any rate – but it wasn't. It put her in a bad mood, and when she got to the studio she stumped in with a heavy heart.

The rehearsal process was now, officially, in full swing. Day jobs had been relinquished, the minuscule amounts that passed for wages were being doled out weekly, and Quentin Faulkner was dabbling in his own brand of alchemy. He had, it was clear, some interesting ideas. He had a fine reputation in New York as the choreographer of some well-reviewed, even groundbreaking pieces of ballet. The problem was, for the dancers working with him, that he was the ditherer from hell. Today the company, severally, were giving him their all, but by three o'clock Quentin's face had clouded over. He was standing, hunched, beside the tape recorder, chewing the skin around one thumbnail. 'Okay, I've got it,' he said, moving forward in a surge of decisiveness. 'We've got to scrub the last section.'

Denise planted her hands on her hips. 'Where from?'

'From Natasha's entrance. I want to stick with you three for this passage.' He indicated Denise, Johnnie and Luc. Erik and Pascale, he had already mentioned, were to have a *pas de deux* in the next section.

Natasha rubbed a hand across her mouth, staring at Quentin. 'You're joking, right?'

'It's just not gelling.' Quentin grimaced, shook his head.

'So what are you saying – scrap it?'

'Scrap it.' He nodded. 'Right, people, let's go from the top of the slow sequence.'

Natasha remained standing exactly where she was. Quentin noticed her, and clicked off the tape recorder again.

'It's not the way you're doing it, Natasha, it's just that section. Thematically it's jarring, okay?'

'Then rework it,' said Natasha. 'I mean, can't it be changed so that it does fit in?'

Finger over the Play button, Quentin looked at her stonily. 'This is an ensemble piece, baby. If you want a fucking star vehicle, go and dance *Swan Lake*.'

Natasha retreated to the changing room. Instinct screamed at her to walk out altogether, but she knew she was treading on thin ice. She leant against the wall, clenching and unclenching her fists. She would have to talk to Milan, that's all, she told herself. He'd see how bloody ridiculous this was. And if he couldn't do anything about Quentin, at least he might remember when casting his own piece.

There was one window in the changing room and beneath it a wooden bench. Natasha sat sideways, her feet drawn up tight beneath her, her back against the wall. She listened to Quentin's voice drifting through from the studio – 'No, no, no. Not like that at all. It's a melting I want, but keep the strength in it, don't just flop. Yes – yes – better, baby. Ya-ya-ya-*paam*. Smooth. See? Yo! You got it!' She heard the squeal of soft leather soles twisting on the wooden floorboards, the thud of even the softest landing and, tinny through the tape-recorder speakers, the music, composed by a friend of Quentin's in New York: synthesized voices in strange pulsing rhythms, snatches of dissonant instrumental phrases – for the dancers, not much more than emotionally barren background noise and a bugger, moreover, to count.

When Quentin had finished and the other dancers came into the changing room, Natasha was still at the window, though now wrapped in a jumper and with a magazine across her knees. This last was purely for show – she'd hardly glanced at it, but didn't want it to seem as if she had been brooding all this time. The dedicated dancer, she knew, would have gone back into the studio and spent the time observing, but it had been more than her self-control could manage.

'We're done for the day,' said Denise, peeling her sweat-drenched leotard down to the waist as she searched about for her bag. 'Milan says he'll leave that last bit of the Stravinsky till the morning.'

'He's turned up?' said Natasha, flipping pages to conceal her interest.

'Jus' now.'

It was lucky that no one suggested a drink: she would have had to explain why she wouldn't come straight away. As it was she hung back, seeming simply unwilling to hurry to get changed, busying herself plausibly with an old pair of toe shoes and a bottle of shellac. She painted the noxious brown liquid carefully over the greyed canvas lining, then stuffed the shoes with pages ripped from her magazine. By the time she'd finished and set them on the window-sill to dry, the changing room was empty. A moment later, she heard Quentin, too, take his leave of Milan. So, unless Victor was keeping uncharacteristically quiet, Milan was out there in the studio on his own.

Natasha tweaked at her jumper, suddenly hesitant. Her anger with Quentin had deserted her, but no bad thing, perhaps. She could explain her feelings to Milan soberly, reasonably: he would be more likely to respect her for that. She took a deep breath and walked to the doorway. Milan was across on the far side of the large room. She had thought he would be locking up but he had stripped off to the old torn T-shirt and jogging pants sawn off at the knees that he often wore for class. Now he was feeding a tape into the machine.

Surprised, and suddenly feeling like an intruder, Natasha dodged back into the changing room. He must be working stuff out for his new ballet – rehearsals were scheduled to start the next week, after all. She heard the machine click. Now the music started. Shit! What should she do? Make a run for it?

It was a thrashing guitar sound, brash and violent. This was odd: Johnnie had sworn to her that Milan was planning on using something classical to contrast with Quentin's piece. Natasha heard the sound of feet moving across the floor: she crept to the doorway and looked again. 'Honey, you haven't seen him dance,' Denise had said to her once. 'You think he's impressive in class? That's nothing. He's just keeping the motor ticking over.' Natasha had doubted her but now, peering out into the big room, the doubts dissolved.

It was a solo, that was clear: the way he covered the ground, made use of the space, left no room for absent figures. The style of the piece was quite extraordinary. As explosive as the music, the movement scythed the air, passing through freeze-frame images of agony, and then twisting onwards in a spiral of manic, tearing force, battering the body through space. Natasha watched the lean spare muscle of his limbs, perfect in their control, imprinting shape after shape on the air, expressive of a pain, a torment so savagely painted it terrified her; she could taste it. *This* was Milan dancing: the barriers were down. She knew she should not be a witness to it and yet she was rooted to the spot.

It was when the movement brought Milan around to the very back of the room in a series of punishing contorted leaps that seemed to suspend him, for a heartbeat, in space, that he saw her. He landed off-time, and stood, eyes bulging with the effort of his lungs, expression darkening rapidly from shock into anger while the music crashed onward in the still and empty room. He crossed the floor and switched off the tape. Then, in the sudden heavy silence, he faced her. He had caught his breath: his voice, when he spoke, had a terrible calm.

'Spying, Natasha? Or have you forgotten the way out?'

Numbly, Natasha stepped forward into the studio. 'I was just . . .' She gestured vaguely, then gave up the pretence. Her hands dropped to her sides. She said, 'That was incredible.'

'You shouldn't have seen it.' Milan turned away – not, though, to resume his work, but to remove the tape and unplug the machine. He slung the chair it had stood on to the corner of the room where it clattered against the metal legs of another.

Absorbed in thought, Natasha simply watched. 'Why won't you dance on the tour?' she said.

'I don't have to explain myself to you.'

She looked at him levelly. 'Yes, you do.' Seeing Milan's expression brought a flare of anger. She said, 'You know what they say about you back in London? That you're bound to mess up – again. That it's a waste of time anyone taking a job here because you're such a pathetic mess.'

'So why did you?' asked Milan. 'Oh, I remember. To be different.'

The tone was stinging. He had turned his back again. Now he stripped off his T-shirt and, as he bent to his bag, the ridges of his spine stood out between moving planes of muscle. Natasha, regarding him intently, said, 'Don't you want us to get this tour?'

'At any cost? No.'

'At what cost? A bit of effort on your part? Against what cost if you don't? Loss of a chance to all of us. Don't you think you owe us that?'

'Owe you?' Milan faced her, bunching a fresh shirt in his hand. She caught sight of a smear of colour on his arm – a tattoo she'd noticed before. 'Maybe I don't have principles as you might define them, Natasha,' he said, pulling the shirt over his head. 'I left them behind a long time ago.'

There was silence. He wanted her, simply, to leave. Profoundly uncomfortable, and angry too, Natasha still did not move. Milan finished dressing quickly, pulling a second T-shirt over the first. She caught flashing glimpses of the skin along his forearms as they lifted and turned. A thought occurred to her. 'You're clean, aren't you?' she said.

His eyes locked on hers, quite blank. Then his head dropped and '*Christ*,' he said, in a tone thick with exasperation that she hadn't heard before. He looked up. 'Do you really think, Natasha, that I'd make it to class every day if I weren't?'

'People do.'

She was answered with a sharp, questioning glance. 'By now,' said Milan, 'I reckon I'd be pushing a longevity record. Take my word for it, you don't know just how much I was using.'

'Why, then, do you let everyone think your life is still as . . . as it was?'

'To stop them from doing exactly what you're trying to do now.'

'You let Victor in.'

'Victor was there when I *was* living like that. Victor pulled me from the pit more than once. He has seen me in all states and knows what to do.' Milan smiled drily. 'I get no sympathy from him.'

'But it's a neat excuse for hiding yourself away like some god-damned leper,' said Natasha, her frustration rising. 'What are you afraid of?'

Milan lifted his hands from his bag and turned to face her. He folded his arms. There was a pause. Natasha had the distinct impression she was being read, and easily at that. It was a highly unpleasant sensation.

'You think I need help,' he said at last, amusement showing somewhere way back, far behind his eyes. 'And you think that you're the person to help me.' He considered. 'Is this getting round to some sort of proposition?'

There was an unbreathing, unblinking pause. Eyes strained to their widest, Natasha stared at Milan, then stared at the floor. The breath, which seemed to have left her lungs altogether, came suddenly, shudderingly back in.

Proposition?

But the shock was not that he had strayed so wide of the mark, had got her so hopelessly, clumsily wrong. The shock was that he had not; that – as Natasha saw, in a single soul-scalding moment – he was right.

She was, she realized, still looking at the floor. Swallowing carefully, she raised her head. 'Why not?'

'Too many reasons to count. But thank you. I'm flattered.' Milan turned back to his bag, stuffed in the last of his clothes and pulled at the zip.

'Is that a refusal?'

'I'm not worth wasting your time on.'

'Can't I decide that for myself?'

'No.' His tone was light now. 'You really know nothing about me.'

Natasha started forward. 'If you mean the story of all your heartaches and conquests,' she snapped, within a pace of Milan now but meeting the pale gaze fearlessly, 'then no, I don't. And I don't want to. It may surprise you to hear that it just doesn't interest me.'

'I say again, you know nothing about me,' Milan said evenly, then paused. 'And what you want is . . . not in my repertoire.'

'How the hell do you know what I want?' cried Natasha. How could he, when she hardly knew herself?

Milan regarded her gravely. 'You're looking at the shell and imagining there's something inside, Natasha. There isn't.'

He raised a hand, fingers loosely curled, and as her breathing quietened she thought that it would brush against her cheek, but he held the hand suspended, an inch away from her skin. There was no tenderness as he looked at her, only a kind of distant consideration. It was as if he didn't see her. At last when his gaze focused again, though his expression hadn't shifted the eyes betrayed a flash of laughter. 'You know,' his tone had changed, 'you could be good-looking if you—'

'Sod off!'

'There.' Milan smiled. The hand dropped to his side. 'We're both feeling better now.' He dug in his pocket and tossed a bunch of keys towards Natasha. Automatically, she caught them.

'Lock the door on your way out, will you?' he said and, picking up his bag, he turned and left the studio.

Natasha's hand was raised, still, clutching the keys. Her

dark eyes were wide, her lips parted slightly in a perfect expression of disbelief. As she heard, echoing up the deep stairwell, the front door bang behind him, her face crumpled into agonized frustration, and her fists came up to push against her forehead. 'No,' she groaned aloud, pressing the keys against her skin, sharp and cold. 'No.'

What had she done? Anger and ambition had pushed her to speak to Milan about Quentin – but what had she done instead? Thrown herself at him – and been insulting enough into the bargain to ruin any chances she might have had in his ballet. She'd be lucky if he even cast her now.

She shook her head, trying to rake over the confused shards of conversation in her mind. How had he twisted her words against her – again? How had he seen through, so easily, to something she hadn't even recognized herself?

Damn it, how had he turned her down?

Chapter Eight **London, 1970**

The morning of Milan Novák's first expected appearance as a member of the EBT, Dandy Franks broke the habit of a lifetime and got up early. With Laura unwillingly in tow, he bounded into the company office. 'Where's the casting list for *Firebird*, Heather?'

Laura watched as Heather turned him round and propelled him back towards the door. 'Not ready. You'll just have to wait.' She barely came up to Dandy's chest, but she could push.

'What's Max up to? Playing with our nerves?'

'Some things are still undecided.' Heather's hand was on the door now, ready to close it. She had work to do.

'God, doesn't he know us well enough yet?'

'Just keep doing the work, Franks.'

As the door shut behind him, Dandy treated Laura to a gibbering-ape impression. He and Evie were having a hard time of it, she knew, nerves chafing badly against their hopes. For herself, though, there was no tension. As a member of the *corps*, Laura knew with certainty what her fate would amount to – a peasant girl, as always, a royal maiden, a wedding guest – but as the only unstressed member of the household, she felt a little responsibility for preserving the others' mental health.

'Come on. Let's get to class and gawp at Novák,' she suggested, slipping her arm through Dandy's and hugging it as she led him down the corridor. 'We'll have to get a good likeness for the voodoo doll.'

Whichever way you looked at it, Novák's arrival was about to rock the company boat hard enough for the water to start slopping. In press and publicity terms, of course, his advent was viewed as a wonderful coup for a relatively young, independent company. The dancers, however – always, and inevitably, on the look-out for the main chance for their own careers – were less certain. That morning, then, the barres of the rehearsal studio were more closely packed than usual, with no one for once claiming ailments, real or imagined. Laura was surprised, tasting for herself the atmosphere of strained expectation and badly hidden resentment, to feel a fleeting stab of sympathy for their latest Principal Guest Artist.

He was last in. On the dot of ten, the studio door opened and Alexander, who was to take class that morn-ing, entered, followed by the small neat figure of Nadine, and finally Novák. All eyes turned to the new man, and tracked him as the pliable feet scuffed unconcerned across the studio floor. He took the place beside Nadine at the front of the central barre, and craning heads, seeing in the mirror that their curiosity was conspicuous, bobbed back into line.

But Laura, from the back of the right-hand wall, had an unimpeded view and, as Alex began to lead the company through a somewhat unimaginative barre, she took full advantage of it, with uneasy fascination. That Novák was tall, long-limbed and muscled like a runner she knew from having seen him on stage – the only difference now that a fine costume had been swapped for the obligatory worn and washed-out layers of ragged sweatpants and T-shirts. But she was close enough to observe the face, too: the spare flesh drawn across wide, Slavic cheekbones and a fine angular jaw, the strong nose, very straight, and the eyes, fairer than they should have been beneath dark brows, with lids like blinds half lowered. On a more amiable person, the face could certainly have been called beautiful; as it was, Laura saw no more than an arrangement of finely moulded features, expressing graceful but unpleasant self-regard. Her sympathy dissolved.

Barely two weeks ago, she reflected, this man had cut himself off from family, and friends, if he had any, from the entirety of life as it was known to him. Observing the smooth, tranquil face, the story took some effort to believe. But Laura was relieved. In view of her loyalties to her friends, she had been hoping to dislike Novák.

And it looked as though he was going to make it easy for her.

For late August, it was decidedly cold outside, and a watery, greenish sun lit the dancers in slanting shafts through the studio's two long windows. Laura had never known the company, in class – and on a Monday morning at that – work quite so hard. The men flung themselves into their *grand allegro* with a sweaty, tight-jawed determination, less mindful of their joints and straining ligaments than of their egos. The women stabbed their *pointes* to the floor with a precision and energy usually reserved for the stage. No one was coasting. And eyes that would usually have flicked Alex's way for approval now checked, instead, on whether Novák was watching them. He never was.

What the dancers saw instead when they looked, along with his provoking lack of interest in them, was enough to create a bitter spasm of mingled inspiration and depression in the collective stomach. Novák was good, oh, God, he was good. Laura could dislike him, she thought, with all the rightful ire she could muster, yet she had still to admit a technician's appreciation of his skills. Stepping now into the centre space as her group's turn came to attempt the *enchaînement* Alex had set, Laura felt glad she was not a man. Watching Milan Novák in class would be enough to make all but the most egotistical, or unrealistic, male dancer feel tempted to look for another career.

The *enchaînement* brought her close to where Novák

was standing. He leant against the wall beside Nadine, resting his elbows on the barre behind him. They were on Laura's right, two dark heads apart, given space by the other resting dancers as if a repellent magnetic field surrounded them.

Laura sprang into a turning *pas de basque* towards them. She had a little too much rosin on her left shoe and it caught as she turned and gave her a twinge, which sent her momentarily off-balance. Concerned about her ankle, she did not at first register the reaction in those nearest spectators. But as she prepared for and completed the final *pirouette* – on *demi-pointe* for safety – she caught a glimpse of Nadine. She was leaning towards Novák. 'This one . . .' Laura heard the beginning of the murmured comment, and no more. But the accompanying smirk told her all she needed to know.

She held the final position after her *pirouette*, giddy not from the spin but the insult. Feeling the blood burning in her cheeks, she turned her head determinedly in Nadine's direction as she walked to the back corner to make way for the next group of dancers. Her defiance, however, did not find its target: Nadine's attention had shifted elsewhere. But another's had not. Laura's glare met and held the cool, expressionless gaze of Milan Novák.

'THE NEWEST SENSATIONAL star of British ballet was thrown out of Pedro's Nite Club at three a.m. after a fracas with a journalist.'

'Let's see!' said Laura, flailing her free hand as she held a plastic cup under the dribble of noxious brown liquid the machine optimistically called coffee.

Evie stuck her cigarette in her mouth and turned the newspaper round. 'Not the best picture,' she said. 'But, see, he doesn't even look that interested when he's just thrown a punch.'

Laura tilted her head to get a better look. 'Don't know how he can drink till three in the morning and then get to class,' she said.

Evie smiled grittily. 'The man has talents, my dear. I only wish he'd give those bloody photographers a bit less to be interested in. It was like a Harrods sale just trying to get into the building this morning.'

'Darlings.' Dandy appeared, slipping a hand round each of their shoulders and squeezing. Laura spilt coffee and squawked. 'Our lord has spoken,' he said reverently, ignoring her. 'The list. It is up.'

Evie started. 'And?'

'I'm Kostchei,' said Dandy. 'Can you believe it? I mean – a character role! What an insult! Unless, of course, Alexander is doing something radical with the part. Which I very much doubt.'

'*And?*'

'Second cast, darling. Not as much as you deserve but well done anyway.' He bent and dropped a kiss of congratulation and condolence on Evie's forehead.

'Seen this photo of Milan?' said Laura, brandishing the paper under Dandy's nose.

He looked at her coolly, not giving the paper a glance. 'Don't you want to know what you've got?'

'Yes, yes,' said Laura, humouring him. 'Surprise me.'

'I dare say I will,' said Dandy. 'You're fourth cast.'

'Fourth cast?' Laura hesitated, gave Dandy a sharp look. She couldn't think what he might mean – unless . . . 'Fourth . . . *princess*?'

Dandy smiled seraphically. 'No, not princess, darling. Firebird.'

'I THOUGHT YOU WERE GOING to hit the floor the next second. That òr vomit on me. And this isn't a cheap shirt.' Dandy, hunched like a roosting bird on the edge of the kitchen table, fingered his collar protectively.

'Well, I think it's brilliant,' said Evie, yanking the cork from their second bottle of wine with a satisfying *thlock*.

'I think it's bloody mad,' said Laura. She was lying across two chairs, blowing smoke rings at the ceiling. 'It's a massive role. In the old version, at least, the Firebird's hardly off-stage, and . . . and . . .'

'And she carries the entire emotional weight of the ballet,' put in Dandy helpfully.

'Thanks.' Laura frowned at her lopsided efforts and sighed. 'I just can't bear walking round with this feeling everyone hates me. The looks I got in the changing room this afternoon!'

'Don't tell me, a Francesca special,' said Evie, her freckles crinkling in distaste. 'Still, it's better than the feeling that everyone likes you. Then you *know* something's wrong.'

The roles worth getting in *The Firebird* were few, and perfectly clear-cut. The story, a Russian fairytale, was of a Prince, out hunting, who captures the magical Firebird. In return for her safe release she is forced to give him one of her feathers; this he can use to call for her help should he ever need it. Elsewhere in the forest, the Prince finds a beautiful Princess, imprisoned by a wicked magician. He falls in love, and summons the Firebird. The Firebird overpowers the magician and frees the Princess, whom the Prince then marries. The Firebird is seen, finally, at the royal wedding before taking flight and disappearing for ever.

The principal roles, then, were Firebird, Prince and Princess. The magician, Kostchei, though significant, had hardly a dancing part. The *corps* roles were predictable: for the men, friends and servants of the Prince, peasants of the forest and creatures belonging to Kostchei; the women would be peasants too and royal maidens attending the Princess, both in captivity and in the wedding celebrations.

At the first rehearsal after class the next morning, Dandy, Evie and Laura were still nursing hangovers. A frightening pile of cigarette stubs and empty coffee cups in the common room attested to their attempts to rid themselves of the alcoholic silt in their veins, but it was not easily to be shifted. The night's celebrations had been a little desperate in character: though numbered among the lucky names on the cast list, they were all, for different reasons, distressed about their lot. Laura, for her part, wanted promotion – of course she did, more than anything – but this was too much too soon. To be given a chance and to flunk it could do years of damage to a career. She felt sick.

Her Prince, the fourth one just as she was the fourth Firebird, was a soloist named Adam Radford. Laura hadn't danced with him before and felt suddenly and unexpec- tedly embarrassed as they stood together now in the studio, listening to Alexander's precise instructions, all directed quietly and specifically to Nadine and Milan as if no one else were present. Laura snatched a glance at Adam in the mirror. She felt shy of her body and of his hands. And of his hands upon her body, where they would have to be to grip and lift and steady. Under her sweaty arms. Between her legs. She frowned at herself momentarily and hooked a stray strand of hair behind her ear. This was her *job* – and his. At least Adam's was a friendly face, and he was junior enough to be ready to help her, and trust her too. And she was thankful that this was just a principals' rehearsal: the *corps* women were not standing about, boring their ill-wishing, envious eyes into her back.

They had started, confusingly, near the end of the ballet, on the Prince and the Firebird's final *pas de deux*.

Alexander mentioned that it would be the most challenging of the duets and Laura sincerely hoped he was right, since she realized quickly that it was not only technically complex and demanding, but gruelling too. They rehearsed the passage in sections, but the thought of eventually putting those sections together, dancing the whole lot without a break, filled Laura with a kind of nervous disbelief: she didn't know how anyone could get through it and still breathe.

'I hate that straight lift in the second section,' she said to Evie, as they sat in the common room afterwards. 'I just can't get the timing at all.'

'It's very Nadine.' Evie shrugged, picking at her lunch. Though practically the thinnest person in the company, she had started on a new diet regime, which seemed to involve watery cottage cheese and extra nicotine. 'She loves that sort of thing. Alex is bound to choreograph what looks good on her.'

'And the rest of us?'

'Have to cope as best we can, chicken. You're doing fine.'

To those who have, more is given, thought Laura ruefully. Nadine, as the first-cast Firebird, had a role shaped to her strengths. Not that Alexander was the most flexible of choreographers – unlike many, he seemed to enter the studio with everything already worked out clearly in his head. But still, if something did not look right on Nadine, it was changed to suit her better.

One advantage, however, that Nadine lacked was an easy partner. Milan seemed to believe he knew best how to dance her role as well as his own, and did not scruple to correct her or make pointed suggestions, in the full hearing of everyone else. Perhaps here, mused Laura, watching Nadine bristle visibly at their next rehearsal, were the problems of mixing work with romance. Nadine had sunk all her hopes in one man: career, love and revenge. What could be a more heady combination? The stakes were high. And was Milan aware of how much depended on him? Maybe he was – and maybe that was the problem. And, to make matters worse, husband Max had decided to sit in on this rehearsal.

It was a particular lift now that was causing difficulty. The women had to run, the men to swing them seamlessly into the air directly above their heads and to shift, almost instantly, to a single-hand grip. Nadine and Milan had failed to find their point of balance; they prepared to try it again.

'Everyone,' ordered Alexander briskly, casting a rare glance around at the other three couples.

Laura prepared, ran. Adam caught the balance perfectly and lifted her in a single swoop, then removed one hand from her waist, with only a hint of a tremor as the remaining arm took her full weight. She grinned down at him, delighted.

Behind them they heard a voice, lightly accented, thick with sarcasm. 'What do you think I am, a weight-lifter?' it said quietly. 'You have to *jump*.'

Adam brought Laura down carefully, both hands to her waist again, facing him. As he released her, she bent and made a needless adjustment to her shoe-ribbon. She did not dare to look at Nadine.

But as Laura straightened, an unfamiliar grip closed hard about her arm, dragging her sharply to her left. 'Look,' instructed the same voice, still speaking to Nadine. 'Watch what I do here.' Then Milan swung Laura to face him, released her arm and stepped back several paces. The chin lifted, beckoning. 'Come on.'

Laura frowned and glanced at Alex, but saw nothing more than a look of arch attention. Max was amused, and tactlessly showing it, but the lips were buttoned shut. She prepared, and ran.

'See?' said the voice lightly as she was held a moment later, rock-steady above Milan's head. 'As you jump I push you on and up in the same line. *Anyone* can do it.'

Without ceremony he brought Laura – *anyone* – down to the floor and, with neither look nor word of thanks, turned back to his partner. But Nadine, stiff with rage, did glance at Laura. It was a look that dripped venom. Then she, too, turned her back and began her own caustic explanation.

On the stairs after the rehearsal Laura found herself behind Milan as he made his unhurried way down. Not knowing the best form of address, she stuck out a hand and tapped one shoulder. He stopped and smoothly turned to look at her. She was a couple of steps above him; their eyes were level.

And there was something disturbingly odd about those eyes. Laura focused instead on the stub of cigarette drooping from the corner of his mouth and said, 'It would really help if you didn't do that again.' She waited and then, since he wasn't saying anything, added, for clarity, 'Don't drag me into your quarrels. It causes trouble for me and it's not fair.'

Looking again Laura saw that the eyes had widened and she noticed, suddenly, what was strange about them: the pale irises, which seemed unable in this light to decide on their exact colour, were encircled by much darker rings, like a reverse eclipse. They were expressing deep surprise. Quivering a little with spent courage, Laura hurried on down the staircase.

IN LATE SEPTEMBER, RICHARD came to London and brought the news that his father's health was failing. With Oliver settled permanently in Manhattan with a Wall Street job he apparently could not leave, the full burden of caring for an ailing father and an anguished mother fell on Richard. Broad though his shoulders were, he needed a break and had come to London to take it.

He was supposed to be staying with Daphne, but ended up at Bleak House three evenings in a row, arriving always with food, plentiful wine and, despite his anxieties, a fine line in easy, convivial conversation. Dandy and Evie loved him. To Laura, he was a strange, if innocent, reminder of Oxfordshire and it felt distinctly odd to see him installed at the kitchen table, explaining the intricacies of an estate economy to a sweetly encouraging Evie.

'God, he's perfect for you!' she and Dandy chorused, when Richard had left on the third evening – for good this time, as he was due to catch the 8.20 from Paddington the next morning.

'Admit it, Laura,' said Evie slyly. 'Stop playing hard to get. He's won already.'

'My little Hunca-Munca deserves to have men flitting about her like moths at a tulle lampshade,' said Dandy. 'And indeed I must compliment you, darling, on this one. He really is a fine specimen of the young male species.'

Laura was irritated. 'Nothing to do with *me*.'

Her two friends glanced at one another and then turned, together, to her. 'But you must have noticed,' protested Evie. 'The way he looks at you.' And she fixed Laura with a longing, passionate gaze.

'You treat him with such textbook cruelty, darling,' said Dandy, patting her shoulder.

'I do not!' said Laura. 'Do I?'

'You are a little offhand,' said Evie.

'I didn't *ask* him to come to London.'

'Well, fiddle-de-dee,' said Dandy, in his best Scarlett O'Hara voice.

Later, as Laura lay in bed and failed to sleep, their playfulness gave her a quiet and unexpected grief. They had struck a chord. Though she didn't think for a moment that they could be right about Richard's feelings, she nevertheless asked herself why it had never occurred to her to feel anything other than simple friendship for him. It would be perfectly natural, after all: Richard was thoughtful, capable and, if you bothered to notice, undeniably good-looking in a blondish, square-jawed way. Had Max been right? Am I cold? she wondered, curling tight beneath the sheets in discomfort. There's Richard, kind Richard. I ought to feel something for him – but I don't know how.

IT WAS CLEAR THAT BLEAK HOUSE was going to be no more hospitable in winter than an ill-made igloo, though at least the cold kept the chip fat congealed on the ceiling. But it was still only the beginning of October and already clothes laid out the night before felt, by morning, as if they'd been left in an ice box.

The last straw, one weekend morning, was Dandy's discovery of something rampant and green growing up his bedroom wall. He dashed out in his pyjamas, everybody else's jumpers and a nasty, matted poncho and came back trailing a large second-hand electric fan heater. 'This'll do the trick,' he pronounced confidently, the cigarette in the corner of his mouth beating up and down, and plugged the monster into the one free socket in the sitting room.

It fused the lights, twice, then set up a menacing throaty rumble that sounded like a Tube train passing somewhere below, and sent the electric meter into a feeding frenzy. But at least it produced some heat.

Things at work were in equal need of thawing out. The tension between Milan and Nadine in rehearsals had become the subject of general speculation – since Milan did not forbear to voice his comments in full company rehearsals as well as those for principals.

'He's not interested,' speculated Dandy, who had taken to huddling in shadowy corners in the hope of observing something he shouldn't. 'Milan has used her and now he's dumped her.'

'Or maybe there never was anything going on,' suggested Evie, huddling with him. 'Maybe when Nadine made the move he just said a straight no.'

Laura, who was frequently asked for her opinion, preferred simply to listen and to watch. Certainly, whatever it was that had soured in this spotlit relationship seemed to have progressed to curdling-point. But Laura had enough of her own to worry about in rehearsals: it was proving difficult to get an emotional handle on the role of the Firebird. There was no way that a technically sound rendition of the steps would suffice: for the ballet to work the bird had to convince as an emotional creature, her motives and her attachments made clear through this silent expressive language. But, more than this, Laura wanted to make the role her own; she wanted her performance to have something different to say, not risk seeming a diluted copy of Nadine's. It was not enough to be competent. To build on this chance that had been thrust upon her, to avoid a swift return to the *corps*, she had to make her mark.

The problem was that the ballet seemed an unpleasant story of entrapment and exploitation. A hunter captures a wild animal and forces it to promise to help him. When he calls, it has no choice but to come and do his bidding. Laura simply could not feel satisfied with such a reading. A creature treated thus would be permanently in distress – which was not an attractive focus for the ballet.

It was on the bus one morning that she hit upon the answer. The Firebird, she reasoned, might be initially scared when the Prince captures her: she has never been touched by a human before. But, swiftly, she falls in love with him. When he calls on her to help she comes willingly, only to find herself asked to secure the release of a rival. It is a true test of her love, and the happiness of the Prince indeed proves more important to the Firebird than her own. Laura did not discuss her theories: they were a key by which she could unlock the steps for herself, make them more than virtuosic display. In rehearsal, she began to try out variations in gesture, in the use of her head and arms, in the expressive quality of a flight from her partner or a movement towards him. Adam did not complain, and Alexander did not seem to notice.

In this, the distracting tension between Nadine and

Milan, tangible as an electric field, had done Laura a favour. And as the days peeled back, and *Firebird*'s opening date crept closer and closer, tempers and tolerance seemed more and more thinly stretched. The press were panting for Milan's début; it was understandable he might be feeling the strain. But nerves, at least on Milan's side, did not seem the cause of the ill-will. As he shifted himself about the company building, to class and rehearsal, and to Max's office or Heather's for discussion on subjects no one could wheedle out of either of them, he seemed as relaxed, as slackly bored as ever. If Milan knew how generally he was watched, he never acknowledged it. He seemed to move in a separate, parallel world: it was impossible to work out what he might be seeing half the time, let alone what he was thinking. It gave Laura the creeps.

On the Monday of the week before the opening, the four Firebirds and their Princes were called to the upper studio to go over the first *pas de deux* and solos of Act One with Trish, the *régisseur* and Alexander's assistant. Trish wore a purple jumpsuit and a matching scarf across her forehead as a kind of accessorized sweatband. She was forty-four and had been a moderately successful dancer. She was scared of Milan, and Nadine despised her. The atmosphere was fraught.

Adam and Laura were having difficulties with a fiendish series of supported leaps and were buried in discussions about grip and impetus. Suddenly Nadine's voice cut through to their corner of the studio: 'You do that once more and I'm leaving.'

As one, Laura and Adam snapped round. Milan, at whom the rebuke had been directed, did not appear to be listening. The steady gaze was focused somewhere in the middle distance.

'Christ!' Nadine threw up her hands in exasperation, and paced to the side of the studio and back again.

Then Milan did speak. 'This is the right way,' he said, his voice devoid of emphasis. 'We discussed it before.'

'Discussed it?' Nadine snapped. 'Don't make me laugh! We never discuss anything.' She grabbed his hand roughly and clamped it to her waist. 'Come on. Again.'

Laura saw a muscle flick in Milan's cheek, but his expression was impassive.

They repeated the sequence, which represented the final moment of capture for the Firebird. Nadine had a series of desperate movements to execute as she attempted in terror to escape from Milan's grasp; then, defeated, she was tossed up to his shoulders, his head lowered and she arched across his back, before being brought spiralling around him, with dizzying speed, to the floor. It was this last move they had struggled with – and this time, from the first instant of the descent, Laura could see that it wasn't right. Nadine dropped too fast, the angle was awkward, and she seemed to fight against the momentum instead of using it. When her foot hit the floor, there was an audible, sickening crunch.

For a brief moment the studio was utterly silent. Then Nadine's face contorted, her mouth opened, and as she screamed, her legs crumpled beneath her and she slipped through Milan's grasp to the ground.

Laura darted forward and was kneeling beside Nadine before anyone bar Milan had had a chance to move. She found him opposite her now, his hands working quickly and carefully to turn Nadine onto her back, the injured foot no longer under her weight. He looked up. 'Go and get the physio,' he said calmly, detaching Nadine's clutching fingers from his T-shirt, 'and call for an ambulance.' Laura stared at him aghast, and then stood up. She found Trish beside her, wringing her hands, and the other dancers clustered behind. She pushed her way between them and ran from the studio.

The hard toes of her *pointe* shoes beat the floor as Laura raced along the corridor, a trail of screams echoing in her wake. 'Bastard! You bastard!' Nadine was shrieking now, her voice catching with agonized rage. There could be no doubt where she laid the blame.

WHEN THE PHYSIO ARRIVED and Nadine had been carried from the studio, the rehearsal resumed. Evie and Dandy had disappeared, but Laura, Adam and the third-cast couple – Francesca, who had also been given first-cast Princess, and a senior soloist named Mike – picked up the thread again, with a trembling, distracted Trish, and made the best use they could of the time remaining. Drama or no drama, rehearsals were now precious. Laura was amazed, however, when twenty minutes later she saw Milan slip back into the studio to join in with as much, partnerless, as he could and to observe the rest with apparently untroubled concentration.

They finished at six, and Laura, sweaty and exhausted, found herself sickened, still, by what she had seen. It hardly mattered what she thought of Nadine: like most of the others, she was reflecting that it could so easily have been her.

She gathered her belongings, slung in a corner of the studio, and buried her face in her towel. Raising her head, she found Milan standing a little way off, surveying her impassively.

After a brief silence he said, 'It wasn't deliberate. What happened earlier. I didn't—' He broke off, perhaps disconcerted by the absence of reaction. Laura was carefully holding her expression as bland as his. He began again: 'You looked as if you thought—' and again he stopped. He turned and left the studio.

It was a half-hearted disavowal and it hadn't worked: Laura didn't particularly believe him. What was odd was that he had bothered to say anything to her about it at all.

After a shower, unable to face the common room, Laura sat on a radiator in the corridor outside and smoked a cigarette. The whole building seemed to be holding its breath. Reaching for the packet again, she heard footsteps and looked up to find Dandy stalking towards her. 'Any news?'

He shook his head. 'Heather says she's still in Casualty.'

'Does Evie know?'

'You bet. She's in quite a state.'

Evie, it turned out, was in Heather's office, having a brandy. This was a crisis in Evie's life, no less than in Nadine's. As second cast she was in line to step into Nadine's place, should Nadine be pronounced unfit to dance at the première. And premièring a new ballet was a chance big enough – but partnering Milan Novák in his first performance since his defection was the stuff of which ambitious dreams were made.

Evie looked fragile and so pale against the dark leather of Heather's enormous bucket chair that she seemed almost translucent. The rings on her fingers betrayed her with a soft, clinking tremble as she cradled her glass.

'Take her home, you two,' said Heather to Dandy and Laura. 'And make sure she gets some rest tonight.'

But by the time they reached the flat, rest seemed out of the question: Evie wanted to talk. The three of them sat at the kitchen table, wine open, chain-smoking.

'You know, I keep thinking of everything – right back to my first lessons. All the years of training, all the times I've wanted to give up – it was for this. *Could be* for this.' Evie pulled on her cigarette, inhaling deeply. 'It's going to be the biggest opening this company's ever had. Thanks to Milan. If it was me up there . . .' She shook her head. 'I can't bear it. I need to know. But I don't want to show *them* I'm like this. I have to be cool. Nadine might be okay. It could come to nothing.'

Dandy, deadly serious for once, pursed his lips. 'Nadine's not one for phantom injuries. I wouldn't be surprised if the physio had to beat her over the head with a crutch just to get her to hospital.'

They turned in towards one. But when Laura got up a couple of hours later to go to the bathroom, she noticed a sliver of light still showing beneath Evie's door.

THE NEXT MORNING AFTER first rehearsal, Laura had just emerged from the changing room when she narrowly avoided colliding with a red-faced and running Heather. 'Thank God! There you are,' she panted, leaning a hot hand on Laura's shoulder. 'Can you come with me for a minute?'

Laura frowned, but nodded and followed her back along the corridor.

'Max wants a word,' said Heather as, passing through the swing doors, they started up the stairs.

Laura tried to ask about what, but Heather would not be drawn. Her features were set in an expression more than usually grave. Laura wondered what she might have done wrong. It was with mounting tension that she approached Max's door.

He called her in at the first knock. The office was, as

she remembered, small and dingy; sitting at the centre of it behind his large, messy desk, Max appeared fairly small and dingy too. He did not, though, seem angry.

He leant back till his chair creaked perilously onto two legs and touched the wall behind him. There was no beating about the bush. 'Nadine has broken her foot,' he said, matter-of-factly, 'so I'm going to move you into the first cast.'

Laura met the bulbous blue gaze, utterly perplexed. The words took a second to sink in. It was the longest second she had ever known.

'Me?' she said at last, in a voice that seemed to struggle up from somewhere near her knees. 'But what – what about Evie?'

Max lifted his eyebrows, with no hint of concern. 'What about her? She'll stay as second cast, where she is. We'll sort out what happens to Adam later. I may just give him a few performances with Francesca. Four casts were always a bit more than we needed, strictly speaking.'

Today is Tuesday, thought Laura, numbly methodical. The first night is in precisely one week's time. And changing partners was no small step: everything, but everything had to be reappraised. The trust, the vital intuition that told you exactly where your partner would be without you needing to look, the knowledge that prevented hesitations, mistakes and *accidents* took time to develop. It took a damn sight longer than a week.

'Well, don't look so frightened,' said Max, with scoutmaster joviality. 'I got the idea when he used you to demonstrate that time, remember? You looked good together. So, first rehearsal this afternoon. I don't need to tell you how hard you're going to have to work. We'll arrange extra sessions for you with Trish, of course. And – you may as well know – I'm going to get some flak for this decision. We both are. You have *got* to prove me right.'

Max had risen from his chair and approached Laura round the desk, eyes glistening stickily. Now he leant down, prodded a finger beneath her chin to tilt it and kissed her lightly on the mouth. She hardly felt a thing.

Two minutes later she was in the lavatory, chucking up what felt like her entire intestinal tract.

On her way back to the common room, she met Dandy emerging from the physio's office. 'What was all that about?'

She looked up at him, feeling beaten hollow, still hardly comprehending. 'He's given me first cast.'

Dandy was silent, his face entirely unreadable. Laura held herself firmly, withstanding the urge to collapse in tears on his shoulder. At last he opened his mouth. 'Christ,' was all he said. Then he looked at her and smiled, a little too brightly. 'Congratulations, Hunca-Munca. This is your ticket to stardom.'

'I JUST DON'T UNDERSTAND, though. Why on earth does he want me?' Laura pleaded into her coffee. Dandy had ordered her to grab her coat and they'd headed for the nearest decent café. She was glad to get out of the company building.

'What?' said Dandy, who had recovered his irony. 'Apart from the fact that you're screwing each other senseless, and it's something you made him promise when you had his dick in your mouth?'

'Yes, yes,' said Laura impatiently, 'apart from that.'

'Well, apart from that . . . Look at it this way. It's a major gamble. But if you pull it off, it's all the "a star is born" business. Everyone will have come to see our charming little Bohemian friend. So if they discover you at the same time it's two supernovas in one.'

'As opposed to Evie, whom they already know.'

'Along those lines I'm afraid, yes.'

There was a brief pause. 'God.'

'Thank you, darling, but "Dandy" will do. The flip side, my love, is that of course if you mess up, you could be putting the whole company into a fatal financial tail-spin. Don't worry about it, though.' He patted Laura's hand absently.

They had three espressos on the trot, then, buzzing and a little nauseous with the overdose, headed back for the studios.

As they walked, Dandy, whose arm was draped around Laura's shoulders, hugged her to him, saying, 'This is going to be very hard for Evie, you know.'

'Dandy!' Laura pushed away and halted, staring at him furiously. 'For God's sake. What do you think I *am*?'

THE NEWS TOOK LESS TIME to get round than a bad smell in a packed lift. As soon as she was back in the building, Laura noticed conversations stop when she approached; faces turned to stare at her, Sphinx-like; whispers bristled on the air as she passed.

Evie getting the part the company could have accepted: it was logical; it was what second cast meant — you were next in line. But for *Laura* to be plucked almost straight from the *corps* felt like any one of them getting it. And this brought them face to face with the fact that they hadn't — and that they would have killed for the chance. Suddenly, mysteriously, people who had never got on with Evie had become her champions, and there was even a ground-swell of whispered sympathy for the previously vilified Nadine.

Only once did Laura stoop to answer a half-heard comment in the changing room. 'Tell me — just tell me,' she said, looking around her at faces averted, half seen, surprised at her own vehemence, 'if Max had offered it to you, would you have said no? Eh?'

No one had looked back at her. There was no need to answer.

There were, too, plenty of congratulations, but none gave the impression of sincerity. Laura found she preferred on the whole the people who said nothing. The wind, suddenly, was blowing cold about her. Was this what it meant to be going up in the world?

WITH HALF AN HOUR TO GO before the rehearsal, Laura had fled from both changing room and common room. She was making her way via a circuitous route to the studio when she caught sight of Milan. He was standing a corridor's length away, outside Heather's office, the finely muscled back propped against the wall, the profile lowered beneath a tangle of black-brown hair. Even at this distance, she gathered from the brooding stance that the door was resolutely shut, that he was waiting, and that neither fact was doing much for his mood. Laura hesitated, but then fancied it might be better to speak to him now for the first time as his partner rather than in full view of the company in rehearsal, and started forward again. At that moment, however, Heather's door opened and Max emerged, still speaking over his shoulder. From inside the room, Heather's voice replied. Max shut the door behind him and found himself facing Milan. He jumped. 'Ah!' he said, with an uneasy look, badly concealed. 'Just the person I wanted to see.'

'A little late, perhaps?' said Milan. The quiet voice carried faultlessly to Laura down the smooth-painted corridor. 'What is this? Are you mad? It's some joke, yes?'

Laura had seen Milan irritated in rehearsal. But this,

she realized suddenly, registering the biting chill of the tone, was Milan angry. She saw that Max, too, was taken aback. And that, over Milan's shoulder, he had spotted her. 'Perhaps we could talk about this later,' he said, laying a restraining hand on the younger man's sleeve. With wrist-cracking violence, the arm twisted free.

'I want,' said Milan, his voice still hardly raised, 'to talk about it now.'

Max sucked in his lips. 'Go on.'

But Milan did not immediately speak. Restlessly he turned aside, pulling at his mouth, then in a burst of exasperation struck the heels of his hands against the window-sill behind him and flew round to Max again. 'She's a child,' he said. 'Any fool can see that. You've watched her in class, I take it?' His head bent in close to the director's. 'An *inexperienced – talentless – child.*'

Max considered. 'I have been watching Laura for a long while. She has great potential. I believe she'll rise to the challenge.'

'Do you? What are the odds you'd offer me? And you're taking a gamble with *me*, here. Do you think I left Czechoslovakia in order to dance with . . . *that*?'

'Milan, Milan.' Max's tone was wheedling. He ventured to touch him again, placing a soothing hand on his shoulder and preparing to lead him away. The hand was once more shaken off. 'Let's discuss this in my office, hm?' pleaded Max.

There was a short silence. Then Milan grudgingly assented and the two of them started away from Laura down the corridor.

Long after they had gone, she found her feet still planted on the same spot of linoleum. Her breathing required concentration. Her thoughts, in the meantime, had to stagger where they would. And they seemed, from the discomfort caused no matter which way they headed, to be shod with spikes. *An inexperienced, talentless child.* Laura's chin lifted and her brows drew delicately together. A third of it was undoubtedly true, another third merely a semantic quibble – and the rest? Talentless? It was quite possible, even probable in the sense demanded of her now. And it was a judgement served by the most gifted dancer she had ever in her life encountered. The one, moreover, on whom she would have to rely completely. She hardly understood the shock – but she understood the hurt and the anger, and through it, Laura trembled for herself.

HE WAS A LITTLE LATE, but Milan turned up to the rehearsal. Whatever had been said within the confines of Max's office, he had not, at least, refused to go on working. He took his place alongside Laura without a word. She was at pains not to acknowledge him either, observing him instead with covert enmity in the glass.

Unluckily, the full company was called to this afternoon's rehearsal. Laura felt eyes constantly on her back but never, when she turned, did they meet her face. The studio air, as the dancers waited, shimmered with silent hostility, like heat rising. Evie, coming in earlier, had shot not a single glance in her direction. She felt the smart of that still. But none of it, she knew – not Evie, not Milan, not the waves of ill-will emanating from the *corps* – must take a hair's breadth of concentration from the task before her. She was not sure, now, that her knotted muscles would remember even the simplest move.

Alexander was clarifying a point of phrasing with the musical director at the piano. He must have had a hand in Max's decision – *Firebird* was, after all, his ballet. But he had said nothing to her. Encouragement was not his style. Laura, absently stretching her legs in turn, pondered her position. The general disapproval of the company she had only to face out. If she could block it from her mind she had nothing to fear, with one significant exception: if he chose to, Milan could get her injured. Had yesterday's accident been Nadine's fault or his? And if his, had it been carelessness or malevolence? Double work was a dangerous game – the very best of partners could not retrieve every slip – and trust was everything. How could she trust Milan now? Besides, even if he arranged no accidents, he might still wreck her performance – that was fairly easy for any partner. Deliberate mistiming, insensitivity to her centre of gravity, the quirks of her personal technique: any man with enough strength could fling his ballerina about and make her look terrible, with little discernible harm to himself. Would Milan stoop to this? Might he think it would serve his petty purposes, proving to Max he was right? That Laura might not herself be the architect of her own success or failure she found deeply disturbing. And when Alexander clapped at last for the dancers to take up their positions, Laura placed her hand within Milan's cool grip with a heightened sense of foreboding.

Act Two, final scene: together the Firebird and the Prince battle against Kostchei's evil creatures to rescue the Princess and her maidens. The presence beside Laura now was so different from Adam: not simply taller and stronger, but sharper too, lighter on his feet, and with a precision of movement that made her other, respectably accomplished partner seem distinctly clumsy.

But it didn't help. The hours of mounting anxiety had taken their toll: Laura quickly found her ankles had turned to jelly, her neck and shoulders to solid slabs of tension and her arms seemed to have been transplanted from a scarecrow. She struggled on a balance, resorted to *demi-pointe*, and in a supported *pirouette*, flung Milan a hefty blow to the stomach.

He had been closer than she expected. Still, it was a novice's mistake. Unwinded, he nevertheless turned from her abruptly and walked away. Laura was relieved that he didn't descend so far as to appeal to the assembled dancers, but he glared at Alex, as if vindicated.

Alex, sitting in his accustomed butt-clenched, fastidious pose before the mirror, showed only wry surprise though Trish, beside him, darted Laura a small, anxious smile. His command was simply that they repeat the passage.

'Don't push so much. I can't turn that quickly,' Laura urged as she struggled under Milan's sliding hands through a series of twisting *piqués*, the other dancers whirling in a blur about them.

'*You're* telling me how to partner now?' he said in her ear.

'I'm just saying I could get hurt.'

They were face to face, breathing hard, as she held a freeze-frame *arabesque*. The pale gaze stirred, searching hers sharply, suspecting an accusation. Then she turned away once more, bringing her lifted leg round in front of her, the whip-thin quads contracting viciously as she held the limb without a tremble. The muscles, at least, had begun to respond again.

LAURA DID NOT HURRY BACK to the flat that night. Persuading Trish to give her a late rehearsal, she went over the final Act solo in bone-grinding detail, and afterwards stayed on in the studio alone, working feverishly, and allowing nothing but the work to enter her mind.

It was past eleven o'clock before she unlocked the front door of Bleak House and crept in. The hallway was dark, but from behind the pushed-to kitchen door she heard the murmur of voices. They were, she realized, three friends no longer: there were two, and there was one – and it was she who was the stranger in her home.

They had heard her come in: the kitchen door was pulled wide and Evie stood silhouetted in the yellow light. Beyond her, Laura saw Dandy sitting with his back to the wall, knees drawn up beneath his pallid face, lashes cautiously lowered. She hesitated, then stepped forward swiftly – but Evie stayed her with a warning hand. 'I'm sorry, Laura,' she said, her voice changed, Laura realised, with recent crying. 'I know – I know it's not exactly your fault but—' The thin neck pulsed as she swallowed. 'You can't stay here.' There was a note of appeal in her voice. Please, it said, the advantage is all yours, now make it a little easier for me.

Laura found she couldn't answer, or meet, after a moment, Evie's greyed and washed-out gaze. It was left to her simply to nod, and hasten to her room to begin packing.

LAURA COULD NOT MOVE OUT for another two days. She took the first room she saw at a manageable price that had not already, between the publication of the advert and her telephone call, been snapped up. While she waited, she spent the intervening days contriving to leave home as early as she could in the mornings, and come back as late as she could bear to at night. At work, Evie avoided her, and Laura avoided Dandy. She didn't want him to feel torn between them; she didn't want to risk forcing him to make a choice, or to compromise his loyalty to Evie. Laura had what Evie wanted; it was only right that Evie should have Dandy.

And yet, how Laura could have done with him now. How badly she needed someone to confide in, someone who understood her fears, and with whom she could discuss her difficulties with Milan. Daphne, she felt instinctively, would simply not understand. And who else was there? She lingered in the shower at work, turning the warm, forgetful water on her face. She no longer ran for trains, eager to reach her journey's end, but stood, content to be carried at the escalator's pace, her eyes gazing numbly across the figures floating past. The city bustled round without touching her. It was not new to Laura to feel alone. But it was new to have lost such friendships. And to have lost them in getting what she wanted.

It was a voice down the phone line from Oxfordshire that shone a faint light at last in the darkness. She had had to ask for help from some quarter: with almost every waking moment spent in the studio, or travelling to or from it, the prospect of moving house unaided seemed impossible. So Laura had rung Richard. She had had no right to, she knew: his father was not expected to last many more weeks now, and in any case why, with such a busy life of his own miles from London, should he drop everything for her? But she turned to him because there was no one else she felt she could ask – and because she knew he would agree to help.

The room she had taken was in Kentish Town: it was small, seemed smaller with the brownish paint, and sickly in the light from the traffic-stained window. Limp curtains flapped in the draught through the flaking frame and proved, when drawn, not to cover the full width. There was a single bed, a deflated, lumpish sofa, and a small electric stove. Above it all, a bare hanging bulb provided a staging post for the dusty spider's threads strung, corner to corner, across the ceiling.

'Jesus.' Richard, his massive bulk filling the room, swung about on the spot. Armfuls of bags swung with him. 'Why didn't you just go back to Daphne's?'

Laura, setting down a box, did not reply. It had occurred to her, but she had not known, when it came to it, how to ask. She had been Daphne's charity case for five years. That was enough. She had moved out and moved on, and besides, this was no temporary phase: she would have to learn to live alone, and to like it. Still, it was an effort to stop her heart from sinking as she looked about her.

The bedstead, Richard discovered in sitting on it, dipped in the middle like a hammock; he tipped the mattress onto the floor and with little apparent difficulty lugged the iron frame downstairs and propped it in the grim yard behind the house. Then Laura unpacked two mugs, teabags, and boiled a pan of water. They spoke little as they drank, side by side on the sofa, and to her chagrin Laura found herself endeavouring not to cry. She felt too needy, too grateful. She blinked carefully and said, 'This chance, it should be the best thing in the world and instead it's the worst. I've lost my friends and now my home too.'

'Don't do it, then,' said Richard. 'Tell them to find someone else. They could, couldn't they?'

'Of course. But . . .' Looking at that steady, agreeable face turned to hers in such reasonable inquiry, Laura felt too weary to explain. 'It doesn't matter,' she said, and tipped her head instead to lean it against the solid mass of his shoulder. Slowly, unseen, a solitary tear escaped and slid across her cheek.

THERE REMAINED NOW ONLY three more days before the first performance. Saturday Laura spent, as she had spent every day since Max's recasting, battling with Milan in the company's rehearsal rooms. It was an unequal fight. The shaking nerves that had all but prevented her from dancing in that first rehearsal had gone, but still her improved work brought no thaw in Milan's attitude. Stepping as daintily among his arrogant sensibilities as through a minefield, she avoided, remembering Nadine, the head-on challenge. When Milan insisted on a move or sequence being executed his way, as he frequently did, Laura bit down her irritation. It both helped and did not that he almost invariably turned out to be right.

Undeniably, then, he knew how to partner. Within the very first hour of working together he had pinpointed, with a cold technician's skill, her centre of gravity, her habitual point of balance; his touch now, four days later, communicated complete assurance in every move; the strong grip shifted with clinical precision from Laura's limbs to her torso, catching, steadying, lifting and turning. Laura felt passages that had seemed difficult or awkward with Adam flow more smoothly and more naturally than she had imagined possible. But alongside the improvement came frustration: if this skill would only bend itself to her needs what might they, together, achieve? Instead, she felt in Milan's accuracy an unspoken rebuke: since she failed to meet his standards, he would not use his advantage to help her. He would use it, rather, to display her errors in starker relief.

This afternoon they were rehearsing their first Act One *pas de deux*. Half-way into a lift, Laura found herself suddenly on the way down again. Releasing her, Milan backed off, shaking his head. 'No. Still not right,' he said grimly, burying his fingers in his sweat-drenched hair.

It was a complicated move, involving Laura being caught from a leap, turned in the air and swung, with lightning change of grip, into a fish dive. There was nothing desperately wrong: it was an intrinsically awkward sequence, more difficult for the man, and requiring great strength. Milan, though, seemed not to find this a problem – except that Laura's timing was not quite as he wanted it.

Laura rested her hands on her knees and drew a couple of shuddering breaths. With three days to go this kind of fine-tuning was a luxury they could ill afford, but she knew the short shrift such a view would get if expressed. Her muscles were clogged with fatigue, her sodden clothes cooling quickly against her skin; she felt harassed, frustrated, ready to cry with the urgency of it. Hanging her head, she sank her teeth hard into her lip.

'Why are you doing this?' Milan was demanding now, and he repeated a movement of head and fluttering hands Laura was using just before the leap.

Straightening, Laura debated quickly. This gesture did not affect the lift: Milan was making a needless challenge. Why should she, this time, drop it to please him? Gathering what remained of her ragged nerve, she said, 'The way I – I see it, the bird can't simply be terrified all the way through this section. It's more interesting if she's intrigued as well as afraid . . . Th–that's what I'm trying to get over, anyway.'

'But what,' broke in Alexander from his perch by the mirror, 'is all this acting you think you need to do, child? The steps are perfect as I have given them. You are simply the paint on the canvas. It is I who hold the brush.' He laughed, and his cropped beard split to show a flash of white enamel. 'My God, if I relied on you to *think*!'

Laura, flushing in anger, returned her gaze determinedly to the floorboards. She waited for Milan to heap his scorn, too, upon her head.

A moment passed. Looking up, she found him considering her, with something a little like curiosity. When he spoke it was simply to say, 'Still, don't turn too soon as you jump,' and to extend his hand for her to try again.

This time, it worked, and as Milan swung her back out of the fish dive – the room, dizzyingly, righting itself again – Laura was met, spinning on *pointe* to face him, with a sardonic raising of the dark brows in recognition of success.

For an instant she thought it might be a breakthrough. It seemed at last a flash of honest communication – and besides he had just, tacitly, refused to side with Alex against her. But when she directed a smile to him she was met again with bland indifference, and the hands on her body for the rest of the rehearsal were as efficient and impersonal as ever. When finally Alex dismissed them, and Milan turned from her as usual without a word, Laura quit worrying through sheer exhaustion and went home to bed.

That night, *Firebird* tormented her in restless dreams. She was in the studio, but the walls had pressed back to admit countless rows of faceless spectators. It was the Act One *pas de deux* again, the fish dive was approaching. Laura leapt, her timing split-second perfect – but where

Milan's arms should have been there was empty air, and she felt herself falling like Icarus to a floor that seemed suddenly fathoms beneath her. Insensible of the impact, she lay crumpled like Nadine and, looking up, saw Milan standing above her, the muscled arms hanging loose from the broad beam of his shoulders – and beyond him, in the gallery window high in the studio wall, Laura saw the worn face of her mother, looking down. With a half-cry to the image already gone, she sat up – and found herself in the drear light of her little room, bathed in sweat.

The dream did not fade as Sunday's dawn thickened into a cold October morning, and when Laura arrived at the company buildings and walked into the lower studio she flicked her eyes up to the gallery window, and was relieved to see a clear and empty oblong of glass. But later in that long and exhausting day, something moved her to glance again, and this time, with a jolt of bitter shock, she did see a figure there.

Unwilling, but defiant, Laura held the fixed gaze. Nadine Kelly stayed exactly where she was, staring down, whey-faced and still as a waxwork.

THREE HOURS LATER LAURA left the building. As she crossed the small courtyard, heading for the main road, a diminutive figure stepped out from the shadows. Nadine had waited for her. Immaculate as ever, the tight-drawn brown hair caught the sheen of the street-lamp. The thick collar of her coat was turned up against the autumn chill, framing her face like an Elizabethan's. Within, half shaded, half lit, the fine features were held in careful composure.

It was the first time they had faced each other, alone, since that awful meeting in Max's flat. Remembering, Laura's cheeks darkened with the old humiliation. She saw Nadine, remembering too perhaps, twitch her mouth into a taut little smile. Then it disappeared and she said, 'So, my dear, you must be very pleased with yourself.'

The tone was honeyed enough, but Laura knew well the sting that lay behind it. She chose to say nothing, but stood and waited.

Nadine glanced down at her own feet, hidden beneath faultlessly elegant black trousers. 'It will heal in three months,' she said, 'perhaps two.' She looked up to Laura again, and the smile had returned. 'Oh, yes. I shall be back, my dear, and you needn't think that you'll be partnering *him* for two seconds once I am.' She paused, studying Laura's face. 'You think you're doing just fine, don't you? Well. That's him, dear, not you. This fuss everyone makes about him, it's for a reason, you see. And, of course, you'll get mauled by the critics. A shame, really, that you're being put next to such a talent. How can you hope to hold your own?'

She's desperate, thought Laura steadily. And she's afraid. That's all it is. If Evie were here in my place she would be saying exactly the same.

She waited until, spurred by no response, Nadine fell

silent. Then, sidestepping neatly, Laura set a straight and confident path away from her, towards the reassuring noise of the street.

YET WITH ONE DAY ONLY NOW separating Laura from the opening, the words burned like acid in her mind as Nadine had hoped they would – and how could they fail to, since they echoed, exactly, certain thoughts of Laura's own? Her mental landscape was cratered with confusion: hope dissolved into fear; fear brought desperation; desperation the knowledge, once again, that all she had, all she could cling to was this great and terrible task before her; and then, finally, ambition stirred afresh and with it a longing that somehow she would do it, even without Milan's help. Somehow it would come right.

At times Laura believed she would buckle beneath it – the hope as much as the despair – and at others that it buoyed her up, and that she could bear everything, even disaster, and come through. And this turbulence rocked her back and forth through succeeding punishing hours, through rehearsals and stage calls, last-minute costume fittings, and the long, lonely quarters of the final sleepless night.

Now at last it had washed her here: to her solitary barre an hour before the curtain was due to rise. Shored up only by a worn and trembling resolve, Laura felt sick with the effort of it, and sick at the thought of what was to come. If even in her best moments in the studio she was no match for Milan, how much worse would she be numbed and blacked-out with nerves?

She watched her limbs, swaddled in thick layers of fraying wool, move through the familiar warm-up movements, as if they belonged to someone else. Then she saw herself head back to her dressing room, where the scent and the sight of flowers overwhelmed her – roses from Max, carnations from Trish, lilies from Richard and Daphne. Feeling sick, she piled them all in the tiny washbasin and sat before the mirror, where the bright bare bulbs set her wan face looking back at itself like a paperthin ghost. She applied her make-up; she dressed. The costume was beautiful – a scarlet tutu, filmed with layers of orange and golden netting, the bodice encrusted and sparkling with sequins and edged with feather trimming. There were thread-thin bands to tie around her slender arms, trailing feathers too, and a plumed headdress. This was too heavy: throughout the dress rehearsal the previous night she had feared for her balance and felt as if someone was leaning on her from above, hard.

The dress rehearsal had been a shambles. The dancers had been hopelessly unfamiliar still with the set: most had had only one proper stage call – a farcical affair that had seen more of the scene-shifting crew on stage, half the time, than dancers, while missing bits of the set were belatedly tested out. Laura's personal nightmare lay with her first entrance: she was to descend a flight of steps concealed in the appearance of a craggy rockface. Since it had been the last piece to leave the workshop, she had still not had a chance to practise on it; it was perilously steep – and before an audience, she would not be permitted the luxury of looking down.

She dared not think of it now. The half-hour to curtain-up was called as she fixed her headdress, hair coiled beneath it with an army of pins and enough lacquer to make her a fire hazard. At the fifteen-minute call she was finishing another set of stretches; at the five, she went down to the stage and tried out some *pirouettes* while the lights were still up.

She had glanced about without success for Milan. Now, as she made her way behind the high wooden construct at the back of the stage, buttressed with rough-cut staves and secured with weights, she caught sight of a distinctive dark figure in the wings opposite. He seemed relaxed, flexing his feet easily in their soft calf-boots, the *faux* jewels of his thick Russian-style Prince's tunic wink-ing dully as he shifted. Loose in his grip hung the double curve of a slender hunting bow, and his eyes were lowered to it, without apparent attention. Watching him, Laura fluffed up her tutu, tested her shoes against the floor for the twentieth time, and listened absently to the strains of the overture. Despite the limbering her skin felt damp and cold.

Now it was time. Laura turned her back on Milan and, with the utmost care, mounted the makeshift steps at the back of the painted crag, trying not to think of the mirroring set of steps at the other side. Head up. Don't look down. Don't even think of falling. She concentrated on the music – the final bars before her cue – then, launching at last into swift movement, stepped out into the arching gap at the head of the stairs. The glare of the lights struck her a warm and blinding blow. Beyond them, she sensed the dark space; unseen, the countless watching faces. She was on.

She made it down to the stage, hardly aware of a single step beneath her feet. There was no floor, out there, no ceiling, no front or back, no up or down – it was pure, free-falling adrenaline. In a rush of panic, she submerged herself in her role, tried to breathe through each step and through each nightmarish combination the emotions and the sense of the story. It was all she could cling to.

Her first solo. Milan there, somewhere, to her right. No one else on stage – though plenty of figures, she was dimly aware, standing sullenly in the wings. A spin; her toe caught fractionally on a seam in the stage flooring. Laura missed her balance, felt herself straining to push her weight forward, but it was no use – she was toppling, toppling irretrievably backwards . . .

And then she felt the warmth of a presence close behind her, and she wondered who else had come on-stage, but a voice murmured, 'It's okay,' and a firm hand, held to her waist a crucial fraction early, steadied her, righting her again. Ahead, she was aware only of the uplit face of the conductor, his arms flailing her perfect, chosen, tempo. And behind, felt rather than seen even as she twisted towards him, was Milan – but hardly the Milan of the rehearsal studio.

In that single moment of crisis and rescue, the barricade, constructed so carefully between them, had crashed down. Laura realized she could sense instinctively where he was, as if his body had become an extension of her own: she could have moved in perfect unison with him if they had been a stage apart and blindfold. Without conscious effort, she found she was anticipating perfectly where he wanted her to be; the hands that steadied her, the arms encircling her waist were pliant, confident and trusting, pulsing with life. They were locked, it seemed, in a spiralling helix, their movements inexorably linked. And as the music swept them onward, without a spoken word passing between them, they began to test a little at the edges of the steps, to pull at the phrasing, to breathe more freely through the weaving melodies.

Laura could have laughed with the joy of it, if she had had a gasp of breath to spare.

Escaping into the darkness of the wings she wanted nothing but to be out there again. Heaving to fill her desperate lungs, shaking numbed limbs, she waited eagerly and then plunged back into the hot pool of light, believing, for those precious moments, in the Prince, in the Princess, in the evil Kostchei, in the magical creature she was supposed to have become.

★

THE NOISE WAS DEAFENING. Standing perfectly still, Laura seemed to hear the rush of an ocean of water in her ears; she was swimming to the surface, gasping for breath. Her body felt flayed of a layer of skin; it tingled all over, shrinking almost from the very touch of the air around it. And as the sensation rushed back, so did awareness of all the aches and the pains; muscles that had felt tireless while the orchestra played, now seemed stripped, scraped and mashed with a meat-pounder.

She focused for the first time, dazed and smiling, on the auditorium. It was not for her, though, she knew, that this grinning, whooping crowd was going wild: it was for Milan. She could hear the distant rumbling as hundreds of feet in the gallery and gods stamped on the floor beneath the seats, drumming their thunderous approval.

He was standing beside her, his right hand at her waist, his left enclosing her left hand, held out to the side. Though his head was up, his back impeccably straight, she could feel the lurching movements of his rib-cage: he was still out of breath from the final scene. She leant against him a fraction, and pressed her hand where it covered his on her waist to communicate her relief – and her thanks.

They took their bows together, and then Milan handed her forward, with the traditional chivalry, to acknowledge the crowd alone. When a pageboy appeared with a bouquet, he intercepted, and presented it to Laura himself. The noise of the crowd surged with delight, and the magnificent smile, the open, vivid gaze that shone upon Laura then, as Milan lifted her hand deftly and held it to his lips, was one she had never seen. She smiled readily in return.

They retreated behind the curtain for the last time. The audience, accepting reluctantly that there was to be no more, let their applause fade finally into rustling chatter as they wakened to themselves and prepared to depart. Screened off by the curtain, the stage was lit again with the worker lights. Laura turned to Milan, clutching her flowers still, and saw him for the first time in the reality of ordinary light, the painted lines about his eyes, the rivulets of sweat cutting glistening paths down cheeks and forehead, the dark hair as soaked as if he had just showered. She was, she realized, beaming stupidly, thanking him, though she hardly heard the words, fighting the impulse to start forward and cling to him in relief and gratitude. He, in his turn, buffeted by milling dancers, stagehands and crew, was standing, a still figure in the surrounding mayhem, regarding her with a slight frown: it was as if he were searching for something in her face. She heard his name all about: people were calling him; soon he would be swept away on a tide of congratulation to the waiting celebratory reception.

So she pressed him, quickly: 'What? What is it?'

The frown dissolved and, maddeningly, she saw the accustomed smooth control return. The hooded gaze remained on her, clear and untroubled. 'Laura,' said Milan softly, 'you know you mustn't try for four turns in that last *pas de deux*. I said before, you're not quick enough, and you throw the timing out for the whole of the next phrase.'

Laura's eager expression had frozen, and began now to slide. Was that all he had to say? After more than two hours of the rawest exertion, much of it in each other's arms, after finding at last a physical rapport such as she, at least, had never dreamt of, after those glorious, exultant smiles in front of the cheering crowd. Had those smiles been simply a calculated display for the punters, and now all that remained for Milan was to give his inexperienced little partner notes? She could not believe it. And yet how like him: how crushingly, damningly like him!

Beyond Milan Laura saw Dandy heading towards her through the mêlée, his talon-gloved fingers outstretched. In a shiver of scarlet feathers she shook her head, thrust her bouquet, hard, into Milan's stomach and stalked off the stage.

WHAT SHE NEEDED WAS a few minutes' solitude. They seemed, however, determined to elude her. She had hardly got into her dressing room before Max burst in, brimming and sweaty with smiles; after him Alexander, who brushed cold lips against her cheek and said she had made an admirable *start*; and finally, just as she was shutting the door and wondering if she could at last get out of her still-damp costume, there was another knock and a dusty blond head appeared. 'Richard,' said Laura, mustering a final scrap of enthusiasm.

He stooped and gathered her to him in a vigorous hug; she had to strain her head back to avoid smearing make-up on the immaculate lapels.

'Daphne's gone,' he said, releasing her. 'Instructed me to tell you how fantastic you were, but she said she expected the last thing you'd want would be some old trout cluttering up your dressing room. I quote, needless to say.'

Laura smiled. Dear Daphne. Beneath the teasing humour lay unerring foresight. Richard, however, did not share it. He settled himself on the sofa. Laura tipped her tutu and sat too, before her mirror, and reached for the cold cream.

The worst extravagances of black and gold around her eyes were hardly off before there was another rap on the door. Laura held tight to her temper. 'Yes?' she said, watching in the mirror as she tore off a fresh wad of cotton wool.

It was Milan, still in costume. On seeing Richard he hesitated for the briefest moment, but registered no surprise. He looked instead to Laura's reflection; she hadn't turned her head. 'I have to put in an appearance at this reception, but afterwards I'm going to head someplace else for a drink. Do you want to come?'

Too little, and far too late. Laura glanced at him in the glass. 'Thanks, but I've got other plans.'

There was a short pause. Then Milan gave the smallest of nods, and disappeared, clicking the door shut behind him.

'The great man himself,' said Richard flatly. 'Not exactly, something tells me, a bundle of laughs?'

'Look – could you just—' Laura stopped herself, and formed a deliberate smile. 'Could I meet you in twenty minutes or so? I need to wind down a little and take a shower.'

'Of course.' Richard got up, bent to drop a kiss on her grease-smeared forehead, and softly left the room.

MID-MORNING THE NEXT SUNDAY, Dandy walked into a small café just off the Kentish Town Road and slapped a pile of newspapers on the table. 'You little star!'

Laura leant back in her chair. A secret smile crept over her face. 'They're okay?'

'Okay?' Dandy's mouth twitched with amusement. 'You could say that. Same story as the dailies, basically. Milan is God's gift to just about everyone who lives and breathes and you are the amazing and unexpected find of the decade. Together, the greatest partnership since Romeo and Juliet. And rather, one hopes, less tragic. Ah-ah.' As Laura reached for the papers, Dandy pulled them out of reach again. 'I really don't think you should be reading your own press, do you? You'll stop talking to the likes of me. Although,' he added, slinging himself into the empty chair, 'given my latest piece of news, perhaps I'm not so far behind.'

He looked at her slyly, waiting to be asked. Laura purposefully went back to her coffee.

'You're impossible, Douglas.'

She sighed. 'Come on, then, what is it?'

'Well . . .' Dandy's eyes half closed in feline satisfaction. 'Max has said yes. He's letting me choreograph something for the new year. Just a short piece but it's a start. Because it will, of course, be a roaring success and then he won't be able to stop me.'

Laura grinned. 'That's brilliant!'

'I know.'

She had never seen anyone look so smug. She told him so. 'Well,' she said then, 'have you decided what the piece is going to be?'

'Certainly. A *pas de deux*. For you and Novák.'

There was a short pause. Then, 'Wow,' said Laura, a little lamely. Her spirits were managing to sink and rise at the same time. It was a curious feeling.

'This is pleased and honoured, is it, this odd expression?' inquired Dandy, waving a spidery finger at her nose.

'Sorry, Dandy. Of course I'm pleased. And honoured. And I wouldn't want anyone else to be dancing with Milan, which must mean I'm happy about that, too. it's just . . .' Laura let out a weary breath. 'Rehearsing *Firebird* with him was enough of a strain. This is creating something new so it'll be worse and . . . I kind of feel I could do with a break before facing it again.'

'Of course *Firebird* was a strain. You had a week to get used to one another and an awful lot riding on your joint success. Now you've got something to build on.'

'Not, I'd wager, the way Milan sees it. He still treats me like I've got a bad case of buboes.'

'Hmm.' Dandy pondered. 'And yet you dance together so sublimely.'

'He could dance well with anyone.'

'Not the way he dances with you. It wasn't the same with Nadine, it isn't the same with Francesca. You two have something special.' Dandy slapped a hand on the pile of newspapers. 'You'd be stuck together anyway, after those notices. And *I* certainly can't give you a choice. You and Milan are the only bloody reason Max is letting me do it. The ignorant hordes won't stampede for tickets to a Dandy Franks ballet – *yet* – but they will to see the new star partnership.'

Laura nodded. 'My ambition, I assure you, is turning joyous and grateful somersaults. The rest of me will cope.'

'Course it will, little one. And, you never know, between us we may be able to melt Glacier Novák.' Dandy smiled archly. 'It could even be fun.'

LAURA AND MILAN, TAKING their turn with the second and third casts, had given three performances since the opening night. Their new sixth-sense of physical communication had endured past that first performance, but in every other way, Laura knew, they were as far from an easy relationship as ever. Milan hardly spoke to her, and when he did, it was almost always to make some terse request, correction or criticism.

It wasn't simply depressing; even considered purely in the light of hard-headed ambition, it was, Laura felt, an opportunity lost. The most illustrious and enduring partnerships in the dance world had invariably been based on an emotional as well as physical rapport. How could you create works of art together when you couldn't even hold a proper conversation? Milan's coldness would become, in time, as much a weakness in their work as any technical fault, and Laura couldn't see why making an effort to improve things seemed beyond him.

Turning this over again in her mind as she waited in the wings at their next performance the following Wednesday, Laura remembered with a sudden guilty pang how brusquely she had refused Milan's offer of a drink on the opening night. He had given her ample cause to be angry, but still, that was the closest he had come to apology or friendliness and she had rejected the gesture out of hand.

It was with a mixture, then, of guilt and irritation that she saw him now waiting in the half-dark to her left, watching the dancers on stage. Francesca O'Connor, affectingly doe-eyed as the Princess, was begging her captor for her liberty and Dandy, whose make-up for Kostchei had in his new-found optimism become positively operatic, was thoroughly enjoying making a vicious refusal.

Treading carefully, Laura picked her way towards Milan. She halted at his shoulder, facing, like him, the glare from the stage. He had not moved or turned his head but she knew he was aware of her. And she, for her part, was studying covertly the stark profile, the sharp contours of the face outlined against solid black shadow. Without moving she whispered gently, 'Aren't you going to complain to Max? To be cast opposite a talentless child for a second time . . .'

He would not know she had overheard that conversation, and as a tease it was perhaps a little more barbed than she'd intended – though Milan's peaceful expression took it, for a moment, without a flicker. But then he faced her, and Laura saw with astonishment that he seemed uncomfortable. Their eyes locked only for an instant before he moved noiselessly away, disappearing into the deeper darkness at the back of the wings, heading for the stairs. Laura turned to watch Francesca and Dandy again, wishing, heartily, that she had said nothing at all.

By the interval, she was still feeling guilty. She had only repeated his insult to her, it was true, but she had intended, this time, to be friendly – and she had bungled the chance. Seeking an excuse to speak with him again, she discovered it in a query – genuine but minor – about

the taking of the feather in Act One. She had only now
to find Milan. Reaching the top of the steps from the
under-stage passage, she caught sight of him at the far end
of the corridor, walking away from her. Swiftly, she
followed.

Tracking him around one corner, Laura came round a
second just in time to glimpse him disappear into his
dressing room. And, with a flick of loose chestnut hair,
someone followed him in. Someone who had evidently
been there already, waiting.

Laura reached the door as it swung shut – hard,
perhaps from a kick. But in the instant before it closed she
saw into the room and there, in the large wall-mirror,
glimpsed a reflection.

Painted wood slammed across in place of it. Laura
stood winded, as if by a blow to the stomach. One hand
sought her midriff and, with the other palm-flat on the
corridor wall she turned, carefully, to retrace her steps.

The image was still before her. Of Milan standing,
turned to face his visitor. And – moving swiftly, surely
towards him, her face uplifted, the blue eyes bright and
eager – of Francesca O'Connor. Laura had seen Milan's
head lower, his fingers sliding deep into the shining hair.
He had been about to kiss her.

She stopped now, gripping the handle of her own
dressing-room door. What was it to her, after all? She had
simply wanted to speak to him. It could wait.

★

AFTER THE INTERVAL, LAURA had to make her way under the stage to come up in the prompt side wings for her next entrance. Down in the cold subterranean passage, she found Marco and two other soloists some way in front of her, mid-conversation, their voices ringing along the empty tunnel.

'. . . not a single one of the *corps* girls that wouldn't screw Novák soon as look at him. They're simply *dying* of jealousy. But poor Colm!'

'Poor Colm, my arse!'

'But someone should *tell* him.'

'If he hasn't worked it out by now he doesn't deserve to be told.' This was Marco. 'Hey, d'you think they're a threesome? Can't see Novák going for it, somehow.'

Gales of cackling laughter gusted back to Laura as the three dancers reached the end of the passage and disappeared round the corner. So it was general knowledge, she thought queasily. How long had it been going on?

Laura reached the end of the corridor herself, mounted the narrow steps and opened the felt-buffered door, still thinking. She was disturbed, and not at all sure why. Except, perhaps, that she had been faced with the crassest evidence of what she should anyway have known: that Milan was not as cold with everyone as he was with her. Did he dislike her so very much?

Twenty minutes later a flying *grand jeté* brought Laura back into the darkened safety of the wings. The impetus took her stumbling to touch against a clear patch of cool brick wall. She leant there struggling to take air more deeply into her gulping lungs, then turned, leaning still, and lifted her face to watch the two dancers she had left on stage.

The hunter Prince had found his captive and suffering Princess, and had fallen in love. It was an exquisite *pas de deux* Alex had choreographed for them, full of tender, melting movement, floating lifts and anxious caresses. Under the stage lights, Francesca became a glowing nymph in a milk-white shift, her lustrous hair hanging loose, draping across Milan's shoulder as he held her close against him. Laura observed them both with fresh eyes, noticed, as she had never troubled to notice before, that somehow Francesca's body managed to fit delicate womanly curves into a dancer's slender shape, that beneath the diaphanous folds of her costume rose softly swelling breasts where others had hardly more than rib-cage, that even the perfect oval face seemed girlishly full were others were hollowed and haggard. Laura watched Milan's hands track across the fabric, along the well-turned limbs, the soft, sweetly flushed skin, and she saw again, in her mind's eye, his fingers in Francesca's hair, his head bending to hers . . .

How strange, she declared to herself, that life should mirror art thus, feeding into it, feeding from it. It seemed voyeuristic to watch them now, enlightened as she was, and she wondered whether the as-yet ignorant Colm would suspect the truth if he were in the wings beside her, rather than down in the green room, waiting complacently for his next call. Poor Colm indeed. His wife snatched so easily, so expertly from under his nose, and he was the last to see it.

But Laura had to shift her thoughts quickly from this reality: the music was rolling towards her cue . . . With a last shake of cooling limbs, she launched herself back onto the stage, back, as she crossed the threshold, into the quilled skin of the Firebird. In the love-triangle portrayed on stage, only one person now was acting, only one was having to conjure emotion out of nothing. And that was her.

Still, Laura found that the Firebird's jealousy stung her hard tonight: she felt it, deep and raw, within her, and startled but pleased at its force, she gave herself up to it, pushing her limbs through their wild twists and contortions and finding a strange respite, for once, in the exhaustion of her work.

The curtain calls seemed interminable that night. When the last was over, Milan left Laura's side immediately as usual, weaving swiftly through the bustle on stage. But as she glanced after him this time, Laura was gripped by a sudden urge to delay him. She hastened to follow. 'Milan?'

At the edge of the wings he stopped and turned. 'Yes?'

Laura looked up at him blankly. What was it she had intended, earlier, to ask? She could think, only, as she looked at him now that perhaps Francesca was waiting downstairs, and he was on his way to her. She hoped the thought wasn't obvious. As the silence lengthened, the confident sweat-glossed face regarded her with growing curiosity.

'The wedding,' she said at last, a little desperately. 'That section before the Maidens' Variation. You and Francesca are passing far too close to the dais. I'm worried we'll collide as I come across.'

The curiosity tightened into weary irritation. But Milan said levelly, 'It's because you're starting those *posé* turns early. You shouldn't get up to the back till we've moved downstage. Still ...' He inclined his head the merest fraction, in expression of a favour granted. In two strides he had disappeared.

Laura made her way limply through the wings in his wake, bouncing the by now familiar bouquet, upended, against her legs. When she reached her dressing room and pushed the door to behind her, for once she turned the key in the lock. And, sitting at the mirror, dragging at her face with the cotton wool, pulling off the colour in stripes, smearing the red and black and gold like warpaint across her cheeks, she found it mingled with a sliding film of greasy tears.

Chapter Nine **Paris, 1989**

On 1 October Renée arrived on the five-forty flight from Heathrow.

When she caught sight of her friend emerging through the arrivals gate, Natasha realized with considerable surprise that she was, after all, glad Renée had come. She had been in a furious mood for days, and knew that it was the dangerous kind of anger that was but a whisker away from grief. Renée, though, would expect her to be her old self; and perhaps she would rise to the challenge.

They took the RER into town. 'You're lucky,' Natasha told Renée, 'that I've moved. I did have a *chambre de bonne* the size of a postage stamp on a corridor with five psychopaths and no shower.'

'No *shower*?' said Renée.

'And there wouldn't even have been enough floor space for you to lie on. I was planning on dangling you over the balcony at night.' She fixed Renée with a beady, bird-like stare.

A room had come free the week before in the block where Johnnie lived, out in the 10th. It wasn't large, but it had its own small bathroom built into one corner. It was, by comparison, heaven.

'Thank goodness,' said Renée.

They dumped Renée's things at the flat, then went out again in search of beer. By the time they sat down in a café Natasha had learnt everything about Jonathan, Renée's boyfriend, that anyone bar a long-lost relative might want to know. He sounded safe and boring and sweet – right up Renée's street, thought Natasha, and then reprimanded herself for being so snide. It's only because you're jealous, Taylor. And then she was appalled. Could she really be jealous of one of Renée's relationships?

'Sorry,' said Renée. 'I want to hear all your news too.'

'You don't,' said Natasha.

Renée laughed and, inadvertently, went straight for the jugular. 'Come on, what's the legend really like? And who are you sleeping with?'

'He's an arrogant, patronizing bastard. And I wouldn't sleep with him if you paid me.' Natasha remembered, too late, that that hadn't been the question.

Renée eyed her consideringly. 'Okay.'

'And you can stop looking like that right now,' Natasha said, jabbing an accusing finger. 'Anyway, what do you want to know? My life is very boring. I go to class, I go to rehearsals, I go to the gym. Oh, and I go for beers. Plenty of them.'

'Who with?'

'The company – all except Novák. They're a decent crowd.'

Renée was unconvinced. Just to get away Natasha stalked over to the bar to order sandwiches. When she got back she pumped Renée for news of the other people from their year at the Institute. It was depressing – most had got jobs, and decent ones too. Natasha lit up, and puffed through a cigarette at double speed.

'Well, this is going to be a fun couple of days, I can see,' said Renée, leaning back as the food arrived. 'Look, Natasha, you can tell me now, or you can tell me when you've had a few more beers. What's wrong?'

Natasha glared at her sandwich, dropped ash on it by mistake and cleaned it off with a paper napkin. She looked up at Renée. And sighed. 'Okay, so it's Milan. I've not kept on the right side of him. And I'm shit-scared he's going to give me a raw deal in the show.'

'What did you do? Or need I ask? You mouthed off at him, right?'

'I kind of . . . We kind of—' Natasha winced. 'He thought I was coming on to him.'

'And were you?'

'No, I wasn't – and then I kind of was. And then he wasn't interested.'

'Wasn't *interested*?'

'No. Okay?' Renée, Natasha saw with annoyance, was smiling. 'What?'

'Now let me remember the Natasha Taylor agony-aunt advice.' Renée put a finger to her temple. 'If a bloke's not interested it's his loss. Not worth wasting your time on. I *think* I have that right.'

Natasha glared at her.

'Only teasing. But you seem . . .'

'Like I said, he's an arrogant, patronizing bastard,' said Natasha. 'And I told him a few home truths. So *other* than the possibility of having mucked up my casting chances, I'm telling you I couldn't give a toss. Right?'

That sympathetic, disbelieving gaze could hardly have been more irritating – but Natasha felt comforted, too. Just to have told someone what had happened diminished it somehow, made it loom less large and less claustrophobically in her head. She had thought she was going mad.

Renée was tactful enough, at least, to make an effort to change the subject. She chatted brightly about how well Madame seemed to be doing since the gala, and how rumours were circulating that she and Alex really didn't get on and that there was going to be a storm about it sooner or later. 'I guess it could get Madame into hot water with the board,' said Renée lightly, pulling a slice of salami out of her sandwich and chewing it. 'They think the sun shines out of Alex's arse. Or that's the impression I've always had.'

Second only to Renée's blissful love-life, the things in the world Natasha least wanted to hear about were the Institute and her mother. She nodded, shrugged, gnawed at her baguette and, leaning sideways, grabbed a newspaper that had been discarded on the next table. She scanned the front page. East Germany again, and South Africa. Her French was getting a lot better. She glanced down the articles, reading parts, guessing the rest.

Looking up, she found that Renée had stopped talking and was watching her. 'What?' she said abruptly, her fag and her sandwich suspended, in the same hand, in mid-air. It'd be something about Milan again. She steeled herself in readiness.

But Renée said, 'You're the only person I know who eats and smokes at the same time.'

Relieved, Natasha stuffed the end of the bread into her mouth and tore off a chunk. 'Bull,' she said round it. 'I'm just the only person you know who does it in public.' And then, to her own astonishment even more than Renée's, she burst into tears.

THE FIRST REHEARSAL FOR Milan's new ballet was scheduled for the next day. He'd told the company nothing about it, other than that he wanted them all to attend.

'Do you think there's any chance he'd let me watch?' Renée had asked when she had discovered she was not allowed to comment on Natasha's startling, if very brief, breakdown of composure and was casting about for something different to say.

'No,' Natasha had replied bluntly, in between aggressive

sniffs. Whether he would or would not, she didn't want Renée sitting there and analysing Milan's every word, in the light of him being The First Man To Turn Down Natasha Taylor. And, for her own part, she was finding facing him each day difficult enough as it was without an audience.

Natasha wanted to be off-hand, relaxed, neither soliciting Milan's attention, nor – and this was the harder part – shying away from it. She tried to remember exactly how she had acted towards him *before*. She couldn't. And what made matters worse, she had begun to notice him watching her at odd moments. He would be talking to Victor, then would look across at her. Only for a second, and the glance was utterly blank; she could read nothing in it. She was surprised that, possessing a habitual expression as infuriating as that, he didn't more often get punched in the mouth.

Perhaps he wanted her to apologize. Well, that wasn't her bag. And, besides, the idea that he was laughing at her – feeling sorry for her, maybe, certainly thinking less of her – preyed on her mind. It brought her anger boiling up against him. Anger and resentment. Why had he informed her of what she wanted only to tell her she couldn't have it? Why not just leave her in ignorance? Yes, a voice in Natasha's head replied sardonically, in that strange state of ignorance that had made her dash after him down public pavements without having a clue as to why she was doing it. Maybe Milan had saved her from making a spectacle of herself. The thought was hardly cheering. And it was one she tried very hard to squeeze out of her mind on those occasions, like now, when Milan was standing just a few feet away from her. They had convened for the rehearsal, and he was explaining the background to the new ballet.

'No title as yet,' he said, turning his blanched gaze around the small assembly. 'The music's some Bach – I'll play it to you in a minute. But first I want to outline the theme.' It was, he said, the lonely journey. The central figure would be seen passing through different relationships as it passed through life: with its parents, whom it rejected; with its first love, who left it; with its child, who replicated its own rejection. And by the time the person turned back to its parents, completing the cycle, they were dead. 'I have an image of people turning away from each other,' Milan said. 'A lack of communication. Look.' He beckoned Denise and, taking her shoulders, squared her up to face him. 'You're talking to me, but,' and he turned his back on her, 'I'm busy looking at someone over here. Now I want your attention.' He faced her again and Denise, understanding, turned away. 'That's right. The opportunity's gone. See?'

They did. Natasha was surprised. She had thought Milan's piece would be more abstract, less narrative than this.

'And the main person?' said Johnnie.

'Ah, yes.' Milan folded his arms, the fingers splayed

across the well-worn cotton of his sleeves. 'I want the main person,' he said, 'to be Natasha.'

Johnnie, Denise, Erik, Luc and Pascale: they were all looking at her. And she was looking at Milan – in shock. The shock held Natasha rigid, then melted into a pointed grin. Wrong again, Taylor, she told herself. Aloud she muttered, 'Thanks.' But Milan had turned his back, already busy with the tape machine.

JOHNNIE LEANT OVER, HIS stomach resting on the green baize, and lined up his shot. With one perfect swing of the cue, he hit the white against the black and the black against the cushion, doubling it back within a hair's breadth of a cluster of reds and into the centre pocket.

'You bastard,' said Natasha appreciatively. Though she wielded a mean cue herself, she had to admit she was no match for Johnnie. And as the loser was buying the beers, it was getting expensive.

They were in the back of a bar in the 9th, not far from the rehearsal rooms. Outside it was a bright late-October day, slashes of clear blue sky showing above the streets. But Natasha liked the seedy half-dark and the smoke of the bar. And she wanted some information out of Johnnie. 'When, for starters,' she said, hooking her heels over the rung on her stool and watching as Johnnie lined up his next shot, 'are they going to tell us where we're performing? Less than a month to go, and we don't even know the size of the stage.'

Johnnie grinned, sliced his cue through smoothly and watched the balls kiss and drop. The light from the low lamp caught the shine on the skin of his head, his tonsure of close-cropped hair. He straightened and let the cue run through his fingers to rest on the floor. Then he folded both hands on top of it. 'Truth is, kiddo,' he said, 'no one's known it. Victor's been waiting to hear how much dough we're getting from the Ministry. There's a small theatre he's found, out in the eighteenth, but the management have been throwing their weight about because we couldn't confirm. Milan went off an hour or so ago to try to get the keys. He hasn't seen the place yet, either.'

Even to Natasha, the last-minute nature of all this seemed quite incredible. And now that she had her big-time début set up – no thanks to Quentin – she was more than ever determined that all should go ahead smoothly. Straight from school to the main role in Milan Novák's new ballet. That would be something for her mother to read about in the papers. But, thinking of the tour, a question occurred to her about what she had seen that painful day three weeks ago in the studio. In trying to block out the conversation that had followed, she'd blocked the query from her mind too. What exactly had Milan been rehearsing, and why?

'The solo Victor wants Milan to include in the programme,' she said now. 'What is it?'

Johnnie circled the table, weighing up his options. 'Bit of a wild piece,' he said, bending to a shot, and then changing his mind. 'Nightmare to perform, it completely flattens you. The title's "The Fallen" – set to some pretty dodgy thrash rock. The choreographer's idea was based on Lucifer in hell, apparently – the fallen angel, you know? A nice bit of biblical torment.'

There could be no doubt, then, that that was what Natasha had seen. She frowned, thinking, and – getting a chance at the table – promptly missed the pocket. 'Shit,' she said and went to the bar.

That was the third beer and they were coming round quickly. On an empty stomach, Natasha's head, as well as her wallet, was feeling the effects.

'One more game?' offered Johnnie.

Natasha nodded and tapped the white towards her with her cue. Out of the corner of her eye she caught sight of a figure striding through the bar. It stopped at the table, and faced them along its full length.

'I have them!' said Milan. He was holding aloft a jangling bunch of keys.

Natasha's beer-swilled brain was slow to comprehend, but Johnnie said, 'That place in the eighteenth?'

'The very same. Come on. We're going on an inspection.'

Unsure whether she was included in the invitation, Natasha nevertheless set down her cue and followed. What the hell? She wanted to see the stage.

Outside, blinking against the light, she spotted a battered Favorit with atrocious paintwork, parked illegally.

She hadn't even known Milan had a car. She soon discovered he hardly did – it was too generous a description.

'So did the Ministry stump up the cash, then?' Natasha looked across at Milan. There was so little space that his knees were practically either side of the steering wheel. Johnnie, nominally in the back, had jammed his large face through the gap between their shoulders.

'We're okay for the home run,' Milan replied, eyes glued to the road. Suddenly his hand, thrusting across towards her door, knocked Natasha backwards in her seat.

'Hey!'

But he was already furiously winding at the little black handle. He leant over to shout at a car pulled up alongside.

Natasha caught Johnnie's eye. 'Don't ask,' he said, out of the corner of his mouth. 'Grammatically incorrect but insulting enough to get us rammed.'

Slapping hand over hand onto the wheel as he spun it into a dizzy right turn, Milan centred himself back in his seat. Sinking her teeth, hard, into her bottom lip to stop herself from giggling, Natasha wound up the window again.

They were heading north, through the 18th *arrondissement*. The theatre, when they reached it, looked modest from the outside but funky. In the foyer, posters advertised avant-garde exhibitions, cellar cabarets and installations. Milan stalked straight through to the auditorium; Johnnie and Natasha followed.

Inside, they felt rather than saw the space. It smelt vaguely of stale fags. Soon, Natasha's eyes adjusted to the dimness. Though the stage was unlit, she could see grey shapes of flats up towards the back, presumably from the current show.

'It's tiny.'

Five hundred seats, maybe, at a guess.

'It's perfect!' Milan, below her, strode down the shallow gangway steps two at a time. Reaching the front row, he sat and propped his feet on the edge of the orchestra pit. Natasha made her way down after him. The scene of her début, she thought, a little tipsily, but with a suitable sense of moment. Heading round to the side, she swung herself up onto the stage.

'Get the workers on, will you?' Milan called.

Natasha plunged into the darkness of the wings and felt her way around. More by luck than judgement, she swiftly found the stage manager's board and flooded the stage with a harsh blanket light.

The rake didn't look too steep. 'We'll need to get a floor down,' she heard Milan say. Johnnie replied but she couldn't make out his words.

Standing in the wings, Natasha concentrated on look-ing about her. A large mock fountain stood pushed against a far wall, supported with slats of chalked-up plywood at the back. Further along there were three metal rails, fatly packed with costumes. The wardrobe department, perhaps, was having a clear-out: the costumes were neither new nor spectacularly clean and seemed fitted for some flamboyant but flaky production of *Don Quixote* or *Cyrano de Bergerac*. Padded doublets, pantaloons and lace ruffs jostled each other for space; in a vast cardboard box beside them she found a selection of rapiers, large feathered hats in lurid colours, and *commedia dell'arte* masks with pendulous noses.

Milan and Johnnie, she could hear, were deep in a tedious discussion about sight lines. Natasha was free to investigate. There was a store-cupboard, in which she found a full head mask of some ape; she pulled it on and was almost overwhelmed by a smell combining, somehow, mothballs and curry. Looking further, she found halberds, hessian smocks with grisly bloodstains round the neck; dresses dripping with diamanté, patchworked with foul American-tan gauze that was supposed, when worn, to look like bare flesh; a Spanish finned helmet and a jousting helmet with elaborate crest that wobbled dangerously; a jester's hat with bells . . .

Natasha decided to stick with the ape's head. She teamed it tastefully with a small ruff and a lion's body suit and, thus bedecked, emerged onto the stage.

The conversation stopped. There was a moment of stillness from across the footlights and Natasha wondered, mustily, if she was about to be scolded. But then, through her inadequate eye-holes, she saw Milan appear on the stage – having got there, apparently, in a single bound – and race past her on his way to the wings. From which, a moment later, came the sounds of wild rummaging.

'My God!' Johnnie shouted with laughter. Natasha spun round, went blind, and, adjusting her headgear so that she could see again, found she was being greeted by a beak-masked cavalier dressed from head to foot in hideous turquoise. The swashbuckler, folding his cloak about him, bowed with extravagant courtesy. Natasha, carefully, responded. Johnnie promptly got hiccups.

And then, struggling around a swinging scabbard and the trailing lion's tail, which Natasha presently had the sense to drape over one shoulder, they began to dance. It aspired to be a tango, of a rather wild and innovative variety, although from the liberal and flourishing use of the turquoise cloak, the *paso doble* could also have been partly to blame.

Johnnie, getting the hang of it quickly, came in with a rollicking vocal accompaniment at the top of his lungs. He put his continuing hiccups to percussive use, with effective but occasionally oddly timed results.

Natasha was dimly aware that the beer must have been very strong, but was too busy enjoying herself to care.

They twirled and lunged. At the bottom of an arm-draped back-bend, Natasha's head fell off. 'Go on,' hissed Milan, his voice unsteady with laughter, and she could see, in the glittering gaze behind his half-mask and the smile beneath it, a curious, childlike delight.

Surging towards a lift, they half overbalanced and Natasha, laughing so much her stomach hurt, clung to Milan's shoulder as they turned. Out of breath, their faces were inches apart; Milan's arms were around her, his hands on her back. They separated again as he spun her out with a whipped unfurling of an arm, gripping her fingers' ends white, then releasing them and, as she toppled, shifting sideways to catch her expertly at the waist. He laughed aloud, bent his head towards her and she, laughing too, and thinking that that was what he intended, kissed his unmasked lips.

The effect was immediate. Milan straightened as if she had struck him and relinquished his grip, so that Natasha stumbled backwards and almost fell against the proscenium arch. Johnnie stopped singing. And one of the doors at the back of the auditorium opened.

Through it walked a man, middle-aged, stout and not at all friendly. He spoke in rapid French. Milan, as he replied, removed the hat and mask and cloak, instantly in control, serious, business-like. It was one of the administration staff, no doubt, and they had been caught with costumes that didn't belong to them. Natasha, thankful for once that her French was still not all it should be, hurried into the wings to change. Enough harsh words were sounding in her head as it was: she needed no one's help to feel sick and ashamed.

She had been a fool.

Just as she had caught sight of what Milan, relaxed, might be like – the Milan she had been seeking all along – she had brought his defences clanging down again like metal shutters across a store-front. Glimpsing his friend-ship, she had pushed it beyond her reach. And what would he think of her now? She could imagine all too well.

Shit. *Shit*.

THE PAPERS WERE FULL OF events in Eastern Europe. Natasha had begun to follow the developments daily. The trickle of people coming out of East Germany, which had started in August, had swelled into a flood. Thousands were crossing into Czechoslovakia and taking refuge in the West German embassy in Prague; thousands more of those left behind were staging anti-government demon-strations – and the government had expressed a willingness to discuss reforms.

The Novák Company, which usually found it easy to forget their leader's country of origin, had been made to remember it again. 'Milan,' Luc had said one day as every-one took a brief break between class and the morning's first rehearsal, 'there's a few of us want to go to Berlin. If we go on a Sunday, we can take the Monday off, can't we?'

Natasha, frowning in concentration as she followed the rapid, rumbling French, saw Milan's jaw tighten. 'No,' he said.

'Come on – this is history happening here.'

The cold stare widened. 'What are you planning on? Chipping a chunk off the Wall?'

'That kind of thing.'

'It's not a sideshow.'

'But we can go?'

'Of course. You just won't have a job when you get back.'

And with that, Milan had left the room. Eyebrows had been raised, but in silence. The subject was not mentioned again.

There was, besides, plenty of cause for everyone to be irritable. Victor, who had gone ahead and confirmed the US and European tour dates assuring all backers that Milan would dance, had just admitted his tactic to his employer. It was a last-ditch attempt to force Milan's hand, and he was not, it appeared, to be easily forgiven.

Natasha rang Denham to prepare her father for the likely outcome. 'Dad, I may well be home for Christmas. You needn't cheer.'

'But it's allowed if I'd like to, I hope,' said Richard. 'And when will you be due back in Paris?'

'There may not be any job to come back for.'

'Hmm.' There was a brief pause, and Natasha reflected with fond amazement on her father's ability to react to dramatic news as if it were the reading of a shopping list. 'No bad thing, perhaps,' he said at last. 'I can't believe that outfit is—'

'What?'

'Good enough for you.'

Natasha laughed, incredulous. 'Dad! What do *you* know about it?' She wondered suddenly if Richard had been talking to her mother.

'Not much, of course,' he said. 'But, look, it'll be lovely to see you. And Daphne will be delighted. She misses you more than she'd admit.'

'Her mind's going.'

'I'll tell her you said so.'

Natasha smiled into the receiver. She was pinched, suddenly, by a longing for home. Denham and Daphne and solid old Dad, who never quite understood his sometimes raging, always resolute daughter. But he invariably tried.

In rehearsals, the proximity of the opening night had replaced the usual atmosphere of steady dedication with one of palpable tension. It was worst with Milan: the black looks he cast at the world made Natasha berate herself, again, for the stupidity that had channelled a fresh gulf between them.

She knew he had ample cause for bad temper, right now. Time was short, Victor in desperation had pushed their argument into the public arena, and how the situation in East Germany made Milan feel none of them could tell, though they strained to imagine.

But still Natasha couldn't help taking his sourness personally. Even the prospect of the show opening in just over two weeks' time couldn't lift her mood. When possible she kept out of his way; but when forced, in rehearsal, to be near him it pained her that he seemed as distant as if he were sleepwalking, and often, through some angry, struggling dream she couldn't fathom. What was worse, she had no right to expect it should be otherwise. The misery of it dragged at her, a sickening ache.

BUT MAYBE IT WASN'T SIMPLY misery. The next Tuesday, exactly two weeks before the opening, Natasha started the day with a dull pain behind her left eye. By the afternoon she felt limp and ragged, and by six o'clock she was convinced she was going down with flu. She went home and, falling gratefully into bed, slept deeply. When she awoke, it seemed as if it should have been morning, and yet it was still profoundly dark. Her head had ceased to ache. She felt about for her alarm clock, but couldn't find it, rolled over in the tangled sheets and dozed again.

And woke again some time later, with the suddenness of having been disturbed. Before she was fully alert Natasha was listening, sharply, to something in the darkness. It was a buzzer, sounding insistently in the room directly below hers, Johnnie's room. He must be out, because the buzzer sounded again, long this time, as if it were being leant on. Natasha pulled back the bedclothes and, shivering in her thin T-shirt and leggings, crossed to the window.

She opened it and put her head out – rather too

quickly: her vision swam as she peered into the gloom beneath. The street light on the pavement opposite was spluttering through its usual attempt at a strobe effect, and in the flickering orange glow, she caught the edge of something billow out from the doorway of her building and disappear. A figure, leaning against the stone post of the entrance, rolled on its shoulder pavement-wards, and then, cringeing down as if taken by a cramp, was sick.

Some drunk, she thought with a shudder, and was about to shut the window again when, taking one last glance at the figure, she made out the shape of it turning its face up towards her. In an instant Natasha darted to the door, threw it wide, and raced to the staircase.

Her blood pulsed in her ears as she flew down, each step icy against her bare toes, willing herself not to think or she would miss her footing. At the ground floor she flung herself down the hallway to the high double doors of the entrance. The lock was stiff: her sleepy fingers struggled stupidly, but at last it turned.

Pulling back one narrow door, she was just in time to witness the waiting figure retch again, with scraping though now unproductive violence, into the gutter. She stood and watched, feeling strangely lightheaded, then reached out to steady him as he pushed his weight off the leaning shoulder and reeled towards her.

She thought, once inside, he might sink down the wall onto his heels – and probably sleep there for a good few hours until the drink wore off. But he stayed standing, and it wasn't until he passed under the harsh glare of the hall light that she saw the condition of his face – and realized why he was holding his hands gingerly a little way from his body.

'My God,' she said softly.

'Nothing to worry about,' said Milan. He tried to smile, and then thought better of it. 'I won't be sick again. If you could just . . . I think I need to sit down.'

Natasha led him to the staircase and he lowered himself onto the bottom step. There was a cut above his left eye, which was swelling gently; blood from his nose had dried across his top lip; fresh blood was seeping from grazes on his cheek and forehead. His hands hung limp between his knees, the fingers bruised, the knuckles scraped and raw.

'What happened?'

'Out at an unfriendly hour, that's all.' He was, she saw now, utterly sober. 'There were three of them. Not far from here. I thought Johnnie might be in.'

'Well, I'll have to do,' said Natasha briskly. She looked at him for a moment. The shock had cleared her head; the aches of the afternoon had left her. She said, 'Can you walk? I'm on the third floor, I'm afraid.'

He stood up with some difficulty.

'Where's the dog?'

He shook his head, muttering, 'At home,' and she wondered, as she often had, just where that was.

By the time they reached her room the worst effects of the blows to his stomach were wearing off and Milan was standing straighter, moving with a little more ease. She loosed his arm. 'That one's the most comfortable,' she said, nodding towards a soft chair by the window.

While he sat, she fetched warm water and cotton wool to clean the cuts. None were too deep but there had been a deal of blood, from his nose most probably. His clothes, filthy enough with grime from the street, were streaked and spotted. Swabbing as gently as she could, Natasha surveyed the face before her; the eyes were closed and, though he winced a little, he did not speak.

When she was done, she retreated to her bed and sat on top of the covers, a blanket drawn around her legs for warmth. The bedside lamp glowed rosily through its coloured shade; by its light she watched the unmoving figure in the chair. His head rested against the back, his bruised fingers curled over its arms; she could not tell if he was sleeping. It was a little past three o'clock.

She felt privileged. He had not meant her to see this; he had come for Johnnie. But, in his extreme need, she had been given another chance to show that she could be a friend, that he no longer needed his defences with her, because she was not a child. She was strong enough to build the barriers within herself, so that what she had asked for, and he had refused, would not be demanded again. But she wanted his friendship: she could not go so far as to deny herself that.

Soon after the half-hour Milan opened his eyes. Natasha still watched, her face in shadow. She said, 'I'll run you a bath. You'll be less sore tomorrow,' and, without waiting for a response, went to do it.

She ran it hot, as hot as she thought his battered skin could bear, and found some salving oils for the water. A heady, thick steam rose softly, veiling the mirror and the chrome with a fine-beaded mist. Milan hesitated when she showed him into the room. She closed the door behind her to keep in the heat and seated herself on the stool in the corner. 'Don't worry. I'm only going to wash you.'

Milan tried again to smile, and succeeded, though she could see the pain it cost him.

The clothes he pulled off with some difficulty, but quickly; Natasha did not move to help him. There were fresh bruises, she saw, on his stomach and back. And, under the skin too, the sinews and muscles were sharply delineated – she watched the tension as he gripped the sides of the tub, then, leaning on his arms, lowered himself slowly into the water.

Natasha knelt beside the bath and lathered her hands. She took his nearest hand, palm up, and cast her eyes over every inch of the scarred flesh, the tracks along his forearm. He sat motionless, submitting himself, tranquil, to her scrutiny. Turning the arm she saw again his tattoo, and studied it properly for the first time.

It was a bird of some sort. Feathers in flame colours – crimson, yellow, orange – fanned out across the skin. But at its base there was a horizontal smudge of darker colour.

It looked like a mistake in the design. Or something older, underneath. Natasha glanced up, and found Milan watching her, his gaze resting gently on her face, the hollows of his eyes shadowed darkly, one lid pressed half closed with the swelling. She thought she saw a pleading in the look, and then he turned his face into her hair, speaking some words she didn't understand, and then her name, in a tone so soft the pulse within her missed its tread.

An invocation, it had struck like the chiming of a bell, and rung true. Her decision, so carefully made, was in that instant undone. Moving her hand gently to his cheek, Natasha turned Milan's face towards hers. Her fingertips brushed lightly across the still swollen lips – then she held them to her own. And discovered that she had not, after all, been mistaken.

After some moments she drew back from him to continue with her task. The capable fingers working gently, she washed his arms, his back, his hair. She found him a bathrobe, held out a towel as he emerged, sleek-skinned, from the water, stood back to let him dry himself.

When he was done, she took his hand. He suffered himself to be led by her as if, commanding for so long, he had finally yielded his place. She brought him back into the larger room, not, though, to the armchair where he had sat before, but this time to the bed. Unsure of what was possible with the battering he had taken, she was tentative, her fingers tracing the contours of his skin with an exquisite, searching care. But it was not just concern for his injuries: endangered pride, too, made Natasha hesitate. He had rejected her before. What, now, had changed?

Before long she found her answer in his hands, his breath, his lips at her throat. She met there a need that matched her own and bettered it. The hunger she recognized – it was the mirror of all she had felt over the past days and weeks and months. And it was a hunger of such shuddering force that a bruised body's pain could be engulfed and swept away.

What had changed? Here indeed was the answer: nothing. Simply, the sought had, unknown to Natasha, been all along the seeker too.

'CHRIST, WHAT HAPPENED TO YOU?'

Johnnie's glance as Milan entered the studio became a swift double-take, and then a wince.

'That bad?' said Milan, unconcerned, crossing to dump his bag beneath the piano.

'Frankly, yes.' The grazes and cuts had clotted red, the bruising showing blue, veined with small floods of purple. The swelling above the eye had lessened a little, but the lid was still half closed.

Milan declined to elucidate, though with the evidence so visible it was hardly necessary. He was taking class today and concentrated totally on the work.

Natasha, with a new ease of spirit, did not find it difficult to do the same. He had left her early that morning. When she had woken he was already up, dressing himself by the dull light of dawn seeping through the half-open shutters. She had watched the strong, lean body as it went about its mundane task – as ill-used, in a way, by its owner over the last twenty years as it had been by those three men last night – and her skin had secretly felt again the warmth of his hands and of his mouth as if he were still beside her.

At last, ready to leave, Milan had stood and surveyed her, her hair lying dark against the pillow and against her pale skin. Natasha could see the tension in his stillness, but did not wonder what impulse he held in check. Then, wordlessly, he had turned from her and gone. She saw now that he had been home, to pick up fresh clothes and his neglected dog. And, looking at him from her accustomed distance, acknowledged no more than on any other day, she felt the familiar longing and with it a fresh one, born of knowledge.

The day was long and arduous. Natasha, throughout, had no occasion to speak to Milan of anything other than work; she did not look for one. But at the finish, when weary bodies were wrapping themselves up ready to head out into the night, she hesitated, uncertain what to do. Milan solved her problem, crossing to where she stood leaning against a barre. He said, 'We should talk. Will you – come to my place?' She agreed, and waited for him as he spoke to Victor, and then Johnnie, and as the other dancers, one by one, called their farewells, slung bags over aching shoulders and left.

The first days of November had brought with them bitter cold, and as Natasha and Milan walked, the rain that drove sideways into their faces was trying hard to thicken into sleet. Despite it, they spoke fitfully of work and more particularly of Milan's new ballet. The dog ran between them, his eyes angled up to his master. Between them, too, the unbroached subject hung heavy on the air.

The route they were taking led them to the 17th *arrondissement.* When at last Milan stopped in the doorway of an apartment block, it was in a little scruffy side street not far from the Place de Clichy. Putting his key in the lock, he opened the door and then stood aside to let Natasha through. She touched her fingers to his midriff as she passed, but felt him contract away. It gave her a shudder of foreboding.

Passing through a hall she came into a courtyard, where the dog, knowing its home, led the way to *escalier* C. Milan's apartment was on the second floor. So this, thought Natasha, was the home he guarded so jealously. As a place of mystery it was somewhat disappointing. Neither smart nor especially large, it was, nevertheless, of a decent size and comfortably furnished. In the living room, where glass doors gave out onto a balcony, one wall was covered with framed photographs: shadowy black-and-white views of streets and squares, flights of stone steps, jumbled rooftops. No people. Natasha stood surveying them.

'Prague,' said Milan behind her.

'All of them?'

She turned and saw him nod. He had brought things from the kitchen. 'Brandy?' he said. 'It's the only drink I've got.'

She took the glass and, when he offered it, the bottle too and poured herself a finger's width.

Milan had taken her place before the photographs, his back towards her. Damp from the rain, the bleached hair curled and tangled at the nape of his neck. Natasha, reaching up, spread her fingers gently through it, cradling the curve of his skull in her palm. Then, hesitating only a moment, she moved her hand round to touch his cheek. A second later she felt the smart of fingers clamped on her wrist and found Milan facing her. She twisted free and stepped back, breathing quickly. 'Don't tell me,' she said, after a moment's silence. 'Last night was a horrible mistake.'

'Certainly not horrible.'

'But a mistake, nevertheless?'

Milan dropped his gaze. He held a glass too. Turning it once, he set it aside on the table, and looked back at her. 'I can't let anything more happen between us, Natasha. It was only a mistake in so far as I didn't want to hurt you.'

'How very thoughtful.' She felt her grip on her drink

tighten. She glanced down at it. When she spoke again her voice was studiedly level: 'But I'm afraid it won't wash, Milan. You can't pretend you feel nothing for me. I don't think even you act that well.'

It was the boldest test she could have ventured. Yet, though she saw the pale eyes widen a little, the rest of Milan's face held its blank control. 'You have a brave line in bluster,' he said at last. 'But you presume a great deal, Natasha. You know nothing about me.'

'You've said this before, remember? And I said I wasn't interested in a tale of your misdeeds. Well, I take that back. Enlighten me, if you think it will make so much difference.'

She heard rain beating against glass as the wind outside changed direction. Milan crossed to an armchair and sat. Natasha, still standing, put down her drink. She clasped her hands behind her back, where he couldn't see them. And waited.

'In my twenties,' Milan began at last, 'I fell in love. It wasn't . . . a good experience. And from what has happened since, I have learnt not to attempt a repetition.' He paused, not looking at her. 'In the years since,' he said, 'however much I have tried – or thought I was trying – I have succeeded in nothing but using people. It's done me no more good than it's done them. So now I choose to forgo what brief pleasure there might be in order to avoid the pain.'

'Until last night,' said Natasha. 'Which was, as you

have already pointed out, a mistake.' She saw a flinch, immediately checked. She said, 'What happened to you that was so terrible?'

'The person I loved betrayed me. And someone else, who loved me – I betrayed her.' Milan smiled wanly. 'A neat little triangle. And a just punishment, you might say. Except that the innocent party suffered more than I did.'

'A pattern you seem to want to repeat,' said Natasha caustically. 'So, let me get this straight. Because you messed up once, you're going to stick yourself in solitary for the rest of your life? Forgive me if I'm not impressed. What would you call it – bravery? Self-flagellation? Don't you realize that each blow you aim at yourself strikes me too?'

Milan sat perfectly still. He didn't answer.

'It's not even,' Natasha said, 'as if this self-denial seems to work. You may have kicked the drugs, but I wouldn't say you're exactly sorted now, would you? You can't even bring yourself to go on stage. What happens when you can't get through class any more, either? What if the money runs out and the company folds – again? What then? How will you fill your days? How long will Victor stick around for you?'

'I don't look that far ahead.'

'Maybe you should.'

Milan looked sceptical. 'You're offering to be nurse-maid to an old man, are you? It's really very touching. Perhaps you should apply again in a few years.'

'Damn you!'

'I won't be bullied, Natasha.'

'And I won't be fobbed off like some dumb child!'

There was a charged pause. Then Natasha said, more gently, 'Milan. I'm not going to throw hysterics and say that I can't live without you because if I have to, I will. But I won't let you tell me that last night meant nothing, either. It's equally stupid.' His head had dropped. Now he raised it again and Natasha thought she saw the ghost of a smile. She said, 'Let me in, will you? Just for a while, knowing something of your history, knowing how – and how quickly – you predict it will end. I'll be dipping a toe in the water, at my own risk. If either of us wants out, they only have to say.'

'I won't let you make yourself that vulnerable.'

'Stop telling me what you'll allow me to do! If you're worried about hurting me, it's too late. If you hurt me down the line it's only as much as you'll do by keeping me away. Let me take my own risks.'

She was standing beside him. Now she sat, carefully, on the chair arm. 'I'm not asking for your soul, Milan.' But part of her knew that she was; and seeing, with shock, the look he gave her then – a look darkened with fear not for her, after all, but for himself – Natasha could almost have sworn that she had it.

Chapter Ten **London, 1970**

'Whooa! Run that one by me again.'

'She – has – left – him,' Dandy enunciated clearly, pushing aside a curtain of greying dance tights strung across the middle of the bedsit. 'Francesca O'Connor has left Colm for Milan. Hardly what you'd call surprising really. There *is* an awful lot to choose between them and none of it in Colm's favour, I'd say.'

Laura emerged through the washing behind him, bearing two plates of her finest spaghetti bolognese. When the line was up, the bed was the best place to eat; she'd already put out the cutlery on the eiderdown. Now, as she sat, gave Dandy one plate, and drew the other onto her knee, she gave his news uneasy consideration. The atmosphere in class that morning had certainly been fraught: Milan had seemed as unconcerned and shut off from the world around him as ever, but Francesca had looked, for once, pale and pinched. Colm, significantly, had been absent. Still, it didn't add up. She said, 'Why, then, doesn't Francesca seem a bit more blissful? Is she regretting it already?'

'Poor Francesca.' Dandy smiled wickedly, twirling his fork. 'Milan was furious when she told him, and he broke off their little liaison on the spot. And now Francesca is running round after Colm in desperate contrition. Needless to say, he doesn't want to know.'

As Laura prodded her food, a mess of different emotions did their own tangled-spaghetti impression somewhere uncomfortably near her stomach. She was no friend of Francesca, but half of her boiled with indignation that Milan could so casually pick up a woman and drop her again, shattering a marriage in the process. The other half seemed, inexplicably, to be pleased the affair had ended. *That* she put down to lingering resentment over the bed-bugs episode, and berated herself for nursing such a petty grudge. 'What beats me, though,' she said now, 'is how Milan has the gall not only to show his face in class, but to look so damned unruffled while he's doing it.'

Dandy shrugged. 'Why should he take notice of what anyone else thinks? He never has before. He doesn't notice, for instance, that at least a dozen women are queuing up to be next in his bed.'

Laura remarked that she thought he noticed it very well. 'He knows that for some poor, misguided types, arrogance is a turn-on.'

'Let me guess. You still don't like him much.'

'Do *you*? Anyhow, is it compulsory?'

'Certainly not, though you've got to work with him. And you're swimming against the feminine tide.'

'So, with plenty to keep him busy, he won't notice a lone dissenter, will he?'

Dandy chewed contemplatively. Then he said, 'I'd be surprised if Milan touches any of them with a barge pole. Once bitten and all that. Declarations of undying love are not what he's after. I think he wants something far less complicated.'

'Well, he made breaking up a marriage look remarkably simple.'

'Laura Douglas, you Victorian matron!' Dandy crowed with delighted laughter. 'Francesca was hardly unwilling – she made the first move, I'm told. And, anyway, you might as well say she was wading into someone else's marriage too, give or take a bit of paper. Milan is not an unattached man.'

Laura was sensible of a certain contraction – of shock. 'Oh?' she said carefully.

'You have to promise not to tell anyone. I did but – feel honoured – I've decided you don't count.'

'I don't,' said Laura. 'Feel honoured, I mean. Well?'

'Have you seen Milan's tattoo? Rather crude black lettering, round about here?' Dandy waved a fork at the top of his left arm. 'Of course you have. It spells "Anežka" if you haven't worked it out, and she, dear heart, is Milan Novák's sweet patootie. Been together since they were teenagers, apparently. She's still over in Czechoslovakia.'

'Close relationship.'

'Don't sneer. You're getting very cynical and I'm not sure it's entirely becoming. Anyway,' Dandy leant forward, as if in danger of being overheard, 'the plan is to get her out. They'll never let her go legally. She was heavily involved in all that stuff two years ago before the Russians rolled in. So Milan's pretending he's not still in touch because the Czech authorities are keeping close tabs on him apparently. And meanwhile he's working his butt off to lay glamorously secret plans for her escape. That's why it's so important we don't blab.'

'How do you know all this?'

Laura listened to Dandy's proud explanation with a sinking heart. She had expected the source to be shaky at the very least, had half expected the whole story to be some concoction brewed up in the boys' dressing room by over-imaginative brains subjected to one too many Sean Connery movies. But the reality was different: the person who'd told Dandy was Nadine. 'We're quite the firm coffee-shop pals, now, m'dear,' said Dandy in answer to the arch look Laura managed to give. 'If I'm going to be as big as I fully intend, it makes complete political sense. *She* may be old news but she has contacts squeezing out of her ears. Besides, I'm getting quite fond of the old cow.'

Nadine, Dandy explained, had friends in diplomatic circles and had helped in the arrangements for Milan's defection – this was the connection that had brought him to the EBT. 'I gathered,' Dandy added, 'that the Anežka story came out as explanation for his refusal of Nadine's advances. So I was right about *that* all along.'

'But he didn't refuse Francesca.'

'Quite. For Nadine it was insult to injury, as they say. You can imagine how delighted she is with them both.'

'So. He probably just cooked up the whole story as an excuse for Nadine.'

'Possibly.' Dandy frowned, considering. 'Somehow, though, I don't think so. Getting a tattoo is just a little beyond the call of duty.'

Typical Dandy, thought Laura. Carried away with his own imagination. Anežka could easily be an old girlfriend, firmly consigned to the past. She put her plate on the floor, the pasta still only half finished. If it were true, after all, Milan wouldn't have messed with Francesca, would he? An echo of Daphne's voice sounded then in Laura's head: 'This is nineteen *seventy*.' She supposed she might, after all, have a childish view of love.

LAURA'S INTEREST IN MILAN'S emotional life was, of course, purely professional: she didn't even like the man but she was performing with him three times a week and they were about to create a new ballet together. The fact that professional interest didn't altogether explain the clutches of virulent anger that were troubling her, mingled at times with a vague sort of anguish, was unsettling – and was something she left largely unexamined. She was over-tired, she knew, not sleeping well, working extremely hard and, to cap it all, suffering from increasing pains in her weak ankle. But she would get through: it was just a question, she thought automatically, of discipline.

And discipline that would be required in increasing amounts with intensive rehearsals added to the routine of classes and performances. The next morning, with a bag in one hand, a coffee and a fag in the other and much apprehension in her heart, Laura pushed through the door into the upper studio, her ankle and several other parts of her already aching from a two-hour class.

The lights weren't on. Outside, rain was sheeting down from a grey and grit-stained November sky. Dandy and the notator, who was to write down each move as they set it, hadn't yet arrived. But Milan was there, in a tatty black hooded tracksuit, a towel slung around his neck, leaning against the closed and covered grand piano in the far corner. When he looked up, Laura mumbled a hello, hurrying to cross the room and dump her bag by the chairs.

She eyed him in the mirror over the rim of her coffee cup. She wanted to know whether what Dandy had told her last night was true – as if she might be able to tell, somehow, now that she knew what she was looking for. Was Milan really loyal, whatever his need for temporary comforts, to a long-time love? He didn't appear to be pining, but then, as Dandy had told it, subterfuge was a vital part of the plan for reunion – and must not life behind the Iron Curtain teach you that your true feelings were best kept out of your window display?

Coming out of a nose-to-knees warm-up stretch, Milan caught Laura watching him. Swiftly, she looked away, finished the last of the coffee, slung the polystyrene cup in the bin and busied herself with putting on the lights. The next moment Dandy appeared, with the notator and an enormous tape machine in tow. Laura was relieved.

But the feeling did not last long. Dandy, with hardly a word of preliminary chat, began to expound the theme he'd chosen for the *pas de deux*. It was not to Laura's liking. 'Love,' he said, plugging in the tape machine. 'In all its forms, good and bad, shown through the paradigm of a single relationship. We'll see it develop from first awakenings, through passion, to final, violent destruction.'

Laura, face averted, grimaced feelingly. Anything, please, anything but that.

Then Dandy played them the music: popular songs, of dramatically different styles, providing some chronological as well as emotional progression, from the gentle courtesy of the Ink Spots, through Billie Holiday and Elvis to Janis Joplin and Jimi Hendrix. 'Getting permission to use all this stuff is going to be hellish,' he said, clicking buttons on and off with his long fingers, 'but I've got Heather working on it, cursing me even as we speak.' Finding the place he wanted on the tape, he turned. 'As you may have guessed, you can forget tutus and the classical convention-alities. There'll be no bravura smiles in this number.' And, with that, they set to work.

For someone in the throes of creation, Dandy cut an unlikely figure. He sat slumped in an uncomfortable plastic chair, swathed in a mound of jumpers and at least two scarves, one hand working his cigarette in and out of his mouth, and the other supporting that arm, the elbow cupped in the free hand. His bony nose was tilted upwards, and he studied them down it inscrutably through long lashes. Occasionally he got up to show them what he wanted, clomping around in his outdoor shoes.

'Right. Go over there and then head down here,' he said now, pointing to the back corner and then the opposite front one with his cigarette. 'I want something fast and angular. Nasty.'

The vagueness took some getting used to. Put off by Alex's sterile habit of creating everything in minute detail in advance, Dandy instead had left all but the broadest decisions unmade so that the piece could grow, as he saw it, organically, so that he could look at the bodies before him and see more possibilities than the mind could conjure in isolation. Improvising, for the dancers, meant taking big risks, and it was difficult at times to hold on to dignity. Laura dreaded Milan's scorn, but was surprised to find in him a new reticence. He simply worked alongside and with her, with an intensity of concentration and commit-

ment to Dandy's ideas that she found surprising. It came
to her, after a while, that these men liked each other.
They were an unlikely, but effective, combination.

At the end of the session, finding themselves the last
two left in the studio, Dandy turned to Laura with a grin.
'There, Hunca-Munca,' he said, twitching a stray frond of
hair back from her face, 'that wasn't so bad after all, was
it?'

It wasn't so bad. Rather the reverse: Laura came away
from the rehearsal fairly buzzing with excitement. In the
world of choreography, this was *haute couture*; the movements were moulded so exactly to her shape, to her
strengths, her preferences, and yet it was the most challenging work she had attempted, too. Unlike Alex, Dandy
required them to think and trusted them enough to know
that much would come of it, from their mistakes as well
as their successes. As the rehearsals progressed, he watched
them with increasing satisfaction.

'That!' said Dandy, pointing with his cigarette. 'That
thing you did then – brilliant! Do it again.'

'What was it?'

'Your leg came up here; Milan, you turned her round.'

They tried. It didn't work: they overbalanced and to
stop Laura hitting the floor, face first, Milan had to snatch
swiftly at her waist. He hugged her to him, her legs and
arms dangling free, and Laura found that they were both
shaking with helpless laughter. Milan staggered and she

blurted out, still laughing, 'P-put – me – down!' Bouncing her first a little in his arms, he dropped her neatly to the floor.

Dandy watched with amusement, both palms flat to the top of his head. 'You won't believe this,' he began, 'but there was something in that little disaster I think we could use . . .'

Once a substantial part of the middle of the piece was complete, Dandy then bowed to sequential logic and went back to the beginning. The next rehearsal was devoted to the earliest section, in which the lovers-to-be progressed from cold formality to childlike shyness, and thence to tender, trembling first gestures of desire. Laura was delighted: Dandy was covering such a wide dramatic range, from lyrical innocence to stark, violent fury, that it was an unprecedented chance to show audience and management just how much, as an actress, she could do.

'Okay, that's coming,' Dandy said when they had completed, a little uncertainly, a newly set phrase, 'but I want you to try the *bourrée* round the other way. *Yes*. And what we're building to here is a kiss. It's the turning point, the cataclysmic moment – neither of you is going to be the same again, okay? You're both young innocents, you've never even imagined before what a kiss can be. Take the whole of that phrase for it.'

They danced the section flat-out for the first time. It had a rapturous, undulating grace of a kind quite new to

Laura – a fresh sensuality expressed in movement deceptively simple, requiring inch-perfect control, steely strength and an almost telepathic knowledge of your partner. It was working magnificently. And when Laura turned and was gathered into Milan for the kiss, she was so buried in her character that it was the most natural thing in the world. She swam up through the movement towards him, his head bent and the next instant his lips had sought, and found, her own.

'That's great – just right,' came Dandy's voice, from what seemed like miles away, as if Laura had drifted out on the tide without knowing it and he were still on the shore. 'That moment of revelation, Laura – quite still – was perfect, spellbinding. I couldn't breathe watching you, darling. Now, I think the move behind her was right, Milan. But I want you facing the front too – see, like this.'

Laura, her brain numbed and reeling, looked at Milan in the mirror. His hands, as he listened to Dandy, were still at her waist, where they had come to rest after the embrace. She could feel the warmth of his palms, the small pressure of each fingertip on her lean little body. A thought struggled up through the fog to the surface of her mind, absurd in its raw simplicity: it was that she had never been kissed that way before. Milan's mouth – the mouth she knew so well curled in sardonic amusement or brutally flat in its lack of expression – had become, suddenly, shockingly, a blind sensation against her skin, its light touch, driftingly tender at first, hesitant as the story demanded, had deepened quickly, insistently, in gathering desire. Also, of course, as the story demanded.

What the story did not demand, however, was the ache Laura had felt suddenly dragging at her core, as if the kiss had reached down inside and wrenched at something buried deep. The feeling had not lessened as Milan pulled away. Laura was watching Dandy speak and gesture now without understanding a word he said. But it was not, of course, she thought steadily, that she felt anything for Milan. It was simply that no one had ever kissed her that way. Right?

Wrong. Somehow even the inexperienced soul can make a distinction.

Dandy had turned to spool back the tape, hunched intently over the machine. The notator was bent to her scribbling pencil. But Laura sensed one pair of eyes on her – she could feel the look as if it had the same skin-heat as a touch. But she couldn't meet it. He'd kissed her as if he meant it and now he was probably laughing, seeing she couldn't handle it. The casual, calculated ease of it! He was as technically accomplished in this as in his dancing. And Laura's green passions had risen to the illusion like a silver fish swimming to the bait. She could see the hook, and she could not help herself.

As Dandy pressed the button and the music filled the studio once more Laura, with effort, recovered her equilibrium, and found herself moving eagerly into Milan's arms as they tried the sequence again. Part of her watched herself in dismay.

BUT THE TIME FOR PRETENCE and denial, Laura realized, was finally and irretrievably over.

That night, standing in the wings, hidden behind her disguise of Firebird costume and make-up, she watched Milan before his adoring public with new and painful vision. The blazing strength and speed, achieved with little appearance of effort and none whatsoever of strain, transfixed her, along with an auditorium of others. The fine proportions, muscular shoulders, contours of back and torso and arms, the thoughtless grace in the simplest turn of the head set trembling a basic, animal desire that Laura no doubt shared, in some measure at least, with half the audience too.

Had she admired only the body, though, she might with happy honesty have called her instinct lust. But she could not pretend that was the sum of it: what she felt for Milan was altogether more dangerous. And thus to dance the role of the Firebird tonight, knowing at last what she knew, was for Laura a peculiar exquisite pain. The desire she had acted out so often she recognized now as her own desire: the fantasy had engulfed her and followed her into what was laughingly called real life, and her only release, her only expression of the power of all she felt, was to be found on stage. She shed a snakeskin that night before a crowd of strangers; she dug her nails deep into the crusted outer layer of herself and ripped and ripped, stripping down to the naked seeping mess beneath. The world had shrunk to a pool of blazing light on a melting floor. Drenched, she tore through the air as never before, twisted in Milan's arms, sprang at him, clung to him hungrily. She could have overbalanced him several times, she must have bruised him countless more, but the arms remained steady about her, battling when necessary, bearing her up with perfect control.

Laura came to only when the performance was over and she stood before the curtain, Milan beside her, as the packed theatre went wild. He turned to her in gallant acknowledgement and the smile, as ever, was for the crowd. But above it the pale flat-stone eyes were lit strangely. Before them Laura felt shattered and hopelessly exposed: she had no energy left to dissemble and knew that if Milan had not already seen through her performance tonight, he could read everything now in her face. He would think her another Francesca, foolish and ripe for the picking. Her own public smile plastered over the turbulence, Laura was livid with herself for making it so easy for him; and livid with Milan for seeing it.

Once the curtain calls were over, she was first off the stage, hurtling headlong through the wings, down the stairs and to her dressing room, dodging obstacles inexplicably blurred. In the shower she scraped at herself with virulence, desperate to wash away her stupid, unkempt feelings. It was no use, but the blast of water served to calm her. Afterwards she dressed quickly and sat in front of the mirror to remove the last layer of make-up still silting her face.

She was half-way through the task when, with no preliminaries, the door opened. It was Milan, hair damp and ruffled from his shower, the stub of a cigarette wedged between his lips, his Prince's splendid marriage costume changed for an old sweatshirt and threadbare jeans. He leant back on the door to shut it and then shifted to the side, propping himself against the radiator. Laura waited for him to speak, neither turning round nor pausing in what she was doing. But he said nothing, simply watching her in the mirror, calmly, as if his presence had been required.

It seemed to Laura inevitable. She wished she could tell him to go away but she couldn't trust herself to say a single word. Her heart was beating wildly against her ribs – it seemed impossible that he couldn't hear the thudding. She felt almost afraid of him or, perhaps, it was what he made her feel that she feared – and that he could use her as he had used Francesca and never know, and it would break her.

Softly, Milan pushed himself off the wall. There was a stool beside Laura, a scarred old thing. He slung it nearer and sat, silent still, his eyes still bent on her reflection.

Laura watched in the mirror, too, her slight fingers working quickly and surely with the cotton wool, cream and tissues. More desperately as the minutes passed, she willed him to speak. He didn't. He simply watched. And, though it cost her great effort, Laura took pains not to hurry. Make-up removed, she tidied her belongings on the tabletop, then brushed out her brown hair, loose against her shoulders. In the glass the ring of bright bulbs reflected oddly in her eyes, the skin glistened taut across the small bones of her face. She could hardly bear to look at herself – but still less at that other face, more dimly shown in shadow.

Laura got up, reached for her bag, ready to go. Turning, she met Milan's steady, disarming gaze unreflected for the first time.

Then he spoke. 'I'm coming with you,' he said, and got up from the stool.

There had been no challenge in the look or words, no attempt at seduction, just a simple statement of fact. Confused, Laura followed him out into the corridor. There he stopped, nodded, as if to himself, then held up a finger to indicate that Laura wait and turned from her, sloping unhurriedly away.

A moment later he was back, his battered jacket slung over his shoulder like a towel. There was an equally battered small leather suitcase in his hand.

Laura looked at it, struggling to think. 'Going somewhere?' she asked.

Milan's expression didn't change, but his eyes seemed to brighten. 'Yes,' he said mildly, 'your place.'

Not what she'd meant, but Laura said nothing.

It wasn't until they had left the theatre and were walking down towards Leicester Square that Milan added, 'My landlady threw me out this morning.'

At that Laura stopped abruptly, and two people behind barely missed cannoning into her.

STILL FURIOUS, LAURA SWEPT A tangle of papers and clothes off her sofa, making room for Milan to sleep there. To be so used, so presumptuously counted on . . . and then to be *told* what was happening was to be insulted twice over. Milan had read her feelings, decided to make use of them, but only because it would save him paying for a night at a hotel. And the worst of it was that Laura *still* hadn't been able to bring herself to tell him to get lost. Instead, she had barely spoken on the way home and she was now white and tight-lipped with rage – and clinging to her anger as the last chance to save herself from worse humiliation.

'It should be okay,' she said curtly, nodding towards the ancient broken-down sofa. 'I'll find you some blankets.' And she pushed past, hardly looking at him, ripping the washing from the line as she went and slinging it in the corner.

Returning with the bedclothes, she asked if he was hungry. Milan shrugged mildly, and she took that as a no. She was ravenous, but was damned if she was going to press him to take her food. She announced that she was going to bed. He nodded and turned his back to arrange his bedding.

Now Laura hesitated. It was mad: Milan had walked past her a thousand times in the wings when she'd been naked, in the middle of a quick change; he'd gripped every intimate curve and angle of her body in the name of work. But something stopped her from changing for bed in front of him. She bundled up an old T-shirt and pyjama trousers and took them instead to the bolted privacy of the bathroom.

Some minutes later, safely installed in bed, Laura pulled the eiderdown to her chin and reached for the lamp switch beside her, shooting a glance across the room. Milan had stripped off to his jeans and covered himself with a blanket. He was, it seemed, perfectly happy to go to sleep without having laid a finger on her, hardly having looked at her. Simmering anger, despite itself, acquired a scum of frustration. What the hell was he doing? She flicked the switch.

Street-lamp light seeped in through the thin curtains. It was cold. Laura lay stiffened and alert, breathing shallowly. After a while she heard Milan shift – he was uncomfortable, inevitably, stretched out upon lumps of horse-hair and broken springs. She heard him shift again, and then get up. Her stomach knotted in anticipation. But when she stole a glance she saw he had dragged his blanket onto the floor and settled there. She could see that he had folded his hands behind his head and, from the glisten that caught dimly in the half-light, she knew his eyes were open, trained on the ceiling.

Laura's anger not only required that she find sleep quickly, as if utterly untroubled, but also efficiently prevented it. Thoughts of all she could and should have said whipped about, stinging and unchecked, in her head. At last, however, the anger subsided and, lulled finally into quieter contemplation, Laura recognized the arrival of quite another feeling. Disappointment.

She wondered now, not daring to look, what *he* was thinking, staring so stoically at the ceiling? Listening attentively, she caught the sound of deepened breathing. He was staring at the ceiling no longer. He was asleep.

LAURA HALF WOKE; SHIFTED. She heard an unfamiliar noise, blearily sensed movement, and her eyes snapped open.

On its side, an image of her little bedsit. The curtains were drawn back: a thin damp light, hardly worthy of the time of day, made it through the window with effort. And it illuminated, in the centre of the room, a crouched figure, head bent, tousled hair hanging down over the brow. He seemed to be arranging something on the floor; then he straightened and picked his way across to where a small pan was heating on the only ring of the Baby Belling that still worked.

'I'm making coffee. Do you want some?' Milan knew

she was awake without looking; Laura wished he would look at her now. But his tone, at least, was gentle.

'Lovely. Thanks.' She sat up in bed, pulling the eiderdown under her arms, and leant back against the wall. The anger of the night before had drifted away into hazy memory; she simply watched Milan with interest now, unable to settle to this view of him – of all people – in her home.

Two plates were laid out on the floor. Two knives, two forks on the hairless green carpet. And between them platters of food: cuts of roast ham, thin slices of some waxy, dry cheese; honey; butter; a big loaf of rough bread, brown crust showing through a thick coating of flour. Sudden anxiety gripped her. 'Was this stuff in the fridge? It isn't mine.' The fridge was shared, stealing food a serious – though not ordinarily tempting – offence.

Milan did look at her then and, to Laura's amazement, his face broke into a warm, reassuring smile. 'I got them,' he said. He poured coffee from the pan into a mug and pushed it towards her. 'Here.' She would have to get up to reach it.

So. He had crept out while she slept and bought breakfast and prepared it, waiting for her to wake. She saw a paperback propped open beside him on the floor. How long had he been up?

Straightening her T-shirt and trousers Laura clambered out from under the eiderdown and reached for a jumper.

It was cold. She found her electric heater and plugged it in: the meter would need feeding soon.

'Don't drink yet.' She had the coffee mug half-way to her lips. Milan said, 'It's *turecká*, Turkish coffee. You have to wait for it to settle or you'll get a mouthful of grit.'

Laura put down the mug and stretched herself on the floor opposite Milan, the food between them. Her hunger of the night before resurfaced quickly at the fresh smell of it as Milan broke the bread and handed her a piece, prepared another with butter and cheese and meat and gave that to her too, watched her as at last she sipped her coffee, waiting for approval. The smile had not returned, but there was a constant light of pleasure in his eyes, and his face bore an expression more open, more relaxed than she could remember having seen. Laura drank in the sight as if it were as liquid as the coffee: she seemed to be looking at a changed man.

Along with last night's hunger had reawakened the muscles, ligaments, tendons and joints Laura had strained on stage last night to the limit of their endurance. Her old foe, the weak left ankle, was stiff and sore. Dragging her eyes reluctantly from Milan she looked at it, pointing and flexing the red, damaged toes. Milan looked too and, swallowing the piece of bread he was eating, he stretched out his hand, pushing his thumb into the arch, encasing the foot in his wide, careful grip, rubbing in a circular motion at the muscle. Then he cleared the plates and mugs aside, and drew Laura's foot onto his lap.

Leaning back on her hands Laura watched him slide the cotton cloth up and over her knee, and begin to massage her calf. His touch was deft, sure, the fingers strong; her muscles, knotted and aching, tried to flinch beneath it and, finding they could not, instead melted. From time to time Milan glanced from his work to her face, his light gaze sure, appraising.

And as the moments dropped away the working touch mutated, so gradually Laura almost doubted what she felt until she was certain at last that the push to loosen muscle had drifted into something else. Then, stretching out his arm towards her, Milan buried his fingers deep in the soft hair at the base of her neck and drew her to him. The fair eyes, so close now, showed neither pride, nor calculation – only a peculiar look of certainty. The next moment he was kissing her.

I am lost, Laura thought. This is the path to ruin and I know it and follow willingly. And then she could hardly think any more.

LAURA WOKE FOR THE SECOND time that Sunday morning to the same rainsoaked light in the same grey room and felt herself reborn to a new reality in which joy and fear were mingled inextricably.

She could feel Milan's breath, even and slow in sleep, on her shoulder; his arm lay heavy across her stomach. She was where she had needed and longed to be. And it terrified her.

That it had been, for him, a casual passing pleasure could not have been told from his touch. But that he felt the same – the paltry same – as he had with Francesca, Laura knew as certainly as she knew her own feelings. What she had now to discover was how to live with what little he had given her, in the knowledge that he might give nothing more – and in the knowledge, too, that even if he did, it could never be as much as she needed.

Gently, gently, Laura lifted his arm and shifted herself from beneath it. He stirred and turned, but did not wake. She dressed swiftly, put on her coat and took some money. She had no clear idea of where she might go; she knew only that when he woke, he would leave, and she did not want to be there to see it. Should she write a note, she wondered. No – there was nothing in honesty that she could say. At the door, she cast one last glance across to the sleeping form, then turned the handle silently and left.

Outside it was still raining, the water sliding in greasy sheets down shopfronts and bus shelters, across pavement, gutter and tarmac road. Laura felt painfully alert: the smells of fumes and passers-by and garbage bins tingled in her nostrils. Her wanderings were aimless. When she saw a bus pulling up to the kerb she took it, not knowing where it was heading. It wove into town, and deposited her at last in Trafalgar Square. And so, climbing the grand grey steps, she let the maw of the National Gallery swallow her up, and moved into its calm, quiet chambers full of dead faces, hoping to lose herself among them.

It didn't work. And when she got home, just as she had expected, Milan was gone.

WITH NO APARTMENT OF HIS own to return to, where Milan went that night remained a mystery. Laura saw him the next morning in class as usual and, as usual, he seemed locked in his own impenetrable thought-world, hardly looking to right or left throughout the entire two hours.

A rehearsal with Dandy was scheduled afterwards, on the other side of a coffee-and-fag break. Laura was dreading it. Being ignored today in class was one thing; being ignored by someone two inches away with his arms wrapped around you quite another. When those same arms had last held you, naked, in your own bed. She wished, trembling a little as she leant against the coffee machine, that she could block out the memory.

When at last Laura pushed apprehensively into the rehearsal studio, Dandy was there before her, and the notator – and Milan. 'Sorry, am I late?' she said, not looking at him. And then, as Dandy said no, she did look, and Milan flashed her a vivid, lit-up smile. She wanted to take the nearest chair and sit in it to catch her breath. Instead she choked on her cigarette smoke, putting down her belongings, and Milan, as he came up to pat her on the back, was laughing softly.

She knew, then, that the rehearsal would go well.

Dandy seemed pleased at their progress, his veiled smile conveying an unspoken steady confidence that spurred them on to push harder at the limits of what they thought possible, to take delicious risks, voice even the craziest ideas.

The end of the session brought satisfied exhaustion. Dandy and the notator left and Laura was on her way after them when she heard Milan speak her name. She stopped, watching as the door swung back and forth on its hinges before her. When she turned her head Milan had already crossed the studio and now, with one hand on the towel and bag at his shoulder, he dipped the other gently beneath her chin, lifting it to meet his lips. Carried belongings slithered to the ground, and they stood there for some time.

It was hard, almost, to remember there were other things to do, other rehearsals to go to. Racing up the stairs to the locker room, with an immoderate cheeriness in her heart that had silenced the voices of realism, Laura half caught sight of something as she rounded a landing corner. She backtracked a few steps to the swing door leading off into the passageway, and glanced again through the port-hole window.

This was the same passageway in whose wall the gallery window was set, giving a view down into the studio Laura had just left. To one side of the window, turned away from it, her back to the wall, stood a small woman of unusually upright bearing. Her eyes were lightly shut, and one hand pressed the base of her throat as if she were struggling to swallow.

The sight of her flushed out Laura's optimism. After a hair's breadth pause she started up the stairs again but, reaching the next landing, halted once more and turned, both hands on the metal banister. Nadine, somehow, had seen her and had emerged from the passageway door. They faced each other now across the narrow channel of empty air at the stairwell's centre, Laura above, Nadine below. Laura's eyes flicked down to where, through the iron grille, she could see Nadine's injured foot. It was still strapped but its progress was no longer of moment. Since *Firebird*'s success Nadine's contract had been summarily terminated.

'Trying to avoid me, my dear?' The voice echoed coldly.

Laura said, 'I shouldn't need to try. You have no business being in the building – let alone watching a rehearsal.' And the rehearsal was not all, Laura knew, that Nadine had seen.

'I am still Max's wife.'

Irrelevant – but instinct advised Laura not to respond.

Nadine went on, 'You, my dear, have now *everything* that should have been mine. If you planned it, it was subtly done. If not, you have been far too lucky.' She surveyed Laura thoughtfully. 'But, then, luck doesn't last.'

'Meaning what, exactly?'

'Meaning you won't keep hold of it all for long.' And

a brief, wintry smile appeared as Nadine added, 'You must, my dear, know that.'

It was, apparently, all she had wanted to say. She began then to descend the stairs at a stately pace and Laura, at a pace correspondingly unstately, crashed on up to the locker room attempting valiantly to laugh. The woman had an unfortunate taste for melodrama. What had that little pronouncement been? A threat? An indication of some inside knowledge? Max was very pleased with her, Laura knew; she didn't fear a sudden cooling of management support. So was it, rather, to do with what else Nadine must have seen, to do with Milan? Nadine could speculate about Milan's intentions, of course, but could know no more than Laura herself – unless Milan had confided in her. Impossible. Another option, then. Nadine knew the story of Anežka. Did she still believe it, even after what had happened with Francesca? And Laura wondered afresh whether the romantic story Dandy had told her could possibly be true.

GIVEN HER CONVICTION THAT Milan felt little for her, it was hardly necessary to find out. Laura wondered afterwards whether the fact that she still felt driven to try meant that a part of her subconsciously entertained some wild and foolish hope. If so, it was a hope swiftly quashed.

A couple of nights later, at a newly pleasurable hour of the very early morning, Laura lay awake. Beside her, between eloquently rumpled sheets, a body was stretched out on its stomach, its arms crossed on the pillow, its dark head upon them turned towards her. By the soft glow from the street Laura could see that the eyes rested on her with a warm, lucent gaze. And beneath the cheek, a patch of skin on the upper arm was marked with blurred and thickened blue-black lettering, like a brand.

Milan caught the direction of her attention and rolled onto his side to prop his head on one hand, removing the other arm's clumsy decoration from her sight. 'Your heart on your sleeve,' she said, speaking softly into the still room. 'Don't be coy.' She smiled, but it was a sign only that she was steadying herself very carefully. Then she said, watching him, 'I know about Anežka.'

The dark-ringed eyes snapped wider. 'What do you know?'

'Dandy has struck up a friendship with Nadine. Feel fortunate he only told me. Usually he's as leaky as a sieve. And don't worry. I won't tell.'

'Nadine!'

'Hell, as we all know, hath no fury . . .'

Milan had flopped onto his back, both hands raised to screen his face. The plain anguish told Laura everything she had wanted – or feared – to know. She was glad to have this moment, unobserved, to collect herself.

She made quick work of it: she had more to say now, having her answer, and she must say it swiftly or risk not saying it at all. For, one thing she had pledged herself: if she were to have a chance of surviving, of reaping as much as she could in this short harvest, knowing her stores would have to last for many barren winters to come, he must never know she felt a whit more than he did. More than that, she had calculated: he must be made to believe the opposite of the truth.

And so now, as Milan groaned gently, his face still hidden by his hands, she said, 'It might, I suppose, have helped if you'd told Francesca too. But, then, perhaps you imagined, with a married woman, that you'd be safe from complications. Well, I can assure you, in *case* you were worrying, that I, by contrast, am refreshingly heartwhole.' She had sat up a little, her shoulders against the cool wall behind her, and she was listening to herself, half appalled, wondering where on earth the bright tone had come from. She said, 'I am not about – or ever likely – to declare my undying love. In fact, you will be relieved to hear, you have found someone who appreciates the short-term, no-strings affair as much as you do. So, while you are waiting for Anežka to arrive, I may just be your ideal uncomplicated pastime.'

The face was still covered, but she had the impression that behind the hands lay acute attention. She imagined – and was glad not to see it – that there lay, also, relief. What she did see, glancing down, was that her fingers had formed nail-dug fists around handfuls of sheet; she released them slowly and looked back to Milan.

The arms at last had lowered. He rolled and leant up on one elbow, his face impassive. After a minute spent studying her, the lips curled in a considered smile. 'What time we have, then,' he said, 'must be wisely used.' And, reaching out his strong and expert fingers, he drew the sheet gently back from her body.

IT FELT LIKE A HIDDEN VICE, an addiction. A relationship, conducted entirely in secret, in which the racking emotions unleashed had, agonizingly, to be concealed even from the object of their inspiration. Laura, affecting insouciance when she had hardly felt so far from it in her life, knew she was doing herself harm, was suffering already, and with no prospect but of suffering more. Still, to give it up seemed fully as impossible as to cease, on a whim, to breathe.

The lack of sleep alone was debilitating enough: all Laura's reserves of energy were called upon to keep working at the same bloodying pace. But as days were filled with class and rehearsals, and evenings filled frequently with performances, it was as often as not well into the night before she and Milan could discard their professional restraint and greet one another as lovers. And Milan, as he had said, seemed as keen as Laura to use whatever time they had to mine this seam of pleasure until it was spent. She marvelled that for one whose heart lay elsewhere he could seem so passionately engaged.

Exhaustion, though, was not Laura's sole physical enemy. The pain in her ankle was now increasing steadily, almost by the day, and discomfort ominously had spread to the longitudinal arch of the foot. In performance, adrenaline had been blocking it out, but now the pain had reached such a pitch that it broke through all barriers, and though Laura tried to make no allowance for it in her movements, whispering aches in her good foot told her that she was not succeeding. The company physio was worried: he bound the ankle in thick tape strapping for class and rehearsal and had taken to subjecting performances to anxious analysis from the wings. Laura, trying to mask fear as well as pain, felt accompanying mysterious soreness in her neck and arms, back, thighs and knees and, convinced that she was falling apart, faced the calamitous spectre of imminent surgery with lonely disbelief.

Not a wince, of course, made it across the footlights. Offers were flooding in from a galaxy of companies wanting to poach not just Milan but Laura too. Max, citing contracts, refused even the briefest guest appearance. Milan's contract was numbered in months only, and while Max had hold of the goose, he wanted to keep the golden eggs for himself. So the EBT circus rolled on, and to the world, Laura and Milan's partnership seemed unshakeable – and exclusively professional.

Milan had taken a flat in Earl's Court but he rarely spent time there and Laura never did. The secret world of their relationship was contained almost wholly by the four brown walls of Laura's tiny, shabby bedsit. Sometimes the room seemed to her as unreal a place as the stage.

Remembering later, it seemed always night there – or always Sunday. Sundays were precious; entire, delicious days spent together, sometimes barely leaving the house, sometimes venturing out to a cold and wind-blown park, nervous in case of off-duty journalists, but walking, nevertheless, wrapped in each other's arms.

Through it all, Laura was glad of one thing: she could be under no illusion that Milan might love her back. That knowledge was small and hard as a stone deep within her. To survive it, she had to deny herself thought of the future or the past. She had searched for an option and found none that was not worse than what she had now: what use was further thought? And whatever Milan's reasons for wanting to be with her, she did not wish to know them. Nor to know how plans were progressing to bring Anežka to the West. The present was all, and when they were together, Milan's need seemed as convincing as her own.

Still, the strain of it made Laura cry, happy and miserable at once. The tears were shed alone; to Milan she was breezy and confident. She had what she wanted, and if it was breaking her she had chosen to be broken. Would the relationship end before she crumbled? She could hardly think straight enough to care.

There was no one, of course, in whom she could confide or seek advice. And she was sunk so deep in enforced loneliness that she might not have realized how desperate her need was, had not an opportunity presented itself. In the dam-burst of relief, she hardly stopped to consider whether she should take it up.

It was the beginning of a late November afternoon: there were just another ten minutes to go before the next rehearsal when Heather put her head round the common-room door. 'Laura? There's someone for you in reception.'

Making her way swiftly downstairs, Laura had not been able to think who it might be. And when she saw the tall, fair-headed man waiting, she felt dismayed as if to put on an act for him, too, would be another burden. But then Richard said, 'Hello, gorgeous,' and squeezed her in such a steady, affectionate embrace that she stayed breathing quietly against him, soaking up his warm, fresh smell, and felt glad that he had come. 'I'm in town to see the lawyer about Father's will, so I thought I'd show my face,' he said, releasing her at last and leaning one solid forearm on the reception desk.

Laura still couldn't think of Richard, somehow, as master of Denham. She asked after Lydia. Richard smiled. 'Oh, bearing up, thanks. I've packed her off to the States to see Bro.' He studied Laura. 'You're looking a bit weary. Performing tonight?'

Laura shook her head.

'Well, then can I take you out to dinner?'

He could, and she told him so.

LAURA ORDERED LEMON SOLE, with leeks and new potatoes, then hardly touched it. Richard grappled energetically with a steak. The restaurant was quietly, unstuffily expensive, the wine list extensive, the quality high. It was an evening Laura would ordinarily have enjoyed. Yet she was unsettled: Richard seemed from another world, which barely existed for her any more, and she realized just how buried she must be in her work, and in Milan.

When he looked up from his plate and found her watching him, Richard gave a wide, cloudless smile. 'You've changed a bit, you know,' he said, planting an elbow on the table and returning what he'd recognized as an assessing gaze. 'I don't know what it is. You look so pale, sort of . . . ethereal. Your eyes are very bright.'

In his simple candour he was more accurate than he knew: Laura felt, somehow, that she had been fading into a wisp these past few weeks and here, sitting opposite, was her anchor, splendid, steadfast Richard. She felt something trickle down the side of her nose and, dabbing with her napkin, knew that she was about to tell him everything. 'I'm in love, Richard,' she said. 'It's someone in the company. I'm so happy and it's killing me.' And, through a quiet flow of tears, with her gaze lowered to the tablecloth, she told him the story, explaining, more than once, that he should not mention any of it to another soul. She tried also, as she thought, to anticipate his criticisms by saying that she knew she shouldn't put up with such an arrangement, but if he were in her place, wouldn't he make the same choice?

Richard, throughout, had kept very quiet. 'I'm sorry to have gone on so,' Laura said at last, suddenly aware that she had been speaking uninterrupted for some time. Confident, though, of comfort, her eyes lifted to his face.

What she saw there gave her a shock so great she drew in a breath. Richard's expression, drained of all its habitual gentleness, was hardened as a mask of solid oak. The sight of it sent through Laura an involuntary shudder.

'You have no idea, do you?' he said softly, shaking his head and looking at her, his brown gaze frighteningly level. 'My God, I hope you don't, or I don't know what I'd think of you.'

Laura stared, wide-eyed, struggling to understand. 'What on earth do you mean?'

'I don't want to hear how – how much you love this guy. That's all.' He had reddened quickly. Now he pulled the napkin off his lap and pressed it, crushed under his large fingers, on the tablecloth. 'That's all.'

'Richard?'

'I'm going,' he said simply, standing up and feeling in a pocket for his wallet. 'You can finish your meal if you want to, but I'm afraid you'll have to do it on your own.'

'What? Richard – what is it? What have I done?' As he threw down some notes Laura reached for his arm, but with stinging speed it was pulled away.

'Don't,' he said doggedly. 'Don't give me that . . . *That*. Any more.'

And, with a final glance that chilled Laura like cold sunshine from a suddenly heatless sun, he strode out of the restaurant.

Milan did not come to Kentish Town that night. In bed alone, Laura curled under the blankets, tensed against batterings of anguish. Dandy and Evie, it seemed, had been right all those months ago; and she knew what she had possessed only now that she had lost it. An old, old part of her felt bereft. She had never been so alone in her life.

TWO WEEKS LATER ON A SUNDAY afternoon, someone rang the buzzer for Laura's bedsit. It had already not been a good day. For once, though Laura and Milan were in the room together, they kept resolutely apart within its small space, moving about each other with unwonted care. Milan was on edge, unwilling to talk, to touch, even, it had seemed at times, to look at Laura. Outwardly, Laura accepted this strange pariah status without a murmur, but inside her head a thousand conjectured explanations presented themselves in anxious succession. Was he angry? Was it something she had done – or not done? Was he tired of her and working up to telling her so? From behind a mask of calm she watched him narrowly as she went about her mundane tasks.

When the buzzer sounded, she was sitting cross-legged on the thin carpet, hammer in hand, and had been beating the ends of a new pair of *pointe* shoes, to soften them into a wearable state for the next day. The noise startled her. She looked across to Milan, who was lying on the mattress with a book discarded face-down on his chest: his eyes were open, alert, trained on the ceiling, but since he did not move, she knelt up beside the window and peered out. At first she could see no one, and then a bearded man in heavy spectacles and a mangy sheepskin coat stepped backwards off the front-door step into view and looked up towards the window.

'Who on earth . . .?' Laura muttered. It was someone, she imagined, for another flat who had rung her buzzer by mistake. Her puzzlement, though, roused Milan: he was up and at her shoulder in an instant, and a second later had left the room and was clattering down the staircase to the front door.

Two minutes later he returned, with the mangy sheepskin in tow. 'Vlasta,' he said to Laura, indicating the man, as if this would mean something to her. 'This is Laura.'

The man called Vlasta nodded energetically. '*Ahoj.*'

He was smiling; automatically Laura smiled back, but she felt distinctly uneasy. Milan had invited this person, or had at least passed on her address, without her knowledge. She noticed there was a silence and, wondering if it was awkward, looked up again.

'So.' Vlasta studied his fingernails. He grinned

momentarily, like a shrug, then dropped his gaze to the floor. Milan regarded him, then shifted his gaze, wordlessly, to Laura.

They seemed to be waiting. Laura's unease deepened. They couldn't, surely, be waiting for her to withdraw? This was a bedsit – there was nowhere else to go, unless she locked herself in the bathroom. She turned her attention, studiedly, to her *pointe* shoes, her thoughts treading carefully through the implications. This man was not British. He had some business with Milan, to be spoken about in private. That he was Czech, and that his business concerned Anežka, was the only explanation Laura's brain could light on. Had he brought news? And had Milan been on edge because he was waiting for it? Laura, her fingers tensed around the hammer's shaft, weighed it carefully, and struck harder.

Vlasta had sat down on the sofa. Milan began to speak to him in what Laura presumed must be his native tongue. Vlasta shook his head, mumbled his reply into his coat collar; Milan pressed him further.

This was too much. Laura's ragged nerves could not stand it. She flung down the hammer, which dinted the skirting board and thumped to the floor. Two pairs of eyes turned to her, one neutral, one black with irritation. 'Are you going to tell me what's going on?'

Above the curling beard, Vlasta's face reddened. 'I'm sorry,' he said quickly. Milan, though, turned away and pulled his coat from the back of the door. 'Okay. We'll go,' he said to Vlasta. He did not look at Laura again.

For a long while after she had heard the front door bang shut, Laura sat perfectly still. There were several little tasks she had it in mind to do, and felt she was about to do all of them – but could not move. Was Anežka on her way? Would she turn up, one day soon, in London? Even – and the thought made Laura feel sick – turn up here unannounced, as Vlasta had? Why not? After what Laura had told him, Milan could have no idea how it would affect her.

Some time later Laura left the house and walked fast, feeling cold, furious and afraid. There was a chattering voice in her head and she was anxious to still it.

When she got back, Milan had returned, alone. She found him slumped low on the sofa, the shoulders of his heavy winter coat hunched up about his ears. His fingers were interlaced over his brow, as if shielding his eyes from some non-existent harsh light, and she couldn't tell which way his gaze was turned.

As she took off her own coat, framing questions silently in her head, he neither moved nor spoke. At last, choosing not the most obvious but the most pressing question, she said, 'Is it me?' She was standing simply before him, her arms hanging by her sides, her brown hair, rough-edged from the wind, lying about her shoulders. She felt exhausted. Slowly, Milan's pale fingers split apart. The eyes behind them, she saw with shock, were thunderous.

Her voice, though, did not fail her when she spoke again. 'The problem – is it me?' she repeated.

'Yes.' Milan blinked slowly, and refocused his gaze straight ahead, as if dismissing her. 'The problem – is you.'

Remembering, as ever, the story she had spun him, Laura held tight to her composure. 'Why did Vlasta come here?'

'Don't ask about what doesn't concern you.'

Didn't concern her? It was almost laughable. 'Is it Anežka?' she said. 'Will . . . is she . . .'

In a spasm of irritation Milan pushed himself out of the chair. The coat swung against his legs as he turned round, raised a hand to his hair, and then turned again. His expression was a strange one of struggle. And anger. 'Yes, she's coming. Okay? *Okay*?'

The words chilled Laura to the marrow. She turned away quickly to hide her face; she did not trust it not to betray her. And she hadn't the courage to ask any more.

TWO NIGHTS LATER, AT SOME still, small hour of the early morning, the phone rang. Laura heard it in her dream, an unrecognizable noise of alarm, and then woke to it, echoing shrilly in the hallway downstairs. Beside her, Milan started awake at the same moment. He hauled himself immediately from the bed, pulled a towel around him and left the room.

Alone in the half-dark, Laura lay desperately still, every part of her straining to listen. The ringing had stopped, but she could not hear Milan's voice. Perhaps he had not reached the phone in time, but then the single bell of the replaced receiver sounded, and she heard his soft bare footfall on the stairs.

The orange glow from outside, filtered through thin curtains, picked out the dark mess of hair and, beneath it, dark hollows for eyes as Milan came back into the room. His expression was unreadable; she watched him dress, quickly and silently. And then, without a word to her, he left. Laura, without a word either, or even a sob, turned her face into the pillow.

Later she watched the darkness drain from the sky, leaving behind it a sickly looking winter's morning. She had not slept again. She was sitting at the window, a blanket drawn tight around her, her knees tucked up beneath her chin. It felt like sitting at a ship's porthole, looking out on a wrecked landscape, and yet the street below was the same as ever, grey, gaudy and littered. Dry and unregarded between her fingers lay a scrap of torn paper, a telephone number scrawled on it in Milan's hurried hand. She had found it on the floor – Vlasta's number, perhaps? Or another secret contact? How long, she wondered, had the date been set for Anežka's escape? How often, when she and Milan were together in this very room, had it been, unspoken, on his mind?

Last night, at least, he had told her a little more about

the plan. Anežka was to be driven across the border to Austria in the boot of a car. She would tell everyone in Prague she was going to visit a relative, then take a train into the countryside and meet the person who was to drive the car – whom she did not, for security, know – at a specified hour of night in the shelter of thick woodland. She could take nothing with her. The boot was to be shared with another person, also unknown to her, and the fit would be so tight that Anežka had been given the dimensions in advance in order to practise a suitable posture. This much Milan knew, and this much of what he knew he had passed on, in the strictest imaginable confidence, to Laura. Listening, she had found the whole scenario one of inconceivable terror; Anežka herself, even more than before, seemed unreal.

She would not, though, remain so for long. Perhaps that phone call had been to say that the plan was in operation – she was on her way. Or perhaps, even, it had been from Anežka herself, ringing from Austria. Was it possible? Laura had an idea she could not wholly erase from her mind, irrational though she knew it to be, that Milan would come back this very morning with Anežka. And yet in a way it was true. He would come back with her firmly beside him in his imagination, knowing in all probability that the simplest of train, bus or plane journeys was now all that lay between them.

By nine o'clock, in spite of fatigue so dragging she felt sick with it, Laura had got herself ready to leave for class.

There had been no tears, no throwing or smashing: she had simply packed her practice clothes, her shoes and towel, and now, with apparent calm, she picked up her keys and opened the bedsit door.

She did not expect to find Milan standing on the other side. He had just reached the door as she swung it open, but still it seemed as if he had been there all the time – or else was some unearthly apparition. She gasped, starting backwards.

He looked terrible. His lips were paler than she thought living flesh could be; his eyes seemed to have sunk deeper into his face, so that he peered out at her from the midst of bleak shadows. But then he had, she told herself, been up most of the night. Maybe she looked the same.

'Go to class,' Milan said quietly now, standing aside to let her pass him to the stairs.

Laura didn't move. She said, 'What's happened?'

He paused, saw she would not come out, and moved past her into the room. 'Go to class,' he said again.

She wanted to shrug and go – she could see it happening in her mind's eye. She managed the first, hesitated, then came into the room and leant back on the door to shut it.

Milan was propped at the window's edge, hugging his arms across his chest. His head lolled against the frame, eyes lowered to the street.

So, thought Laura, willing herself into some semblance

of stepping-stone logic, if Anežka was out, he had to end this little affair. Milan rolled on his shoulder to face her. He seemed to need the wall's support.

'Look, Laura. Will you just . . .' Reluctantly, his eyes dragged from the furniture, the floor to Laura's face. 'Don't worry. Just go to class.'

'No.'

She saw a flash of anger, far off. He said, 'Well, I will.'

As he started forward, Laura caught hold of his sleeve. 'For Christ's sake, Milan! Tell me what's happened! Don't be such a bloody coward! Or is she just going to turn up here, like Vlasta did, so that you can introduce us, huh?'

It made contact so fast, the blow, that Laura did not know what had happened. She found her vision suddenly fixed on the side of the room, and an ice-sharp heat spread across her cheek. Then she turned back and saw the hand, open, still raised.

They both stood motionless save for the ragged movement of breathing. It was Laura who spoke first. 'Okay,' she said, with biting control. 'You can go. You can just go. Right now.' And, turning about the room, she began to grab every belonging of Milan's that she could see, tossing them together in a heap. 'Here's your stuff. All your – *fucking* – stuff. Now get out.'

She was pushing at him, bent, in her fury, on nothing but getting him out of her sight. To think that she had sat here as day dawned, waiting with fatalistic acceptance for the arrival of his lover! Milan must have been amazed at her – if he'd thought about her at all. Even for the supposedly heartwhole it showed a marked lack of self-respect. Christ! The mound of clothes she took and hurled out onto the landing. Milan was still in the middle of the room, buffeted but not shifted by her shoving blows. Now she managed, at last, to push him to the door. He was speaking to her gently, but the words didn't penetrate. She wanted him out; he had to get out; she couldn't bear to look at him—

The door slammed shut. Laura's hands lay flat against it. She leant on them, her arms stiffened before her, head hanging. Tears, she realized, had been coursing down her cheeks; she'd not felt them. She was trembling. The room was silent.

Then, through the door a voice, quietly: 'They've got her in jail.'

Laura didn't move, struggling to make sense of the words. She bent her elbows until her forehead rested on wood. She whispered, 'What did you say?'

He spoke gently, quickly. 'Anežka's still in Prague. In jail. She was arrested before she could even get the train.'

Laura's eyes were shut, the tears seeping out beneath her lashes. She opened them, looked at the door handle, slowly moved her hand to it and closed her fingers around the chipped wood.

Opening the door, she waited behind it. Milan came in and stood against the wall just inside the room. His face was livid white, all its smooth assurance gone, and when at last he spoke, the tone was flat, spent and weary. 'If the authorities aren't aware of the escape plan, there may be some hope. We don't know what evidence they have. Maybe they picked Anežka up for her samizdat work.' He looked away, then back to Laura. 'It happens. They just hold people, and later the case is abandoned. Let me see your face.'

Laura realized that it was still stinging, and that she hadn't noticed. She brushed her sleeve roughly across wet cheeks. 'It's fine.'

Milan stretched out his hand, but she flinched away. Hope, he had said. *There may be some hope.*

'I'm going to class,' she said, and looked about her for her bag.

'AH, LAURA, DO YOU HAVE a minute?'

Laura turned. Heather Spinks was leaning into the corridor from her office doorway. Laura made her way towards her.

'It's just a call we got from the *Sunday Express*. They want an interview.'

An interview. Laura tried, with some difficulty, to focus her mind.

'They want to do a feature,' said Heather. '"New Golden Girl of Ballet" – you know the type of thing. They're ringing back at two. What should I tell them?'

Laura supposed she would do it. She said so.

Heather put her hands on Laura's shoulders, studying her face. 'Hey. Are you okay? You look awful.'

She smiled. 'Thanks, Heather.'

'I reckon you should see a doctor. Just get a check-up – for me, will you? And come and talk if you need to.'

Laura nodded vaguely. Heather smiled, reassured, and retreated into her office.

THERE WAS A REHEARSAL THAT afternoon. Milan, who had not been to class, nevertheless turned up on time, looking hunted. He and Laura exchanged no glance or comment except those demanded by the work, and in the moments of greatest physical proximity were still a thousand miles apart. It recalled, for Laura, in painful parody, the earliest days of their partnership. How she moved her limbs she couldn't, afterwards, remember. She felt utterly, lifelessly drained.

That night there was no performance for her; at six she went home alone. Letting herself into the bedsit, she was surprised to find Milan there before her. The powerful frame sat, folded and hunched, on the sofa. The head was back; the eyelids, closed, looked grey, as if so thin that the colour beneath showed through. Something under Laura's ribs contracted in pain at the sight of him, but she was powerless to help – and he powerless now, she knew, to do anything but hurt her.

She had considered her position. With Milan's longed-for reunion delayed, even though perhaps only temporarily, nothing in essence had changed. And yet they had both faced the reality of Anežka's coming in a way that would colour everything now. Milan, in his mind, had broken with Laura already, and Laura, who all along had told herself there was no choice but to hang on as long as she could, knew that she had come to the end. All that puzzled her now was why Milan did not make it easier for himself. Why did he not simply take his things and leave?

At the noise of the door shutting behind her, he opened his eyes. Laura said, 'Any more news?' He shook his head.

She put down her bag, took off her coat, but did not sit. 'Why don't you speak to the media?' she said. 'Set up a campaign over here to publicize the case?'

His face contracted impatiently. 'You have no idea,' he said. 'If the authorities knew I was in touch with her, it would be all the evidence they needed to prove that Anežka had been planning to leave. They'd convict her like that.' He snapped his fingers. The hand hovered for a moment, then dropped. 'It is my fault this has happened. It is my punishment for—'

'For what?' said Laura icily. But he didn't need to say. She, Laura, was his sin. He had betrayed his real love with, among others, the shallow, tawdry substitute of their affair. 'Your punishment?' she echoed spitefully. 'Are you the one in prison, Milan? And if she's so precious, why the hell did you leave her in the first place, eh? Why don't *you* sacrifice something for a change? Why don't you go back to Prague for her now?'

'I should.'

The tone was so cold, so even, that she looked at him quickly. His eyes, cast down, were hidden beneath thick lashes, and a little colour had appeared, at last, on his cheeks. He was not joking.

Her throat uncomfortably tight, Laura said, 'Don't drag this out, Milan. You have a flat. You mustn't come here any more.'

He didn't look at her but put his hand to the sofa-arm and stood up. 'Of course.'

NAÏVELY, PERHAPS, LAURA HAD not anticipated that the journalist would ask whether she and Milan were more than professionally linked. Was it standard speculation, she wondered, taking a hurried sip of her coffee, or were there rumours abroad – and so far abroad that they had reached *Sunday Express* ears?

'There seems such a chemistry between you on stage,' the journalist, a woman in her thirties with a hard lean smile, was saying now. She looked hopeful.

Laura managed somehow to laugh, and said, 'It's a purely professional relationship.' And remembered, with a sudden, private spasm of grief, that she wasn't even having to lie any more.

They were in Heather's office, which Heather had temporarily vacated, seated on the tan leatherette of

Heather's couch, affecting relaxation and bonhomie. Laura, who had spent much of the last three days, or so it felt, in surreptitious weeping, was wearing a good deal of eye make-up and feeling frightful.

'And when will you run this?' she asked ten minutes later, as the photographer tweaked at the arrangement of her skirt, a peasanty, flounced affair bought especially for the occasion.

The journalist shrugged. 'Not this week. Next, maybe.'

They were all done by eleven. They had to be: Laura had an appointment to attend. She had been feeling steadily worse, and had taken Heather's advice.

IT SNOWED WHILE LAURA WAS in the doctor's office. She came out into the street to find big chunky flakes zigzagging down, whirling and chasing each other on the freezing eddies of air. She felt them against her face as she set off along the pavement. They stung a little, and then ran, like tears.

It was curious: she hadn't noticed on her way to the surgery that there was a park just around the corner, though she had come by the same route she was retracing now. It was only a small patch, scrubby and rimed with the mulch of dead leaves, blistered railings showing black between the bushes. Laura found an empty bench, damp and splotched with bird droppings, and, disregarding both, sat down. And stayed there a long time, too, until the cold seemed to have made her as solid and immovable as the wood beneath her.

The doctor had been kind enough but, lacking sympathy, had stumbled instead into humouring patronage. It was the age-old story. How can you pretend not to have known? his infuriating smile seemed to say. Laura didn't bother to tell him that she had put it down to stress, this month's lack of bleeding. Stress and recent loss of weight. You're not pleased, Miss Douglas? Well, and his eyes had flicked to her unringed hand, I *do* see. Perhaps he disapproved, Laura thought blandly, but concluded that, on the whole, it was more likely that he didn't care.

Her knees, chilly beneath new skirt and old worn winter coat, were pressed girlishly tight together; she sat on the bench's ridged edge, hands thrust deep in pockets, head hunched low between her shoulders, a picture of taut and joyless contemplation. What could Milan think, she reasoned, but that this was a deliberately laid trap? That despite all she had told him she had sought to bind him to her, against his will, with ties of blood. She shuddered, and took a rasping breath of air, so cold it stung in her mouth and nostrils. And where, oh, where, did this leave her career?

When it began to get dark, Laura stirred with some difficulty, and shifted her frozen body from the bench. She rode the Tube home, seeing nothing and no one around her, and when she reached the door of her bedsit she hardly knew how she had got there. Still in her coat, she sat by the window. The light was off, the shadows pushing out from each corner to fill the room, engulf her. She fancied she might drown in them, and leant back so that the dimming light from the outside world would not fall on her face. The street-lamp had broken: it flickered once and failed. Above the shopfronts all was stained a dark, gathering blue. She watched as the shadows crept and shifted.

And in a moment, seemingly, it was late. Very late, most likely, but she could hardly tell. She crossed to the door and felt her way down the stairs to the phone in the hall. She dialled, carefully, and held the receiver to her ear, gripping it in both hands.

It rang and rang and rang as she listened. There was no answer.

DAPHNE STOOD SILHOUETTED IN the window, wisps of her grey-streaked hair spun shining silver against the Little Venice sky. 'You've been to work?' she asked, cigarette-holder hovering.

Across the room, perched on a velvet chair, Laura shook her head. 'Told them I was ill. I didn't have a performance yesterday and Evie will dance tonight.' She took a steady breath. 'I'll go in on Monday.' It could have been worse, coming here. On beginning to explain her predicament, she had found, with considerable relief, that Daphne already knew something of Milan. Richard had mentioned him, she said; tactfully, she had elaborated no further. As Daphne evidently knew, Laura had neither seen nor spoken to Richard since the night he had cast her that look of blazing, wounded contempt, and had turned on his heel in the restaurant.

Now Daphne, trailing silken sleeves and smooth good-will, glided across the room. 'Darling,' she said, settling in the chair next to Laura's, 'I know this is . . . a blow. But if you're only a month gone it's hardly a catastrophe.'

Laura clasped her cold fingers tightly in her lap. 'You mean,' she said, her voice harsh with quiet bitterness, 'get rid of it, and he need never know. Of course it's what I should do. I can't even imagine telling him. How could I convince him that I . . . that it wasn't deliberate?' Invol-untarily, painfully, her hands began to twist. 'But part of me . . . part of me says I've suffered enough. Oh, by my own choice, that's certain – but I've had all I can take in making it easy for him.' She was crying a little now, and her fingers jabbed savagely into her abdomen as she lifted her face in blind appeal. 'He did this too, Daphne! Why the hell should I go through it by myself?'

Daphne reached out and, taking the hand, smoothed its fingers between her own. 'I'm not suggesting that,' she said softly. She paused, and then looked at Laura with tender, serious concern. 'My darling. Do you not think, whatever your decision, that he has a right to know?'

THE NEXT DAY WAS SUNDAY. In the morning, Laura took the Tube to Earl's Court. Daphne was right: Milan must be told, and to put it off was to prolong the agony. After all, she would be asking for nothing: she would not face Milan with the suggestion of keeping the child. That in destroying it she would destroy all she could ever hope to have of him was a thought that hovered at the edge of her consciousness, too painful to acknowledge. Keep the child, after all, and she must forfeit her career. And what else had she? What else had she ever had?

The train carriage was almost empty. An elderly man at the far end by the driver's cab seemed asleep; a few seats along from Laura, a woman was flicking desultorily through a newspaper. Laura noticed with a vague surge of interest that it was the *Express*, and then remembered that her interview was not due for printing for another week at least. She wondered how on earth she had managed to talk to that journalist with such apparent calm. It would be like reading about someone else.

As the train rattled through the tunnels, drew into stations and out again, the journey began to seem dreamily interminable, and Laura longed that it should never end. But at last Earl's Court swung into view, and the train deposited her at her unwelcoming destination.

The flat was five minutes' walk away, on the ground floor of a red-brick mansion block. Lugging herself along the pavements, feeling heavy and stupid with nausea, Laura wanted desperately at each step to turn back. Still, she located the block, stepped into the tiled porch and, finding the right bell, pressed it.

It had not occurred to her that he might be out and several minutes elapsed before the lack of answer, the still-shut door registered fully, and anxiety at the prospect of seeing Milan slewed round into anxiety at not.

At that moment, the door opened with a heart-tightening click and sudden swing. A paunchy middle-aged man emerged, registered surprise at Laura's presence, then sidestepped past her and turned into the street. Just before it swung shut behind him, Laura caught the heavy door and slipped inside.

Gloomy hallway; polished floor. An old lift shaft in front of her; stairs; cold echoing space. Turning to her right Laura found the dark-wood door numbered '1'. She stood before it, gathering her courage. Then lifted her fist and rapped cleanly.

Silence. She strained, but could hear no shuffle of movement within. She knocked again. Nothing.

It was then that a desperate urgency overcame her. Her palms drummed frenziedly on the wood as if to beat a way through it; she seized the handle and rattled it fit to drop off. Instead, it turned. The door, unlocked, swung open before her.

That he was out she could tell before she even crossed the threshold: something smelt empty about the rush of air swept up by the opening door. Advancing a little way, she found herself occupying a short length of corridor that served as a hall. Doors led off it, before her and on each side. It had no feel of home; there were no pictures up, no coats left hanging. But, glancing through the half-open bedroom door on her way along the passage, it took the beat of a long second for Laura to realize that there was more to the emptiness than that.

There were signs that he had been there: a pile of old practice shoes, thin and battered, on an armchair; a sweater she recognized hanging off the bed; the sheets ripped back on a skew – pulled as someone had got out. Signs of hurry. Drawers half open; bottles and boxes pushed aside on tables and surfaces. It was eerie: the objects, so still, spoke as eloquently of movement as a blurred snapshot.

With gathering dread, Laura lurched from room to room: each was the same, marked with signs of hurried, disordered leave-taking.

The sitting room was the barest space of all: there was just an ashtray, full, in the middle of the carpet and beside it an open newspaper. As Laura scanned the room her eyes grazed the paper only for an instant, but recognition drew them back. She walked across to it, then bent and snatched it up. A photograph of herself filled almost half the open page; legs curled up; skirt arranged so carefully across the leatherette couch. Beside it the title letters blared with appalling oversized relish: 'Ballet Star's Tragic Love Triangle' and, beneath, 'True Sweetheart in Commie Jail'.

For a long time, Laura stood, waiting for her eyes to clear of this bizarre, fear-hazed hallucination. She blinked:

it was before her still. She crossed to the window, hoping the brighter light would show her her mistake.

There was none; this was her interview. She could even recognize a few of the subjects she had talked about: how challenging Dandy's new piece had been to work on; a passing reference to Miss Lawrence's school. But the rest . . . The meat of the article concerned Milan. Milan and *Anežka*. It was written as if Laura were being quoted, explaining that her relationship with Milan (relationship? she had denied it) had been passionate but doomed – his real girlfriend was in Prague. And explaining how tragically it had all turned out: Milan had tried to arrange for Anežka to follow him to the West, but the Czech authorities had caught her and now she was awaiting trial. '"The cruelty of it makes me sick," says Miss Douglas, with generous sympathy for her rival . . .'

The lies screamed up at her from the dead, dry paper. Staring at them, sunk in a kind of panic-drenched stupor, Laura swayed as she stood. It took a wrenching effort to make herself think. Milan was not here. He had left. Before he had gone he had seen this article. And he had no way of knowing that it lied, that she had not told them everything.

Abruptly, then, in a single boneless movement, Laura sank to her knees, her coat billowing out around her, the paper drifting unnoticed to the floor. Her thin hands came up to cover her face. Behind them, shattered at last and despairing, she burst into tears.

★

'LAURA, LAURA. WILL YOU LISTEN to me just for a second?'

She hiccuped, gripping the phone so tight to her ear that it hurt. Dandy's voice was steadying. 'I haven't spoken to any journalists, okay? It wasn't me, and if it wasn't you—'

'*If*—'

'Since it wasn't you it must have been someone else, all right?' She heard him take a drag on his cigarette. 'Now, you'll be able to explain this to Milan as soon as you've both calmed down.'

'But where is he? I went to the studios, but they're locked up. I don't know where else to look.'

'Fret not, my little one. It's a show of theatrical temperament. He'll report for duty in the morning, just you see.' Another drag. 'Look – do you want to come round to mine?'

'Can you pick me up?'

'I'll send a taxi.'

'No . . .' She was almost whispering into the phone.

Dandy paused, and when he spoke again his voice had changed. 'I'll be there in twenty minutes.'

THE FOLLOWING MORNING, REPORTERS and photographers surged in a rib-crushing pack towards Laura as she arrived at the doors of the EBT studios. She was thankful Dandy had made her wear dark glasses, even though they seemed ludicrous on this grey December day. Her eyelids were taut and swollen. She kept her head up, said nothing, and pushed for the door.

Milan did not appear at class or rehearsal. As the hours passed, Dandy's calm began to ebb. There was his ballet to consider: the première was now only two weeks away. And wild rumours had begun to circulate. The press, staking out Milan's deserted Earl's Court flat as well as the studios, had quickly got wind of the situation, and were speculating that he had returned to Czechoslovakia – even that he had been bundled onto a flight by the Czech secret service.

'*Might* he have gone back?' Heather asked Laura. The question was gently put, but her bright eyes betrayed its urgency.

Laura considered. 'I should,' he had said, when she had told him to go back to Anežka. She looked up at Heather numbly. 'It's possible.'

There was only one other person now she could think of to contact, and it wasn't until she got back to her bedsit that night that Laura saw how she might go about it. Somewhere lay the scrap of paper she had found that final night – the night Milan had learnt of Anežka's capture. She had thought then it might be Vlasta's number. But where was it now? She ransacked her room, hurling clothes out of drawers, books off shelves and tipping the contents of the wastepaper bin in a spreading heap on the floor. At last, incredibly, she found it: stuffed under a small plastic plant pot on the window-sill. Water had splotched the ink and made it run, but the figures were still just legible. She ran down to the phone.

'Is he with you?'

'I'm sorry?' The voice sounded surprised; guarded. She recognised it as Vlasta's.

He was playing dumb. Laura cajoled and even begged him for information, keeping a dogged grip on what remained of her composure, but he would not budge an inch.

'Let me see you, then. Please.'

He demurred. Thinking this signalled that Milan was there with him, Laura pressed harder. And so was half surprised when at last, quite plainly against his better judgement, Vlasta gave way. Laura scribbled down an address in Stockwell, and five minutes later had left the house.

Snaking in a dimly lit tunnel under London, under the darkness of a cold winter's evening, Laura journeyed from north to south, across the river boundary, and was disgorged at last half-way along the Clapham Road. From there she plunged at driven pace into the thick-shadowed side streets, hanging on grimly to the knowledge that this evening's destination was, perhaps, her final hope. Was she on her way to a meeting with Milan? It was possible he could be there – or have been there, and have absented himself because she was coming. For the thousandth time Laura's spirit writhed in wretched distress at what he must think; at what pain and fury kept him from granting her even a hearing. Her route to him, then, would lie through Vlasta. But she would have to tread carefully. Vlasta held her in suspicion – as he had every reason to. But in her efforts to convince him of her honesty she must not reveal too much. Would not Milan have emphasized – to this man who also knew Anežka – how little, by comparison, he had cared for Laura and she for him?

Under her third knock the door was opened cautiously. Vlasta's bearded, unsmiling face appeared round it, spectacle lenses winking in the light from the landing. He moved back grudgingly to let her through and Laura sensed, as she stepped into the apartment, that he was alone. She fumbled in her bag for the article. She had torn it from the paper: it was folded now into a thick tight square.

Leaving Laura to follow, Vlasta retreated into the living room. It was scruffy, cluttered and airless, the atmosphere bitter with the smell of strong cigarettes and the window resolutely shut. Before the sofa a low table stood covered in books and papers; Laura cleared a space among them and spread out the crumpled pages of newsprint.

Vlasta sat and read. And pulled at his beard. Shook his head. Sucked his breath between his teeth. '*Ježíšmarjá.*'

'I've no idea where they got it from. I said nothing about it.'

He looked at her owlishly.

'Honestly.'

He grunted, looking back to the paper. 'Who *did* you tell?'

Laura's lips pressed together. She had given Richard no more than the vaguest outline, had mentioned no name, no details – it could not be him. She said firmly, 'No one.' After a moment's pause she added, 'I'll put out a statement, denying everything. Is there any chance the Czech authorities won't get to see the article?'

Vlasta said nothing. His look was withering.

So, thought Laura, this, if nothing else, means certain conviction for Anežka. Milan thinks I have put Anežka in prison deliberately. And he knows that in court Anežka will discover he has had a lover. A lover he enabled to betray her. Struggling against her desperation, Laura said, 'Vlasta. Just tell me where he is. He needs to know the truth.'

But, obstinate and unyielding, Vlasta refused to alter his plea of ignorance. Laura began to believe him. She was thinking furiously. If Milan had chosen not to tell Vlasta, his closest ally, where he was heading, perhaps it was because he was set on a course he knew Vlasta would not condone. Or . . . perhaps it was because he had been given no choice.

Steeled with every last ounce of determination, Laura made a rapid decision. She reached out to grip Vlasta's arm, resolve printed clearly on her pale, intent face. 'You must help me, then,' she said, and her fingers, unnoticed, crushed yellow-white against his sleeve. 'Please. I'm going to look for him. I want to go to Prague.'

Chapter Eleven **Paris, 1989**

'He's said yes?' The question was posed in a low voice, in soft, rapid French. The tone was faintly incredulous. 'He's actually going to dance?'

'You're behind the times, Luc. He told Victor three days ago,' said another voice and, passing Luc and Natasha both, Denise bounded up the wide aisle steps and swung herself into a mid-row seat. 'This,' she said, settling complacently, 'I have to see.'

Natasha followed Luc into the same row and took a seat herself. They had been rehearsing all afternoon, marking out the pieces for the first time on stage, getting used to the dimensions of the place, to the rake, to the layout of the wings. There was only one piece from the programme that hadn't yet been run through.

A call sounded from the back of the auditorium; Victor hovered, half in and half out of the doors, conducting conversations on both sides. He stuck his head inside now, and shouted down to the stage. 'Milan, they want us out!'

The solitary figure there, his yellow hair straw-like under a gantry of lights, looked up and shaded his eyes with one hand. 'Tell them ten minutes, Victor. What's the big panic?' He thumbed his feet unhurriedly into their soft kid shoes, stripped off his sweatshirt and slung it, spinning, into the wings.

The theatre management, who had a different show to present to the public in two hours' time, evidently acquiesced to a final ten minutes' rehearsal; Victor came fully in through the swing doors, leaving them slapping on their hinges behind him, and lumbered down the aisle steps to where the rest of the company had gathered, a single row of eager spectators for Milan's first official run-through.

Natasha was nearest the end of the row. Victor wedged himself into the spare seat beside her. 'I have you to thank, I believe, for this,' he said, nodding towards the stage.

Natasha cast a glance down to Milan, and then up again. The dark gaze was speculative. 'Me?' she said. 'I don't think so.'

In answer, Victor offered only a smile. It looked knowing.

That she and Milan had become lovers, Natasha knew Victor was aware (whether the rest of the company had noticed, she'd hardly stopped to wonder). But, though they had talked a good deal, she hadn't persuaded Milan into this, if that was what Victor implied. The worst of Milan's black mood had lifted in recent days, it was true, even though the pressures Natasha supposed had caused it were still there: the show's opening was imminent – only three days away, now – and, while events seemed speeding towards momentous reform in East Germany, nothing of hope had happened in Prague. Milan was hardly light-hearted – she could see a desperate concern beneath the usual sardonic control – but there seemed in him less struggle than before. If Natasha had been a part of the struggle, a part which had now resolved itself, then perhaps, in that small way, Victor was right.

Down on stage Milan had shaken his legs, windmilled his arms from the shoulder sockets and now, taking up position not far from the backcloth, he signalled to the wings that he was ready to start. Beside Natasha, a row of faces, set low in the seats as bodies sprawled and lounged and legs draped over the row in front, already showed rapt attention. Victor, at her other side, sighed with satisfaction and a relief that was clearly, after three days, still keenly felt.

As the sound burst from the auditorium's speakers and the figure on stage began, masterfully, to move, the company remained in a motionless tableau, a little slacker of jaw, a little wider of eye than was their custom, the spell broken only, some time later, by a start and a muttered expletive from Luc who had let a cigarette burn down to his fingers. Watching Milan, he'd forgotten he was holding it.

Natasha, no less than the rest, watched Milan in awe.

Greater familiarity did not detract from the impressive power of this display. She was reminded, inevitably, of the last time she had seen part of the solo, when she had first seen Milan dance full-out, that strange, painful afternoon. '*You're looking at the shell,*' he had said then, '*and imagining there's something inside, Natasha. There isn't.*' It wasn't true. There was too much inside, if anything; too much that he was afraid of, that had kept him away from the stage, and away from her, for a while, too.

Perhaps that was what Victor, understanding more than she did, had meant. Perhaps in accepting her arguments, in letting her in, Milan had conquered the selfsame fear that had barred him from performing. And, on the evidence of their relationship at least, it had been a chimera: Milan had shown no sign thus far of the destructive tendencies of which he had so solemnly warned her. On the contrary, their relationship had deepened further than Natasha had thought possible. And she had felt not the least trace of anxiety: the same world that had seemed so recently one of battling anger and uncertainty now showed itself full of golden-flooded vistas, and the future a place of air and light and warmth. Sitting in the auditorium now, Natasha smiled towards the stage, and felt Victor notice it and smile too.

A few moments later the Novák Company, strung out in their lounging line, erupted into wild applause.

Their revered leader retrieved his sweatshirt, took a bow and, with an ironic grin that sank the lines on his face into crevasses, raised two fingers the impolite way round. His gaze strayed to the end of the row and found Natasha. She saw a whisper of a private smile she understood, and then he advanced beyond the lights to the lip of the stage and dropped, noiselessly, into the auditorium.

'And now we have to get out,' said Victor, levering himself from his seat. 'Who's coming for a drink?'

They all were, Milan, to a few raised eyebrows, with them.

'The crew will be striking the set through the night,' he said, when they had settled, squashed for the most part onto the benches of a single booth, the overspill on stools crammed around the table's end. 'I want everyone in for nine tomorrow.'

'Dress rehearsal on Monday?'

Milan nodded. 'Two, if we need them. There'll be some press photographers.'

'Not just photographers,' said Victor, who looked, on his stool, like a bear sitting on a cotton reel. 'They want to interview you.'

'Christ,' said Milan flatly. 'Warn them, then. Questions on this production only or they'll be out on the pavement before they can reach for their tape recorders.'

'And how are the company coffers?' said Johnnie. 'Ticket sales?'

Victor shifted. 'Going very nicely. The management's already talking about adding another week or even two.'

With the implications this held for expected time off,

the dancers' approving grins quickly turned to interest in the froth on their beer. Quentin, an unfailingly poor judge of the opportune moment, raised a finger and said, 'I just . . . Can I just mention, I'm not happy with the last few phrases of the middle section of my piece – you know, after the electronic pulse comes in? The shapes need to be tighter.' As he described, in tireless detail, the source of his anxiety, the beers around the rest of the table were lifted in perfect unison, and only when they headed down again did the drinkers, thus fortified, come in with their challenges, denials and weary assurances. It became an unhappily involved discussion.

Natasha, filtering out much of it for the sake of her temper, glanced after a while across the table and saw that Milan, nursing his glass, was similarly listening to no one. But neither was he daydreaming: his eyes were cast with more than casual attention towards the bar. Natasha turned to see what had drawn his interest. A television was bolted to the wall behind the counter and Milan was staring at the screen with a frown of urgent concentration.

Then he rose, leaving his stool rocking, crossed to the counter and rapped on it for attention. The proprietress, a tank of a woman with over-orange hair and startling eyeshadow, ignored him for as long as humanly possible and then, looking up, gave what was evidently the incorrect response. Throwing an expletive in her face, Milan turned on his heel and strode out of the bar.

Johnnie, Natasha realized, had seen it too. Beneath a

furrowed expanse of forehead his gaze held hers, alarmed
and questioning. Then, without hesitation, they pushed
their way off the bench and hastened after Milan. Emerging onto the street, Natasha at first thought he had
disappeared altogether. Then Johnnie spotted him, on the
far pavement, already some distance away, and running,
his coat flapping behind him. They set off in parallel,
dodging from the pavement to the gutter and back again
as they swerved to avoid collisions.

About them, shops were beginning to close for the
night. They saw Milan dog-leg left down a side-street,
right, left again, and then plunge suddenly into an electri-
cal hardware store. Thwarted by traffic lights, hopping,
cursing and then sprinting, it was some moments before
Natasha and Johnnie plunged in after him. He was at the
back of the shop. The assistant, hovering beside him,
looked ready to cry.

'Jesus,' Johnnie breathed, supporting himself against a
washing machine. 'He'll be lucky if they don't call the
bloody police.'

At least Milan seemed, now, to have what he wanted.
He was crouching by a television screen, remote control
in hand, a look of ferocious concentration on his face.
Standing a little way behind, Natasha watched with him.

It was film of a massive demonstration. A river of
young people, numbering thousands, flowed down a wide
street, high banks of ornamented buildings on either side.
Above the rooftops the black night yawned; below, light

spilt from shop-fronts and street lamps onto faces flushed with cold, onto banners, and anoraks, scarves and winter hats, and onto the white helmets and batons of riot police ranked, heavy-booted, in a cordon across the road ahead. A little distance from this grim barrier the demonstrators halted, and sat down. Candles were lit and placed in a diminutive, haphazard front line of resistance across the iron-grooved tramlines. Then the film cut to another scene: protestors standing eye to eye with the riot police, treating with them, offering them flowers. The police, on an unheard order, surged forward.

Johnnie stirred. 'What is it? Berlin again?'

'No,' said Natasha, turning from the screen as white batons, stark against the evening shadows, rose and fell upon bent heads and backs and vainly shielding arms. 'That isn't Berlin, Johnnie. That's Prague.'

AN HOUR LATER NATASHA WAS sitting, her legs drawn up, on an armchair in Milan's apartment. He had been pacing for some time across the far end of the room; now he stood, outlined against the long panels of glass that shielded them from the balcony and the cold night air, his hands up, pressing against the frame on either side, his bleached hair ragged and grimed with street dust. He was quite still, but there was something in the set of the shoulders, the rigid lock of the half-bent arms, that spoke of knife-edge suspense. Contemplating him, Natasha found, with surprise, that she preferred the pacing. They had caught the radio news a short while before: the demonstration had taken place the previous evening, one student reported dead, many badly beaten. The film they had seen, student-shot, had been smuggled out of Prague immediately and thence across the border. Within the city, the police savagery had inflamed where it had meant to frighten: calls had been raised for a general strike.

Listening to all this, piped through a little box in the sane, steady newsreading tones of *France Info*, Milan had shown no clear emotion; he had stood, his arms crossed, his features heavy-drawn in the soft lamp-light. Nor had he, either then or in the long minutes since, offered comment. Natasha was startled now when, face still turned to the glass, he said, 'A lot will depend on the factories – and the army. The government's weak, but it'll fight.' The fingers shifted a little on the wood. He added, 'This could be the beginning. Or it could be disaster.'

Natasha said, 'You want to be there?'

There was a pause. Somewhere below, gears crunched and a car began to manoeuvre. Milan turned sharply from the window, dropped into a nearby chair and took up the cigarette packet that lay on its arm. A match fizzed into life. Shaking it out, he looked across at Natasha steadily. 'What help would I be? Go back to get beaten up so I can say I tried? I might as well just ask those bastards who did me over in the tenth to have another go.' He smiled disparagingly. 'I would have nothing to lose. Those kids you saw tonight are risking everything. And when I was in their position, twenty years ago, what did I do? I thought of my career and kept my head down.' The dark-ringed eyes were wide and unforgiving; they seemed, tonight, from where Natasha sat, a bitter, smoky shade of grey. Milan said, 'And then I ran.'

'You regret that?'

'I should have stayed and done what I could.'

'But they would have stopped you dancing.'

'So? What does that matter?' he said grimly. 'Compared to what people have been through there every day for the last twenty years, what the hell does it count for?'

Natasha, her knees still drawn up, had her arms clamped hard about them. She said, 'And what would it have counted for, precisely, if you'd been through it too? You have a talent – God knows, that's an understatement – and you had to make use of it. Don't you think your work has been the best contribution you could have made?'

'Contribution to what? I can spill my guts on stage, and do a few performing monkey tricks into the bargain. Maybe I do them better than most but that hardly increases their value.' Catching Natasha's look of pure astonishment, Milan cast his eyes to the ceiling, rubbing his face. 'Look, leave it, will you? You don't understand.'

'No,' agreed Natasha vigorously. 'I don't know what it was like. And yes, I have no right to talk about it whatsoever. Fine. But I know a little, pathetically little, and I want to know more. Milan.' She willed him to look at her again. He did, and she went on more gently, 'Tell me. Tell me what to read, at least. Don't just batter me with my own ignorance. I *want* to understand.'

And so, rising, Natasha held out her arms and Milan piled them high with books: histories, novels, collections of letters and plays. And, while he kept the radio close by him, and later dozed fitfully in the armchair, Natasha, overwhelmed, retreated to the bedroom and began to read. Her education on the subject of Milan's past had begun.

How MILAN HAULED HIMSELF through the technical rehearsal the next day – what reserves of strength, mental and physical, he found to call on – Natasha never knew. Drained by the long, watchful night she found it difficult enough herself, though she had only her own costumes, her own roles and stage placings to concern herself with; Milan had his and everyone else's, and the set, the lighting plot and stage crew too.

He had hardly slept yet there he was, through the long hours of the morning, the afternoon and beyond, dispensing orders, criticism and occasional words of encouragement, pacing the stage with the black-out boys, climbing to the flies with the technicians, dropping back into the auditorium to view the effects and call further instructions to the stage manager or the lighting box.

By the time the dancers began their stop-start run-through, Milan had settled in a row just more than halfway back from the stage, dusty boots propped on the seat in front, hands resting lightly on his knees, gaze always and acutely on the scene before him. To one side of him Quentin was watching too, and he handled the New Yorker's itchy, fussing tension with apparent unruffled calm. Fits of temper, indeed, were notably absent: throughout the day all were treated with the same exact and exacting basic civility; and while the relentless orders to repeat and repeat and repeat were mercilessly given, and the verdicts often scathing, still a theatreful of egos were handled with skill and, when necessary, judicious restraint. If it hadn't been for the small transistor radio Milan kept close beside him, Natasha might have forgotten that there was anything other than the Novák Company to claim his attention that day.

For her own part, she kept her professional distance. It was hardly possible to do otherwise: the dancers had few enough breaks, and Milan, it seemed, none at all. In the afternoon, when a long discussion about the lighting for Quentin's ballet had drawn what seemed like the entire crew into a discursive huddle on the stage, she took the opportunity to slip out to the foyer and put through a call to England, knowing that at this hour on a Sunday she might well find her father at home. She was in luck.

'Just to let you know,' she said, when the customary greetings and enquiries were over, 'that I won't be back for Christmas, after all. We've had a fortnight's extra performances confirmed this morning, which means only two full days off. And straight after New Year we fly to the States.'

'So the company lives to fight another day. Congratulations,' said Richard cheerfully. 'We'll miss you like crazy, of course, but I only say that because I know it won't bother you in the slightest. Can you book me a ticket?'

'You're coming over?'

'To see you in your début production? I'll say I am. Would a Saturday night fairly close to Christmas be all right? Then I can bring you seasonal greetings at the same time.'

Natasha pretended to consider. 'It's selling out, you know. I'll see what I can do.'

Replacing the receiver she realised that she had made no mention of Milan's new place in her life. It had been on instinct, somehow, and it was only later that Natasha worked out the reason: she was about to dance the main role in his new ballet and she didn't want anyone jumping to casting-couch conclusions. Hardly likely in Richard's case, but her mother might somehow get to know ... Natasha didn't want to risk it. Rapturous reviews, she was determined, were to be the first Laura heard of her progress. By the time Richard came to Paris, the reviews would have been and gone. She would tell him then.

BY TUESDAY, THE NEWS FROM Prague seemed tentatively hopeful. Various opposition groups had united

under a new banner, Civic Forum, and under the leader-
ship of a dissident playwright named Václav Havel. The
young man believed killed in Friday's demonstration had
turned out to be alive, but public outrage at police
brutality had not lessened and thousands had taken to the
streets in fresh demonstrations. Actors and students, meanwhile, were touring the provinces, spreading news of
events in Prague and the planned general strike.

Looking back later, Natasha could not divorce the
opening of the Novák Company's first production from
the background of this news. Back in London, in her old
life, the events in Czechoslovakia would have been just
another headline, but refracted through the person of
Milan, it was her personal ambitions and concerns that
seemed puny and unimportant. She could not have
relinquished them, or afforded them any less fundamental
a place in her heart, but she had glimpsed a little of their
relative worth compared to the efforts of others elsewhere,
and had felt an unaccustomed stab of shame. She would
never have imagined it possible.

Tickets for the first performance had sold out some
days before; by six o'clock, when the box office opened,
the queue for returns snaked right out of the theatre and
into a side-street. Victor, trailing in and out of dressing
rooms, wardrobe, green room, down to the stage and up
again, was noticeably pleased. Quentin's nerves, however,
remained tautly unassuaged: he darted from room to
room, dispensing last-minute notes and making ragged-

toothed attempts at encouragement. The dancers, making up, dressing and limbering, were either ignoring him or bristling.

Natasha – one of the ignorers – shared a first-floor room with Denise and Pascale. Johnnie, Erik and Luc were in residence next door, and Milan had a dressing room of his own below, just a few yards from the wings. There was a universal sense of occasion, anticipation, anxious and confident by turns. But Natasha was aware, too, of a personal landmark reached. It was for her, alone of all the company, a baptism into the properly professional world. She didn't remind them.

Still, some remembered unaided: emerging from her dressing room to head to the stage for a final warm-up, Natasha found Johnnie on the landing, using the metal stair-rail as a substitute barre. After an appreciative whistle he said, 'Behold the débutante. Hey, kiddo!' Half-way down the stairs, she stopped and turned. 'You scared?'

'Shitting myself,' said Natasha, with dignity. She raised an eyebrow. 'And you're not, I suppose?'

He swore comfortably in answer, and leant with a broad smile over the rail as she carried on down the steps.

Passing Milan's door, Natasha did not knock; nor had she sought him out in the hour or so before that. But twenty minutes later, retreating from the stage, limbs nicely supple and not over-warmed, she spotted him at the back of the wings, talking to the assistant stage manager. He was dressed in a white bathrobe, his feet pushed into makeshift slippers – an old pair of battered ballet shoes, flat as pitta breads, heels trodden down. As he spoke, Natasha saw his eyes flick her way past the man's shoulder and signal to her, wordlessly, to wait for him. A moment later the man moved on and Milan set his course for where she stood. Beneath the loosely tied robe was what passed for his costume, consisting – as near as decency and a scrap or two of cloth would allow it – of nothing but muscle-defining body-paint casting dark terracotta shadows in the grooves of his ribs and around the contours of his abdomen, arms and back. Natasha knew from the dress rehearsal that the overall effect, *sans* bathrobe, was of stark, dramatic magnificence. But body-paint, she observed as he reached her now, did not mix well with white towelling.

Smiling, he took Natasha's hand and led her to a quiet corner, out of the way of the ropes and pulleys and hurrying crew, away from the dulled murmur, too, of the crowd gathering at the other side of the lowered tabs and safety curtain. He had decided to speak, Natasha guessed, to each of his dancers in turn, like an officer with his troops before battle. But the attention he focused on her now was lit by a tender warmth the others would not see. He said softly, 'I shan't patronize you with encouragement. You know how good you are.'

'Yes.'

Milan's smile deepened a little: it was communication of a different sort, that did not need words to answer it.

But at length he added, 'I just wanted to thank you.' And as her expression queried it, 'For being contrary enough to join us despite all the warnings. It took faith. Of a peculiarly warped kind.'

'I wasn't the only one.'

The peroxide head inclined. 'I'll be thanking Johnnie later.'

'Not with your hands there, I hope.'

Milan looked. They had come to rest at Natasha's boyish, spiky hips, on the clinging gown that was her costume for Quentin's ballet. And now they shifted, subtly, on the fabric. They knew the contours of her body very well.

Natasha laughed softly and said, 'And how are you?'

'Ask me when it's over.'

Watching him walk away, Natasha reflected that she had pictured her début many times over the years, but she had never once imagined it like this.

IN THE EVENT, THE NOVÁK COMPANY'S first performance was a whooping, roaring, programme-waving, seat-thumping success. The little auditorium was packed with bodies of all ages and several nationalities, and they greeted Milan, according to their theatre-going pedigree, either as a much-missed returning hero or as the latest heart-stopping sensation of the stage. In practical terms, the distinction was academic: *The Fallen* was performed to a collective holding of breath; the ovation afterwards seemed to threaten the stability of the building. But the appreciation was not reserved for one man: Natasha, as the leading dancer in Milan's new ballet, felt the rapt attention of a thousand eyes upon her and reeled at the heady thrill of live performance. The evening seemed to pass at intoxicating double speed.

When it was over, the company took each of the many curtain calls together, in egalitarian single-line formation. Natasha, on Milan's left, watched him lead them forward to bow and back again, sweat trickling down the brick-dust make-up that made such startling contrast, under the lights, with his yellow hair. Depsite the attempted insistence of his colleagues, he refused to acknowledge any of the applause alone. When he did at last break ranks with a single step forward, it was to raise a hand to still the audience, and then to dedicate the night's performance, in precise, elegant French, to the courageous efforts of the Civic Forum. The crowd, brought to pin-drop silence by his announcement, heralded its end with a fresh outbreak of riotous applause. 'They don't know what the hell they're clapping for,' Milan muttered out of the side of his smile, as he stepped back into line and reached for Natasha's hand at one side and Johnnie's at the other. 'But maybe . . .' as he led them forward and swung their arms up and over into yet another bow '. . . some of them,' he said upside down, 'will read a newspaper tomorrow.'

When the curtain finally fell and Quentin had skittered

onto the stage in a flurry of unexpectedly physical gratitude, Milan began to move swiftly and methodically
among the dancers and crew, taking his personal congratulations and thanks to each individual in turn. His face,
vivid and animated and now, in the ordinary light, a very
peculiar colour, shone among the crowd of bodies, among
the smiles and excited conversation, among the hands
raised for high fives or flung wide for relieved embraces.

He came to Natasha last of all. Amid the noise and the
hubbub, he faced her quietly. The teeth flashed white in
the weathered, terracotta face. Then he kissed her, properly and at length, and when they broke free of one
another and turned, Milan's arm resting lightly, still, across
Natasha's shoulders, it was to greet a small, appreciative
audience. In the faces about her, in the grins of genuine
goodwill, Natasha saw that the rest of the company had
known about them for some time, after all – and she
cursed them for it fondly, grinning too. Then Milan, with
a last squeeze of her hand, and a sharp look of approval
that caught everyone in its range, departed swiftly – in
search of a radio and the international news.

RICHARD'S VISIT DID NOT HAPPEN. It had been booked,
as requested, for the Saturday before Christmas, but with
three days to go before his planned crossing to France, he
was struck by a virulent bout of flu and had to take to his
bed. His ticket for the Novák Company's show, however,
was not allowed to go to waste: it was passed to the

occupant of the East Wing, who journeyed to Paris in his stead.

After that Saturday night's performance, Natasha was called down to the stage door. Waiting for her in the shabby vestibule she found an exquisite picture of bony, wrinkled elegance: the shining white hair was drawn back in an immaculate chignon, and beneath it the figure was cloaked in a sweeping midnight blue evening coat, which fell to the ankles and which, on anyone else, would have been too much. On Daphne Devereux it was hardly enough.

'Darling,' said Daphne, greeting her with graceful theatricality, 'you're quite revoltingly talented – did anyone ever mention it? No, I shan't come up. I don't wish to be mistaken for a groupie.'

But Natasha insisted – and prevailed. She led Daphne up the stairs and into the green room which, but for a litter of stained cups and spilt ashtrays, was quite empty.

After a brief and unsentimental summary of Richard's state of health Daphne sat on an ancient ottoman and surveyed Natasha in thoughtful silence. Natasha was perched on the counter that served as a bar, swinging her legs.

'It's most disconcerting,' said Daphne at length. 'You're looking positively radiant. Whatever is the matter?'

Alarming and wholly predictable perspicacity. Natasha, caught unawares, felt herself flush. And then, because there was no way around it, she gave Daphne the news she had been planning to give Richard. Hardly an announcement, hardly anything so formally momentous, but something that she had wanted her father to know.

Unexpectedly, half-way through the short speech, Daphne got up with some energy and crossed the room, ostensibly to examine a framed poster on the far wall. Her back was to Natasha, the blue velvet falling clear from her straight shoulders. Something about the set of them was peculiarly eloquent.

Natasha, drawing rapid conclusions, felt a flash of anger. 'What?' she demanded. 'It can't be because he's *older* – Christ, Daphne, not you! I just don't believe – or because he's my boss, is that it? You said yourself a minute ago you thought I had the talent. D'you honestly think I'd stoop so low?'

Daphne turned then and Natasha saw, with considerable shock, what she had never seen before: the grey eyes were brimming with unshed tears. 'No, darling,' Daphne said, her voice crisp and controlled. 'Nothing like . . . that. I'll tell your father. I am—' She halted, smiling and frowning at once. 'I'm so *glad* that you're happy.'

And, without waiting for a response, she swept from the room. It was several moments before Natasha had gathered her wits enough to go after her. She clattered down the concrete stairs and shot past the stage-door man's sentry-box office, but too late. Stopping, panting, in the street outside, she could find no sign of Daphne there or by the taxi rank around the corner. She stood in the shadows of the cold dark street while the taxis edged in their queue along the kerb, peeling off from the front as fares came to claim them. Eventually she turned away. And then turned back, her eyes wide. A taxi sped from her, its rear lights fiery in the blackened street. Dimly, through cross-currents of thought, she had glimpsed the person getting in, a fleeting image only, the back of the head, a reaching arm, a pale, ungloved hand. Natasha shivered, and swore that her mind was playing tricks on her. For it had not been Daphne, but a smaller, neater figure, with brown hair, just lighter than her own. She had been convinced, for the briefest moment, that it was her mother.

Walking slowly back into the theatre, Natasha met Milan emerging from his dressing room. Fresh from the shower, his face was scrubbed its usual colour and his hair was tangled and darkened with damp. He began to smile but, reading her face, stopped. 'Natasha. What is it?'

He had taken her shoulders in a gentle grip. Steadying herself with some difficulty and a little inward impatience, Natasha forced herself to smile. 'Nothing,' she said, and cleared her throat. 'Absolutely.'

She was a better actress than she knew. Milan's smile returned. 'Johnnie's declared a desperate need to shoot some pool,' he said. 'Want to come?'

★

THERE WERE ONLY FOUR OF them that Christmas, though it felt, at times, as if a pack of partygoers three times the size, bent on hedonistic disorder and conspicuously enjoyable consumption, had descended without their noticing it. It was amazing, Natasha reflected, what could be done with a bit of determination and the right supplies.

The venue was Milan's apartment in the 17th; the party comprised Milan, Natasha, Victor and Johnnie, and there was much, besides the season, to celebrate. In Czechoslovakia, the Communist president and prime minister had resigned, and Václav Havel seemed set to become the new head of state, with full democratic elections a well-nigh certain prospect for the coming year. In honour of all this, the little household near the Place de Clichy celebrated, in the Czech fashion, on Christmas Eve. And carried on celebrating long into the night – so long, in fact, that they came out the other side and called it morning. Milan, Natasha discovered, held his drink frighteningly well, while the others laughed and lounged and hiccuped, and wove their way about the apartment with meandering aplomb.

Unjustly, if foreseeably, he seemed also the least affected when the two days of holiday quickly, and for some painfully, rolled into work again. Compromising the quality of one's performance was not in any way to be tolerated, Christmas or no Christmas. It was as well, for those with weaker heads, that there were only a few Paris performances still to be given. Ahead, the day after New Year, lay the flight to America.

And in between, of course, another party. A proper party, with a real crowd this time, and antisocially loud music and a barn of a place to hold it in. The end of the old year, the beginning of the new, and the imminent embarkation for a tour that stretched endlessly ahead had to be marked; the company rehearsal space in the condemned building in the Pigalle had to be bidden farewell. It was a happy coincidence.

By ten, the room was packed. The entire staff of the theatre, backstage and front, seemed to have turned up, in addition to friends, friends of friends, and a few Pigalle neighbours. Milan, sitting cross-legged on top of the rickety grand piano, was engaged in what looked like a savage version of German whist with one of the lighting technicians. Against the pounding from the speakers, the flip and slap of cards dealt and laid down and taken up again, the grunts of frustration and crows of triumph were played out in eloquent dumbshow. Money was changing hands. He was thoroughly enjoying himself.

Across the other side of the room, perched on the back of a half-dead settee that had been wheeled out of the changing room for the occasion, shoulders propped against the wall and shoeless feet plunged deep in the squashy upholstery, Natasha and Johnnie sat side by side like birds on a wire, their heads cast back against the paintwork, their hands nursing drinks and cigarettes.

After a while Johnnie, who had been watching the piano, rolled his head towards Natasha. His voice only slightly slurred, and at a volume to compete with the music, he remarked, 'He's happy.'

Natasha looked over. 'Yes.'

Johnnie said, 'It's your doing.'

'And Mr Havel's. Among others.'

Uncushioned by hair, Johnnie's head rolled back to observe. 'All the great man's birthdays have come at once,' he said. 'There's been a revolution here for him, never mind where else.' He took a slug at his bottle. 'And you?'

Natasha considered. 'What – you mean, am I happy?' And when he nodded she grinned a wide, sharp-toothed grin and rested her head, comfortably, against his shoulder. 'Ah, Johnnie,' she said. 'I never imagined what it was, before. I never imagined.'

She had not spoken to Daphne in the few days since her visit, or to her father. It seemed easy, with the beer and the constant distraction of company, to put them out of her mind.

BY THE LAST HOUR OF THE OLD YEAR, Natasha had been drawn onto the dusty dance floor. The room was hot with unchoreographed exertion, the windows thrown wide to the black December night, with a blasting two-way traffic conducted through them, of music on the way out and cold air on the way in. Not everyone, however, was dancing.

'Come *on*.' Milan leant contemplatively against a barre and Natasha dropped the exhortation in his ear as she hustled past, hip to hip with Fabrice, the company pianist.

The eyes lit with mischief, a hand darted out, caught hold of her wrist and swung her round. 'Come on *you*,' Milan countered, pulling Natasha in towards him. 'At this rate we'll be starting the New Year singing along to "Joe Le Taxi". Will you come outside? I want to see the night a little.'

Natasha, whose partner had shimmied off to pastures new, grimaced and huffed and pretended to be put out. But, grabbing sweater and coat, she followed him all the same.

It was spectacularly cold. Few stars showed above the street lights, but the sky was clear and cloudless, and the dark roads sparkled with the beginnings of a frost. Hugging arms about one another for warmth as much as affection, Natasha and Milan walked fast, matching each other stride for stride, leaving the noise of the party blurring and fading behind them. Milan's dog had been found a new home – with Luc's mother – until after the tour. It seemed strange to be without him.

They covered considerable ground. Spurred on by the biting air they walked right down to the river and then turned eastwards along the bank. Beside her Natasha felt

Milan smile, his profile bright and sharp against the shadows. This new year, she reflected suddenly, was to be the best of her life.

They crossed onto the Ile de la Cité, and reached at last a little park jutting out into the Seine, thick with trees. Here they stopped and sat on a bench, Natasha fidgeting, hunched against the cold, her reddened fingers jammed under her legs. Voices carried on the air from the banks of the river; it was probably close to midnight.

But, as they sat, Natasha watched Milan's smile seep stealthily away. There had been more to this escape than the party's music or a breath of fresh air. New Year, she could imagine, brought reflections that Christmas did not, of a painfully sober kind. It did not take much for her to guess, now, at his thoughts.

'Why not go?' she said, tipping a nudging shoulder towards him.

Milan stirred as if, lost in reverie, he had hardly heard her.

'Go to Prague,' she murmured.

She saw the smooth lids lower, and rise again. 'How can I?' he said.

'How can you *not*?' She took his hand from where it lay on the cold bench between them and rubbed it encouragingly, saying, 'Go taste the atmosphere – it won't wait for you.'

'I'm never going back.'

Natasha set down the hand and let her breath out, all

at once, in frustration. For several minutes she listened to the distant shouts and laughter, the wind above, singing to them, echoing strangely as if the night were some vast cavern. Then an idea came to her. After an evening's beer she did not hesitate to voice it. 'That person you told me you loved,' she said quietly. 'She was in Prague, wasn't she?'

If the question troubled Milan, he gave no sign of it. He sat quite still, looking straight before him, then shook his head. 'There was someone in Prague,' he said. 'And I had loved her, but—' He stopped; his brows lowered. 'It wasn't her I meant.' Then he looked at Natasha quickly and smiled. 'But you're right. That's partly why I won't go.'

Natasha nodded, thinking. 'Tell me about her, then,' she said, and after a silence: 'Go on – I can't get colder than I am already, and you'll have to talk to take my mind off it. Please?'

He didn't want to, she could see that. But, slowly, without looking at her, he began to speak. 'We . . . had been together since we were at school – young idealists, you know? It binds you so strongly, finding ambitions together. It's hard to untangle the person from the dreams.'

'And the dreams were?'

'Mine, only to dance. But she – Anežka – wanted to fight the system. She had political hopes. She got in with a militant student group. They ran incredible risks – in 'sixty-eight they thought they were winning.' Milan shook his head, took another draught of air. 'After the Russian invasion she encouraged me to leave. I had the opportunities, tours abroad. She was to follow.' He stopped again. Elbows on knees, he had his fingers laced before him, the knuckles white. Now his head bowed to rest on them. 'For me, it was over between us before I left Prague. Only I hadn't told her. We'd been together so long that I couldn't make the break. I thought ... somehow I thought that, once she'd got out, got settled in her new life, I could tell her then. I owed her so much.'

'So what happened?'

Natasha thought he wouldn't answer. Then Milan looked up and released his fingers, staring out across the little park. He said, 'I fell in love. Truly in love. You might think you know what it is, and then when you meet the real thing . . .'

Natasha wanted to say that she knew, but something in Milan's expression stopped her, and she sat still and silent as he went on. 'It was someone in London. And someone to whom I was just a passing fling. She made that abundantly clear. Only now I was in a difficult position. What would happen when Anežka arrived? It tortured me. But when the time came, of course she didn't arrive – someone leaked the plans and the police picked her up. At the start we had hope – we didn't know how much they had on her, and there was a chance they'd have to release her without charge, though she still couldn't have

tried to cross the border again for a long while. I felt—'
He drew a long breath. 'I had some mad guilt complex.
Somehow I thought this was all punishment for my not
loving Anežka any more, for my loving someone else. I
remember feeling that even before . . .' He paused.

'Before what?'

'Before this woman – the one I loved – blabbed to the
press about Anežka being in prison about to stand trial,
and how I'd been trying to get her out. Giving the police
their case on a plate.'

'My God . . .'

'Anežka served seven years,' Milan concluded flatly.
'Because of that. Because of me.'

There was a long pause. Then Natasha said, 'You have
to go back.'

He turned sharply, his expression bleak with anger.
Natasha raised her hands to his cheeks. 'You're in pain,'
she said. 'My God, I can see it's so raw, it makes me want
to weep. And this is after all these years? You have to face
it, Milan – you must. And if you'll let me, I want to come
too. I want to find this other part of your life. Let's look
for Anežka together – if you can stand it.'

She released him, and the head dropped low. A
muffled voice said, 'I was so sure I could never feel so
much again.'

'Then lay the ghosts, Milan – they're hanging on to
half of you and I want the whole of you for myself. I'm
greedy that way.'

He paused, thinking, shook his head. 'It'd take a month to get visas, maybe two. And there's no break in the tour schedule. It's impossible.'

'So cancel half a week in ... I don't know – where are we in March? Copenhagen, or Munich. Why not? Just a couple of dates.'

'Everything looks so simple to you, doesn't it?' Milan looked up at last, but she saw there was no scorn in the remark, only a gentle curiosity.

And then, with a crump and a fizz and a noise like gunfire so sudden it made Natasha gasp, the sky to the north-west was all at once ablaze, pocked with sparks of glittering flame, giant chrysanthemums of stardust blooming and dying in showers above the Place de la Concorde. Milan turned to watch the display. After a minute, he said, without looking round, 'Victor will hate you. Hate us both.'

Natasha, watching the fireworks too, let a slow grin spread across her face. 'Happy nineteen ninety,' she whispered.

Chapter Twelve **Prague, 1971**

In the first days of 1971 Laura took a flight bound for Prague. It was a flight into the unknown; she had no knowledge of the city, or of this country, almost exactly at the centre of Europe, whose capital it was. Neither did she know how to search for a man who might not even be there, and who, if he were, almost certainly did not wish to be found. The odds against success were immaterial, most rational thought, indeed, unhelpful. Laura knew only that she had to try.

The landing was made in thick fog; the aeroplane's passengers saw nothing of the city on the descent, only dull choking cloud pressing up against the windows. The airport building, when they reached it, turned out to be a plain, flimsy box in a sea of white. Armed with an address where Vlasta had arranged she could stay, Laura struggled past the uninterested hostility of the customs officials and hailed a taxi.

Prague. Praha. Milan's home town. As to what kind

of place it was, the ride through the outskirts hardly enlightened Laura further: she saw houses and apartment blocks, square, solid and unremarkable, on either side of the wide grey road they were taking, and beyond these nothing but a hinterland of opaque vapour in which vague shapes lurked, veiled by the clinging fog like furniture under dust sheets. Only the foreground existed: the flats of a stage set. There, traces of old, sullied snow lingered on roof-tiles and the edges of pavements, surfaced with a fixing layer of ice. It was bitterly cold.

Twenty minutes later the taxi drew up by a kerb. Laura, fumbling with the unfamiliar currency, got out and looked about her. They were still, she supposed, on the airport side of town for they had not even grazed the city's centre. She found the apartment block she wanted, located the correct name among the confusion of bell-buttons and, after announcing herself into the intercom, was admitted. Dusk, already, was gathering.

'So,' Šárka Vacková, the woman Vlasta had described vaguely as a friend, settled back in her chair and fixed Laura with a comfortable, assessing gaze, 'you are here, I gather, because you are looking for someone.'

They were seated in a dining room four floors up above the street, where a polished mahogany table stood on a polished linoleum floor and a pair of antlers hung, sharp as giant rose thorns, on the wall. Laura, chewing doggedly, nodded. A plate of tiny open sandwiches had been placed hospitably before her, and a bottle of dark, caramel-coloured beer decanted into a glass. The smell of the food mingled with scents of unfamiliar wood polish, freshly pressed linen and a faint drift of cigarettes. Swallowing now, Laura said, 'I'm looking for Milan Novák.'

'Milan?' The reaction was instant, but hard to read. Šárka turned her head, and exchanged glances with the only other person in the room: a slender, dark-haired young man standing propped against the doorpost. His name, Laura understood, was Karel. Šárka said, 'In Prague?' and turned to Laura again. 'What makes you think he's come back?'

'He's disappeared from his home and his work in London,' said Laura. 'A short time ago, he mentioned to me that he felt he should return to Prague. He had heard that a . . . that a friend of his had been arrested. That's all I have to go on.'

For the first time Karel addressed Laura, his accent thicker than Šárka's, strange with distended vowels, but his speech fluent. 'We have heard nothing of him here,' he said.

Šárka asked, 'Where are you going to look?'

Laura surveyed them. The one face stony; the other gentle. But both, perhaps, putting up a front of ignorance.

'I don't know,' she said. It was the truth, though she saw Karel's eyes narrow. What could he possibly suspect her of? Wasn't her foolish lack of planning, her *naïveté* in this whole sorry business embarrassingly obvious?

'If there's any help you can give me . . .'

'There isn't,' said Karel. Then the phone rang, and he disappeared to answer it.

Šárka smiled softly and pushed the sandwiches a little closer to Laura. 'First,' she said, 'as a foreign visitor, you must register at a police station.' She nodded towards the newly shut door. 'Karel will go with you in the morning. It could be a long process.'

KAREL, TACITURN AND DISTINCTLY unfriendly, would not have been Laura's choice of companion for her first trip into the city. She was surprised, indeed, that he had agreed to come at all, but put it down to Šárka's persuasion. Studying him next morning as they waited in silence at the tram stop, she wondered who he was, and what he did for a living, and why, without any provocation, he had decided to dislike her. He was a year or two older than her, she guessed, but that was despite the build: the high bony shoulders and concave abdomen suggested more the gangling teenager. His skin was the unhealthy colour of raw potato; his hair, by contrast, was black, and hung in heavy natural curls about his ears. She had not yet seen him smile.

To reach the police registration office, they were to cross the city, travelling east into the centre and then directly south, changing trams twice on the way. It was still bitingly cold; the city lay under a leaden sky as under the dome of some great heavy bell. But the fog had lifted and a thin watery sun picked out the faded colours, the dirty, peeling faces of elderly aristocratic buildings. Winding downhill, the first tram took them through narrow streets and squares, and thence across the river, grey-brown and thickened with mud. As they reached the far bank, Laura looked back and saw the castle on the horizon, all width and windows and pale, regimented elegance. And from its centre rose the blackened hulk of the great Gothic cathedral. It was a stately but sinister skyline, brooding and watchful. Laura kept her eyes on it until the tram swung round a corner and it disappeared.

The registration office, in a southern residential district, was supposed to be open for two hours that morning: a notice to this effect was pinned to the door. But the door was locked. After half an hour's wait Karel led Laura back into the street. 'We'll have to try again tomorrow,' he said, with no indication of surprise or annoyance. 'It should open at three. I'll take you back to the apartment?'

Laura shook her head. 'Thank you but I want to explore.'

Rattling in again to the centre of the city, they disembarked together in a broad thoroughfare lined with shops and bars. Karel said he had some errands to run, and prepared to take his leave. 'You'll be okay?' he said, in a tone that suggested it was neither here nor there to him.

Laura smiled. 'Of course.'

With a nod, Karel turned his back, and disappeared down a side-street.

★

Six hours later laura found her way back to the apartment. It had been dark for some time. Karel opened the door. But hardly the same Karel who had left her in the city: all bland indifference had been wiped from his face.

'You were lost?' he said, ushering Laura in.

'No.'

After so long outside, the heat of the apartment hit Laura like a Turkish steam room. Every inch of exposed skin felt chapped and raw with the cold, and now was flooded with a painful rush of blood. She kept her coat on and, greeting Šárka, made her way into the living room and sat huddled on the settee.

An exchange in Czech, bearing the tone of a reprimand, passed between Šárka and Karel. Catching Laura's eye Šárka said, 'We were worried.'

'I'm sorry.'

She waved away the apology. 'As long as you're all right.'

Somewhat surprised, Laura smiled. She couldn't feel her nose. She said, 'I'm fine. Just a little ... chilly.' She looked down at her hands. A short while ago they had been blue, with livid orange blotches; now they were swiftly turning a shiny and unappealing puce.

Karel disappeared into the kitchen. Returning with a cup of steaming tea, he bent and closed Laura's fingers around it. 'You were walking, all this time?' he said, looking down at her with frank incomprehension. 'You hoped to *find* him?'

Laura thought of the hundreds of faces she'd studied as she'd trudged the unfamiliar streets, picking directions at random, half careless of remembering which way she turned in the hope that instinct might somehow lead her to him. She said defiantly, 'I wanted to see the city,' but knew even as she spoke that she was fooling no one. She dropped her gaze. 'I know it was stupid.'

Šárka, with a quiet smile, left the room. It was Karel who sat with Laura while she sipped her drink, watching thoughtfully from the depths of an armchair, his bony feet propped on the coffee table. This time, the silence did not seem hostile.

At last he said, 'You really are so desperate to see Milan?' Laura looked up from her tea at him and was surprised to see something resembling sympathy.

She drained the last of the tea from her cup. Did Karel have information after all? Had he decided now that she was genuine – and therefore to be trusted? Setting the cup down, she said earnestly, 'I would give anything for that.'

But if Karel knew more, he gave no sign of it. He simply nodded, his mop of black curls bobbing, and went to the kitchen to get her a refill.

LAURA HAD NEVER IMAGINED how infuriating, inefficient and downright affronting Communist officialdom could be.

'We were lucky,' said Karel, as they left the registration office the next afternoon. 'Just two trips and a ninety-

minute queue – not bad. It could have taken several days.'
He grinned – an unbeautiful, but utterly winning
expression. Today, for the first time, his mouth had been
quick to smile and much employed in chat. Whatever his
reason for mistrusting Laura before, he seemed to have set
it aside.

Now, as they made their way down the street, Karel
was explaining that he had another errand to run, something to deliver in the Old Town, though Laura could see
no sign of a package, parcel, or even a letter stuck in a
pocket. He did not elaborate. But he added that Laura
could come with him if she liked, and then they would
return to the apartment together. She agreed.

One tram journey and a short walk. Stopping on the
edge of Josefov, the old Jewish quarter, Karel squeezed
Laura's arm, said he would be five minutes, and disappeared. He was fifteen, but Laura wasn't troubled. She
was happy simply to stand before a dull, faded shop
display, and to think. The morning she had spent walking
again, exhausting herself fruitlessly, racking her brains for
fresh avenues of inquiry. She had already tried the National
Theatre, had asked at the stage door, with all the innocence she could muster, whether she might as a visiting
dancer be allowed to watch the National Ballet's company
class. It was a plan that dropped dead at her feet. Having
no English, the stage-door guards tried to speak to her in
German, of which Laura knew no more than a dozen

words. Somehow, still, she managed to communicate her request. Somehow, too, after what seemed like hours of perplexing gesticulation, she understood that without a formal letter of introduction and the prior agreement of the directors, her chances were unalterably non-existent. On the way out she had lingered, her fingers around the handle of the stage door. How many times had Milan's hand enclosed this piece of metal? She had shaken herself: it was a maudlin line of thought. Soon it would feel as if she were chasing a ghost.

The fifteen minutes up, Karel arrived back at her side. Heading west, aiming for the river, they plunged into a plexus of narrow, twisting streets. The area had an aged, fairy-tale beauty, but behind the crumbling façades Laura felt that the buildings were shut against her, their backs turned, their stone shoulders defensively hunched. The city, indeed, seemed more and more to her a puzzle, a maze of artful distractions, with its real life hidden some-where, accessible only through an unmarked door, seques-tered, secretive, shut off from the stumbling foreigner.

How could she hope to get anywhere, then, without a guide? Glancing at her companion as they walked, Laura wondered whether the new, smiling Karel would tolerate a little curiosity. 'Tell me,' she began tentatively, 'is Šárka your – mother?'

He shook his head. 'We're not related. I'm just staying at her place for a while. I come from Hradec Králové, but

I didn't want to go back home.' He shrugged. 'Lots of people stay at Šárka's when they're . . . in a bit of trouble. She's good that way.'

Trouble? thought Laura, but she said, 'And – are you studying?'

'No,' said Karel. 'I clean windows. *Most* days.'

'Oh. Oh?' She had tried not to show her surprise, but obviously failed.

Karel laughed. 'It is not the sum of my ambitions.'

'No. I mean – no?'

'I *was* studying. For my doctorate at Charles University. But I was expelled. For having a mind of my own, you might say. Grave mistake. Especially in a university.' He laughed again.

Laura said, 'What was your subject?'

'Philosophy. I suppose it helps.'

'You didn't want to be a photographer? It is *your* darkroom I'm sleeping in?' Her bedroom, a tiny boxroom off the kitchen, was littered with trays and bottles and piles of photographic paper.

Karel nodded. 'That's my hobby. But if it became my work I'd have nothing to relax with.' He walked on in silence and then explained, 'Some things we want to have more of – and it's better if we don't get what we want. More perfect. It can be like that with people also. That's what I tell myself, anyhow.'

Laura considered the idea. The cold air seemed to have brought some inconvenient water to her eyes. She sniffed surreptitiously as Karel added, 'Anežka Černá was expelled from the university too.'

'Anežka? Milan's . . .' It was hard to say it. 'Milan's girlfriend?'

'Yes.' Curiously, the epithet seemed displeasing to Karel too: Laura thought she saw a wince.

They had stopped, waiting to cross a road. Before them the beginning of a bridge was marked by a dark-stoned Gothic tower, a wide archway bitten out from its base.

'I told her years ago she shouldn't have anything to do with him,' said Karel softly, as they stepped off the pavement. 'He never thought of anyone but himself. And he didn't love her. I could see it. I told her she was with the wrong boy. She thought differently.'

'I'm afraid I think differently, too,' said Laura, hurrying to keep up as they passed beneath the tower and onto the bridge. Blackened statues lined its low walls: saints as sentries, contorted in their strange attitudes of humility or spiritual rapture. 'About him not loving her, anyway.'

Karel said, 'Then he must have changed. Or got Anežka mixed up with Prague. He misses *her*, I'm sure. Who wouldn't?'

He turned suddenly to face her and walked backwards a pace or two, flinging his skinny arms out wide, and disturbing a number of birds that had settled on the wall and the nearest sandstone figure behind him. They wheeled into the air, cawing cries of alarm, and Laura watched them for a moment, then looked about her. Above, on the horizon, stood the castle; to either side the river stretched away, threading the next bridge, and the next onto its sinuous arm like bangles. From the water Laura lifted her face to look straight up into the sky, and, seeing nothing but untextured greyish white, her eyes made patterns of their own, white on white, which swam and popped and spun like catherine wheels.

'He blames himself that she's in jail,' she said, and straightened her head again before she lost her balance.

Karel said nothing. She thought perhaps he hadn't heard.

WHEN THEY GOT BACK, the apartment was bright with laughter and people. A young couple had arrived with their baby: Karel and Laura found them sitting around the dining table with Šárka, talking animatedly over coffee and cigarettes.

Karel greeted the couple as old friends. Laura was introduced; they spoke no English but the man, Zdeněk, had a little French and his partner, whose name was Olga, was fairly fluent so they managed with that. Šárka explained that today they had been evicted and would stay in the apartment until they had found somewhere else to live. Karel could sleep on the sofa and they would have his room. Karel readily agreed.

As the conversation veered once more into Czech, and into, Laura imagined, subjects of which she would in any case know nothing, she watched the baby with curiosity. He was large and alert and energetic; his mother looked frail and exhausted. But Olga was friendly, with a bright smile she turned frequently on Laura. Laura moved to sit beside her and when the boy, Petr, was offered to her, she took him willingly into her arms and felt a strange light-headed misery.

It was a busy evening. Šárka cooked, the phone rang, and a succession of people called, to be whisked into the kitchen by Karel, apparently for private discussions. Some of the callers left again immediately, and others stayed long enough to be brought into the dining room for a drink. Laura heard herself introduced, and smiled and nodded at the friendly faces, but stayed where she was beside Olga, with Petr hanging contentedly onto fistfuls of her hair.

Later, when Olga had taken her still lively son to bed, and had stayed there herself, and when, some time later, Zdeněk had followed and the last of the callers had disappeared into the night, Laura found herself sitting with Šárka and Karel in the small, plain kitchen. Producing a bottle of plum brandy, Šárka poured them all generous shots and Laura was taught to toast her hosts' health in Czech. Then, in the ensuing silence, she turned her thoughts reluctantly to the following day.

'I have no idea what to do,' she said. 'I suppose I should try to find some other way to get into the theatre.'

'What is the point?' said Karel, sitting on the work-surface opposite her. 'If Milan had come back to the National Ballet, they would be telling the world. The prodigal son, you know – seen the error of his ways and returned from the wicked West to be a good socialist citizen once more. They would keep a tight rein on him, sure, but they wouldn't keep him hidden.'

Laura was silent. She took a sip of her drink; it burned its way pleasurably down to her stomach. She said, 'Do you know his family? Can you tell me about them?'

Šárka shrugged. 'Not much to say. He's an only child. I knew his mother well – we were at school together. She died when Milan was a teenager. His father . . .' Šárka hesitated.

'Milan hated him,' Karel put in.

'That's why he was always round here so much.' Scraping back her chair, Šárka turned to look at Karel. She said, 'We could ask Zdeněk.'

Karel seemed unconvinced; he made a comment in Czech.

Šárka nodded. 'I know, I know, but it's worth a try.'

'If he has come back,' said Laura, 'have you any idea whom he might have contacted?'

'I would have said us, first of all,' said Šárka. 'Since Anežka's not here.'

The elusive, mysterious Anežka. These people know her, Laura reflected. She is not simply an absent player in my life, she is flesh and blood somewhere, just as . . . just as Milan is flesh and blood somewhere too.

'Karel?' she said. 'Do you have a photograph of Anežka? I'd like to see one.'

Karel eyed her doubtfully, but then nodded, and lowered himself from the work-surface. He disappeared into Laura's bedroom and returned with a small brown box. He lifted the lid and drew out a photograph. 'That's Anežka,' he said, handing it to her.

Laura looked down. In her hands lay a black-and-white print of a young woman, somewhere outdoors – a park or garden, perhaps? She had been caught as she turned towards the camera: her long hair lifted as it swung; it was dark, and her eyes were dark, too, beneath darker brows. She was laughing, mouth slightly open, lips drawn back wide across small straight teeth. Her features were fine, almost delicate. She looked confident and happy and indisputably real.

As she studied the picture, Laura held her own face firmly blank. Somehow, though she had not known what to expect, it had still taken her by surprise. She had not thought Anežka would be so beautiful.

THE NEXT AFTERNOON, WHEN Karel arrived back at the apartment after a day washing windows, he mentioned that Zdeněk had given him an address for Milan's father. 'There is not a big chance,' he said sternly, seeing Laura's lit face. 'Don't hope too much.'

Still, he could not dissuade her from setting off immediately. And since he could not dissuade her, he went along too. The address took them to the eastern side of the city, to an area of low-rise apartment blocks clustered around a small, charmless park. Karel found the block they wanted and rang Pan Novák's bell. No one was home. 'He may not be back from work yet,' said Laura. 'I want to wait.'

Karel, she asserted firmly, did not need to wait with her. When he reminded her that Milan's father was unlikely to speak anything but Czech Laura flushed and bit her lip. Karel stayed. Side by side they sat on the swings in the park, scuffing their feet in the dirt, watching bus- and tram-loads of people wend their way home in the early winter twilight. A few times they thought they had spotted him, a man of about the age and height Zdeněk had described, but each time the stranger turned off in the wrong direction, to another street or apartment block. They were beginning to attract glances of hostile curiosity; Karel suggested that they take a walk.

Coming back to the park five minutes later Laura spotted a solitary figure heading up the road that skirted its western side. It was a middle-aged man, a little down at heel, with the unmistakable weatherbeaten look of a heavy drinker. Laura squeezed Karel's arm. 'Could be,' he muttered, and started forward across the scrubby grass.

Laura retreated to the corner of the street to watch. She saw Karel approach the man, dipping his head politely, speaking a few words. The man looked startled, confused, and then his face reddened'with anger. He made a sharp gesture and Karel turned away.

'What did he say?' Laura asked, as Karel took her elbow and propelled her swiftly in the opposite direction.

Karel was shaking his head. 'Not a nice man,' he said. 'But, then, I suppose he was a little scared.' He released Laura's elbow and glanced across at her. 'Swears he hasn't seen Milan since he was sixteen,' he said. 'I think it is probably true.'

THE DAYS WERE SLIPPING BY and Laura had nothing to show for them. She tried to put all thoughts of her impending return to England firmly from her mind. As a distraction, she spent increasing amounts of time with Olga, helping with the baby and chatting. Laura's French was improving: they understood one another easily.

'Don't expect to hear a good word about Milan from Karel,' said Olga one evening, as they were preparing to bath Petr together. 'Karel's been soft on Anežka since high school so he was always jealous.' She tested the water and took Petr from Laura's arms. 'And Milan kept himself on the edge of the students' union stuff,' she said. 'He knew it could damage his chances in the National Ballet. It caused resentment – Zdeněk rowed horribly with him about it.'

Laura watched the baby, his fists and feet punching the water. She said, 'What did *you* think of Milan?'

'I could see the ability, right from when we were kids,' said Olga. 'I used to have hopes of dancing myself – oh, only until I was thirteen or so. I was never going to be good enough. But the last time I saw Milan on stage – it was at the National Theatre, the month before he went on tour – I sat there and thought, yes, it was right that nothing should have stood in the way of that talent. Not even – and Zdeněk would hate me for saying it – but not even politics. The way Zdeněk feels about the political struggle, Milan felt about dancing. I could understand it in a way the others couldn't. And there was a bravery in it, too – that's what they could never see. Milan put his dancing first despite what the others thought of him – even Anežka. She disapproved, in her way.'

'But Anežka was . . .' Laura wondered what she might safely say about the attempt to get her out. 'She had plans.'

Olga nodded. 'There's a lot to be done, abroad. There are a few people who are working really hard, of course, but they could do with help.'

'Like Vlasta?'

Olga nodded again. Then she said, 'Šárka's his aunt, did you know? He won't have told you, I suppose.'

'He just said she was a friend,' Laura said, 'and I suppose I kind of half thought . . .' She laughed. 'Well, my mistake.'

She looked down at Petr and smoothed the bubbles back across his pink forehead, away from his eyes. He writhed, pressing his head against Olga's supporting hand, and grinned at her gummily.

'Laura.'

She looked up. Olga's young, tired face was studying her own with grave concern.

'You . . . You're pregnant, aren't you?'

Silently, Laura's gaze widened in astonishment. She glanced back to the child quickly, blushing. And nodded.

'I thought so.' Olga turned back to Petr, blushing, too, but pleased to be right. 'Don't ask me why. I had a feeling . . . And, after all, I've just been through it myself.' She paused, then said, without looking up, 'Have you told Milan?'

Another bullseye. Am I so very transparent? Laura asked herself. 'There wasn't . . .' She swallowed, needing to steady herself. 'He'd already gone.'

Olga lifted Petr onto the towel across her knees and began to dry him. 'So,' she said softly, 'what will you do?'

'I don't know.' Laura turned in search of another towel and found, with a start, that Karel stood slouched in the doorway. He hung his head, then looked at her again with a grimace of apology. Olga, seeing him too, said something sharp in Czech, but Laura put out her hand.

'Just listen,' she said quickly, looking from one to the other, 'Anežka mustn't know, okay? Don't tell her about me at all. Please. I'm not . . . asking for anything from

Milan. And even if he is here . . .' she hesitated, but she knew now that it was true, 'there's no real point in telling him, is there?'

ON HER LAST FULL DAY IN PRAGUE, Karel led Laura up into the castle precincts to take her photograph. They walked from Šárka's apartment, striking up the incline away from the main road to take them the back way to the castle approach, through the trees and past the old formal gardens, and finally through the castle courtyards to the wide forum in front of the imposing gates – a stone-clad plain with magnificent views across the city. It was a clear day: the mists had lifted to reveal outlines lemon-sharp against the morning sky.

Karel directed Laura to stand near one of the ornate green lamp-posts in the middle of the square, where women cast in cold painted metal, their drapery hanging heavy on their thighs as if sodden, stood in permanent classical repose. Laura lifted a hand to trace over their shapes as Karel moved about her. If only she could stay here, she thought. Prague felt curiously safe; reality was beyond its walls. Why leave, then, and face it?

But Prague felt safe only, of course, because here her life had hung suspended, frozen out of real time. If she stayed, the clocks would start again. She was, after all, still pregnant.

Laura felt Karel approach, and turned her head. He had taken off his scarf; now he lifted it and placed it around her neck. The soft wool, warm already, felt comforting as he crossed it under her chin.

A few minutes later they moved to the edge of the square, to the side that opened across the Prague skyline. Laura stood by the wall, looking out. The click of the shutter faded, and she ceased to listen to Karel's comments or instructions. Spread before her, the city seemed to shift, towards her and away, like a softly rolling sea, and she fancied dreamily that she was being carried out on the swell.

When she came to, Karel had finished and was stashing camera and film back into his bag. Catching her eye, he smiled briefly; she replied in kind and turned back to drink in one final view of this bleak, enchanting place. And in those last still moments Laura found that her hands, unconsciously, had come to rest on her lower belly. She held them there, thinking, for a long time before she turned away.

Chapter Thirteen **Prague, 1990**

There was a murmur of excitement from the passengers as the plane banked round, and those not next to the windows craned to see past their neighbours.

'Are we there already?' said Natasha, putting up a hand to shield her eyes from the sun. 'God, it's so clear.'

Milan, in the window-seat beside her, his face turned to the view, sat curiously quiet. The sun streamed across a cloudless sky. As the plane made its turns above the airport, the ancient centre of the city, ringed by the grey tower-blocks of the Communist suburbs, lay sparkling in the crisp spring air. Red roofs glowed warm in the light; cupolas, verdigris-green, and spires like sharp black shoots pushed up among them and the Vltava river, reflecting the sun in its watery scales, slid belly-flat along its winding bed.

As the plane banked again and the window's view slid up to show only empty sky, Natasha sat back, reassured. The city at first sight seemed neither sinister nor forbidding. There was no particular reason why it should, except that she had been aware in the past few days of a growing feeling of dread when she thought of the place, alarmed at the enormity of what she had done in persuading Milan to come back here. She was dabbling in things of which she knew nothing; she could no more know how it felt for Milan to return to Prague than she could foresee how he would be received by Anežka, should they find her.

Natasha had spent half the flight turning over in her mind what scant facts Milan had told her of Anežka. That he had not loved her, latterly, at least. And that, because of the person he *had* loved, Anežka had gone to jail. What sort of a meeting could it possibly be, two decades on? If Anežka were angry with him still, and attacked him with all the details of her suffering, she would be perfectly justified – but how could Milan survive that? She, Natasha, had persuaded him here in the hope of finding some sort of peace: had that been simple *naïveté* on her part? If the trip was a disaster, she must shoulder her portion of the blame.

On a lesser scale, it had caused enough problems already. Victor, having been told nothing of the plan until the visas were confirmed, had practically gnawed his knuckles to the bone in trying to cajole, beg and bully Milan into changing his mind. Two performances in Munich had had to be cancelled, with the loss not only of revenue, but of much goodwill from the venue, and if it hadn't been for the success of the Novák Company's freshly finished tour of the States and the reviews there which, crossing the Atlantic, had whipped European dance audiences into a pre-booking frenzy, the company would have been in danger of losing the Munich dates altogether.

But Milan had seemed immune to Victor's entreaties. When patience finally ran out, he had simply taken the great bear face in both hands and drawn it towards his own, forehead to forehead. 'Victor. Dear Victor,' he had whispered in a voice so barbed with irritation each word had seemed to crunch on bone. 'You can't begin to understand. I realize that. But I *am* going. You *can't* change my mind. And so you may as well bloody shut up about the whole thing.' As Milan had released his grip Victor had stepped away from him awkwardly. 'I know you will sort Munich out.' And Victor had walked out of the room past Natasha, glowering. Natasha, aware of his already well-formed opinion of her guilt, had chosen not to meet his gaze.

Fortunately, the rest of the dancers had been more understanding. The allure of a long weekend without performances was not without its value. 'Go on with you,' Johnnie had encouraged them, volunteering to take charge of class in Milan's absence. 'I'll not spare the rod. They'll be licked into such shape by the time you get back, it'll put you two to shame.'

He'd made it sound as if they were going to be away for a month, thought Natasha now, stuffing the in-flight magazine into the pocket in front of her as the plane finally made bumpy contact with the runway. And they were only staying in Prague for two days. Yet if all did not go well, these two days could well seem like a lifetime.

THE CLEAR WEATHER HELD, and as Natasha and Milan set out from their hotel little more than an hour later, they found Prague's Old Town bathed in a spring light that picked out each scrolled parapet, each stately façade in crystalline detail. They headed westwards, towards the river. It was, by a whisker, still morning.

As she walked, Natasha looked about her in awe. Each way she turned there stood glorious buildings, neglected, many of them, their opulence self-effacingly shabby. On their lower levels, window displays and shop signs were muted or non-existent, and to one accustomed to neon and blaring soundtracks, the streets, echoing intermittently to the rattle of trams, or the occasional car, had an air of dignified, dusty restraint. She looked at Milan against this background, struggled to place him here, and could not.

People passed with quiet tread; where a group clustered three or four deep about a shop front they stood patient and silent. Natasha presumed they had spotted something sought-after or unusual, but coming to the third such group, she saw that these windows held not goods to buy but newspaper articles pasted to the glass, or TV screens rigged up to show, on a loop, student film of the winter's demonstrations. She and Milan stopped and watched too, and afterwards Natasha saw the smiles, still a little dazed, on people's faces as they turned away.

Milan, an odd figure with his bleached hair and his swinging, street-wise stride, was looked at with curiosity, though not recognized. He had changed too much for that, Natasha supposed. She watched him, anxious and pleased by turns, as he stopped to examine each small commemoration they passed in archways or on pavement corners, pools of melted wax, fresh candles, wilted flowers.

For the most part, walking on, he paced beside her in silence, his mind lost in other pictures of this same scene, seeing about him, she knew, other faces. But from time to time he would surface, and begin to point things out, bars, hotels, churches, a theatre, a café, a street name, carved doorways and house signs, directing her gaze this way and that with dizzying, proud enthusiasm. They took a wide circular route and, arriving back at their hotel, Milan went in search of a telephone directory. Natasha took a shower.

'She'll be married, I expect,' he said to Natasha, as she emerged from the bathroom, twisting her hair into a towel. He had the phone in his hand, the directory open on the bed before him; he was flipping its pages, running his finger along lists of names. He stopped at one and dialled, listened, then flew into a rapid burst of Czech. Quickly, he pushed the cradle down with his finger, checked the book, dialled another number. As the calls progressed, Natasha saw his tension ease and the apprehension leave him: from the laughter and lengthy discussion he seemed to have found at least some people he knew.

'Did you speak to her just then?' asked Natasha, when the phone went down at last.

Milan shook his head, rubbing his hands through his hair and grinning. 'Another old friend,' he said, 'but it turns out he's the one Anežka married.' He shook his head again, in wonderment this time. 'Karel Malý. My God.' He looked at Natasha, dragging his thoughts back to practicalities. 'He'll tell her I called. She'll ring here later on.'

Anežka's husband at least, then, thought she might want to talk to Milan.

ANEŽKA DID WANT TO TALK: she rang, and arranged with Milan that they would meet at a bar they both knew at four o'clock that afternoon. Natasha came back to the room after exploring the ground floor of the hotel – which had, in parts, original art-nouveau décor – to find that the call had come through in her absence, and was privately disappointed. She had wanted, for her own curiosity, to be witness to such a significant moment. Later, on consideration, she thought that perhaps it was for the best. Whatever she had seen she would have had no power to interpret. But she hurried to assure Milan that she did not expect to accompany him. 'I'm going to get on a tram and see where it takes me,' she said, brandishing the guide book she'd brought from Paris.

'Take the twenty-two,' Milan advised her. 'Go and look at the castle.'

'I might.'

She left before he did, in case the temptation to follow him and catch sight of this woman might prove too great.

Natasha walked fast, looked at everything, mined the guide book for information every time she paused for breath. She hurried through shaded narrow streets, across cobbled squares and, avoiding the trams after all, crossed the river on foot and climbed to the sprawling castle complex. Everywhere she saw the Czech flag, the smiling-face logo of the Civic Forum, and the distinctive crumpled face of the new president, smiling too. The graffiti shouted slogans she didn't understand, named names she had never heard of – and a few that she had. Still, however far she walked, however many buildings she looked and mar-velled at, the three hours dragged by and felt like twice the time.

She had arranged to meet Milan in front of the National Theatre, a majestic gilded pile back on the Old Town side of the river. As she approached it, crossing the bridge directly opposite, she saw that he was there already, waiting on the steps. And he wasn't alone. Beside him stood a woman, who looked small and slight even in the thick padded jacket she wore against the cold. She was talking animatedly, and her hand, gesturing, reached out to touch Milan's arm. He took and held it, leaning towards her and laughing.

Whatever Natasha's other confused anxieties, the possibility that she might feel jealous had not occurred to her, and it was surprise at herself that gave her a sudden jolt. They had not yet seen her: she wanted to stop and turn about. But still her feet strode confidently onward.

She halted a little below them, on the pavement. Milan turned, and smiled, and switched into English. 'Here, Anežka,' he said. 'This is Natasha.'

The woman came down a step or two, holding out a hand. She was in her early forties, Natasha guessed; dark hair, cut close around her face, made her eyes seem even bigger than they were. The smile was quick and genuine; she shook Natasha's hand warmly.

'So pleased to meet you,' she said, in easy, well-accustomed English.

Natasha returned the compliment, and babbled ineffectually about where she had been, her gaze fixed on Anežka all the while. She saw how she moved and spoke with confidence and good humour; and how a deep, quiet fondness lit her eyes when they were turned on Milan. Bitterness could not have been concealed in such a look. But neither could anything more ardent. Natasha, feeling stupid and relieved at once, breathed freely again.

'I would like you both to come to supper tonight,' said Anežka. 'Will you? Meet Karel and the boys.'

Natasha, glancing at Milan, readily agreed and Anežka took affectionate leave of them both, saying that she would see them later that evening. They watched as she crossed the road and set off along the embankment. Then Natasha felt Milan's hand at the back of her neck and, turning, found him bending to kiss her.

'So, you like my home town?' he said, as they began to walk in the direction of the hotel.

Natasha considered him. He was looking not at her but directly ahead, his expression vivid with happiness. 'I love it,' she said.

It had been right to come. Thank God, it had been right.

ANEŽKA LIVED WITH HER family in an aged apartment block just above Kampa island, a thick spur of land that was not, in fact, an island at all, being joined to the river bank at one end. From the outside, the apartment block appeared derelict; it was the smeared, uneven brown of old shoes and in parts looked positively scabrous. Inside, however, all was in perfectly good order and Anežka's apartment, on the third floor, was spacious and clean, bright with family photos and posters.

It was Karel who had come to the door; Natasha hung back, smiling, as he and Milan greeted one another, then stepped forward to be introduced. Karel was a wiry man, with spectacles and a rambling grey-streaked beard, which parted swiftly in a wide grin. He bustled Natasha through into the kitchen-cum-dining room, where food and wine were already laid out and where his sons, kneeling up in their seats, had turned towards the door. More introductions. Two lean, bright-faced boys, eleven and thirteen, shook hands with her politely and spoke a word or two of hesitant English. Natasha replied with the little Czech Milan had taught her. Laughter and congratulations all round – 'But that's all I know, I'm afraid,' said Natasha, spreading her hands in apology.

'Don't worry, it will be good practice for Tomáš and Honza tonight,' said Karel, and he clasped Natasha briefly on the shoulder. 'We shan't leave you out.'

The meal was a lengthy, convivial affair, the conversation quick and constant, and all but the odd exchange conducted, as Karel had promised, in English. Natasha could detect no sensitivities being nursed: Karel himself mentioned, with gentle self-mockery, that he had married Milan's cast-off sweetheart, and Anežka, pretending to be insulted, teased Milan that Natasha was only seven years older than her eldest boy. 'Should we say it's Natasha's maturity or my immaturity?' asked Milan mischievously.

'Neither,' replied Anežka. 'We should say that the soul is ageless.' And she reached for a fresh bottle of wine.

Tomáš and Honza, who had been struggling to keep pace with the conversation, asking their mother for frequent translations, were then permitted to give their enthusiastic accounts of the events of November and December, which they had been itching to do. They lurched from English to Czech and, when helped, back again, pointing out proudly various photographs pinned on the noticeboard and slipped between the glass doors of the kitchen cabinets.

'Still taking your snaps, then?' Milan said to Karel and, to Natasha, explained, 'He's been a camera-bore since high school.'

Tomáš scurried about the room, collecting prints. Now, the dishes cleared away, he brought them to the table and, squeezing himself between Natasha's chair and Karel's, pointed out his favourites. As the boy chattered, Natasha pored over the photographs. The images were extraordinary. A sea of people, faces intent and alert in the glow of candlelight; bunches of keys held aloft; a woman with a picture of Havel taped to the back of her anorak; a statue, pasted with home-made posters and photographs, and the numbers 68/89 sandwiched together, poignant resonance in the neat reversal. 'Now, at last,' said Karel, 'I can take pictures of absolutely anything I like.'

'Have you kept all your old photos?' asked Natasha.

Anežka groaned. 'We're drowning in them. I'm afraid if he takes many more we'll have to look for a bigger place.'

'Do you have any of Milan when he was younger?'

'I suppose I must have,' said Karel. He frowned, thinking, then scraped back his chair and stood up. 'Come this way.'

Glass still in his hand, Karel led Natasha a little unsteadily to a small room at the back of the apartment.

The walls were lined to the ceiling with shelves, and the scanty floor space was all but obliterated with piles of ancient cardboard boxes. Treading carefully among them, Karel headed for a row of albums in the far corner. He set down his drink on a box and began pulling them out.

'Here.' Without turning, he handed one back to Natasha. 'Look towards the end of that – or perhaps – no.' He pulled out some more, flipping through them and casting most aside.

Natasha opened the album he had given her. It was pasted with small black-and-white photographs, many of them self-consciously artistic; a corner of a parapet against a lowering sky here; an anonymous distant figure posed starkly in an otherwise empty field there. Karel, meanwhile, had moved his drink and, sitting on a precarious tower of boxes, had pulled another onto his lap and was skimming speedily through its contents.

Natasha turned as instructed towards the last few pictures in the album, and came upon one of a group of teenagers standing in what looked like a small square: behind them were trees and a park bench. She peered at the figures closely. On the left, a young man stood slouched in studied indifference, his face half turned from the camera. 'That him?' she asked, twisting the album to show Karel.

He looked up, squinted at it, and nodded, grinning. 'At . . . oh, sixteen or so. Would you have gone for him back then?'

Natasha laughed and, looking at the photo, drew in a sceptical whistling breath. Milan at sixteen had been good-looking, all right, but the bearing and expression spoke of defiant arrogance, little humour, no irony. Much like me not so very long ago, she thought, with a sudden clutch of shame. Hurriedly, she moved on to study the other faces. There, beside Milan, was a girl she quickly recognized as Anežka. She had worn her dark hair long and plaited then, and looked very young in a cotton dress and socks and sandals. At her other side stood another boy; Anežka had a hand linked through his arm as well as Milan's, and, Natasha noticed, she looked by far the happiest of the three.

Glancing up to ask Karel about this, Natasha saw that he had stopped riffling and had drawn a single photograph from his box. The struggle to remember whatever it showed him had brought a stern concentration to his face. Not wanting to disturb his thoughts, Natasha smiled and bent her head again to the album before her.

Chapter Fourteen

Prague and London, 1971

'Here,' Karel leant through the taxi window, pushing something into Laura's hand, 'I hope it's dry.'

She looked down. A photo from the day before – herself up by the castle. She smiled at Karel, aware that tears were brimming in her eyes. 'Thanks.'

'Yes, yes,' said Karel, with embarrassed impatience. He leant further in to kiss her on each cheek, then pulled himself back through the window and motioned to her to wind it up. It was cold.

Šárka tapped on the glass. 'Don't give him any money,' she whispered, through the last crack at the top of the window, pointing to the driver.

'You've paid him?' Laura fumbled for her purse. This was too kind.

But Šárka shook her head. 'He owes me. I got some text-books for his daughter.'

As the taxi drove off Laura looked down once more

at the picture, which bore Karel's thumb-print prominently across one corner. Her visit had not made life easy for them: Šárka had mentioned they would have to write a detailed report for the authorities listing everywhere Laura had gone, whom she had spoken to, what she had said, or, at least, a version of it. Why had they bothered to show such kindness to a stranger? It had been such a pleasure, finally, to be with them that she had hardly faced up to the fact that her visit had been a failure. She had no more idea now of where Milan might be than when she arrived.

But perhaps – the thought occurred to her suddenly – that was exactly the way Karel and Šárka had wanted it. Perhaps their friendliness, as much as their initial reticence, had had a purpose. Laura shifted quickly in her seat to look out of the back window. But the car had turned a corner and the figures, the stretch of pavement, the apartment block had gone.

THIRTY-THREE THOUSAND FEET above central Europe Laura tried to consider, carefully and calmly, her options. Milan lived and breathed somewhere, he *was* somewhere, at this very moment. It seemed to Laura strange that if you wanted to find someone so desperately, the powers of the mind alone could not give you the answer. It should come to you – in a dream, perhaps. It should, but it did not. Quite possibly, as the plane had lifted away from Prague, it had lifted away from Milan too, somewhere in the city, in a street, in a building, in a room Laura could not visualize.

Or maybe he had been in London all along; maybe she would return to find him there. And she would be able to explain, as far as she could, about that article. And she could tell him about their child.

The child she could hardly believe in. She felt sick for large swathes of the day now, and she had come to know a new drained exhaustion that the worst rigours of the dancer's life had hardly taught her. But she did not feel pregnant. Perhaps it was an advantage. She had still to decide what she wanted to do.

It was doubtful that she would have a job at the EBT to return to. She had left a letter for Dandy since in going to Prague she was dealing a second shattering blow to the plans for his ballet. They were to have gone ahead without Milan – Dandy had drafted in Marco to learn the part – and the première should have taken place while she was away, but it would not have done. Max, she was sure, was livid.

Still, the press coverage for *Firebird* would no doubt open doors in other companies. If Laura chose not to have the baby. Dancers simply did not have children – until, that is, they retired. And, besides, who would help her to care for it? She could not afford to pay for help and knew no one who would provide it for free. So the choice was stark: career or child.

Laura waited for her luggage in a daze and drifted

through Customs, the sights and sounds of the airport and of other passengers coming to her as if from a great distance, as if her eyes and ears were the surface of some pool and she were lying curled on the bottom, removed from reality in a silent underwater world.

Approaching the arrivals gate, she was dragged back to the surface in one wrenching moment of panic. Ahead, further down the hall, she saw a pack of press photographers, milling, laughing, eyeing the information board. How on earth had they known? They hadn't spotted her – they were some distance from the barriers. It seemed they didn't expect her quite yet. Maybe she could get through . . .

Keeping her head down Laura passed under the archway, gripping the rail of her luggage trolley grimly, praying.

Suddenly a hand covered hers on the rail and began to drag the trolley off to the side. Not daring to look up Laura pulled desperately against it. The hand shifted, painfully, to her wrist. A voice close at her ear said, 'Don't be stupid, it's me. They haven't seen you. But it might be a good idea to get out of here.'

'YOU TOLD DAPHNE WHICH day you were due back, remember? So I drove up from Denham last night and checked out the flights. Good job I did.'

'Thanks.' Laura wanted to say more: she really was deeply grateful, and amazed that Richard had thought to rescue her. When she had last seen him, after all, he had been storming out of a Covent Garden restaurant. But the speech of thanks would not come: it required a supreme effort just to think.

'Who – who told the press?' she asked.

'Oh, it wasn't you they were waiting for. Some actor was due in from Switzerland. But if they'd seen you – well, it wouldn't have been very useful, would it? As it is, since that statement you put out you've hardly had a mention in the papers. It's lucky – they're all too busy speculating about your friend being a Communist agent.'

Laura looked at Richard then, but his expression was bland. She said softly, 'He wasn't. Isn't.'

Richard gave no response. He rapped on the taxi driver's window. 'Right here'll do.'

Laura opened her bag, wondering whether she had any British cash, but Richard stopped her. 'Just get yourself out,' he said gently.

She waited on the pavement, looking numbly around. Dry trees stood poking through their square holes in the concrete slabs, forked branches scratching the air. Leafless bushes pushed through painted railings. Mulchy leaves were left mashed and brewing in the gutter; a few dry ones brushed along the street towards her, tripping between the dog mess and splattered stains on the pavement. Laura watched them, turned her face, watched Richard pay the driver. She felt wrung out as an old dishcloth, colourless, empty. The last street she had stood on had been in Prague. Yet it didn't matter where she was. Nothing mattered now.

'Laura? Laura!'

She roused herself. Richard was at the top of the steps, about to ring the bell. Daphne's bell. He had, as close as he could manage it, brought her home.

HER SKIN FELT STEAMED. It was warm still, soaked and soft and fragrant. Wrapped in a vast towelling dressing gown, Laura was sitting in the drawing room. A strong drink – she hardly knew what – and a cigarette, ready-lit, had been pushed into her hands by Daphne. Daphne's repertoire of care was small, and confined to what she herself would need in an emergency.

The phone rang. Laura heard Richard's voice in the hall, telling someone firmly that Laura Douglas was not there, and no, he didn't know where she was. And no, he wouldn't give his name. The phone slammed down.

'Leave it off the hook!' called Daphne, from her place on the chaise-longue. She had been watching Laura, and smoking silently, for some time. Now she said, her thread-thin brows contracting slightly, 'Darling, what are you going to do? There is a decision to be made, and if you don't make it soon, you won't have a choice.'

Heads or tails. A career or a child. Both seemed impossible, unreal. How could she go to class? How could she have a child? Laura was amazed at how the minutes ticked by and still she was there. She wanted it all to go away.

The drawing room was heavy with dark patterns and clutter. Daphne had lit a candle and an incense stick. The smell curdled Laura's stomach.

She said, 'I want to get rid of it.' She listened to herself with some surprise.

'Sure?' Daphne leant towards her. 'I mean, darling, needless to say, you've thought it through?'

Laura said that of course she had. Daphne sat back. Something like relief registered on her face. She said, 'Would you like me to make the arrangements?'

Laura nodded. It would be easy. She could drift through it like a dream.

DAPHNE DID HER WORK swiftly and well. The clinic was in Knightsbridge. Laura was due to check in very early in the morning, in case by some mishap the press might get wind of it. She got up in the winter dark, feeling sick, and took a taxi from Little Venice. Alone – at her own insistence.

It was almost light by the time she got there. She was wearing a smart wool jacket and skirt and Daphne had lent her a vanity case. It felt vaguely surreal; she almost wished for a hat and gloves.

The taxi drove away. It was raining, though not very hard, and the front door was blue. There was a knocker in the shape of a fish. It was brass, freshly polished. What if, thought Laura, gazing at the ridges that marked out its fins, what if I ring and no one answers, and the moment doesn't end and I am fixed, standing here for ever? She put out her hand and the fingers seemed to her foreign, as if they belonged to someone else. The bell rang.

Inside the clinic all was polished wood and button-studded leather and aspidistra leaves. It looked like the office of an old family firm of lawyers. A young lady appeared, smiling with professional politeness. 'Miss Devereux?'

Another safeguard. Laura nodded.

'This way please.'

THE OPENING OF DANDY Franks's new ballet was delayed by three weeks. The première, featuring Eve Morrison and Marco Agnelli, received much press coverage, due to the English Ballet Theatre's sensational recent history, and much press praise. The same night Max Norris, the company director, issued a statement informing journalists that the contracts of two of the company's leading dancers – Milan Novák and Laura Douglas – had been terminated. It was, the statement added, purely due to the company's generosity that there would be no legal action taken for breach of contract. And still no word, the newspapers reported, of Milan Novák's whereabouts. The mystery, and the speculation, continued.

Laura had had the papers brought to her room. They

lay now in a jumbled mess on her counterpane; her arms, outside the bedclothes, rested on top of them; her head, against the pillows, was turned to one side, towards the window.

Softly, on crêpe soles, a nurse entered the room, removed a tray, with glass half emptied, and withdrew. Laura stirred and, reaching out one hand to the telephone on her bedside table, lifted the receiver.

After only two rings, Richard's voice answered.

'When can you get here?' said Laura.

HE CAME IMMEDIATELY AND took her back to Little Venice. Daphne was waiting on the doorstep, purple silk kimono pulled about her tightly. 'It's all over now, darling. It's all over,' she said, folding her bony arms around Laura's shoulders as Laura suffered herself to be led indoors.

And it was. But not in the way that Daphne meant.

SEVERAL DAYS PASSED BEFORE Laura admitted that she had changed her mind at the clinic; that nothing had been done. Richard had returned to Denham, not able to leave the estate for long at such short notice. He would return, he had said, the next weekend.

Daphne had stood alone in the drawing room as Laura told her. Laura looked away as she said it: she did not want to see Daphne's reaction, did not want to feel the need to explain. Daphne's response was smoothly reassuring, indicating nothing of what she thought. But she could think what she liked: it would make no difference now.

The truth of it was not what they might assume. The decision hadn't sprung from any sense of communion with the dividing cells inside her – if Laura imagined them at all, it was more with fear than tenderness, as if a tick had snapped its jaws into her belly. And the decision had not even been to have the child: it was neither so grounded in realism nor so positive. She had simply known that she could not go through with the abortion. The consequences could be what they would: the future streamed upon her as blank and cold and empty as the winter sun.

That week Laura moved silently through the flat, unable to settle to a book or letter, unable to sit for long, unwilling to talk. Dandy rang and left messages; she looked at them and put them aside. Daphne neither questioned her nor made demands, yet her eyes spoke of serious concern as they followed her from room to room; Laura looked away. Since to break down was no more possible for her than to take charge of herself, she left those near her with nothing to do. She took walks alone, long walks, often leaving early in the morning, swathed in scarves against the January cold, and prying eyes.

It was clear that she could not continue to live with Daphne for long. And to contact her father, after all this time, was hardly an option. With no job, she could not keep up her bedsit. She had nowhere to go.

On Saturday, Richard returned. Laura knew she should have felt grateful for his solicitousness, but could not. It bore inherent pressure: he had come to see, she felt, how she was 'getting on'. And he still had not spoken a word of Milan, or of their argument. His forbearance bore down on her, weighted with guilt. And yet his face, when turned towards her, showed nothing but mild patience, and a watchful hope.

He suggested a walk on the Heath. Laura did not want his company, but wanted to be out in the afternoon's gusting wind; she agreed.

It was a bright day. The sun, hanging low and large and heavy in the sky, shone like a giant searchlight straight into eyes already tear-stung by the wind. Laura forged uphill, leaning into the blast. Strangers passed in ones and twos, with dogs, some, and some with children. They looked ordinary and unconcerned: Laura wondered how that might feel. Everything had changed: the future of her hopes, once as familiar to her as the top of the hill she was climbing, was now obscured.

At the top she passed a bench and sat down on the grass. Richard, a moment behind, sat beside her. Neither spoke.

At length he said, 'You won't be able to work, will you? How will you support it?' She didn't reply, so he turned to her. 'Laura – think, will you? Think.'

'I've been doing nothing else.' She faced forwards still, but watched, out of the corner of her eye, as he paused and looked down at his hands.

He said quietly, 'Then share some of it with me.'

'Richard . . .' She hesitated. 'You've been a great help. Thank you – for everything. But it's not your problem. It's not Daphne's either – she mustn't worry that I'm planning to stay with her. I don't delude myself that she longs to hear the patter of tiny feet on her Kashmiri carpets.'

A kite had been launched above them. It was gaudy red, with a blue and yellow tail, and it made harsh, guttering sounds against the wind as it twisted and dipped then climbed again.

'You could come and live at Denham,' said Richard, as Laura raised her face to watch it.

'What job could I get round there? I couldn't pay you rent – and I'd be no use on the estate. Thanks, but you hardly need a lodger.'

'Lodger? Laura, you idiot.' Richard pulled at the grass in front of him and threw a handful out onto the air, which tossed it sideways, sharply, then dropped it. 'I'm trying,' he said, 'to ask you to marry me. I'd take the child on as my own, of course, if that's what you wanted.' He swallowed, then turned to face her. 'Could you bear to?'

She looked at him, saw the square brow furrowed anxiously, the brown eyes – almost all iris, no white – locked full on hers in their earnestness. Richard, kind Richard, who had always been there for her since she was a child. God in heaven, thought Laura suddenly, and felt a collapse of inevitability, as if a puzzle she had stared at for years had finally resolved itself.

God in heaven. This, of course ... this was the answer.

Chapter Fifteen **Prague, 1990**

Natasha took the photograph album back into the kitchen. Anežka, fond and amused behind a bluff of maternal displeasure, was shooing her sons out of the room on their reluctant way to bed; Natasha bid a formal good night to each, then, falling back into her seat opposite Milan, laid the album open before him.

'Christ . . .' Milan groaned at the sight of his younger self. Laughing, Natasha beckoned Karel, who had followed her, his arm hooked around the box of photos that had so interested him in the study. 'Haven't you any of yourself?' she asked him.

But Karel's attention was directed elsewhere. He clapped a hand to Milan's shoulder. 'Talking of past loves . . .' he said.

'Were we?'

'*Yes.*' Karel glanced across. 'Sorry, Natasha, but I have something else from ancient history to dig up.'

'Go ahead.'

Karel retrieved a photograph from the box and handed it to Milan. 'Now *there* was a curious episode,' he said. 'She was a nice girl, though.'

'Let me see!' said Natasha eagerly, waving an open hand across the table.

But she did not repeat the demand, stopped in her tracks by the sight of Milan's face. Always pale, it had lost every last trace of colour. Silently, as she watched, Milan held out his hand for more photos. Karel, sitting, fed them to him, picking through the contents of the box, blithely unaware, it seemed, of his neighbour's change of mood. Milan said something in Czech; without looking up, Karel replied, then appeared to ask a question. Receiving no response, he raised his eyes at last, and met the strangest gaze from Milan that Natasha had ever seen.

The next moment Milan's chair fell over. It happened so quickly that Natasha registered this before she realized that he'd stood up. Dragging Karel behind him, he marched out to the hallway and into another room, shutting the door. He had taken the photographs with him. Alone at the table, Natasha sat perfectly still. She wished she hadn't drunk so much wine. It should have been beer; she was used to beer. As it was, her thoughts were a little slow and wouldn't run quite straight. But that there was something terrible in those photographs was abundantly clear; and clear, too, that Karel had not anticipated their effect.

Anežka came back into the kitchen, smiling, unaware.

She asked what had happened to the men and Natasha explained, as well as she was able. As she spoke she saw puzzlement, and then a deepening alarm, cloud Anežka's face. But the next instant Anežka remembered herself and, without comment, began to quiz Natasha gently about her work in Paris.

The conversation passed so seamlessly that Natasha was not quite sure how long it was before Milan and Karel returned. When they did, they both looked the worse for it. Karel seemed to have found himself suddenly, painfully sober; Milan, beside him, wore a pinched grim expression and it was in tones struggling for grace that he apologized to Anežka, saying that he and Natasha should go. Natasha stood up, acutely aware that she was the only person in the room with no inkling of what was going on. The leave-taking, warm if awkward, was over in a moment; then they were outside, in the cold of the night, and Milan was walking.

'Are you going to tell me?' She hurried to catch up with him, hugging her coat tight about her. Flecks of rain showed in the light of a street-lamp, too fine to feel. 'Milan?' she said, coming alongside.

He was walking fast, his face set. Natasha felt ignorant and stupid in the silence. And angry.

'For Christ's sake!'

They had reached the end of a street, where a flight of stone steps led up onto the bridge. At the foot of them he turned sharply. 'Look, just . . .' His head dropped. 'Don't,

Natasha, okay?' he said carefully. 'I just need a little . . .
space.'

'Fine,' said Natasha caustically. She stood and watched
as Milan mounted the steps before her and swung himself
up onto the bridge.

Though the rain was no harder she could feel it now,
blowing across her face. She wondered if she could find
her way back to the hotel from here, and then knew that
that would not do. What right had she to storm off in a fit
of pique? She had brought Milan here, and it was easy for
her because she didn't understand.

Climbing to the bridge, Natasha saw that the old
lantern lamps were lit among the statues and their glow
picked out a blond head bent over the low wall, some
half-way along. He was leaning on his elbows, staring not
out across the water, but straight down, so that his face
was almost lost inside his thick coat collar, turned up
against the river-draught. Natasha hesitated. A couple, arm
in arm, were strolling towards her. She let them pass,
then, treading softly, made her way towards Milan. A few
feet short of him she halted. Some saint or other towered
above her; leaning back against the plinth, she settled to
wait, feeling about in her pockets for cigarettes.

When the first was half smoked Milan shifted, rubbing
at his face as if to rouse himself. Natasha offered him the
cigarette. The water, varnished black, its surface ridged like
sand at low tide, seemed still and glutinous beneath them.

'I'm sorry,' Milan said. 'Karel . . . came up with

something he thought I knew about. I didn't.' He turned the cigarette slowly in his fingers, then held it to his lips. 'Old ghosts,' he added, through it.

Natasha said nothing. She knew about Anežka – precious little, but the bones of what had happened – but this could not be about her. Of what other spectres Prague held for Milan, she had no idea.

He shook his head and straightened. The temperature had dropped, the rain ceased and the cold seemed now to be striking up through the soles of Natasha's boots: the night had hardened, chill and unforgiving.

They set off walking again, across the river, along the embankment and then eastwards, in the direction of the hotel. When they reached its doorway Milan stopped. 'Go in,' he said. 'Get some sleep. I want to walk.'

'I'll come.'

'No.' He put his hands to Natasha's cheeks and, smiling a little, kissed her softly. 'I just need to think. Don't worry. I won't be long.'

A fear, colder than his touch, whispered in Natasha's mind. But she nodded and did as she was asked.

Almost two hours passed before Milan returned. Though she had lain still in the darkened room, Natasha had not slept. She had left the door unlocked for him, and watched as he closed it noiselessly and turned the key. The curtains were part-way open, but the dim glow from the street was shielded from her face; he could not see that she was awake and she did nothing to let him know it.

Sleep did not come to Milan easily, but Natasha watched him submit at last. After dozing briefly herself, she woke again before him. The window held the blue luminescence that comes just before dawn and Natasha, blinking at it, was aware of a dragging heaviness in her head. It was not the wine – she had been awake too long for that and had slept sober.

The plain, serviceable little hotel room glowed dully. Her eyes searched about it without purpose, rested on the chair by the window where Milan had slung his clothes, on the dressing table, the mirror that stood upon it reflecting blankly, and finally on the figure by her side. In sleep, Milan did not look peaceful. Twisted half onto his back, one hand hung, palm up, over the edge of the bed, suspended in mid-air by the straightened elbow-joint; the other obscured his face. He stirred, then, and brought that hand down to the coverlet. Before his eyes had opened Natasha knew he was properly awake: she watched his expression change as memory returned.

Reaching out, she pressed her fingers over his own and said gently, 'Can you tell me, do you think? Not now but . . .' It was for her own sake she was asking.

'It's nothing that changes us.'

'Still . . .'

Briefly, his lids closed. But when he looked at her again, he nodded.

★

BEFORE NINE THEY HAD WASHED and dressed and realized, separately, that any half-formed plans they might have had for the day were pointless. Natasha wished they did not have to wait another twenty-four hours to leave. As it was, she felt in limbo. Milan, in the room with her but hardly present, was sitting now on the edge of the bed, head in hands, his fingers digging hard against his scalp. If this carries on much longer, thought Natasha, gnawing on a nail as she watched him from the corner of the room, and he doesn't go mad, I certainly shall. 'You can't sit there all day,' she said at length. 'Or rather, you can. But please don't.'

He didn't lift his head, and his voice sounded odd, muffled. 'Tomorrow, once we're back, there won't be time to think. Today I can't do anything else.' Then he did look up and his eyes were weary. 'I'm sorry. I'll tell you what you want to know. But not here.'

They walked swiftly and in silence through the town, crossing the river by the same bridge as on the previous night. Natasha wondered where they were heading and took some time to realize that, despite his purposeful stride, Milan had no idea. Across the river, they came to a small piece of parkland that ran parallel with the water. Early flowers bordered the grass and clustered at the foot of trees and bushes, freshly budded; among them wound a path, punctuated with benches. Coming to one Milan sat – and then stood again, as if the discomfort of his thoughts compelled movement. They walked on.

'I once told you, didn't I,' he said at last, 'that a long time ago I loved someone who didn't love me?'

'In London. The person who gave that information to the papers about Anežka.'

'Yes.' Milan paused. After a moment he continued, directing a curious smile to the empty path ahead of them. 'It seems I made more mistakes then than I realized.' He pulled at a branch in passing and broke a twig between his fingers, then let the pieces fall. 'When the article was printed,' he said, 'I contrived to disappear. I went, eventually at least, to Canada. A writer I'd known briefly here had emigrated. He had a country estate where I knew no one would find me. But she – this person – thought I might have returned, by force or choice, to Prague. And I found out last night that she came after me.'

Natasha searched for the implication of his words. 'Came here? For what – some rescue attempt? Did she love you, after all?'

'It wasn't that.'

He still stared resolutely ahead. 'What, then?' Natasha racked her brains for possibilities. Some plot? Had this woman been working for the Czech authorities all along? She frowned and said, 'Is she still here?'

Milan shook his head. They had left the park now, and the street before them sloped gently uphill, lined with trees and cars and old apartment blocks. 'She hardly stayed more than a week,' he said. 'When she couldn't find me, she went back to England.'

A thought occurred. Natasha said, 'You know where she is now?'

'Yes. I have for a long time.' Slowing in pace, Milan gripped his arms across his chest. 'And so do you.'

'I'm sorry?'

'You know her, Natasha. I've not told you before because I saw no point in assigning faces to my past which should mean nothing to you. But now . . . it would be unfair not to. Though, God knows, it's hardly someone you admire.' He had stopped. There was a wall behind him; Milan leaned back against it and looked up at the buildings opposite. 'It's the head of your *alma mater*. It's Laura Douglas.'

The words had the effect on Natasha of a blast. The world turned in on her in a headlong rush. If she was still upright, it was from some miracle of balance, not substance – she felt suddenly, utterly emptied.

'You and . . . *her*?' Trying, without success, to drag two far-separated parts of her brain into collision, she struggled for some semblance of clarity. Milan. And her mother. She steadied herself. His great, soul-searing love. And the person who betrayed Anežka . . . Natasha became aware that she was staring stupidly.

'That's not all, though,' said Milan, shifting his gaze from the buildings to the ground at his feet. 'Karel knew why she came to look for me when I disappeared.' He swallowed dryly and dragged his eyes at last to Natasha's face. 'She was pregnant.'

A car, passing them in the street, made no sound. And when Natasha opened her mouth, her own voice seemed to reach her from a great distance. 'When was this?' she said. 'When? The date, give me the date!'

Milan shook his head, as if it aided thinking. 'Uh – 'seventy-one, early.'

But she had already turned from him.

'No,' she said softly, and began running, hearing the word close and thick in her ears. 'No.' She pelted blindly downhill, her feet clattering harshly against the pavement, hearing nothing of footsteps or calling behind, the walls and windows, trees and pavement blurring around her. She was only aware that Milan had reached her when her shoulders were gripped, the pressure grinding hard into muscle and bone, pulling her up so violently she retched for breath.

'Natasha!' he said, harsh and desperate. 'For God's sake – I shouldn't have told you this way.'

He turned her round. She was helpless to hide the tears coursing down her cheeks, mouth half open, her whole body trembling.

'Natasha.' Milan pulled her against him.

With a wild unearthly screech of terror, she tore at his arms, ducking her head through his grip to wrench herself free. She ran, but her footing was unsure, stumbled, regained her balance, and ran again. Milan could easily have caught her, but he hung back this time, half walking, half running a safe distance behind, waiting for her to stop of her own accord.

Seeing, still, little of where she was going, Natasha recognized the dark expanse of water ahead and was confused; then she struck out left along the river's edge and ran and ran until the cold air clawed at her lungs and she had ceased to know, or care, where she might be.

When he came to her she was curled on the ground, rocking herself obsessively back and forth, listening to a voice repeating over and over: 'Oh, God . . . oh, God . . .'

'It makes no difference. It was a lifetime ago – Natasha, listen to me.'

He dragged her hands from her ears. She pulled them free and curled them into fists at her mouth, speaking through them. 'No . . . no! You don't understand.' Swollen, her eyes lifted to him and swam again. She blinked, summoning every ounce of will to stop herself from looking away. 'Laura Douglas . . . is . . . my mother.'

For a long moment, nothing. He looked at her blankly, as if he hadn't heard, or understood, the words. Then the face before her seemed to darken and the features set, hardening into a mask while the real man shrank from behind them. His fingers lifted from her arms, so slowly that Natasha hardly felt the release. And in that gradual retracting of his touch she saw everything that bound them stretch invisibly across the space between, unravelling, shredding, breaking. She heard a ragged intake of breath, and realized it was her own.

'Why didn't you tell me?' he said, the words measured carefully, plucked on a taut string.

'Why didn't *you* tell *me*?' Natasha blurted. She wiped roughly at her mouth. 'Much the same reasoning, I would suppose. Something in our pasts we wanted to be free of, that we thought had no relevance to us now.' She smiled savagely. 'How wrong can you be?'

He was, she saw, struggling to keep the disgust from his face. The pain of it – the justice of it – winded her like a blow. And everything she knew began to drop away: her father – the man she called her father – Denham, Daphne, Laura, that bank of memories that tell you who you are, all seemed to be wheeling and spinning from her into darkness. Milan among them, the foundation of her new world order; Milan her lover . . . her father.

'Go,' she said. 'Just go. Leave me!'

He did not need any persuasion. He straightened up, his eyes lowered, and she heard, though did not see, his feet scuffing across the dusty ground.

By the time she looked up, he was no more than a pale crop moving against the blackened figures of the nearby bridge, walking swiftly, surely, away from her.

IT OCCURRED TO NATASHA NOT to go back to the hotel. It occurred to her, as she slowly became aware of her stiff, painful joints and the damp that seemed to have crept through her whole body till her fingers' ends were yellow with cold, that there was no getting warm now, nor did she want there to be. She stood, walked haltingly down to the water's edge. It was swilling, liquid black, up the concrete ramp, catching vague reflections of sky and land, fractured and senseless.

The desire to lose herself was a gnawing ache. If she could only slip as smoothly into the water as the swan she saw before her now – gliding on the swell, her hair strewn about her, her clothes billowing, drinking up the tow – she would do it. The heavy water called to her: she had only to mount the bridge, and drop over the side like a stone.

It felt like weakness as she turned away. Her face contorted with contempt, for herself and the world, she trod the short route onto the road that Milan had taken and crossed the river, looking neither to right nor left as she walked, knowing nowhere she might go but back to the hotel.

She was certain, at least, that that was the one place he would not be. She knew that his sole purpose now, above all else, would be to avoid her, and she was glad of it; glad she need do nothing to arrange it herself.

At the hotel door, Natasha passed through the thick red curtain into the lobby, but there her resolve failed her and, instead of proceeding up the staircase, she veered left and made her way into the small coffee parlour where she took a table, sheltered in a corner behind a partition, and ordered the strongest liqueur she could find on the card.

It was green, and smelt foul, sweet and herb-infused. But she drank it down, and the glass was filled and emptied twice more. It was another kind of water in which to lose herself.

The room was practically empty. Sporadically, a waiter swam in among the tables. The citizens of Prague who might once have gathered here knew, now, that life was moving swiftly and momentously elsewhere.

Natasha sat on, alone. Paris seemed a world away. There was no question of going back.

Chapter Sixteen **London, 1990**

Three days after Milan Novák boarded, at Prague airport, a plane bound for Paris, Laura Douglas sat in her office reeling from a series of shocks. Her life, these days, seemed filled with the unexpected, as if its theme tune had passed into a new movement. But was it the coda, or simply a fresh exposition? It would have been useful to know. Laura felt, at any rate, in a permanent state of astonishment.

Figgis had surprised them all. The toadying, spineless boy who had spent several months the previous summer traipsing after Alexander McIntyre in the interests of research, had turned out to be rather less toadying, and rather more of a vertebrate than anyone had expected. And, as a consequence, Laura's phone was ringing itself off the hook.

'*Times!*' called Maria, Laura's secretary, from her desk outside the door. 'And the *Guardian!*' She seemed to find bawling her head off some kind of tension release and had given up ringing through.

'No comment – and no comment!' Laura bawled back, rubbing at her throat with a little concern. It would not do: she couldn't stall them for ever, and besides, she had to decide how she – how the Institute – was going to act.

Figgis's studies had evidently gone rather well. No one, least of all Alexander, had suspected quite how deep he had been digging. And of the incendiary nature of his discoveries, he had breathed not a word. Instead, when the time had come, he had simply bid his subject a reverent farewell, and had hurried off to check, to double-check, and make sure his proof could spring no leaks. After several hours in libraries and many more spent fizzing backwards and forwards through video-tapes, he had evidently weighed up his options and prompted, perhaps, by the smarting memory of being treated as a lackey by his erstwhile hero, he had decided not to publish his research through the originally intended scholarly channels. Instead, he had decided to earn a large amount of money, and get a great deal of satisfaction doing it. The day that Nicholas Figgis commenced a fortnight's stay at a luxury hotel in Bermuda, the first of three splashy newspaper articles with his name on the byline went to press.

'Genius of the Ballet World Shown Up as Fraud' ran the first day's headline. 'Every Ballet Stolen' ran the second. No one knew if Alex himself ever saw the third; by then he had gone to ground, and not a peep had been heard from him since.

It appeared – and Figgis had collected enough corroborating evidence to defy anyone to gainsay it – that every one of Alex's ballets, the basis of his fame and reputation, was plagiarized. Early in Alex's career, still struggling to make his mark in the dance world, his memorabilia-collecting had landed him a bundle of papers that had once belonged to a talented dancer who, in the 1920s, had been committed to an asylum. They appeared, to the average punter, to be screeds of unhinged gobbledegook and strange doodling patterns. But Alex knew enough of the dancer's talent to suspect they might be more. So he had set about decoding them, had discovered that they recorded choreography and that in them he had acquired a stock of unseen and quite brilliant work. He had then used it, systematically, for his ballets, passing it off as his own.

It was no wonder then, Laura now saw, that Alex's choreography had seemed to dry up in the late 'seventies: he had come to the end of the manuscripts. So he had not, after all – as a certain person had so memorably alleged – a single talented bone in his body. Other, that is, than those containing the marrow of his code-breaking skills. They could have made good use of him at Bletchley.

Alexander himself had not been seen since the news broke. He had not come into the Institute and was not answering the telephone at his flat – which was being staked out round the clock by a covey of press photographers. That he was in there was certain (the curtains had been seen to twitch), but he had not slipped out for so much as a pint of milk.

Laura found herself host to a mixture of emotions. Admiration for Figgis and his *sang-froid*. Shock – though not, at bottom, surprise. She had always felt that the talent ran directly against the grain of the man. But did she pity Alex? She was not certain. She had long wanted him out of the Institute, after all, and could you pity, where you could not bring yourself to regret?

But the more urgent question was what the Institute should do as the man's employer. Sack him, on the grounds that he was employed because of his reputation – and now he had no reputation? But his role in the school was as teacher, not choreographer. If he were not a good teacher, why had the Institute employed him? And if he were, on what basis could he be sacked?

Laura sat and watched the spring sunshine creep across her office carpet. She was so tantalizingly near to being rid of Alex and yet could not quite see her way through the final moves to checkmate.

'Madame?' Maria had come to the door this time, a look of concern on her genial face.

'What is it?'

'Not a what, it's a who,' said Maria. 'Mr McIntyre. On the phone for you. Sounding a little . . . strange.'

He sounded more than strange. His voice, beginning high-pitched and querulous, sank quickly to hoarse insistence. His lips were close to the mouthpiece, the breathing shallow.

'You needn't think that I doubt for one moment your part in this,' he said. He was no longer, Laura noted absently, calling her 'Madame'. 'Don't even attempt to deny it. I know it was you who set that bloodsucker on to me. How did you find out? And when, hm? How long have you bided your time, waiting for proof, for me to lower my guard? It takes a warped mind to bear a grudge for so long.'

A grudge? It takes a warped mind, thought Laura, to believe only someone with a grudge would expose such wholesale fraud. She couldn't even be bothered to deny she'd had a hand in it.

'You will regret this, Laura Douglas. You will regret this.'

Go on, then, make me, thought Laura. But she was wise enough not to say it.

AT TEN O'CLOCK THAT EVENING Laura was feeling considerably less bullish. She was at home, in her terraced Victorian villa in deepest Wandsworth, and she was being watched. By whom, she did not know. She had switched off the light in the upstairs front bedroom and had approached the window cautiously from the side and peered out, but had seen nothing whatsoever of a suspicious nature. A cat cut a diagonal, skimming path across the street, tail aloft. Two young boys and, after them, a couple passed on their way to the petrol station and disappeared. The street stood still and empty. Yet this feeling of eyes turned upon her did not fade.

I'm going mad, she thought lightly. This is what it has all been. Life has been carrying on quite as normal and I have dreamt these things, these revelations and exposures – I have conjured them up out of the ether. She laughed a little, and was startled by the sound. A woman, alone at a window, laughing. The night, the chill and grimy street outside, held little that was amusing.

Further from sleep than if it had been noon, Laura made her way downstairs to the kitchen. The window to the garden gaped black in the white wall, framed by fingers of vine and creeper. Hastily, she let down the blind and busied herself opening some wine. If it hadn't been for the wind, she would have felt a good deal better. As it was, strange noises sounded in the eaves and insistent tappings drummed intermittently against the glass. Laura wished heartily for a room without windows, and for soothing music, but she did not have the first and, moving through into the sitting room, decided that the second would not help: if there were sounds to be heard, she would rather hear them.

She sat with the wine till late, though barely touching it, trying and failing instead to work at the budgets spread before her.

It was past one o'clock when at last the doorbell rang.

Laura started, sat for a moment, then placed her palms upon the papers before her and rose. Her heart seemed to have swelled and was beating about in her breast like a trapped bird. She walked into the hallway and, by sheer effort of will, put her eye to the spyhole in the door.

What she saw, at first, made no sense. Darkness, shadows and shapes, distorted by the tiny lens. Then she made out a figure, and saw that it had retreated a little way down the steps and had turned, again, to face her. With steady fingers, Laura drew back the bolts and the chain and opened the door.

At that moment a gust of wind gathered and flung itself at the house; she staggered a little as it reached her. But it did not stir the figure on the steps. Beyond the pool of light spilt from the doorway, the man was outlined in the paler phosphorescent glow from the street, the edges of his clothes whipping and jumping in the blast.

She had seen him in November, on stage in Paris. A few months before that, she had seen him among the crowds at the gala. The pale hair was no shock to her; neither the skin, paler still, hollowed and fissured; but this gaze, buried deep in sockets blackened by shadow, had not met hers for almost nineteen years. And it was at once so different and so much the same that something clutched at her gut with cruel, sharp fingers. She felt the breath leave her silently.

The air whined about them. Tightening her grip on the door's edge, Laura stood back to let Milan pass. She shut the door, and followed him into the sitting room and saw there in the brighter light what she had not at first noticed. That he was almost prostrate with fatigue. And that he was angry.

As she watched, Milan's fingers dug into a pocket and brought out a square of paper, battered and curled. He slung it on the table; it spun on the polished surface then lay still. A photograph. Laura stepped forward and picked it up.

An image of her younger self – in Prague. Milan broke the silence, softly, almost gently. 'Why?' he said. 'Why? Hm? Why?' She turned a little from him. He moved round to face her squarely again, but drew no nearer. The voice was low, barely more than a whisper. 'Why did you not say? Do you know what's happened? Do you know what you've done?'

'*I've* done?' she flashed at him, looking up.

He held her gaze, breathing shallowly; half nodded.

Control regained, and with it all semblance of calm, Laura moved smoothly to place the photograph back on the table. 'You left,' she said carefully.

'After three months, you knew where to find me.'

'By the time you were . . . you had surfaced, there was precious little to say.' She drew a breath. 'And, yes, I know exactly what has happened. She has been to see me. I have sat and achieved, for once, a productive conversation with my daughter.'

The description, though, hardly bore witness to the

event; the grief of it, the anguish, accusation and painful explanation.

'*Our* daughter,' said Milan.

'Ah. Yes. Or rather,' finding herself beside an arm-chair, Laura sat neatly and looked at him, 'no. She is my daughter, Milan. She is not yours.'

He was standing in the middle of the room, his grimy coat still hanging from his shoulders, his hair still sticking up in tufts where it had been messed by the wind. 'Don't play games,' he said.

Laura held her direct gaze upon him. 'You – are – not – her – father,' she said crisply. 'Do you prefer it that way round?'

The colourless eyes narrowed. 'Hasn't she told you? I know. I know you went to Prague – I know you were pregnant. Natasha has no sister or brother.'

It was strange to hear the girl's name from his lips. Laura twisted her own mouth into something like a smile. 'Only by chance,' she said. 'When I went to Prague, the child I was carrying was yours.' Pausing, she hoped he had not seen the tremble in her chin before she stilled it. Swiftly, she went on, 'But I miscarried. Three weeks after I came back to England.'

'And Natasha?'

'Was conceived with indecent haste. Against doctor's orders.' She was looking at her hands now, clasped in her lap: she did not want to see his relief. 'I owed my husband a great deal . . . that I couldn't give him. I thought having a child would help. I was wrong. There – you have your explanation.' She looked up brightly to find that Milan had moved. At the furthest side of the room, he was leaning against the wall, his arms pinned behind him, his head lifted.

He thought for a moment and then said, 'If you hadn't . . . Would you have told me?'

The question stung her into movement. She got up and crossed the hearth-rug, twice, then stood before the mantel. 'Why? What do you think you would have done?' she said. 'Stood by me for the sake of the child? When I miscarried, you would have left. And even if I hadn't, you still would have gone. Don't try to fool yourself. You never loved me. At least you were honest about it – *that* I thank you for. I only wish I could have said the same, with honesty, too. But isn't this the age-old tragedy? One loves where another does not.'

In the mirror above the fireplace Laura saw Milan start. And stare. And then drop into the chair beside him.

She watched as the fingers screened his face and, for a moment, she could have believed it was the Milan of nineteen years ago before her, that when the hands came down, there would not be the ragged lines in his skin, the hollowness about his eyes, the age, the care, the marks of self-neglect.

'Don't worry,' she said thinly. 'It can't threaten you at this distance. It hardly could then, child or no child. I knew you loved Anežka. You didn't exactly hide it, not with your heart tattooed on your arm. Besides, more than once you'd made it clear you felt hounded by the demands of infatuated women. What else could I do but assure you of the shallowness of my feelings?'

The fingers had lowered to rest on the chair-arms. 'You were lying?'

Laura smiled grimly. '"How did I love thee? Let me count the ways."' She stopped, with a small frown. 'I thought I'd been in love before. I didn't know what it was. I was destined, clearly, to be made to understand.'

He appeared not to be breathing now. The lines in his face had darkened, his eyes seemed more deep-set and hooded than ever. Her words, the line of poetry, hung between them on the still air. Then the breath came, and the voice rode on it, close to a whisper, 'Then why did you betray me?'

Laura paused, capturing again, carefully, her measured, even tone. 'I didn't. Barely a paragraph of that article came from the interview with me.' She looked at Milan. She said, 'We had earned ourselves an enemy, you and I. And I believe you had confided in her yourself, though I still don't think she knew until afterwards quite how true the blow was that she struck.'

He was frighteningly still. 'Nadine Kelly.' He said it softly, with no hint of question in his voice.

'I didn't find out until some time after you'd gone. She felt that, between us, we had taken everything she had.'

'And so,' he said, 'I left—'

'Due to a misunderstanding. Yes.' Swift and business-like now, Laura crossed to the sideboard and fetched another glass; placing it beside hers on the table, she filled them both with wine. 'I am explaining my actions, nothing more. Have no regrets on my account. They belong to Anežka, if anyone. Without that article, I would simply have had the parting I had predicted for myself instead of the one I had not. Anežka would have been released. You have lost two decades with her.'

She had moved to place one of the glasses on the bookcase near him. But, catching sight of his face, she halted, the clear stem between her fingers.

'You still don't understand, do you?' he said. 'Did Natasha not tell you?'

'Tell me what?'

His eyes did not stray from her face as, roughly, he pushed up one sleeve. '*Not with your heart tattooed on your arm,*' she had said. She dropped her gaze to it now.

The pale veined skin – and there upon it, in place of the lettering with which she had once been so familiar, was a fine-inked image of a bird, its plumage painted cadmium orange and crimson and gold. A firebird.

'You thought I had found my soul-mate?' Milan said. 'You were right.' There was a brief silence. 'It wasn't Anežka.'

'So who?' She looked at him, and back to the tattoo, and shook her head. 'No.'

'To the depth and breadth and height my soul can

reach,' he said, and she glanced up again sharply, searching his face for the mockery and the lie, and finding neither.

Her eyes were wide. She remembered the glass in her hand and, with concentration, set it down. Then 'Why—' she began, with difficulty. She swallowed. 'So why did you tell me you loved Anežka?'

Milan's light gaze never wavered from her own. 'I didn't, if you remember. I was simply stupid enough to tell someone else. At the time it was – convenient.'

Nadine.

They stared at one another. 'Well,' said Laura at last, 'what a mess.' She retreated to the chair she had occupied before, but, finding she did not want to sit, said to its cushions, 'Still, archaeology does tend to produce a heap of mud.'

'Laura . . .'

'Yes?' She turned, her hands clasped tightly and eyes quite clear. Seeing him hesitate, she said, 'What, Milan? You have good news. You love Natasha. She is not your daughter. Go and be happy – with my blessing.'

'Do I love her?' he asked. 'She is not my daughter but she is yours. Of all people I have chosen your child. Can you swear that is a coincidence?'

Oh, God, oh, God . . . Laura felt herself sway a little, and, stepping forward, reached a hand to the mantelpiece. He had given her a choice – unwittingly. She pressed her fingertips hard into the cold marble. Nail-edges bit into flesh.

'Yes,' she said levelly. 'What are you suggesting – that Natasha and I are alike? She would laugh to hear you say it. Don't torture yourself with ghosts. If you love Natasha, you love her for herself. You *do* love her.' Unintentionally, a slight upward inflection made the words sound almost like a question.

Milan, though, hadn't heard it. He said. 'More than anyone, since—' then stopped himself. 'But you're not a ghost, Laura. I walked away once, when you most needed—'

'Can you imagine what it is to lose a child?' She snapped round, desperate only to silence him. She was not sure how much more she could bear. 'You have begun to feel something of it now, perhaps. A little. More died in me than just that baby, Milan. Though it was some time before I understood it.' She took a breath, and went on more steadily, 'I know what you are asking. Offering. Guilt is a good dissembler. It might even make you fool yourself – but only for a while.' She paused. 'So the answer to your . . . *question* . . . is no. And if you and Natasha had never met, it would have been the same.'

He had been gazing at her intently, his eyes wide, the brow above furrowed as if he were straining to follow an unfamiliar language. But as she watched now his expression altered. A shadow seemed to pass across his face, fleetingly, and disappear. She could have sworn she had seen a spirit leave him.

Rising smoothly from the chair, Milan stretched out his hand to take her own. His touch was warm; he cradled Laura's small fingers in his palm, looking down at them. She wondered what he was thinking and, despite herself, a mad hope flickered into life.

But then he said, 'We'll see each other again?'

And so the knife was driven home. Laura smiled, with some effort. 'I imagine we shall be hard pressed to avoid it. Given the . . . connection.'

'Natasha knows?'

She nodded. 'It was the first truly frank discussion I believe we've ever had. I'm daring to feel we may have reached a modicum of understanding. It's been hard-won, and the difficulties entirely my fault.'

'Given the circumstances—'

'One's child, quite rightly, makes no allowance for circumstances. Don't worry. I intend relations to be steadier from now on.'

He closed his hand around hers and then released it. 'Just one more question, then.'

Laura knew already what it would be. 'At Denham,' she said. 'With her father.'

The pale eyes stirred at the new significance. 'And you think I should – go to her there?'

It was a moment before Laura could reply. But when she did, it was with perfect equanimity. 'If you do nothing else,' she said, 'that you must do.'

★

SHE WAS AT THE WINDOW as he crossed the street, heading purposefully back into the night. His yellow hair, vivid at first against the dark, dulled as he drew further off, and finally was gone. And Laura, letting go of the most iron-willed self-control she had ever mustered in her life, lifted the glass in her hand and flung it, straight and very hard, against the wall.

'*So the answer to your question is no. And if you and Natasha had never met, it would have been the same.*'

The wine ran, blood-red, down paint and paper.

It was over; Milan had gone. As once before, she had assured him of how little she felt. He had not seen that, as once before, she had lied.

TWENTY MINUTES LATER THE phone rang.

The conversation was brief. Laura replaced the receiver and ran through the house, collecting car keys, coat and bag. Then she left.

At this unsocial hour the roads were almost clear, and she made good time. Across Blackfriars Bridge and on up Farringdon Road. She drove steadily, her hands firm on the steering wheel.

The glow in the sky was visible from several streets away and, as Laura drew nearer, clouds of slate-grey belching smoke.

Turning the final corner, Laura saw that several fire engines were already pulled up and the firemen racing about their task. But, fanned by the high wind, the flames had well and truly taken: the church roof was burning and scarlet rods of fire shot up the walls of the tower. From the slatted belfry windows black smoke billowed, and burning specks fizzed out against the darker sky. The Institute was ablaze.

Laura, parking at a distance, got out of the car. She could feel the heat from here and turned her face up towards it as she walked. What remained of anything, now, she wondered. She felt oddly calm.

The police had arrived too. Laura spoke, briefly, with the officer in charge and then retreated to the pavement opposite, drawing her coat around her. The waves of heat in the tower had set the great bell swinging on its wooden wheel. It tolled mournfully, clanging above the crackle and hiss of water on flame, and the shouts, and sounds of men running.

As she watched, a figure emerged from a gate in the church wall. It was a man, his slender arms gripped on either side by officers; they turned him in the direction of a police car parked further along the street. The group crossed within a few yards of Laura, though none of them looked her way. But as they passed she saw the man's blackened clothes and the cloth he held to his forehead to stem the flow of blood.

It was Alexander. His mouth was open and his teeth showed white against his soot-stained cheeks. It took a moment for the thin sound to carry on the gusting air. He was laughing.

Epilogue

'Mummee! Watch me dive!'

Natasha turned, just in time to see the small boy bellyflop gracelessly into the pool. Laughter rebounded from the water, and an enthusiastic round of applause.

'And you let this place stay boarded up when I was his age?' said Natasha, manufacturing a little pique.

Her father sighed inscrutably. 'Yes,' he said. 'School fees and ailing relatives.'

She grinned. 'Pathetic excuse.'

They were at the door of the Bath House – newly refurbished, with heating and lighting installed at vast expense – and they were watching two children, a boy and a girl, splashing and squealing in the water below. The mother, a woman in her thirties, was sitting at the pool's edge, dangling her feet and laughing. Her name was Lucy Fenn, she was widowed, and she had lashings of long, toffee-coloured hair. The only other thing Natasha knew about her was that she seemed to have some budding romantic attachment to Richard.

'Where did you say you met her?' she asked, as she and her father turned and strolled back out onto the grassy slope, shutting the Bath House door behind them.

Richard said, 'At the fête this summer. Lucy's a friend of the Whartons – they brought her along.'

'Well.'

There was a thoughtful pause. 'Well?' echoed Richard, eyeing his daughter sideways. 'You're surprised?'

She turned her head to direct him a shining smile. 'I am. But only in a good way. She's very nice.'

Richard surveyed the view, his hands in his pockets. 'I think so.'

The surprise, on Natasha's part, was deep. She had never, since her mother had left, seen her father as someone who could be part of a couple. She had somehow thought that Laura had been it for him: all of the good and all of the bad in one; an experience so intense that nothing more moderate – and therefore nothing – could follow. If there had been others she hadn't known about them, but now, suddenly, he had introduced her to Lucy. And it seemed the most natural thing in the world.

'Have you told Laura?' she asked.

Richard shook his head. 'Early days.' He frowned a little. 'Do you think I should?'

Natasha shrugged, and shook her head in turn, and for several minutes together they stood, contemplating the trees and, among them, the views of parkland and Hall and distant village. 'I'm going to London tomorrow,' said Natasha, her mind still on her mother. 'And I've been thinking I should see her. Six months is too long. There won't be another chance for a while.'

Richard looked at his daughter. The threads of her face – which in the past had seemed so often drawn tightly together, he thought – had loosened. That sharp look had gone: the dark eyes danced, now, with a new optimism. He said, 'Is he still in Paris?'

Natasha nodded. 'Arguing with Victor about budgets for next season.' She smiled. 'The way he's going, there won't even be one.'

A BURNISHED LATE-SEPTEMBER SUN warmed the little room through brick and glass. Laura set down the dictaphone and sat with her hands clasped lightly on the desk, feeling remarkably content. This autumn's fresh intake of students had done well in their first month; the funding for next summer's gala was secure; the rebuilding work almost complete. Soon the studios rented at Old Street could be vacated and the church next door would echo once again to music and the pounding of feet on sprung wood, rather than to the jangling tools of the construction site. All was well. It was a fine time for her to go.

And that she was to go, at least temporarily, had been the import of the letter she had just dictated. The Institute's board of trustees wouldn't receive it until after she had left, but she was choosing to explain retrospectively to minimize – she was quite frank about it – the trouble to herself. She was leaving the Institute in capable hands: she had had a long and detailed discussion with Ellen Ellmore and it was not as if she would be gone for ever. What was the phrase she had chosen? A 'leave of absence'. She was sure the board would not deny her the liberty. If they did, however, she felt today that she would hardly care.

It had taken her a long time to realize it but, finally, it had come to her that there was someone she needed to see. Someone to whom she owed a sizeable debt of gratitude, who had always been there for her, yet whom she had never truly appreciated. Someone who could show her, now, how to live.

'NATASHA TAYLOR – MY GOD!' Maria chewed delightedly and pointed, remembering. 'Hey, I saw you on that documentary last week. That bloke who runs your company – the old guy – he's *amazing*!'

'Yes, isn't he?' said Natasha lightly. 'Look, I'm not stopping. I just want to know – where's—' She broke off, recalling the unfamiliar term. 'Where's Madame?'

Maria tipped her head to the door beside her. 'No point looking in there. As of this morning it's Ellen's office. Madame's gone away for a while.'

Natasha stared. 'Gone? Did she say where?'

'Well, she said she was going home.'

Natasha waited for the merest hint of a likely explanation to present itself in her head and found herself disappointed. 'Thanks,' she said, and made for the stairs.

AN HOUR LATER, SHE WAS standing before a black front door in Wandsworth. Even now, it had taken a little courage to ring the bell.

After the third try, Natasha retreated a step or two and looked up at the windows for signs of life. The clouds, in reflection, scudded across their limpid surface; beneath, she saw that the curtains were open, the rooms unlit

Natasha had a hunch her mother wasn't simply out. She checked along the street for a black VW. No sign. Slowly descending the stone steps, she stretched out a hand to the arrow-head railings and grasped one, turning her palm around it and thinking.

Laura had said she was going home. Where was home for her, any more, if not here?

THE BLACK VW TURNED OFF the motorway and onto the more scenic route, through Berkshire. The afternoon was fresh and clear with a gentle, cobweb-sweeping breeze, which set pub-signs swinging and gusts of fiery-dyed leaves gathering in little heaps against walls and hedgerows. As Laura crossed the county border, the sky seemed to open out in greeting and the landmarks flashing past became ones she recognized: churches and farmsteads, stableyards and gallops.

At length the road narrowed and curled to the left, crossing a small hump-backed bridge. A little further on and Laura turned, passing between the high pillars of a great gateway and onto a long, gently curving drive.

As the house came into view she slowed the engine and took a lingering look. On a bright day like this, the dusty-coloured stone seemed less dour than she had remembered it; the building, open-faced and sturdy, looked out across the parkland with a tranquil gaze. It had been, once, such a familiar, lonely, angry place, and she had not been back now for eleven years.

Swinging the car round, Laura parked on the gravel in front of the stable block. She got out and, on a sudden whim, decided to take the path through the small arched gate that led to the back of the house, and the gardens. There, among regimented twistings of rose bushes, she found what she had been looking for.

It was a solitary figure, leaning among the blooms. Sturdy gauntlet gloves poked and rummaged between spiked branches and a ferocious-looking pair of secateurs swooped in for the kill. Above them hovered a broad straw hat, secured with a scarf that bent the brim like a Victorian bonnet.

Enjoying the unexpected little scene, Laura stood and watched.

After some time, the figure straightened and turned,

secateurs held aloft, ready for application elsewhere. Observing Laura, it stopped. The bonnet inclined sharply to the side: Laura spotted a whisper of smoke escaping on the air. Then a familiar throaty voice said pleasantly, 'What on *earth* are you doing here?'

'I could very well ask the same of you. *Gardening*, Daphne?'

'It hardly rises to the term, darling. We still have Brett junior, you'll be pleased to know, for the real work. But I've found there is a certain satisfaction in snipping things.' She crunched the secateurs in her hand and looked about for something else on which to use them. 'If you're in need of Natasha she's gone,' she said meanwhile. 'And Richard's off in the Lakes with—' A small coughing fit overtook her and, struggling with glove-thickened fingers, she held her cigarette away. 'In the Lakes. For a week.'

'I wasn't,' said Laura, coming forward. 'Either of them. Daphne . . .'

She could see under the shady bonnet now. Daphne, though her hands were busy once more with the bushes, was eyeing her thoughtfully.

'I . . .' Laura hesitated again. 'Do you think perhaps I could stay with you for a while?'

There was a small silence. Then a silken smile crept around Daphne's cigarette. She stripped off the gloves. She crossed the grass to where Laura was standing, and put them, plus the secateurs, into her hand.

'The roses are covered in suckers. The clematis are

prepared to die to spite me, wretched things, and I'm ready to concrete over at least half the herbaceous borders. Between us, though, Mr Brett and I have left you remarkably little to do. Still, I'm sure you'll think of some way to make yourself useful.'

She stopped, and the fine brows arched mischievously in answer to Laura's smile. 'It'll be fun, darling,' she said, and plucked the gold filter of her cigarette delicately from between her lips. She stubbed it out on the secateur blades. 'Now. *I*'m going to fetch the gin.'

BARBARA ELSE

The Warrior Queen

£5.99

A Pan Paperback Original

Kate Wildburn is in trouble. She's an extrovert, a lateral thinker and a talented pianist. She's also a good wife and mother, who has just one ambition: to be the only faithful wife in the twentieth century. She can't see the attraction of illicit sex. 'Getting used to new people's bits. I think it would be icky.'

Then she discovers that her balding surgeon husband, Richard, has not only got used to someone else's bits, but the bits of someone she knows.

So Kate takes up her bow of gold, dons her 'breastplate of righteousness . . . and ruthless spurs of vengeance'. She won't give up till the battle's won. Richard's so-called Thursday games of squash must stop.

THE WARRIOR QUEEN is a brilliantly subversive look at modern marriage. With her fine ear for male bluster and female bitchiness, and her subtle observations of chaotic family life, Barbara Else has created a true black comedy to entertain — and warn — readers from either of the warring camps.

GAY LONGWORTH

Bimba

£5.99

A Pan Paperback Original

Blessed with good looks, great taste and bad judgement, Bimba is no ordinary babe. In the search for better sex and a brighter future, her life is suddenly taken out of control, away from her desk and into a far darker world.

From London to New York and then to Hong Kong, life is no longer a joke – and it's not just Bimba's sense of humour that's in jeopardy . . .

All Pan Books are available at your local bookshop or newsagent, or can be ordered direct from the publisher. Indicate the number of copies required and fill in the form below.

Send to: Macmillan General Books C.S.
            Book Service By Post
            PO Box 29, Douglas I-O-M
            IM99 1BQ

or phone: 01624 675137, quoting title, author and credit card number.

or fax: 01624 670923, quoting title, author, and credit card number.

or Internet: http://www.bookpost.co.uk

Please enclose a remittance* to the value of the cover price plus 75 pence per book for post and packing. Overseas customers please allow £1.00 per copy for post and packing.

*Payment may be made in sterling by UK personal cheque, Eurocheque, postal order, sterling draft or international money order, made payable to Book Service By Post.

Alternatively by Access/Visa/MasterCard

Card No. | | | | | | | | | | | | | | | | | | |

Expiry Date | | | | | | | | | | | | | | | | | | |

Signature   _____

Applicable only in the UK and BFPO addresses.

While every effort is made to keep prices low, it is sometimes necessary to increase prices at short notice. Pan Books reserve the right to show on covers and charge new retail prices which may differ from those advertised in the text or elsewhere.

NAME AND ADDRESS IN BLOCK CAPITAL LETTERS PLEASE

Name _____

Address _____

_____

_____

_____

8/95

Please allow 28 days for delivery.
Please tick box if you do not wish to receive any additional information. ☐